the
sound
of
rain

Books by Sarah Loudin Thomas

The Sound of Rain

A Tapestry of Secrets

Until the Harvest

Miracle in a Dry Season

the
sound
of
rain

SARAH LOUDIN THOMAS

BETHANYHOUSE
a division of Baker Publishing Group
Minneapolis, Minnesota

© 2017 by Sarah Loudin Thomas

Published by Bethany House Publishers
11400 Hampshire Avenue South
Bloomington, Minnesota 55438
www.bethanyhouse.com

Bethany House Publishers is a division of
Baker Publishing Group, Grand Rapids, Michigan

Printed in the United States of America

Library of Congress Control Number: 2017945769

ISBN 978-0-7642-1961-0 (trade paper)
ISBN 978-0-7642-3118-6 (cloth)

Unless otherwise indicated, Scripture quotations are from the King James Version of the Bible.

Scripture quotations identified NIV are from the Holy Bible, New International Version®. NIV®. Copyright © 1973, 1978, 1984, 2011 by Biblica, Inc.™ Used by permission of Zondervan. All rights reserved worldwide. www.zondervan.com

This is a work of fiction. Names, characters, incidents, and dialogues are products of the author's imagination and are not to be construed as real. Any resemblance to actual events or persons, living or dead, is entirely coincidental.

Cover design by Kathleen Lynch/Black Kat Design

Author is represented by Books & Such Literary Agency.

17   18   19   20   21   22   23   7   6   5   4   3   2   1

For the men who inspired Judd Markley:

Daniel Loudin—brother, woodsman, mountain man
Uncle Judd Loudin—hero of my father's tales
Uncle Harry Markley—coal miner who lived to tell
what it felt like to be buried inside a mountain

🌢🌢🌢

To the roots of the mountains I sank down;
the earth beneath barred me in forever.

Jonah 2:6 NIV

CHAPTER

1

BETHEL, WEST VIRGINIA
APRIL 1954

Judd wanted to take a deep breath more than anything. But the weight on his chest, combined with the dust-laden air, made it impossible. He closed his eyes and opened them again, finding it made no difference. Either he was blind or the cave-in had erased any hint of light. He coughed and spit.

Darkness pressed against him almost as hard as the silence. There should have been the hum of machinery, the clink of pickaxes against coal, men's voices. He moved his hands and felt relief at the sensation of ten fingers brushing against rough stone. He couldn't move much, but at least he knew he was alive.

Continuing to take stock, he found he couldn't move anything below his waist. That must be the weight of the rock and maybe some timbers. Surely his legs and feet were still there. And nothing hurt too terrible—that was good. He shifted his head and realized there was a boot pressed against his cheek. It scared him so bad he cussed. Then he felt awful—that might be Harry's foot. Not Joe's, though—he'd been working that

7

other, narrower seam. He hoped Harry and Joe had time to start out toward the entrance.

Judd found he could breathe a little easier—the dust must have settled. He wished he could reach up and wipe the grit from his lips. He spit again and tried to settle his mind to wait. He'd never been afraid of tight spaces, and maybe it was good he couldn't see to know how bad his situation was. And yet . . . the darkness had become a tangible thing. He could almost feel it brushing across his skin. Fear welled in him, and he gritted his teeth against it. There was nothing he could do, no one he could call out to. He guessed Ma would tell him to pray, but he was a man of action and it wasn't like God would reach down into the bowels of the earth and pluck him out. He exhaled through pursed lips just to hear the sound of air moving and maybe, just maybe, there were words buried in that breath.

After what seemed like an eternity, Judd heard a sound. Or thought he did. It might just be his ears wanting to hear something. A few minutes later, he heard a voice for sure and certain and saw a chink of light. His very being quivered, the sudden burst of hope almost more than he could bear. It took at least another hour before the men got to him, their lanterns flashing against the debris and hurting his light-starved eyes.

"Don't move, Judd, we've gotta get this beam off before we can dig you out."

"Ain't goin' nowhere," he said.

Martin Burr grunted as he shifted some more rock. "Reckon you ain't."

Finally, Judd felt the weight on his chest ease. He took a good breath and thought maybe he did hurt some. He saw Martin's grim face. The older man flinched and told Judd to brace himself. Pain seared his very soul, and Judd didn't know anything more.

When he woke, Judd's first thought was that he was still trapped in the mine. But the astringent smell and the squeak of a nurse's shoes in the hall let him know he was in a hospital. He glanced to his right and saw a curtain drawn across a window. The room was barely lit—must be nighttime. To his left, he could see the shape of another man in another bed. He hoped it was Joe.

Judd took that deep breath he'd been wanting back in the mine and moaned. He'd broken some ribs, sure as shootin'. Once the pain eased, he began to inventory his condition. Both hands worked fine. He reached up to rub the sleep from his eyes and found his right shoulder to be stiff but workable. He felt along his torso until he came to the bandages around his rib cage. Next he wiggled his toes—the left foot seemed fine, but his right leg appeared to be suspended some way—immobile. He was afraid to move around much, tender as his ribs were, but at least all his limbs were attached. That was something.

Footsteps approached, and a nurse stepped inside the room. "Mr. Markley. You're awake."

"Yes, ma'am. And I'm powerful thirsty."

"I'm not surprised—you've been here most of three days now." She slipped over to the side of the bed and held a cup with a straw to his lips. The water slipped over his tongue like the first drink after a day spent in the hayfield. He guessed maybe he hadn't died after all.

"How are you feeling?"

"With my hands." Judd grinned and felt his dry lips crack. He licked them. "Guess I feel pretty good for a dead man."

The nurse smiled. "You're actually quite lucky, Mr. Markley. The doctors thought they'd have to take off that leg, but it looks like you'll get to keep it a little longer."

Judd tried to feel lucky, but found it beyond him at the moment. A sound came from the other bed, and he looked over to see Harry leaning over the bed rail.

"Well if you ain't a sight for sore eyes. I was afeared we lost you."

"Not this time around," Judd said. "You must not be hurt too bad, sitting up there all lively like that."

Harry gave the nurse an appreciative look. "These gals would just about make a dead man sit up and take notice."

The nurse made a harrumphing sound but didn't seem displeased. "I'm going to leave you boys to catch up. Breakfast will be around shortly."

Harry swung his legs over the side of his bed and squinted at Judd. "You're lucky to be alive, son. I was farther out than you and just got knocked around a little, but I thought you was a goner for sure."

"What about Joe?"

Harry blinked once. "Aww, they patched him up and sent him home. He'll be back at it afore the week's out."

"Say, whose foot was pressed up against my face then? If it wasn't you, then who the heck was it?"

Harry ducked his head. "Judd. That was your foot. That's how come your leg's all wrapped up like that. You've got enough steel in there to shoe a couple of horses."

Judd reached down and realized the heavy cast came clear up to his waist. "Am I gonna walk again?"

"Don't see why not. Seems like they wouldn't have gone to all that trouble to give you a dead weight to drag around."

Judd rolled his head against the pillow, remembering the rough scrape of the boot against his cheek. His boot. He was beginning to feel pain all over—in his rib cage, his hips, his back. Seemed like everything but the hair on his head was starting to hurt.

"Son, you don't look so good. I'm gonna get that nurse back in here."

Judd thought to accuse his friend of calling the nurse back so he could get another look at her, but he didn't have the grit

10

to make a joke. He nodded and closed his eyes, grateful that even then, light filtered through his eyelids.

◆ ◆ ◆

The nurse must've given him something to make him sleep. When Judd woke the second time, the first thing he realized was that he felt about half-starved. 'Course, he also felt like he'd been in a tussle with a freight train and lost, but he decided to focus on hungry. You couldn't eat if you were dead, and in the dark of the mine he'd thought he might be dead for longer than he liked to remember.

He pried his eyes open and found Harry sitting beside his bed, staring at him. There was also a tray on a table with a bowl of something that might've been hot once.

"That stuff fit to eat?" he asked.

Harry swallowed convulsively and pushed the bowl toward him. "I et mine and it didn't do me no harm. You need help spooning it up?"

Judd braced himself and pushed up a notch, grimacing as pain shot through him in so many places he couldn't narrow it down to say what hurt. "If I do, I'll ask that good-looking nurse."

He reached for the spoon and tasted some kind of bean soup. It was barely warm, but he swallowed it down and wished for a piece of corn bread and maybe a glass of cool buttermilk. His throat still felt raw and parched from the coal dust. Harry sat and watched like a hound dog hoping for a crumb.

"Harry, I appreciate your concern, but you're crowding me a mite. You want some soup?"

Harry ducked his head and shifted in his chair. "I've got something to tell ya. I been waiting for you to wake up and eat—wanted you to get what rest you could."

Judd swallowed and left his spoon, which was getting downright heavy, in the half-empty bowl. "Spit her out, then."

"It's Joe. I lied about him being alright." Harry fisted his hands on his knees. "Them nurses said you needed time to heal afore I told you, but I don't hold with lying and it's been weighing on me." He lifted his head to meet Judd's eyes. "Joe didn't make it. Looks like he died straight out—got hit in the head and probably didn't know nothing about it." Harry's Adam's apple bobbed and he lowered his eyes again. "I know you was real close to your brother, I couldn't see keeping it from you."

Judd felt like the weight of the mountain was centered on his chest once again. He fought for air as surely as he had in the dark of the mine. Not Joe. Not his baby brother who'd always had dreams enough for both of them. He should have died; he should have found Joe and taken his place. He closed his eyes and focused on the pain in his ribs, his leg, his head—anything but the pain in his heart.

CHAPTER

2

Even though it was August, Judd could usually find a breeze out on the front porch of his brother's house. He'd been living here with Abram, his wife, Lydia, and their children since he came back from Korea in 1952 with the bottom half of his right lung shot away. He hardly noticed the old wound anymore and it hadn't kept him from being hired on at the mine. Harry kept pestering him about when he'd be coming back to work, but Judd had made up his mind. He wasn't going back.

Leaning his crutch up against the side of the house, Judd tested his leg as he walked over to the railing. He didn't suppose it would ever be right again, but he could walk pretty well on his own now. He didn't need the crutch so much as he wanted folks to think he did. It gave him time to decide what he was going to do next. And he was pretty sure he'd made up his mind. He pulled a clipping out of the Clarksville newspaper from his breast pocket and read the ad over again. He'd found the bit of newsprint tucked inside an old western Joe had been reading. Apparently, there were jobs down in South Carolina for a man who was willing to put his back into it. Judd didn't know a whole lot about timbering, but he was pretty sure he wouldn't need to go into a hole in the ground to harvest trees.

And if Joe had been thinking about going . . . well, that was reason enough for him to head south.

He tucked the paper away as Abram stepped out onto the porch and eyed the crutch back against the side of the house. "Getting on any better?"

"I'm gaining ground." Judd leaned on the railing and stared out at the pasture. "Been thinking about where I might go from here."

"You're welcome to stay as long as you want." He stroked his beard. "Been thinking—handy as you are with mechanical things, maybe the coal company'd let you keep the equipment running instead of working the seam."

Judd kept his eyes on the edge of the field where he knew deer were likely to browse. "Put in my application two months ago. Mr. Clarkson said he knew I could do the job, but since I don't have a piece of paper that says I'm 'formally trained' he can't put me on. Coal-company regulations."

"Clarkson always did take comfort in having rules to go by."

"That's so." Judd turned to his brother. "And anyhow, Joe's too close around this place. Thought I might head south and see if I can't learn a new trade. Might get in with someone who'd let me make use of what I know."

Abram settled his bearded bulk into a rocking chair and laced his hands across his belly. "Lydia and the kids would sure be sorry to see you go." He set the chair in motion. "Might be I'd miss you myself." He grinned. "Then again, I hear those Southern girls are nice to look at."

Judd forced a smile. "Yup. Lydia might be willing to part with me if I fetch a new sister home for her."

Abram stroked his beard. "You're what, twenty-seven now? Reckon it's time you found a good woman. Guess none of 'em around here's quite suited you."

Judd smiled in spite of himself. There was more than one lady he'd wooed, but he'd never taken romance as seriously as

14

some of those ladies would have liked. "I might have burned a bridge or two by now. Might need to start fresh somewhere else."

Slapping his hands on the rocker arms, Abram stood. "Lydia sent me out here to fetch you in to supper. Once your belly's full you'll think clearer."

Judd got his crutch and followed his brother into the house, where he could hear eight-year-old James and five-year-old Grace chattering with their mother. He breathed in the aroma of fried chicken and biscuits. Joe could just about eat a whole chicken when Lydia did the cooking. Judd loved his family, and he was grateful for a safe place to heal from the war and now the mine accident, but he felt hollowed out. There was an emptiness not even his niece's dancing blue eyes and strawberry curls could fill. He scooped Grace into his arms, grunting at the stress on his leg. He settled her on an upturned crate in the chair next to him and bowed his head to hear his brother's prayer. But he didn't close his eyes. The world was plenty dark enough with them wide open.

◆ ♦ ◆

The bus ticket to South Carolina took a chunk out of Judd's meager savings, but he wasn't worried. Waccamaw Timber Company was hiring, and he felt certain of a job. He'd refused to let his family see him off, hitching a ride to the station and boarding a Greyhound bus with his duffel bag and little else.

It took a day and a half to travel the four hundred miles between the mountains and the sea. Judd slept little, mostly watching the landscape as it shifted from high peaks and low valleys to rolling hills to a flatness that left him feeling unsettled and wondering if he was doing the right thing. He wished he and Joe could've made this trip together.

"Where you headed?" The man in the seat next to him had boarded the bus just before they crossed the state line into South Carolina.

"Myrtle Beach." Judd wasn't in the mood for conversation.

"Boy howdy, that's where I'm headed, too. Been working up near Chadbourne, and now I'm headed down to close out the year at the beach."

Judd figured this man might be a help, so he stuck out his hand. "Judd Markley. I'm hoping to find work with the Waccamaw Timber Company—they advertised in the West Virginia paper and I decided to come on south."

"Didn't think you sounded like you were from around here." The fair-haired man with sun-roughened skin grabbed Judd's hand, his grip firm. "I'm Hank Chapin and I work for the Heywards—they own Waccamaw Timber. Be glad to introduce you once we get to town. You willing to break a sweat?"

"Don't know any other way to get real work done."

Hank laughed. "What'd you do back in the mountains?"

"Coal mining. I was in Korea for a while, but I've been mining since I was sixteen."

Hank whistled. "Guess you do know about hard work. 'Course, timber's above ground." He winked and elbowed Judd, who tried to smile. "Know anything about felling trees?"

"Not as much as I know about mining coal, but I figure to learn."

Hank slapped his knee. "Good enough. I'll need to run it by Mr. Heyward, but you can count yourself good as hired. Got a place to stay?"

"Nope. I have yet to set foot on South Carolina soil."

"Well son, I think you'll like it. Although it's a mite sandier than what you're used to."

Judd turned to look out the window at the scrubby pines whipping past the window. He'd call this Providence if he believed in such things. But if Providence were real, it would have saved Joe's life. If Providence were real, he wouldn't even be here—a man without a home drifting on a southern breeze.

16

CHAPTER
3

MYRTLE BEACH, SOUTH CAROLINA

Larkin flounced into her father's office at the Waccamaw Timber Company headquarters and perched on the edge of his desk, giving him her most winning smile. "Daddy, everyone's going down to the Pavilion this evening. I'm a woman grown now and I can't imagine why you think I shouldn't go."

Her father looked at her over half-glasses and grunted. "Since when do you do anything because someone else did it first?"

Larkin huffed. She had every intention of meeting her girlfriends—and maybe some young men as well—but she craved her father's approval. "You and Mother should come with me."

George Heyward leaned back in his chair and laughed deep and long. "That's a good one. Your mother at the Pavilion." He looked thoughtful. "Though I'd surely enjoy spinning her around the dance floor a time or two." He got a faraway look in his eye. "Light on her feet, that one."

"Why, Daddy, you sound downright romantic."

He gave her a frosty look. "You still have a great deal to learn, young lady. Now shoo." He motioned her toward the door.

Larkin scooted back out into the wilting late-August heat choosing to believe her father's wish to dance with her mother was approval of her own plans to go out that evening. As she stepped onto the sizzling sidewalk, she saw Hank Chapin headed toward the office with a stranger in tow. The man dogging Hank's steps was at least six feet tall with dark hair and an odd, hitching gait. As they drew closer, Larkin noticed he had the most appealing dimple in his chin and blue-gray eyes that looked . . . tired, she decided.

"Hey there, Larkin. Your dad inside?"

"He is, although I'm not sure about his mood." She tossed her auburn curls and adjusted the straps of her sundress. She was grateful the heat hadn't had a chance to wilt her too much. "Aren't you going to introduce me?"

Hank made a little bow. "Larkin Heyward, this is Judd Markley, lately of Bethel, West Virginia, and soon to become a resident of our fair city."

The man held his hand out and smiled, but it didn't relieve the sorrow of those stormy eyes. "Pleased to meet you."

Larkin gave him her hand and ducked her chin. "Likewise." She looked up. "West Virginia is awfully far away. What brings you this far south in the heat of summer?"

Judd looked across the street in the direction of the ocean and squinted, as though he thought he might see it if he looked hard enough. "Reckon I needed a change."

He looked back at her, and Larkin felt as if he could see past her lipstick, nail polish, and curls to the girl underneath it all. It was unnerving. She pushed hair back from her damp forehead, wishing she'd pulled it back in her signature ponytail. "Well, this must be a change, indeed." She gave him a nod. "Pleasure to meet you, but I'd better be on my way. Good luck with Daddy," she said to Hank over her shoulder.

She walked away feeling the stranger's eyes on her back. As she turned into the car lot, she snuck a look at him, but he'd turned and was following Hank into the office. She felt a stab of disappointment. But that was silly. He was just a hillbilly. With the saddest, truest eyes she'd ever seen.

◆ ◆ ◆

Judd tucked his shirt deeper into his trousers, hoping to smooth out the wrinkles as they entered the office building. Hank had taken him to a boardinghouse and vouched for him so he could get a room without having to pay up front, but he hadn't had time to do more than dump his bag and wash his face. He ran his fingers through his hair and thought about how fresh and crisp Larkin Heyward looked out there on the sidewalk. He felt cooler just looking at her starched dress against her golden skin.

Maybe if you lived around here, you got used to the heat. He crossed his arms wishing he'd had time to change into a fresh shirt. He'd sweated through this one. Goodness knows he'd sweated his fair share over the years, but rarely had it been the result of riding in a truck and walking across a parking lot.

Hank motioned him into an office, where a bull of a man sat behind a desk intent on a stack of paper. He looked at them and pushed his glasses up his nose. He grunted and stood, sticking out a hand.

"Hank, good to have you back. You get everything straightened out up there in North Carolina?"

"I did, I did—it wasn't much of a dustup, after all. Just needed someone to clarify the situation."

The man nodded and peered at Judd, squinting a little as though his glasses weren't strong enough. "Who's our guest?"

"George Heyward, this is Judd Markley—he mined coal up in West Virginia and he fought in Korea. Got to know him on the ride back into town. I'm thinking he'll do right by us on one of the pulpwood crews."

Judd stepped up and stuck out his hand. "Pleased to meet you, sir. I'm not afraid of hard work. Been doing it since I got big enough to tail my brother into the fields."

Mr. Heyward took off his glasses and looked Judd over from top to bottom. "Seems like you had a hitch in your come-along as you walked into the office. Will that affect your ability to work?"

Judd could have sworn the man hadn't looked at him until he was standing in front of his desk. "Broke my leg in a mine cave-in." He thumped the leg in question. "But it's healed up now. I may not run as fast as I once did, but it won't keep me from working up a sweat."

The older man took in the dark circles under Judd's arms and got a sly look around his eyes. "It would seem not." He cocked his head at Hank. "If Hank thinks you'll do, then you almost certainly will. Hank, start him on the loading crew, and if he works out, train him on the saws." He looked back at Judd. "You ever use a chainsaw, son?"

"No, sir, but it can't be much harder than swinging a pickax stooped over underground. And I'm good with just about any kind of machinery."

Mr. Heyward nodded. "You can start on Monday. Hank will get you situated."

Obviously dismissed, Judd stepped back out into the hall. Hank followed him and told him to wait while he spoke to Mr. Heyward. Judd stepped over to the window and watched cars and people go by. The only trees he could see looked something like the palm trees he'd seen in a picture of Hawaii one time, but they were smaller and there weren't any coconuts. The sun was brighter than he thought it could ever be, and people moved slow, like they knew better than to rush in the heat. He watched what had to be folks on vacation drive by in convertible cars and wondered how far it was to the ocean. He had a hankering to walk along the beach and see the surf up close. He'd seen the

20

ocean on his way to and from Korea, but he hadn't been what you'd call paying attention.

"You want me to take you back to the boardinghouse? Or somewhere else?" Hank slipped up on him and slapped his shoulder. "I think the boss man likes you."

Judd didn't much care if George Heyward liked him, just so long as he paid him. "I'd like to see the ocean."

Hank grinned. "I forgot you're a mountain boy. Alright then, I'll drop you down by the pier and pick you up again"—he looked at his watch—"at six. I'll buy you your first seafood dinner."

Judd thought to protest, but when he considered how little cash he had, he opted to swallow his pride. He'd earn a paycheck soon enough and buy Hank a dinner in return.

"Sounds fine."

"Excellent. Come on. Let's get some sand between your toes."

🌢🌢🌢

Judd stood near the sand dunes considering the array of people scattered across the beach. He tried not to stare at the women in their swimwear. Bare shoulders, legs, and even midsections left him wondering what to do with his eyes. He skimmed over the multicolored umbrellas and blankets before resting his gaze on the water. He took a step into the shifting sand and quickly decided he'd best remove his shoes and socks. Rolling up his pant legs, he tucked his shoes behind a clump of sea grass and picked his way down to the surf.

Compared to the rocky soil of West Virginia, the sand felt soft under his feet. And hot—fiery hot. Winding his way past families, couples, and other beachgoers, he reached the cooler packed sand where waves curled and receded. Voices, the crashing of the surf, and even sea gulls blended to fill his ears with a roaring that left his mind fuzzy. He stood where the water could lick his toes and scanned the sea before him.

There were a few swimmers and some children playing near the shore. He tried to take in the extent of the water.

"Let me guess, it's not as big as you thought it would be."

Judd turned toward the voice to see Larkin Heyward standing there, sandals dangling from one hand and a straw hat hiding glints of fire in her russet hair.

"It's not so much that," he said. "It feels like I can't see it proper." He squinted down the beach to where a pier extended into the water. "Maybe if I got up on top of something I could get a good look at it."

Larkin laughed like ice in a glass on a hot day, and Judd felt as though something cool had run down his spine. "Come on, then," she said. "Off to the pier."

She started walking and he fell in beside her. She wasn't in any hurry, and he tried to match his gait to hers.

"Did Daddy hire you on?"

"He did. I start Monday on a loading crew."

She wrinkled her nose, and Judd stuck his hands in his pockets just for something to do with them. "You'll burn up out there. Especially not being used to this heat. What did you do before?"

"I mined coal." Judd wished he had something better to say. Joe would have told about being a coal miner so that it sounded like something special, something interesting even to a pretty girl on a beach in South Carolina.

"Well, that doesn't sound much nicer," she said, pushing strands of hair back from her face. "I do volunteer work. Daddy says I don't need to work at all, but Mother says I'd better keep busy, so it's a compromise."

"What sort of volunteering?" Judd was grateful for the breeze off the ocean. He wished he could lift his arms so it would have better access, but didn't think Larkin would appreciate it.

"I'm a candy striper at the Ocean View Memorial Hospital— it's new."

22

Judd didn't quite know what a candy striper was, but he hated to ask. "That sounds interesting."

"Oh, it is. We wear the most adorable pinafores and do things like deliver mail and food to the patients. Some of the girls think it's a good way to meet doctors." Her gaze slid toward him from under the brim of her hat. "But I'd really like to be a nurse and help people. I thought this would give me a head start if Daddy ever decides to let me go to school." She raised her chin. "Or if I decide to go whether he lets me or not. I am twenty-one now. "

They walked in silence a few moments. "Actually, I was headed over to the hospital when I saw Hank dropping you off at the beach. I'm not working today, but sometimes I go in for an hour and read to anyone who wants me to." She sighed. "Mother says idle hands are the devil's workshop, and she's mostly right."

They finally reached the pier, where Judd took Larkin's hand to help her up the dunes so they could walk out across the rough boards. Although his feet were plenty tough, Judd wished he'd thought to bring his shoes as Larkin slipped hers back on. They strolled in silence out to the end of the pier and leaned against the railing. Judd took in the expanse of the ocean all around them.

"Any bigger?" Larkin asked.

Judd chuckled. "I think it got smaller. Maybe the ocean's not something any one mind can take in all at once."

She looked at him, and a slow smile spread across her face. "Yes, that's it exactly. You can only look at it in bits." She glanced at a narrow watch on her wrist. "Oh my goodness, I'd better scurry. I'm sorry to run off and leave you, but Mr. Wilson will be devastated if he doesn't get to hear the next chapter of *Fahrenheit 451*."

She leaned forward and gave Judd a quick squeeze on the arm, then clamped a hand over her hat and trotted back the way they'd come. She turned and waved. "You can find your way back, can't you?"

He nodded and raised a hand. She smiled almost as big as the ocean and hurried on her way. Judd watched her until she was too small to make out. Their short visit had left him feeling unsettled—it was as though she'd reminded him of something he'd rather forget. He shrugged and wandered back to his shoes where he sat down on the sand to wait for Hank. The thrum of the waves, the voices of children, and the enveloping heat left him feeling stupefied, which he preferred to what Larkin had stirred.

Staring vacantly at his feet, he heard a voice he recognized. "Hey, you old bushwhacker, where you been hiding that girl?"

Judd lurched to his feet and looked everywhere for his brother. He'd heard Joe's voice, he was sure of it. His gaze landed on two men slapping each other on the back while a girl in a strapless swimsuit smiled up at them from a blanket. One of the men spoke again, and Judd realized he only sounded a little like Joe. Only just enough to keep the pain of his loss fresh even though he was so very far from home.

CHAPTER

4

That evening, Larkin bathed and changed into plaid pedal pushers, flats, and an eyelet blouse. She tied her hair back into a ponytail and curled it just so. Then she made sure she left the family's modern, brick ranch well before her father was expected home. Mother raised her eyebrows as Larkin headed toward the back door.

"Young lady, you need to do something with that spider plant on the sun porch. If you don't get your green thumb under control, we're going to be overrun."

Larkin rolled her eyes. "I'll get to it, I promise."

Her mother pinched her lips. "Can I assume you won't be joining us for supper?"

"I'll grab something at Peaches with the girls. Don't worry about me."

Mother shook her head. "Greasy hamburgers and milk shakes." She straightened Larkin's cap sleeve. "Fine then, just don't come home late. You know your father frets."

Larkin dropped a kiss on her mother's cheek and grinned before darting out the door. She'd go pick up Nell and then they'd meet Patty at the diner. Patty's brother Leon was bringing her, probably because he had a big ole crush on Nell, but Larkin planned to stay out of that mess. The top was still down on her 1948 Buick Roadmaster. A graduation present from her father, she adored the seafoam-green car, especially when she could drive it to the beach with the top down. She tied a scarf over her hair and slid into the driver's seat.

Twenty minutes later, she and Nell parked near the Pavilion, primped in the rearview mirror, and hurried over to claim three stools at Peaches Corner. Patty joined them not five minutes after they sat down, and Leon hung around like he hoped another seat might open up. Patty finally shooed him away, although Larkin suspected Nell wouldn't have minded if he stayed.

As they waited for their food, Larkin looked around, feeling the electricity she always did when she had a chance to get out and dance. There would be handsome boys, great music, a breeze off the ocean, and the wonderful feeling that came with doing something she was good at. Larkin didn't consider herself particularly vain, but she knew she was an excellent dancer. Sometimes she wished she'd taken ballet lessons or something like that, but she didn't learn that she could dance until middle school, and by then everyone said it was too late. She bit into the burger a waitress slid across the counter and tried to swallow her impatience along with the food. Nell and Patty would sit and talk forever, and all Larkin wanted to do was dance.

She tapped a toe and bided her time. It wouldn't be long now.

◆ ◆ ◆

Hank picked up Judd right on time. Although Judd had brushed the sand off his feet, he could still feel a bit of grit inside his shoes. He guessed that was just the way it would be now that he'd made his bed so far south of the mountains he'd known all his life. This new way would take some getting used to, and until he did he guessed there'd be some grit to aggravate him.

"You ready for a seafood feast?" Hank rubbed his hands together as he pulled into the lot under a sign that read *Sea Captain's House.*

"Sure thing." Judd was pretty sure he'd never eaten seafood. He'd had plenty of trout, crappie, bream, and bass, but he supposed they'd be eating ocean fish here.

They pushed through the door, and the smell of fried things assaulted Judd. A waitress wearing a ruffled apron ushered them to a table and offered menus, but Hank waved them away. "Bring us two fisherman's platters. And I'll have a beer. Judd?"

"Iced tea," he said. He wasn't opposed to having a beer but wanted to keep his wits about him.

The waitress disappeared with a smile and nod.

"So what'd you think of the ocean?"

Judd leaned back in his chair and wiggled his toes inside his left shoe, trying to dislodge the grains of sand eating into the bottom of his foot. "Impressive."

Hank grinned. "Most folks say it's not as big as they thought it'd be when they first see it."

"I guess it's plenty big enough. Just wish I could get up on a mountain and see it proper."

"Son, you have left the mountains behind. We might round you up a molehill or a sand dune. Or you could always shinny up a palmetto and see how it looks from there."

"Reckon I saw enough. Might like to fish off that pier sometime."

"You made it all the way down to the pier and back?" Hank seemed surprised and maybe a little pleased. Judd opted not to mention he'd had company. "Fishing I can handle. First day we both have off we'll head on out there and see what we can hook. Then maybe, one of these days, you can return the favor by taking me hunting up there in West Virginia. I hear the deer are twice the size of the ones in South Carolina."

The waitress appeared with plates of food, saving Judd from

responding. He looked over the pile of fried stuff heaped on an oval platter big enough to feed half of Bethel. And this was just for him. He dug in, realizing he was near starved enough to polish off the whole thing.

After a few minutes, Hank took a long swallow of beer and pointed at Judd's plate with his chin. "How is it?"

"Almost as good as rainbow trout rolled in cornmeal and fried in butter."

Hank laughed long and loud. "Sounds like we can take the man out of West Virginia, but not West Virginia out of the man." He watched Judd wash some popcorn shrimp down with a swallow of sweet tea. "You'll get a full-on dose of the South when you start loading pulpwood on Monday. Eat up, son. You're gonna need your strength."

After dinner, Hank dropped Judd off at the boardinghouse. He unpacked his few things—clothes in the dresser drawer, toiletries on the dresser top, Bible, and Joe's copy of *The Deer Stalker* by Zane Grey on the bedside table. Then he sat in the only chair in the room and considered what to do next. It was Friday and he had two days to get through until he reported for work. Hank said he'd pick him up Monday and take him out to the jobsite. Seemed like a long time till then.

Judd decided to get out and walk around the neighborhood. Maybe he could find a place to buy some provisions to last him through the weekend. Goodness knows he wasn't going to eat any more fisherman's platters until he'd gotten a paycheck or two. He wished Joe were there to play cards with him. Shoot, he just wished Joe were anywhere.

He went out to the hall bathroom where he washed his face and combed his hair, then headed out the front door. Although his room was muggy enough, he halfway expected to step out into a cool evening breeze, but it was just as hot at eight o'clock as it had been at three. This would take some getting used to. He walked slow—like the locals did—recognizing the wisdom of it in a place where he almost thought he could grab ahold of the air and wring water from it. He marveled that the sidewalk was dry beneath his feet.

Not certain of where to go, Judd set off in the general direction of the ocean without thinking about it. After a few blocks, he realized he could see lights and hear music down there somewhere. It offered a sort of siren song that he resisted at first. But why? Why resist? He tucked his hands in his pockets and ambled on toward the glow and what he imagined was the sound of breakers against the beach.

The first thing he saw was the top of a Ferris wheel turning against the sky. There was also a merry-go-round and a handful of other rides. Judd had seen a traveling circus a time or two, but this was something else altogether—fancier. Across the street was a massive building with an arched roof that said *Pavilion*—the music seemed to be coming from there. Judd felt flustered by all the noise and lights. This was a long way from an evening stroll down a country lane. And the people—they were everywhere.

Drifting with the crowd, Judd thought to make his way through the chaos and maybe see if he could access the beach beyond. He could smell hot dogs, cotton candy, and salt air with an undercurrent of . . . perfume maybe. It was a heady mix. He shoved his hands in his pockets and moseyed, noticing he was one of the few men with long pants and socks on. His mother would have a fit if she could see all these young men clomping around sockless in their good shoes.

A cool hand slipped inside Judd's elbow, and he nearly hollered. He got a grip on himself before he threw the offender to the ground and was almighty glad he did. It was Larkin smiling up at him, lips pink, cheeks rosy, and auburn hair tousled by the breeze.

"You keep turning up everywhere I go."

Judd smiled at the pretty girl and noticed two more pretty

girls with her. What was it about South Carolina and women with soft skin and sparkling eyes? Maybe it was just the heat and how they tended to have more skin showing. He tried to steer his thoughts back into safer waters.

"Just out for my evening constitutional."

Judd's comment seemed to tickle Larkin's funny bone. She laughed, leaning into his side. "Well, we're on our way to the Pavilion to dance. Why don't you come with us? I'll teach you to shag."

"I'm not much for dancing."

Larkin took notice of Judd's limp. "Oh, I'm sorry. Is your leg . . . will it . . . did you get hurt?"

"Mine cave-in." Judd tried to even out his gait.

Larkin's free hand flew to her mouth, and the other two girls suddenly began hovering around him like mosquitoes. They lobbed questions at him until he felt dizzy but never waited on him to answer.

"I'm fine. It's fine. You ladies go on and enjoy your dancing."

Larkin flicked a look at the building where they could see dancers gliding around inside. The look on her face was one of pure longing. "You girls go ahead. I'll catch up in a minute."

Judd found himself passing the Pavilion and coming out on a boardwalk on the ocean side with Larkin's fingers still tucked in at his elbow. How was it that her hand felt cool in this heat?

"You should go on and dance. I get the feeling you want to."

Larkin sighed and leaned on the railing, looking out over the beach and the surf beyond. Families had mostly given way to couples strolling hand in hand or sitting near the dunes, tucked in close to one another.

"I do enjoy dancing ever so much, but I can't abandon you on your first night in town."

"Aww, I was just out getting the lay of the land. I aimed to head on back once I hit the ocean."

Larkin giggled. "I like the way you talk."

Judd felt his ears get hot and turned his face toward the breeze coming off the ocean. "Does it ever cool off around here?"

"Sure—wait until December and January—you'll need a coat."

Judd swallowed a laugh. "I'll be looking forward to that."

"So you plan to stay here?"

Judd blew air. "For now. My plans aren't too definite at the moment."

"Oh. Well, I have plans." Larkin stuck her pert chin up in the air.

"What would that be?"

"I want to help people—like my brother does. He gave up everything to become a missionary. Daddy was pretty mad, but I'm proud of him." She looked almost smug as she said it. She slid a glance his direction. "West Virginia is supposed to have lots of people who need help."

Judd couldn't think what she was getting at. "We mostly take care of our own."

"But Appalachia is such a poor, backwards place. You hear about hillbillies and barefooted children who leave school before the eighth grade—things like that. I want to help."

"Not sure where you're hearing that sort of thing. I suppose there are always folks in need, but no more than anywhere else."

"Well, I read an article in *Ladies' Journal* that says the Appalachian Mountains with their coal-mining communities, rough country, poor roads, and lack of education is an area of greatest need in the United States."

It sounded like she was quoting her blasted article. Judd gripped the railing in front of him and debated whether or not he wanted to make her mad. He tried to think what Joe, who always got along with everybody, would do. He finally decided it didn't matter since he wasn't Joe.

"Well if it's written down in the *Ladies' Journal*, it must be true," he said.

Larkin narrowed her eyes at him, apparently deciding to give him the benefit of the doubt, and smiled. "Exactly. So my plans are to go to Kentucky or West Virginia and help people."

Judd almost snorted, but managed to cough instead. "That so? Reckon they'll be glad to see you."

Larkin turned toward him and grasped his arm. "And now that I know you, you can tell me where to go and who needs help. You're an insider."

"That I am." Judd thought about being buried inside a mountain. "That I am."

"So you'll help me?" She looked at him with soft lips parted, eyes dancing with her plans to change the world.

"Nope."

Her face fell and she looked astonished. "What?"

"Don't look to me to help you. I left for a reason. If you want to go make the world a better place, more power to you. Me, I'm going back to my room and getting a good night's sleep so I can do the work your father is paying me for come Monday."

He walked away, not even caring if his limp showed. He didn't need anyone's pity or help. Least of all a pampered Southern girl who didn't even know the half of his story or the story of his people back home in poor, backwards West Virginia.

CHAPTER

5

Well.

Larkin watched Judd limp away for a minute, then spun on her heel and almost jogged toward the Pavilion. She'd never told anyone about her dream to make a difference in the mountains of Appalachia—to follow in her brother's footsteps by helping people—and now that she had she was sorry. She'd been so sure Judd would not only understand but be excited to help her. They were his own people, for goodness' sake.

Inside the Pavilion, she caught a glimpse of Nell dancing with Leon, who couldn't do the Carolina shag for spit but seemed game to try, so long as Nell was his partner. Patty waved to her from the edge of the crowd, and Larkin hurried to join her.

"Did you get rid of your hillbilly friend? He's handsome enough, but he doesn't quite fit in around here, does he?"

Larkin bristled, though she couldn't say exactly why. "It's his first day in town. He probably just needs time to adjust."

"But he's a coal miner and probably never even finished high school." Patty tossed her sleek, dark hair over her shoulder. "There's adjusting and then there's changing your spots."

"He could've been to college for all you know." Why was she defending him after he scoffed at her?

Patty laughed. "Sure. And when Wayne Gragg gets over here, he's going to ask me to dance instead of you."

Larkin turned to see Wayne weaving through the crowd in their direction. Normally, she'd be delighted to see him. Handsome and with the proper pedigree, her parents had none too subtly encouraged her to see more of him. And she didn't mind most of the time. He was an excellent dancer, was about to finish college with a business degree, and clearly liked her. Although she had a notion he liked other girls, too, and hadn't quite made his mind up about whom he'd settle on. But seeing him walk toward her on this sultry August evening, what she mostly felt was . . . tired.

"There's my best girl. What say we hit the dance floor?"

Larkin pasted on a smile and grabbed Wayne's hand to lead him out as "Sh-Boom" began playing. Larkin tried to focus on the music and forget about the tall, sad man from the mountains who scorned her dream. How could she even think about poor, uneducated children in West Virginia when she could be here, dancing with a handsome guy, breathing salt air, and feeling admiring gazes from around the floor? She put an extra swish in her hips as they danced and was rewarded with a wink from Wayne.

The song ended, and Larkin paused to get her breath. She could feel sweat trickling down her spine but didn't care. Everyone was hot and sticky on a night like this. The band switched gears and started "Stranger in Paradise." Wayne drew her closer without asking and began to slow-dance.

Larkin would have preferred to sit this one out with a cold soda, but she didn't protest. Wayne's hands were hot on the small of her back, and she could feel the sweat on his neck where she clasped her own hands. As Wayne leaned in, Larkin shifted her gaze to the boardwalk so he had no choice but to brush his lips against her temple. She'd let Wayne kiss her once before, but this was not the time or place for that. She let him pull her even closer as a sort of consolation for not kissing him, yet his presence was beginning to feel stifling. She listened to Tony Bennett sing.

"'Won't you answer this fervent prayer of a stranger in paradise?'"

Larkin gritted her teeth. Poor Judd. Here he was, far from home in a place that must seem exotic to him. And what did he have to look forward to? Slaving away in a pine plantation for her father. There'd be red bugs and snakes and the ever-present heat. Larkin's taste for dancing faded along with the final notes of the song.

"Wayne, I'm getting the worst headache. I think I'm going to have to call it a night." She drew back, but he held on to one hand.

"Aw, c'mon. All you need is a soda and the ocean breeze out on the boardwalk." He tugged at her hand. "I'll grab some drinks and we can go for a stroll." He waggled his eyebrows, and Larkin felt something like distaste.

Ducking her chin, Larkin poured on the syrup. "Darlin', I just don't think I can manage it this evening. You are too sweet to want to take care of me, but you go on and have a good time." Patty approached them like she'd been cued. Larkin grabbed her friend's arm. "Patty's just dying for a dance partner and you are the very best. You go on and dance with her. You can even drive her home. I'll be grateful for absolutely ever."

She batted her eyelashes at Wayne as she spoke to Patty. "I've got the worst sick headache and I've just got to go on home. Wayne's going to take good care of you." She tucked her friend's arm through Wayne's as the next song started. "Y'all go on now. Don't let me down."

Patty, clearly delighted, pulled Wayne back onto the dance floor. Larkin backed away and gave them both a little wave.

Wayne looked confused but he'd be fine. They'd both be fine. And now that she was free, Larkin realized she really did have a headache. Maybe she'd drive around a while with the top down and see if she couldn't blow this whole evening right out of her mind.

◊ ◊ ◊

Judd woke Monday morning in a puddle of his own sweat. He'd slept badly since arriving, waking throughout the night, feeling almost like he was drowning in the thick, humid air. When Joe dreamed about heading for South Carolina, he clearly had no idea what he was in for. He levered himself to his feet and staggered to the bathroom where he washed his face, brushed his teeth, and braced himself for the day ahead.

Outside, Judd sat on the top porch step squinting at the new day. What he wouldn't give for a plate of fried eggs and sausage with a couple of biscuits. He'd stopped at a small grocery store on Saturday and bought a few items to tide him over until payday. For breakfast he'd made do with a can of fruit cocktail and some bread with peanut butter. A lunch sack sat next to him with a sleeve of Saltine crackers, a can of Vienna sausages, and an apple. The thermos he'd brought from home was filled with cold water. He'd have to see about getting a hot plate if he was going to keep this up.

Hank pulled to the curb in a beat-up 1947 Chevy truck. He honked the horn and waved Judd over. They rode, mostly in silence, to the pine plantation with the windows down. Judd marveled at how even the breeze was warm.

As they pulled up to the work site, men were already laboring, circles of perspiration darkening their shirts in spite of the early hour. Hank pointed to an area where logs were being loaded onto trucks with a boom. "That's where you'll get started. Chuck Hardee—he's the one with the hat—will show you what to do. You can leave your gear in the truck."

Judd grunted, stowed his provisions under the seat, and walked over to the loading area while doing his best to hide his limp. He filled his lungs. It was almighty hot, but at least he could see the sun and feel the limpid breeze on his cheek. He'd take this over breathing coal dust in the dark any day. He wondered for a moment if Joe ever dreamed of heading someplace cooler.

Chuck turned out to be a cheerful fellow who kept his men moving with a string of stories and jokes that turned the air blue. Judd shook hands all around and settled into the camaraderie of men working. Chuck encouraged him to drink plenty of water from a jug in the shade, and Judd had a notion that what he drank ran right on out of him as he helped hoist and position log after log. His boots would probably start squishing before long.

Around noon the men seemed to instinctively know it was time to break for lunch. Everyone started drifting toward the shade where they fished out lunch sacks and boxes, sprawled out, and took their ease. Judd had never seen men work so hard and rest so thoroughly. In the mine, even when they rested, there was a tension to it. An awareness that there was a mountain hanging over their heads.

Judd grabbed his lunch sack and settled against the tire on the shady side of Hank's truck. Chuck moseyed over and flopped down beside him.

"I'm thinking you might work out."

Judd nodded and opened his sausage tin.

"I can tell you ain't afraid of hard work. Hank says you was a coal miner back in West Virginia." He laughed and took a bite of a sandwich. "I'm betting it was a mite cooler down there under the ground."

"It was. 'Course, being able to stand upright is its own reward."

Chuck slapped his thigh. "Son, I tell ya, I admire a man who'll brave the bowels of the earth, but me, I gotta have open space."

He waved an arm indicating the trees and land around them. "But not working a-tall is my long-term goal."

Judd smiled. He liked Chuck—he reminded him a little of Harry. "You been doing this long?"

"Too long, but it pays the bills and keeps me out of the wife's hair." He peeled back the bread from his sandwich and looked inside. "If only she could cook."

Judd took a look and couldn't see much of anything between the slices of bread. "What kind of sandwich is that?"

"Jam sandwich," Chuck said with a sigh. "Sometimes she gets in a hurry and just jams two pieces of bread together." He grinned and slapped his thigh again. "But she's awful purty and she takes good care of the young'uns, so I just eat what she gives me."

Judd offered Chuck a cracker with a sausage on top, and the other man took it with a wink.

Chuck slowly climbed to his feet. "You sit here for a spell. I've gotta get back over there and see can't we get that new skidder sorted out. It's been acting up." He shook his head. "Give me a good team of horses any day."

"I know a thing or two about mechanical parts," Judd said. "Be happy to give you a hand."

Chuck shrugged. "Can't do worse than the rest of us. Come on and give it a look-see."

Judd washed his last sausage down and followed Chuck over to the piece of equipment used to snake logs out of the woods. It looked like a bulldozer with tractor tires and a winch in back. He'd never worked on anything quite like it, but the prospect of getting some grease under his nails made him smile.

"Hydraulics quit on us," Chuck said. "Fellas took the floor-board up to make an adjustment this morning and can't get it working again. I'm afraid they've fouled it up good, but I hate to tell Mr. Heyward. We haven't had it even a month yet."

Judd watched several men wrangle with the machine, cussing

and using tools in ways not strictly intended. Chuck watched with him.

"Whatcha think?"

"Mind if I take a closer look?"

Chuck hollered at the men, "Make a hole and let West Virginia take a look at it."

One fellow who'd been beating on the skidder with a wrench looked particularly aggravated and made a sweeping *Help yourself* gesture. Judd checked the floorboard, poked around under the dash, noticed the hydraulics lever was up, and flipped it back down.

"Try 'er now."

The aggravated man hopped in the seat with a skeptical look, fired the skidder up, and lifted the front blade with ease. He looked surprised, then glared at Judd. "Coulda figured that out in another minute."

Judd shrugged and limped back to Chuck. His leg hurt from all the activity, but he was bound and determined not to show it. "Good as new," he said. "Easy to forget to put the disconnect lever back down."

Chuck grinned. "Say, you wouldn't want to take a look at a chainsaw I've got in the back of my truck, would you?"

Judd spent the rest of the afternoon tinkering with various pieces of equipment and getting most of them into working order. Chuck slapped him on the back when quitting time came. "You, sir, are a prize. I told Hank he did alright bringing you on the crew. Now I'm gonna tell him he needs to make you a mechanic. You're wasted limbing trees and loading logs."

"Motor's a motor, more or less." Judd scuffed a boot in the sandy soil. "Always did have a knack with moving parts. Been making things go since I was old enough to hold a wrench. Will it matter that I'm not what you'd call formally trained?"

Hank walked over from the foreman's shack. "Hear the good Lord did us a favor sending you down south. I'll talk to Mr.

Heyward this evening and I don't think he'll be opposed to promoting you to mechanic."

Chuck elbowed Judd. "There you go."

Hank headed for the truck. "Ready to call it a day?"

Judd nodded and swung into the passenger seat, trying to focus on the fact that he might get paid to use his talents at last—Joe would be proud. He melted against the seat inside the stifling truck. Leaving the windows down hadn't made much difference that he could tell. He felt utterly wrung out but didn't want Hank or any of the other men to see it. Once the truck started moving, Judd appreciated the breeze, warm as it was.

"First day go alright?"

Judd nodded and wished he had more water. He'd drained his thermos hours ago and had been almighty grateful for the jugs Chuck had ready for the men. Tomorrow he'd drink the company water and save his own for the trip home. Maybe to pour over the top of his head.

Hank chuckled. "You'll get used to it. You're not the first one to come down from the mountains and find our weather sucks the marrow right out of your bones."

Judd grinned in spite of himself. "Thought maybe I was hiding it pretty good."

"Son, you look like a half-drowned hound dog. Give it a year, you'll go back home and wonder how you ever stood the cold."

Judd stiffened at the mention of going home. "Don't aim to go home, so that won't be a problem."

"No? Not even for a visit?"

Judd rubbed his palm down his dusty pant leg. "Got a brother and his family back there. Not much else. Parents died a time ago and my . . . well, not much to pull me back anymore. Thought I'd let you'uns make a Southerner out of me." He'd almost mentioned Joe, but couldn't bring himself to say his baby brother's name.

Hank nodded and seemed to sense this was uneasy territory. "So how come they call you Judd?"

"It's short for *judge*. My name's Uriah, but when I was a tyke, everybody said I was solemn as a judge and it stuck." He didn't add that the *g* was dropped because Joe couldn't say it right.

"And now you're a regular barrel of laughs." Hank quirked an eyebrow at Judd, who fought the smile tugging at his lips.

"I suppose I'm still a bit on the solemn side. Took after my ma that way." He tilted his head back against the seat, enjoying being still for a moment. "She was a fine woman."

"Well, we sure are glad you decided to come south. We'll try not to kill you your first week out."

"Appreciate that," Judd said.

CHAPTER

6

Nothing was going right at the hospital today. Larkin flounced into the nurses' station with her empty tray. Mr. Wilson was cranky, the new patient in room 126 wasn't even awake, and the other candy striper on duty was hogging the maternity ward.

Nurse Enright gave her a disapproving look. The head nurse could freeze a fresh cup of coffee with that look of hers. Larkin offered a weak smile in return.

"Do you need help with anything? Seems my usual tasks have run out already."

Nurse Enright exhaled sharply through her nose. "As usual, there are bedpans to clean and floors to disinfect. And I suppose you could carry out old flowers and water plants since you're supposed to have a green thumb. That peace lily in the waiting room is near about dead." She looked over her glasses. "If you can stoop to do such as that."

Larkin pasted a smile on her face. "I'd be happy to." She grumbled to herself as she went to fetch the watering can and a trash bin. She'd start with the plants, that being the least offensive task. Although it meant refilling her can umpteen times, and patients often didn't want flowers removed no matter how dead they were. She should probably just go on home, but that would give Nurse Enright too much satisfaction.

She started with the lily, kneeling down to remove dead leaves, aerating the compacted soil, ruffling the few remaining leaves, and adding water. Why people seemed intent on killing houseplants was a mystery to her. It really wasn't hard to keep them healthy at all. Then she headed for the rooms to remove spent bouquets. She tried to cheer herself by counting how many vacant rooms there were. It was a good thing when people didn't need to be in the hospital. Absorbed in her work and her thoughts, Larkin almost missed hearing the small voice coming from room 126.

"Nurse? Can I have some water?"

Larkin looked around. She was the only one within earshot and getting some water certainly fell within her duties. She set down her watering can and trash bin and stepped into the room.

"I'm not a nurse, but I'll be glad to get you some water."

The frail woman who looked to be in her thirties smiled up from her pillow. "That'd be fine." Her voice was whispery and soft like a breeze through pine branches.

Larkin grabbed the little pitcher from the table and went for ice, then added water. She bustled back into the room and poured some into a cup with a bent straw. She held it for the woman to sip. She raised her head and drew on the straw, closing her eyes as the cool liquid slid down her throat. "Oh my. That is delicious." She patted Larkin's hand with fingers dry and fragile as corn husks. "I thank you."

Larkin set the cup down but didn't want to leave just yet. "What's your name?"

"Lillian Ashworth. I'd be glad if you'd call me Lill."

"I'm Larkin Heyward and I'm delighted to make your acquaintance."

Lill smiled and glanced toward the window. "Look at me.

Have to come all the way to the hospital just to meet someone new. I have hardly been out of the house since I got sick."

Larkin pulled a chair over to the side of the bed. "Where do you live?"

"Over in Daisy—been there since my grandmother died and left me the prettiest little house. I loved visiting her there—she was just about the only family I had." Lill rubbed her shoulder like it ached. "I'm not sure what will happen to the place once I'm gone."

"But you can go back there when you're well," Larkin said, patting her new friend's hand.

Lill wrapped her fingers around Larkin's in an iron grip. "Honey, I don't much expect to get well."

Larkin wanted to ask what was wrong with her—usually she found out from the nurses, but Lill was new and no one had filled her in.

"Are you wondering what's wrong with me?" Lill's dark eyes sparkled even though they were sunken above high cheekbones. "Cancer. Scared the stuffing out of me when the doctor first told me, but turns out you can get used to just about anything. And now I'm just tired." She released Larkin's hand. "And ready to tell this bad old world goodbye."

Larkin wasn't sure what to say to that. She'd faced patients who were intent on giving up before and had tried to encourage them, but Lill seemed different. She fought an urge to tell this woman who should have decades ahead of her that maybe it was all right to let go—to wave goodbye and move on to—what? Larkin had been to church often enough, but she wasn't all that clear on what came after a person died.

Standing, Larkin began to tidy the room, chattering on about how nice it was to live at the beach and how hot the weather had been this summer.

"Honey, you need to light a minute."

Larkin froze as she fluffed the curtains. She turned to look at Lill. "What?"

"Just sit back down here and be quiet with me. You're wearing me out just watching you flit around."

Larkin laughed uneasily and sat in the chair, tucking her striped pinafore around her legs. "Yes, ma'am."

Lill laughed and it sounded like wind chimes in a soft breeze. She pinned Larkin with her gaze. "I might be older than you are, but I'll thank you not to 'ma'am' me. Now, what do you want out of life?"

Larkin cocked her head. "Life?"

"I don't have time to talk about things that don't matter, so I thought I'd cut to the chase." She waved a feeble hand in the air. "You're young yet. Unmarried, I'm guessing. Your whole life ahead of you. What do you want?"

Larkin leaned forward, suddenly glad to have been asked. "I want to help people." She talked with her hands. "Not just bringing people water or cleaning the floors, I want to really make a difference. Educate children, feed people who are starving, make sure everyone has a roof over their heads—things like that. My brother, Ben, gave up a good future with our family business so he could go be a missionary, and I can't think of anything better."

Lill watched. She had wiggled her way a little higher in bed. Larkin noticed her scalp through her thinning hair.

"Then you'd better go do it." Lill pointed at Larkin and kept that unsteady finger in the air.

"What?"

Dropping her hand back to the white sheet, Lill repeated herself. "Go on and do whatever it is you think you're meant to do. I wanted to be a WASP, but I let friends talk me out of it." She sighed and plucked at the sheet covering her thin frame.

"A what?"

"WASP—Women's Air Force Service Pilot." Her eyes got a faraway look. "Can't you just imagine? Flying planes from factories to air bases during World War II. Some of those women even flew simulated missions. I got to ride in an airplane one time and I just knew flying is what God made me to do."

Larkin could picture Lill in an aviator's helmet with a white scarf in stark contrast to her tan skin and dark hair. "Why didn't you do it?"

Lill refocused on Larkin. "Fear. Fear of giving up the good job I had. Fear that I might not be accepted or, if I was, that I might fail." She gazed out the window as though picturing herself soaring among the clouds. "The only thing I wasn't afraid of was dying, and now here I am, doing that anyway."

A nurse came into the room with a blood pressure cuff and thermometer. She smiled absently at Larkin and spoke to Lill. "Time to take your vitals. Won't hurt a bit."

Larkin squeezed Lill's hand and moved toward the door, but not before she thought she saw Lill roll her eyes at the nurse. "You remember what I said."

Larkin picked up her watering can. Indeed. She was going to remember this for some time. Who needed Judd Markley's help? If she was meant to serve the poor of Appalachia, then nothing and no one could stop her.

◊ ◊ ◊

After a week on the job, Judd felt like he was adjusting to South Carolina. Of course, being switched to mechanic was a big help. Not only did it mean a little more pay, it was also a heck of a lot easier on his leg. And it gave him satisfaction to know that he was doing the job the mine foreman had refused him. He guessed he was living Joe's dream, but it didn't satisfy the way he'd expected. He still woke up in a pool of sweat every few nights, fighting to shake a dream about crawling around in mine-deep darkness looking for Joe. Maybe there was something more Joe wanted, and once he figured that out, he'd find peace.

Hank ferried him around between several jobs, and then on

Friday afternoon, the third of September, he ended up back on the job where he started. One of the trucks needed tuning up. From his perch under the hood, Judd noticed the men were livelier than they had been. He guessed it was the start of the weekend. He understood their enthusiasm, but in his short time on the crew he learned that cutting timber was no time to let your guard down. He wished they'd save the horsing around for later.

"Great Caesar's ghost," Chuck hollered. "Show some care, man."

Judd glanced at the foreman and saw him standing as though frozen, face ashen. Ducking out from under the hood, Judd looked toward the crew. The skidder operator, a man named Pete, was notching a tree. Didn't look like anything out of the ordinary to Judd. Pete was just cutting a tree. Except, as Judd looked toward the top of the tree Pete was working on, he saw that an already-felled tree was hung in its top. Then, as though a giant hand tipped it, the already-felled tree swung suddenly free and plummeted to the ground. One minute Pete was there with his chainsaw, and the next there was nothing but treetop. It was like a magic trick Judd had seen once. Only he knew this was no trick. The whole crew ran toward the downed tree.

Judd drew up next to Chuck, who was panting. "He knew better than to jump in there like that. Who gave him a saw?"

Mike, one of the regular cutters, hung his head. "Told him it weren't a good idea, but he hopped off the skidder and grabbed my chainsaw when I hung that first tree. Said he'd show me how it's done."

Chuck cursed and began directing men to cut away branches. "Mike, see can't you get on in there and find Pete. We'll start cutting in case we need to carry him out."

The look on Chuck's face made Judd feel carrying Pete out was the likeliest scenario. Mike shoved through the branches

and hollered back after a couple of minutes. "He's breathing."
There was a softer exclamation that Judd could barely hear.

"What's that, son?" Chuck called back.

"Better make a stretcher."

The men cut away the bulk of the treetop. Once exposed,
Judd could see that Pete's right leg was bent at an unnatural
angle. He swallowed down bile and the memory of his own
broken leg. Pete moaned. Blood ran down one side of his face
where a branch had scraped the skin away, and he cradled his
right wrist against his chest.

"Hang in there, Pete. We'll get you to the hospital lickety-
split." Chuck rubbed his forehead and turned to Judd. "You
can fix machines. How are you at fixin' men?"

Judd swallowed. "We had fellers get hurt in the mines a time
or two." He tried hard not to think about the men who'd died in
the mines. "I'd get some cloth and wrap that arm he's favoring
tight to his chest." He looked at the bent leg, closed his eyes, and
looked again. "From what I understand, you don't want to move
that leg any more than you have to. Get a straight stick and lash
it there so it'll keep things from moving around. Hold a handkerchief up tight against his head. That's gonna bleed and bleed."

Two men came running up with a makeshift stretcher. Chuck
laid a hand on Judd's arm. "Sounds like a good plan. We'll
gather the supplies; you get on in there and get started."

Judd blanched. "Me? I was just giving advice. I'd rather
not . . ." He trailed off as he looked into Chuck's tight face.
"Yes, sir. I'll do what I can."

Judd picked his way through the pine branches and crouched
down beside Pete, who was repeating a string of curses like a
mantra. Judd shook out a clean handkerchief, made a pad, and
gave it to Mike to press against the worst of the cuts on Pete's
head. Pete cursed louder and looked at Judd like a coyote with
one foot in a trap.

Judd licked his parched lips. "Pete, just so you know, I broke my leg maybe worse than this once and, well, it hurts like the dickens, but I reckon you'll live. Now, if you'll let me, I'm gonna get you situated so we can haul you to the hospital."

The fire went out of Pete's eyes. "That why you gimp around?" Judd nodded as somebody handed him torn strips of fabric. "Am I gonna be a gimp?"

Judd almost smiled but caught himself. "There are worse things, but maybe not." He glanced at the bone sticking out through a tear in Pete's pant leg and was surprised to find it less disturbing than before. "Looks like a good, clean break. All you'll get is a nice long rest in a cool hospital bed with pretty nurses to look after you."

Pete grimaced, making his bloodied face look even worse. "You might be lying to me, but I'll take it." He closed his eyes.

Judd began to wind strips of fabric around the arm that might be broken but at least didn't look it. Then he took stout sticks and tied them into place against Pete's bent leg. He almost felt used to the odd angle by now, although he heard Mike go over and throw up in a pile of cut branches. He looked back at Pete and supposed he'd gone on and passed out. Which was best.

They finally got the injured man loaded on the stretcher and hauled him to Hank's truck where they'd made a sort of pallet in the bed.

"The two of us can ride back here with him," Chuck said, climbing in.

Judd struggled a little with his bum leg, yet he managed to hop in, as well. They sat on either side of Pete's head, and Judd pressed a fresh handkerchief to the injured man's temple. The bleeding had slowed, thank goodness, and Pete slipped in and out of consciousness. Judd tried to enjoy the breeze as they drove, slow and careful, to the hospital. He wondered if it really was worse to die beneath the ground than above it.

◊ ◊ ◊

Larkin was just about to leave when she saw Hank Chapin's truck pull up to the emergency entrance. Her earlier weariness evaporated as she hurried over, afraid something had happened to Hank. She was relieved to see him hop out of the driver's side and hurry around to the back. She craned her neck to see where he was headed, and Judd's face popped into her mind's eye. It was easy to get hurt logging and he was so new . . .

Hank saw Larkin and waved her over. "Hey gal, can you let 'em know we got a man here with a real bad leg break and a knock on the head?"

Larkin peeked at the men climbing down from the bed and saw that one was Judd. He saw her and nodded without looking the least bit pleased. But of course he was concerned about the hurt man. Larkin rushed through the doors and waved orderlies out with a gurney. She saw blood as they transferred an injured man over. He groaned and his color was ashy. Larkin didn't recognize him, but then she only knew a few of the foremen and supervisors. She trailed after the group as they took the man inside the hospital.

Bringing up the rear, Larkin saw a shiver run through Judd as he hit the mechanically cooled air inside the building. She enjoyed air conditioning at home but felt certain Judd's room at the boardinghouse wouldn't have it. She was still wearing her pinafore, but pulled her striped cap out of her bag and pinned it back on as she caught up to her father's new hire.

"Is it bad?" She laid a hand on Judd's arm and kept her voice low.

He looked surprised to see her. "I forgot you worked at the hospital."

She bristled. "I volunteer—you know, helping people."

He almost smiled. "That's right, you're going to change the world." He sounded more impressed than mocking, and she relaxed a little.

"So, the man you brought in?"

SARAH LOUDIN THOMAS

Judd pursed his lips and ran a hand over his short hair. Larkin had the notion it would curl if he'd let it grow. "He's tore up, but he'll live. Leg's broke pretty bad, maybe his arm, too."

"And his head injury?"

This time Judd did grin. "His head's pretty hard. Probably what kept him from getting hurt worse."

"You got that right." The other man from the back of the truck stepped over and clasped Judd's shoulder. Larkin knew she'd seen him before but couldn't place him. "Chuck Hardee, ma'am. We met last Christmas."

Larkin smiled and nodded. "Of course, I remember. You and your lovely wife were at the company party. How is she?"

"Sassy as ever. I'll let her know you asked after her."

Hank joined the group. "They're pokin' and proddin' him back there. Doc says they may have to operate on that leg. Says whoever stabilized it did ole Pete a favor. If the bone had shifted around, could have done a whole lot more damage."

Chuck slapped Judd on the back. "This boy knows how to fix more than motors. He's the one clumb in there and trussed Pete up like a Christmas turkey. Son, I don't suppose you could teach my wife to cook?"

Judd grinned and ducked his head. "My ma made sure all us boys could cook before she died. Said we might be too ornery to catch wives, so she figured we'd better be able to feed ourselves."

Larkin found her annoyance with the lanky mountain man waning. It would appear he'd already made quite an impression on the lumbermen. Maybe the conversation she'd shared with him had happened on an off day. He'd only just arrived and was probably feeling out of sorts. Plus his mother was dead. She decided to forgive him.

"You have brothers?" she asked.

The light in Judd's eyes dimmed. "One brother."

"Oh, the way you said . . ." Something in his face made her

trail off. Now he looked mad again. "Well, if you gentlemen will excuse me, I'll see if the nurse has any news I can share with you." She spun on her heel and stalked off.

Judd Markley was an enigma, and she didn't have the time or the inclination to unravel him.

CHAPTER

7

Judd watched Larkin stomp off and felt bad about snapping at her. She had no way of knowing she'd put her foot smack-dab in the middle of the biggest regret of his life. He joined the other two men seated in orange plastic chairs that looked like they might throw a man to the floor if he dozed off. He sat as though the weight of that felled tree were on his shoulders. Joe didn't even make it as far as the hospital. Here he was being celebrated for binding the leg of a man he was pretty sure didn't like him, when he'd failed his own kin completely. He drew cool air in through his nose and wondered if this artificial air might hurt him. He halfway hoped it would.

Hank stood. "Fellas, it's getting along about suppertime. What say I drop Judd off at the boardinghouse on the way back to get Chuck's car?"

Chuck nodded and stood, seeming eager to be on his way home to that wife who couldn't cook. Judd had seen the affection in the other man's eyes. He suspected she had other positive attributes.

"You comin' back here?" Chuck asked.

"Soon as I get a bite to eat. I'll call Mr. Heyward and fill him in. We ought to have some sort of emergency contact for Pete back at the office. He married?"

Chuck shrugged. "Pete never did warm up to anybody much. Tight-lipped."

Judd leaned his elbows on his knees and noticed a sorry-looking peace lily in the corner of the room. It was near about dead, except for some green shoots in the middle and one brave bloom that almost floated over the pot. "I don't mind waiting here till you get back. It can be awful lonesome in a hospital."

"If they do surgery, he won't know whether he's alone or not for a good while, but if you want to stay you're welcome to it." Hank considered Judd and added, "I'm sure Pete will appreciate it."

Judd didn't know what Pete would think, he just knew he'd been glad to have Harry with him when he woke up in that hospital bed. And he didn't exactly have a full social schedule.

The other men left, and Judd sat staring at the floor some more. There were magazines on an end table, but none of them held any interest. He stood and stretched. His leg ached from working all week, and sitting in one position too long made it worse. He walked over to a coffeepot and poured himself a cup. He carried the burnt-smelling liquid to the window and stared out. It was still a long time until sunset, but it seemed like the day had stretched on longer than it should. He rubbed his jaw and felt the beginnings of stubble. Tomorrow was Saturday— maybe he'd go until Monday morning before he shaved. Didn't have anyone to clean up for.

"Would you like a sandwich?"

Judd spun around and found Larkin standing behind him with a little cart. She had a tray of sandwiches, some cups of fruit, and a plate of cookies. "Sometimes we bring refreshments out if folks have to wait a while."

Judd's stomach gurgled. It had been a long time since lunch.

"Well, seeing as how my belly's gnawing at my backbone, seems like a sandwich wouldn't go amiss."

Laughter sparked in Larkin's eyes, but she seemed determined to fight it back. "Would you like ham and cheese or egg salad?"

"Ham would be fine."

She handed him a sandwich wrapped in waxed paper. He sat and peeled the paper back, biting into a triangle of bread and meat. It wasn't half bad, although a summer tomato would go a long way to brightening it up.

"Fruit cup?"

"Sure thing." Judd accepted the cup and set it down on a side table. "You gonna join me?"

Larkin pinked. "We're not supposed to . . ."

"Nobody else around and you sure do have a pile of sandwiches there. Shame to let 'em go to waste."

Larkin glanced around, sighed, and plopped down next to him with a sandwich in her hand. "Nurse Enright will have a conniption if she sees me, but oh well." She picked at the paper around her sandwich. "Is Hank coming back?"

"Yes. He took Chuck back to get his car."

"And you stayed?"

Judd chewed on a bite of sandwich, thinking whether that required a response.

"I was in the hospital a spell with a busted leg. Shame to leave somebody on their own."

Larkin nodded. "The doctor's operating on your friend's leg now. He may not wake up fully for a few hours yet."

Judd nodded. "Them cookies up for grabs?"

Larkin laughed softly. "Oatmeal—I made them myself." She finally took a bite of her egg-salad sandwich and wrinkled her nose. "Hospital food will keep you from going hungry, but I wouldn't necessarily recommend it."

Judd laughed and it felt good. As a matter of fact, it was the first time he could remember feeling this sort of lightness around his heart since before Joe died. There was a night, a few days before the cave-in, when Joe came over and they sat up playing cards and telling lies until Abram told them to either go to bed or take it outside. They'd gone out on the porch, where Joe produced a jar of moonshine. They'd sipped and talked softly until the wee hours. Joe had been spinning dreams about how he was going to see the world. He wanted to start by seeing the ocean and then maybe he'd sail right on across it. After that he'd get a girl—maybe in France or Spain—and after they had some fun, he supposed he might marry her and have some kids.

For the first time, the sorrow of thinking about Joe failed to outweigh the sweet. Judd had made it as far as the ocean for his baby brother, and while he didn't know that he was going to sail on across it, he had met a girl. Judd looked at Larkin and debated telling her about Joe.

Before he could speak, she stood and dropped her sandwich on a lower shelf of the cart. "I'd better get moving. I told Daddy I'd be home in time for supper."

She started away, then backed up and handed Judd the plate of cookies. "For you and Hank when he gets back. Pete might even want one later on." She smiled, and it occurred to Judd that she was just about the prettiest girl he'd ever seen. "You can return the plate next time you see me."

He watched her walk away, the sash on her dress tied in a bow around her narrow waist. He bit into another cookie. She was the boss's daughter. He'd best get his mind right and focus on other things.

▲ ▲ ▲

Judd got back to his room Friday night in time to take a quick shower, and now he was lying on his bed trying to sleep, sweating again. He'd seen one of the other lodgers with a fan in his window—with his first paycheck in his pocket, he thought he might go out and buy one.

He'd had a chance to speak to Pete before he left. The logger had thanked him and even got blubbery about it. Judd chalked it up to the medicine he was taking. Pete's effusiveness almost made him wish he'd left earlier.

Judd rolled over and tried to find a cool spot on his pillow. He could smell the ocean and imagined he could hear the surf. It wasn't exactly the sighing of wind in tall pines, but it was soothing nonetheless. What the heck. Maybe he'd go see ole Pete again on Saturday. He didn't have much else to do.

Buying a fan and visiting a more sober, grumpier Pete carried Judd through lunch on Saturday, at which point he felt at a loss for what to do next. It was Labor Day weekend and Myrtle Beach was teeming with tourists in their shorts and bathing suits. It was like the whole town was desperate to have some fun before summer ended. Wiping sweat from his forehead as he got off a sweltering bus, Judd wondered if summer ever really ended around here. He dropped his fan off in his room and decided to walk down to the beach. His leg hurt and sometimes exercise helped.

Without meaning to, Judd found himself at the Pavilion. There was a crowd there already, dancing, drinking sodas, eating popcorn, and nursing sunburns. After circling the building twice, Judd finally realized he was looking for Larkin. Which was ridiculous. He headed for the surf, tucked his hands in his pockets, and started walking. Next thing he knew, he was at the pier they'd visited his first day in town. Hard to believe he'd been here just over a week now. West Virginia seemed farther away every day.

"Hey there, Judd. You look like a proper man of leisure."

Judd turned to see Chuck leaning against the railing with a fishing line in the water.

"Told my wife I was gonna go see Pete. And I did, but he was sleeping. Figured it'd be a waste to come all this way for nothing." He indicated his pole with a jerk of his chin. "Care to wet a line?"

"Don't have any tackle."

"I got a spare here." Chuck indicated a rod lying at his feet. "Be right glad if you joined me."

Judd picked up the rod, pulled some bait from a bucket next to it, and flipped the line out into the water. "What're we after?"

"Oh, snapper, grouper, sea bass—flounder'd be nice. I ain't particular."

"Is there a trick to it?"

Chuck glanced at him out of the corner of his eye. "Yeah. Wait."

Judd grinned. "Now there's a trick I'm familiar with."

They stood in silence for a time, the rhythm of the waves, beating sun, and voices of tourists lulling Judd into a sort of meditative state.

"I hear Miss Larkin visited with you a spell yesterday evening."

Judd jerked his line even though there was nothing on it. He glanced at Chuck feeling like he'd just awakened from a nap. "She brought me a sandwich." Seemed like the gossips were just as busy in Myrtle Beach as they had been back in Bethel.

Chuck reeled his line in and replaced his waterlogged bait. "She's a right purty girl."

"Can't argue with you there."

"Just so you know, Mr. Heyward doesn't much hold with the workers fraternizing with his daughter. Hank gets away with it some, but there's not much gets by the old man."

Judd felt his stubborn rear up, but decided he didn't care to light a fire under anybody just then. "I'll remember that."

"You're a good fella and a better mechanic. If I had a daughter, I'd be steering her your way pretty hard." He looked at Judd and wrinkled his brow. "Say, you don't have a girl back in them hills, do you?"

"I do not."

Chuck nodded. "Well, just thought you should know. About Larkin."

Judd felt a nibble on his line, waited a moment, and set the hook sharp. Chuck whooped as Judd started reeling something in that felt pretty big.

"By golly, you got a flounder. We're gonna eat good tonight. Reel her on in and I'll get her in the cooler."

Judd watched the flat fish sparkle in the sun as it rose from the sea and was almighty grateful for its distraction. Fish out of water, indeed.

CHAPTER

8

Larkin hadn't seen Judd for two weeks, but she couldn't stop thinking about West Virginia and how she could be a help to those poor children living in the backwoods of Appalachia. Never mind the way Judd's blue-gray eyes and dark hair kept coming to mind, as well. The way he would almost smile, like he was secretly amused but didn't want to let on. She straightened her pinafore and carried a fresh pitcher of water to Lill's room. She'd learned that Lill's cancer was in her bones. Her outlook wasn't good, but the woman was so perpetually cheerful, Larkin couldn't resist her in spite of the heartbreak she sensed in the offing.

"How are you feeling today, Lill?"

"Larkin, aren't you looking lovely? Might there be a young man who's caught your eye?"

Larkin noticed that Lill didn't answer her question. Veins showed through her pale skin, and her cheekbones were more pronounced than ever, but she smiled all the same.

"How about I find you some ice cream?" Larkin wanted to give her new friend pleasure one way or another.

Lill shook her head and waved at a chair near her bed. "Can't hardly taste anything anymore, and I'd a whole lot rather you sat down here and talked to me. Everyone's in such a hurry—the doctors, the nurses. I understand they have pressing matters to tend to, but sometimes I wish they'd just stop and look at me a minute."

Larkin set her pitcher down and pulled the chair closer, taking Lill's thin, dark-veined hand. "I'm in no hurry."

"Is that so? I'm glad. Seems like I was always rushing after something and now I can't think what it was."

"Were you ever in love?" Larkin was embarrassed as soon as she blurted the question. Surely it was too personal. But Lill didn't seem to mind.

"I thought I was once. He was such a pretty man—fine hands, and he played the piano beautifully. He charmed my mother right down to her toes. I think she was more disappointed than I was when he started traveling to play music."

"What happened to him?"

Lill shrugged, her thin shoulder brushing against her hospital gown. "He said he was going to New York. Then I got a letter saying he was headed for California. That's the last I ever heard from him."

"He just didn't come back? Didn't write?" Larkin thought about Ben and how devastating it was for him to suddenly be absent from her life.

Lill pressed her fingertips together and then flung them wide. "Gone. Just like a puff of air. Sometimes I think I imagined him. And now that Mother is gone it feels that way more than ever."

As Lill finished speaking, Larkin noticed her skin looked ashy, and beads of sweat popped out on her forehead. She closed her eyes and her lips moved without making a sound.

"Are you alright?"

Lill opened her eyes. "No, I don't suppose I am, but I'm not going to die right this minute." She offered up a brave smile and reached out to stroke Larkin's ponytail where it fell over her shoulder. "Feels like corn silk. And such a pretty color with that copper in it. My sister Althea wanted yellow hair. Probably would have looked good on her, too."

Larkin grinned. "How many of you were there?"

"Just us two girls and Mother. Our father was long gone by the time I was old enough to talk." Her smile slipped. "I'm the last one left to tell the tale. Mother died—probably of cancer, but she refused to see a doctor. And Thea was hit by a car when I was just a teenager. She was walking to work."

Larkin started to ask for more details but sensed that was all Lill had to say on the subject. She smiled and straightened Lill's coverlet. "I'll see you again tomorrow."

"I'm counting on it."

Larkin tiptoed out of the room, satisfaction and sorrow swirling through her in equal parts. It was good to sit and talk with Lill—to let her know she was seen and heard. But while Larkin might have a knack for reviving the plant in the waiting room, she was afraid Lill was another matter entirely.

Judd felt like he was getting the hang of being a mechanic for Waccamaw Timber Company. He didn't even mind the heat as much as he did at first, although he was pretty sure he'd never come to appreciate how flat the land was. And homesickness still punched him in the gut from time to time. He'd even had the terrible thought that Joe might not have been too smart to want to come south, but he shook that off. If Joe couldn't live his dream, Judd would do it for him. He owed his brother that much.

He'd gotten into the habit of visiting Pete of an evening now that he was home from the hospital. Turned out he had a sweet, quiet wife, but no children. Judd had a notion it was a hardship to them both that they were still childless after several years of marriage. He wouldn't exactly say Pete had warmed up to him, but he was glad to have someone to play cards with and always asked about what was happening at work. Judd considered his visits a sort of penance, although he didn't waste a lot of time considering what all he needed penance for.

He liked walking down to the beach now that it was quiet and empty. The tourists went home after Labor Day, and the locals didn't venture down there much, so he could appreciate the absence of people up against that throbbing ocean. The Pavilion was closed, so there was no chance of running into pretty girls out for a night of dancing. Especially not running into a pretty girl with a ponytail and eyes that reflected the sea. Nope, not at all. Judd's life had settled into a routine he could manage, and he might even go for half a day without thinking about Joe or the mountains back home or how much he missed the sound of a creek tumbling over rocks on its way to the valley below.

So when word came that Mr. Heyward wanted to meet with Judd after work on a Tuesday evening, Judd felt a little uneasy. If the mine owner ever met with someone back home, it was usually bad news. Maybe things were different in the South. He hoped so.

Mr. Heyward reclined in his leather desk chair, gazing out the window at a cloudless blue sky. This late in September there was an occasional hint of cooler air, but Judd had learned to appreciate the air conditioning.

"You asked to see me, sir?"

Mr. Heyward spun around and faced him. "I did. I've been hearing good things about you. I even hear you've been teaching some of the boys out there on the job how to do what you do. You planning on leaving?"

Judd schooled his expression. He had no idea where this was going. "No, sir. Just seemed like it'd be good for someone else to know."

"Right you are." The older man slapped his hand down on

the desk and then waved Judd into a seat. "I have a matter to discuss with you."

Questions percolated through Judd's mind, but he kept quiet.

"The state forestry commission has been after me to partner with them in preserving woodlands." Mr. Heyward squinted and scratched his chin. "'Course I'm mainly interested in harvesting woodlands, but I'm not opposed to playing along with the state boys if it makes things easier in the long run."

Judd nodded and tried to relax. Wherever this was headed, he didn't seem to be in trouble.

"Have you seen this L'il Smokey nonsense?"

Mr. Heyward pushed a sheet of paper across his desk, and Judd leaned forward to pick it up. There was a drawing of a bear in a hat and britches showing a pine seedling to two little cubs. It read, *Smokey says, "Protect little trees to keep our nation strong."* He laid the paper back on the desk.

"Can't say as I'm familiar with that."

Mr. Heyward drew the paper closer and peered at it. "Nonsense, mostly. But it is good to try and keep idiots from burning all the trees down. They think that Bombing Range fire back in June got started when some fool threw out a cigarette. Burned more than ten thousand acres before they got it under control." He looked wistful. "Could've gotten a whole lot of pulpwood out of that stand."

Judd paid close attention. He figured if he hung in, things would become clear.

"At any rate, Carlton Hunter wants me to send him someone who can learn all there is to know about timber management. Then that someone can come on back and teach the boys in the company how to be responsible timbermen." He grinned. "There's even a chance whoever I send might learn something worth knowing."

Judd began to have a notion where this was headed. He made

some encouraging sounds to keep the one-sided conversation going.

"So what I'm thinking is, if you're willing, I'll make you our liaison to the forest service. You spend three days a week over there learning whatever they want to teach you, and the other two days you come back to catch up on anything that needs fixing and share your newly acquired knowledge with the boys." He squinted at Judd. "What do you say?"

Judd took a breath and rubbed his chin where he could feel the day's bristle sprouting. "Well now. Sounds interesting."

George Heyward leaned back in his chair and laced his hands across his rounded paunch. "I know what you're thinking."

Judd was surprised, since he hadn't finished thinking it himself. "What's that?"

"You're wondering how this will affect your bottom line." He leaned forward and braced both hands on the desk. "What if it meant a ten percent raise in your pay?"

Judd raised his eyebrows by at least ten percent. This required less thinking. "Then I'd be proud to go learn what Carlton Hunter wants me to know."

"Excellent." Mr. Heyward clapped his hands and stood. "Come to dinner at the house tomorrow evening around seven o'clock and I'll introduce you to Carlton."

Judd rose to his feet and took the other man's outstretched hand. His clasp was warm and firm and his smile was genuine. All of a sudden, Judd found he liked George Heyward. And it had nothing to do with an increase in pay. Maybe he'd done the right thing coming south, after all. Joe would be proud.

CHAPTER
9

Larkin hated it when her father had business associates over for dinner. The conversation would be all about timber and the price of pulpwood and the state of the economy. Her mother would fuss over the food and tell Larkin to mind her manners—as if she were a child. Once in a while there'd be a wife along and they could talk about something a little more interesting, but Larkin didn't hold out much hope.

Digging in her closet, she pulled out a sleeveless blue-and-white-striped dress with decorative buttons down the bodice and a big bow at the waist. She didn't wear it often because the bow was bothersome, but it'd be fine for this evening. Hopefully dinner wouldn't last too long and she could change early.

"Larkin, can you come help me with the table setting?"

"Coming, Mother."

She slipped into the dress and quickly tied the ridiculous bow. It wasn't quite right, but it would have to do. She quickly refastened her ponytail, dabbed on some Stormy Pink lipstick—what a name—and hurried downstairs. Once there, she mostly agreed with her mother every time she asked if something looked all

66

right. The flowers on the table, the candles, the napkins, the pound cake on the sideboard—actually, that looked particularly delicious. Larkin noted that there were five places set, so maybe there would be a wife coming, as well.

"It's all lovely, Mother. Daddy can't help but be pleased." She plucked a sprig of bougainvillea from where it had fallen on the cloth and tucked it in her palm to dispose of in the kitchen.

"Augusta, we've arrived."

Larkin's mother jumped and smoothed her skirt. She spied the bow at Larkin's waist, made a face, and quickly retied it before hurrying out to greet her husband and his guests. Larkin trailed after her, trying not to look as bored as she felt.

Sultry air billowed in with the guests standing at the bottom of the wide staircase. Larkin shifted a bit so she could get a better look around her mother, who was kissing her father on the cheek and holding her hand out to the first of . . . two men. She vaguely remembered the gentleman greeting her mother—she thought he worked with the forest service. Then the second man stepped forward to take her mother's hand and Larkin almost choked. It was Judd. What in the world? Her father never had the working men to the house.

She had a sudden notion that Judd was secretly a coal titan who had posed as a common worker to learn about her father's company from the inside. And now, duly impressed with the inner workings, he was prepared to become a partner with Waccamaw Timber Company. Which, she realized, would explain his reluctance to offer to help her educate the children of Appalachia. And it would make him an appropriate suitor. She squashed that second thought and fiddled with her bow. Oh, why hadn't she worn the pink organdy?

"Carlton Hunter, this is my daughter, Larkin. Judd, I believe you've already met."

Larkin held out her hand to the older man and smiled. She looked at Judd from beneath her lashes. "We have met. Judd was most kind in caring for a member of his crew who was injured and had to be carried to the hospital."

Judd nodded and flushed but didn't speak. He tucked his hands behind his back, denying Larkin a handshake. She decided that was just like him and hooked a hand through his elbow mostly to see if she could get a rise out of him.

"Let me show you to the dining room."

She motioned with her left hand and realized she still had the flower tucked away there. Judd noticed it and plucked it from her grasp before she could think what he was doing. He stuck it in a pocket with a grin. Blushing, Larkin thought she saw her father smile, which was odd. Her mother escorted Carlton into the dining room, and they all took their seats except for Larkin, who slipped into the kitchen to pick up a cut-glass pitcher of iced tea.

Reentering the room, Larkin thought her father looked thoughtful and Judd looked uncomfortable. Men. Who could fathom them? She began filling glasses, starting with her mother. Judd rubbed his palms against his pressed slacks as she poured amber liquid into his glass. Was he nervous? Finished, she settled the pitcher on the sideboard and took her seat.

"Bow your heads."

Larkin's father asked for God's blessing on the timber company and all the men it employed. Then he asked for good weather, improving markets, and several other things before finally blessing the food. Larkin snuck a peek at Judd and found him obedient in prayer. Finally, it was over and they all said "Amen."

Daddy lifted the platter of fried chicken and offered it first to his wife and then to Larkin, who passed it to Carlton. Judd helped himself to a thigh, started to reach for a second piece, then seemed to think twice about it. Creamed potatoes, fried okra, and sliced tomatoes made the rounds, along with a basket of angel biscuits. Judd took moderate amounts of everything, although he looked a little skeptical about the okra. Larkin hid her amusement.

"Carlton, I think you'll find Judd to be a fine addition to your team," her father said at last.

"I hear you're a solid mechanic," Carlton said to Judd.

"I always liked tinkering with machines. Have ever since I was a boy."

"Well, as eager as I am to teach you about timber management, I might also have some tinkering you could do."

"That'd be fine," Judd said, taking what looked to Larkin like a cautious bite of okra. He chewed and gave the tiniest nod.

"Do you like the okra?" Larkin asked him.

He looked at the food on his plate. "I like most anything that's fried." He speared a few more pieces and ate them. "This is mighty fine."

Her mother dimpled. "Why, thank you. I know you work hard all day, so don't hold back. There's plenty."

Judd nodded and seemed torn between picking up his chicken and cutting into it. Larkin daintily lifted a chicken leg to her lips and smiled at him. He relaxed and took a big bite.

"So you're going to be Daddy's liaison to the forest service?" she asked.

Judd swallowed. "Looks that way."

Carlton stepped back into the conversation. "We've been after your father to send us a man for years. Guess he had to wait and ship one in from up north."

"West Virginia isn't exactly the north," Larkin said, hoping Judd hadn't been offended. "Most of the state is below the Mason-Dixon Line."

"Well, we'll be glad to teach this mountain man our Low-country ways. You spend much time working in timber up there in West Virginia?"

Judd settled his fork on his plate. "We cut wood for the stove, and there's a sawmill over in Evergreen, but nothing like what goes on around here. Those mountains make it a mite harder to haul the wood out all at once."

Daddy nodded. "And now Carlton wants us to do more of this selection cutting. Best I can tell it's about making more work and less money."

"Now, George. It's about preserving forests for future generations. You want your grandchildren to enjoy the beautiful pine plantations of South Carolina, don't you?"

Daddy cut his eyes at Larkin, then Judd. "My grandchildren will do just fine. And there are more than enough trees to go around. So long as idiots stop setting fire to them." He patted his lips with his napkin. "Now, this forest fire prevention business makes sense to me."

"Say, maybe you could sponsor a Smokey Bear costume."

"A what?" Daddy wasn't one to brook silliness.

"The L'il Smokey campaign. They're developing a costume for a man to wear so he can go to schools and fairs and things like that to tell people how they can prevent fires. If you sponsor it, we'd put the name of your company right there on all the posters."

Larkin watched the wheels turn in her father's head. He did enjoy publicity.

"Well now, that is something we might could discuss further." He pushed back from the table a notch. "A fine meal, Augusta. I think we'll enjoy coffee and dessert in the den."

He stood and motioned the other two men to follow him. Larkin saw Judd look at the platter of fried chicken with longing. She ducked her head to hide her smile.

"I'll bring a tray in shortly, Daddy."

Her father patted her on the shoulder as the men left the room. So much for Judd being a coal titan. He was more like a pawn in her father's latest game of chess.

◊▲◊

Judd lay on his bed that night, fan stirring the heavy air that wasn't quite as thick as when he first arrived in August. He laughed softly. He thought George Heyward might have noticed how friendly Larkin had been, although he hadn't put as much distance between the two of them as Judd would have expected. He figured Mr. Heyward was the sort to think Judd was good enough to keep the forestry commission happy but not good enough to try to do the same for his daughter. He rolled over to look at the exotic purple flower he'd stuck in a jelly jar with some water when he got back to his room. When he'd seen it there in Larkin's hand as she greeted her guests, he almost laughed out loud. Clearly, she'd forgotten she had it, and the oversight set him at ease immediately. He'd only been thinking to help when he'd taken it from her, but now, seeing it there on his bedside table, he felt a tenderness he couldn't quite account for.

And the way she'd eased him through dinner— making sure he didn't make a fool of himself with that okra or the way he ate. He used to be the one looking after Joe like that—keeping him out of trouble and smoothing his way.

Sighing, Judd rolled onto his back and stared at the ceiling. Although he hadn't seriously considered courting Larkin Heyward, he had wondered if being invited to her father's house might make it possible. But how could it? He was just a working man who happened to fit a particular need. He picked up the jelly jar and set it in the window, next to the fan. It almost glowed in the streetlight from outside.

Judd marveled at how people tolerated having lights on around them all the time. He hadn't been properly in the dark since he'd arrived. He would have expected it to bother him, but then again, it was a relief to close his eyes and still be able to see light through his eyelids. Not like in the mine. Not like the day his brother died. That day he'd been utterly blind even with his eyes wide open.

Looking through the glistening jar, Judd could see the stem of the flower there. He looked again and swore he could see roots beginning to sprout—fine little hairs swaying in the water. Huh. If it kept going maybe he'd get a pot and some dirt and see if he couldn't make it grow.

CHAPTER

10

On a Friday night in early October, Judd finally noted a hint of something cool in the air. He'd promised to go play cards with Pete and he wasn't looking forward to the evening. He'd much rather be outside, enjoying the beginning of what felt like autumn. He sighed and resigned himself to listening to Pete complain. Spending a month in a cast would wear on anyone, Judd knew, but Pete really played it up, and Judd was pretty tired of hearing how rough life was. As he rode the bus out to Pete's neighborhood, he thought over the past two months and how his own life just might be looking up.

He'd come to enjoy working with Carlton, who gave him free rein to tinker with departmental equipment. He was particularly taken with the fire plows, which were not unlike the plows he and his neighbors used to break up the soil back home. Of course, these weren't for planting corn and beans—the plows were to cut fire breaks in hopes of stopping wildfires. He'd also fashioned a two-row tree planter out of scrap that worked better than the nine-hundred-dollar store-bought one that only planted one row at a time.

Thursdays and Fridays were spent working with the Wacca-maw timber crew—fixing chainsaws, adjusting equipment at the sawmill, and supposedly passing along timber-management advice, although Judd found most of the boys poor listeners when he offered up information he'd learned earlier in the week. Still, Carlton and Mr. Heyward seemed pleased with the arrangement, and Judd just counted his lucky stars. Goodness knows it was the first time he'd felt lucky since he woke up in the hospital.

He hadn't seen Larkin for a couple of weeks—at least not more than in passing—which was probably just as well. There was nothing for him there and no need to get stirred up by pretty pink lips and a swaying ponytail. Although he did plant that sprig of a flower from the night he had supper at the Heywards', and it was sure enough growing right on up the wall outside his window. Might even bloom before long. He'd heard Hank say Larkin was known for her green thumb—maybe it was catching.

Judd got off the bus and walked a couple of blocks to Pete's house. He turned in at the bare yard littered with castoff magnolia leaves. Man, he missed lush green hayfields and brilliant fall foliage.

"About time you got here."

Judd looked up to see Pete leaning on a crutch on the other side of the screen door. "Good to see you too, Pete. I brought you a sandwich from the fish market." Judd snagged the screen door and thought how its squawk sounded just like the home-place in West Virginia. He pushed down a pang of homesickness.

Pete almost smiled. "Hand her over. Sally's a fine cook, but you can't beat fried fish, and she says it messes up the kitchen too much." He opened the grease-spotted bag and inhaled the aroma. "Appreciate it."

Judd nodded. He'd already eaten his food, though he didn't understand why they called it a sandwich when it was a sack of two fish fillets with three slices of white bread. He couldn't

74

figure out the math, but he ate it all anyway. Pete was busy assembling his own sandwich of sorts, and Judd sat back to let him eat.

Sally appeared with two glasses of sweet tea and a sweeter smile. "It's so nice of you to visit Pete like this. And bringing him fish—don't you beat all."

Judd felt his ears warm. "It's nothing, ma'am. When I was laid up, more than one person helped me pass the time."

"Well, we're awful grateful. Can I get you anything else?"

Pete grabbed her arm and spoke with his mouth full. "Hey, how about break out that jar from under the kitchen sink? Judd and I might need us something a little stronger than sweet tea tonight."

Judd saw concern flicker across Sally's face. "Are you sure you should be drinking while you're still laid up?"

Annoyance lit Pete's eyes. "It's not like I'm going anywhere. Now bring that jar and some glasses."

Sally set her mouth in a straight line and disappeared, only to return a few moments later with the requested items. She put them on the card table and left without making eye contact. Judd considered the clear liquid and debated whether he'd have any. He'd surely tasted corn liquor more than once, but it wasn't always a good idea to drink it unless you knew the source. Pete reached over with greasy fingers and unscrewed the lid, pouring a measure into each glass. He held his up toward Judd.

"To a pair of gimps playing cards."

Judd wasn't sure he wanted to drink to that, but he took a tiny sip and found the liquor to be much better than he'd expected. Pete watched him intently.

"Good, right? You probably thought it'd be little better than paint thinner." He took a deep swallow. "Yes sir, my source makes the finest, smoothest 'shine around. He does a peach wine Sally in there isn't opposed to sampling now and again, but this . . ." He swirled the liquid in his glass. "This is what men drink." He tossed back what was left and poured another measure.

Judd lifted his glass to Pete and took a proper swallow. He was surprised by how good it was. He didn't plan to drink any more than what was in his glass right then, but he found he didn't dread getting the portion down. Pete, apparently, intended to make up for Judd's caution. He took a swig and smacked his lips.

"You gonna deal them cards?"

Judd began dealing the ten cards they'd need to play gin rummy. If Pete kept drinking the way he was, he wasn't going to offer much competition this evening. Sally appeared with a plate of hoop cheese and Saltines. Judd thanked her and took some while Pete pretty much ignored the food. Play started and Pete seemed to need all of his focus just to make out his cards, leaving conversation at a standstill, which suited Judd just fine. He was more than content to provide silent companionship.

After losing three hands in a row, Pete threw his cards down in disgust and sloshed some more moonshine in his own glass as well as Judd's. "Aw, let's just drink and talk. Don't get to talk much these days."

Judd tidied the cards and crossed his right ankle over his knee. He picked up his glass, but it was mostly just so he could look at it. He ate another cracker with some cheese. "What you want to talk about?"

Pete leaned in as close as his leg, still in a cast, would allow. "How about them Heywards? Hear you got invited to the big house a while back."

Judd took a small sip. "I did. Mrs. Heyward fries a mighty fine chicken."

Pete swatted at the air, and it occurred to Judd that if it were possible, he would have missed. "Not talking about food. Tell me about old man Heyward."

Judd shrugged, not sure what there was to tell.

Pete emptied his glass and leaned his head back. "He ever run that prodigal Ben to ground?"

Judd had been thinking about how to extricate himself from the situation and head back to the boardinghouse, but Pete's words drew his attention. "Who's Ben?"

Pete got a cagey look and wagged a finger at Judd. "Now, now, don't you go thinking you can get me to let the cat out of the bag." He swung his head toward the kitchen. "Sally, bring me one of them knitting needles so I can scratch this leg."

Sally appeared, and Judd decided this was probably his best chance to leave. "Ma'am, sure do appreciate the refreshments, but I'd best be getting on back now."

Sally squeezed his arm and looked like she understood. "We're surely grateful for the time you spend with Pete. Gets awful lonesome around here with just me for company."

Pete gave his wife a stricken look. "Why, Sally, you're the best company a man could ask for." Tears pooled in his eyes and he looked at Judd. "And you, Judd. You're the only one who gives a hoot about me." Tears escaped. "I don't deserve either one of you."

Sally slid the remainder of the moonshine out of Pete's reach and gave Judd a pleading look. Judd nodded and stood.

"Right you are, my friend. You're one lucky man to have a wife like that. I'll be seeing you soon."

Something hardened in Pete's eyes as he watched Judd walk to the door. "I am lucky. Not like that sorry son-of-a-gun Heyward. His luck will run out one of these days. Things could be a whole lot different around Waccamaw Timber Company if he ain't careful. Especially if I get my hands on a certain something out there on that land he stole from my daddy." He squinted. "You ever go treasure hunting?"

"Never had occasion to."

"Well, you ever take a notion to lend me a hand, you just say the word and I'll make sure you get your fair share. To blazes with George Heyward."

Judd clicked the screen door shut behind him and started the walk back to his bus stop. It had been a strange evening. He wondered who Ben was and what exactly it was Pete had against George Heyward. He wished he'd left before Pete got started on treasure talk. Judd figured he was deep enough in Pete's business without offering to help him dig deeper, but dang if he wasn't curious.

·◊◊

Larkin dragged herself from her car toward the house. Lill was failing fast, and the effort to remain bright and cheery was about to do Larkin in. Not that she was fooling Lill, who sometimes seemed downright excited about coming to the end of herself and the beginning of something new. Still, Larkin felt the need to put a good face on the situation, and it was exhausting.

She thumped down on the bottom step leading to the back door and stared vacantly at a camellia blooming there, dropping spent blooms at her feet. It was a Debutante Camellia— her mother planted it the year Larkin had her debut. Oh, that seemed ages ago now. She sighed, thinking she'd cut some blooms for Lill.

Something fluttered beneath the bush, and Larkin leaned down to get a better look. Pushing a branch aside, she saw a Carolina wren lying there. It fluttered one wing and then subsided. Larkin gasped, fearing she'd just seen it die. It must have crashed into the plate-glass window above. Hands shaking, she reached down and cradled the bird. It was warm, but she couldn't feel any movement. Was it possible to feel a bird's heartbeat? Cupping her hands, she held it to her own breast and tried not to cry. It was only a bird. Everything died eventually. She'd bury it if nothing else.

But even as Larkin tried to think where to lay the little bird to rest, she thought she felt something. A Scripture she'd heard once, maybe in Sunday school—goodness knows her recent church attendance had left much to be desired—came to her. It was something about how not even a sparrow died without God knowing it. She couldn't remember exactly how the first part of the verses went, but she did remember the last bit: *"You are worth more than many sparrows."*

She'd never questioned her worth before. Of course, she was worth more than any number of sparrows—or wrens. But sitting there, feeling what she dared hope might be life stirring in her hands, it occurred to her that life was precious. Period. This bird was a miracle. And yet, if the Bible was to be believed, she was worth more than the miracle she felt moving against her palm.

Larkin eased her hands open and saw a black eye blinking up at her. She crouched down under the camellia and nestled the bird in some ivy growing there. It sat for a moment without moving, then turned its head from side to side as though trying to get a better view of her. It ruffled its wings. Hopped once, twice, and flew, landing in a live oak deeper in the yard. Larkin heard it sing and felt her own heart take flight.

◊ ◊ ◊

As soon as she walked in the house, Larkin could tell something was different. "Mother?" she called.

She heard a rustle in the den and Larkin pursued it. Sticking her head around the corner, she saw her mother dab at her face with a handkerchief while tucking something away in her embroidery bag.

"Mother, are you crying?"

"Just some dust in my eye. It's nothing." She stood and smoothed her skirt. "I was thinking we might have chicken salad for supper. Your father called to say he'd be late, so I thought we'd keep it simple."

Larkin cocked her head. "And I'm early. What were you reading?"

Larkin's mother moved to look out the window as though admiring the perfectly groomed landscaping. "Nothing important."

Touching her mother's elbow, Larkin leaned around to look her in the eye. "I could have sworn you were holding a letter."

"Oh, sweetheart. Your father would have a fit if he knew you'd seen . . ."

"What? Seen what?"

Mother whirled back to her chair and fished the letter out, thrusting it toward Larkin. "It's from Ben."

Larkin shrank back. "But Daddy said we weren't to communicate with him." She eyed the letter with longing and reached out a tentative hand.

Her mother pressed the paper into Larkin's palm. "There are others. He sends them to a post-office box so your father won't know." She choked on tears. "How could I not keep in touch with my only son? The hardest part is never being able to share what he writes."

Larkin sank onto the floral-patterned sofa and unfolded the letter with trembling fingers. It was dated a week earlier.

Dear Mom,

I'm in the eastern Kentucky coalfields now. The raw need among these good people is enough to convince me I was right in defying Dad. They have strong faith, sure enough, but it's a sort of superstitious, hellfire and brimstone faith. I'm trying to convince them God is good and loves them, but they have suffered so much I can understand why they think He must be angry.

They've begun mechanizing the work in the mines in earnest, which means there are fewer jobs and the ones available are more technical. Too many men have too much time on their hands without gainful employment. It is easy for them to make poor choices.

In addition to sharing the Good News with those who will listen, I urge locals to let me help them patch their roofs, mend their fences, and feed their children. But convincing them to let me help is often more work than tarpapering what passes for a home here. I have rarely encountered such stubborn pride. Not that they don't have reason to be proud of their heritage, their passion for family, and their willingness to do hard work when given the chance—rather, it is their unwillingness to allow an outsider to offer them so much as a dipper of water. I often have to "trick" them into allowing me to help, convincing them that they are actually doing me the favor.

It helps that I have become good friends with a local matriarch they call Granny Jane. I was able to offer her relief from terrible bunions by providing her with a pair of loose-fitting slippers and some aspirin. She is by no means healed, but tells me she feels so much better she could "dance a jig." As a result, she has forbidden anyone to treat me shabbily and so the locals suffer my presence for her sake. I wish I could introduce Granny Jane to you— though from very different backgrounds, I think you would charm one another.

I hope that you, Dad, and Larkin are all well. I'm glad to hear Larkin is volunteering at the hospital. I would ask you to give her my love, but know you likely won't for fear Dad will find out we are corresponding. I will continue to pray for the day he forgives me for following my calling and we can all be together again.

> *Your loving son,*
> *Ben*

Larkin read the letter so quickly, she wasn't sure she even knew what it said. It had been two years since Ben finished college with a degree in business and then . . .

They'd been having a celebratory party with friends, family, and some of Daddy's most important business associates. The backyard had been a wonderland with flowers, tables of food, punch, and probably something stronger for the men who gravitated toward Daddy. Larkin remembered the delight she felt seeing her father with his arm around her brother, slapping him on the back and introducing him to important people. Everything had been perfect until Daddy tapped his heavy crystal glass with a fork and drew everyone's attention.

"It's entirely possible I'm the proudest man on the face of the earth today," he said, beaming at Ben. "My son is now in the perfect position to follow in his grandfather's footsteps and in mine, as well. Waccamaw Timber is his legacy and his future."

Larkin glanced at Ben and saw a look of pain cross his face. He started to lift a hand, then simply hung his head, as though waiting for a fatal blow.

"I'm proud to introduce you to the new vice-president of Waccamaw Timber, Ben Heyward."

Applause and even a few whistles rang out as Daddy reached for Ben and tugged him up in front of the crowd. Ben pinched the bridge of his nose, then held up both hands, calming the crowd.

"Folks, I appreciate your enthusiasm and your well-wishes. I'm deeply honored that my father would entrust me with the company my grandfather trusted him to run." He looked toward his father, whose smile was slipping. "But as I discussed with him when he first mentioned this possibility, I feel strongly led to enter the mission field. As much as it would please me to remain here with my family, there are other people who can run Waccamaw Timber better than I can." He took a deep breath. "But there aren't nearly enough people to carry the Good News to people in need all over the world."

By that time, Larkin's mother had joined her and was holding her hand so tightly it hurt. Larkin watched her father's face turn red. She thought, for a moment, that he would simply turn and walk away, but something set him off. Maybe he couldn't stand to see the pity in the eyes of men whose respect he craved.

Daddy threw the crystal glass in his hand against the trunk of a live oak tree, sending amber liquid spraying over several guests who gasped and sidestepped. "No son of mine would dare dishonor his father and his heritage like this." He stepped closer to Ben and held a shaking finger in his face. "You are no son of mine." Then he turned and stomped into the house.

The next twenty minutes were among the most uncomfortable of Larkin's life as guests either slunk away or tried to offer comfort that was really just a thinly disguised attempt to get more information. What would Ben do now? Who would George name to be second-in-command? Was there anything they could do to help?

Larkin tolerated it, but Ben handled it all smoothly, assuring everyone that God had a plan better than any they could come up with on their own and reminding them all that his father had run the company largely by himself until now and could certainly continue to do so.

Once everyone left, Larkin, her mother, and Ben went into the house, but before Ben could cross the threshold, Daddy was there, blocking the way. "You aren't welcome here."

"I had hoped we could discuss this calmly," Ben said.

"There's nothing to discuss. You don't live here. You don't belong here, and I'd thank you never to darken my door again." Daddy slammed the door and that was the last time Larkin had seen Ben.

She knew he planned to head north but had always wondered where he went from there. She'd sometimes imagined him in Africa or China, but the fact that he was in Appalachia delighted her. The article she'd read about the poverty and suffering in the region had touched her deeply, and now that she knew her own brother was there, trying to help, she wanted to go more than anything.

She lowered the letter and looked at her mother. "Do you have others?"

Mother looked worried but nodded her head. "I keep them hidden inside the punch bowl on the top shelf of the pantry." She grasped Larkin's arm in an iron grip. "You may read them, but you must never let your father know." She hung her head. "He would feel it was a betrayal. Maybe even an unforgiveable one."

Larkin nodded and scanned the letter once more. She felt a deep longing to join her brother. To meet this Granny Jane and to help the poor people of Kentucky. As much as she loved her work at the hospital, this somehow seemed ever so much more important. Now she didn't need Judd Markley. All she had to do was write to Ben.

CHAPTER

11

Judd whistled as he cleaned the spark plugs in the old Ford truck. It was Friday again, the weather was the best he'd seen it since coming to South Carolina, and he was planning to do some exploring over the weekend. He'd been feeling almighty homesick and figured a good cure for it would be to get more comfortable with the place he'd landed. Carlton was going to take him and Hank to the Francis Marion National Forest to see how they'd used even-age management practices to restore the forest after years of uncontrolled logging and rampant fires.

It was technically a working trip, but Carlton promised some hunting and fishing along the way, which made it sound like mostly a good time to Judd. Especially now that the weather had cooled off enough that he could breathe the air rather than swim in it. They'd sleep out Saturday night—something Judd hadn't done since before Korea. Yup, he might could get used to this place if he tried.

"You ready for a hurricane?" Chuck slapped Judd on the shoulder and leaned against the side of the truck.

"Is one coming?" Judd had heard about hurricanes and didn't

much relish the idea of being around for one. He'd seen hail, blizzards, torrential rain, and even a little ole tornado one time, but a hurricane struck him as something mightier than all those put together.

"Aw, probably not. Papers say this storm they've called Hazel has knocked the stuffing out of Haiti, but it's supposed to stay on out there in the Atlantic." He squinted at the crystal-clear sky. "Might fling some rain at us if we're lucky. Dry as this summer's been, a little rain would be a fine thing. Keep the forest fires down, if nothing else."

"You reckon Carlton'll cancel our trip?"

Chuck shrugged. "Doubt it. Although I wouldn't much want to be sleeping out if the wind and rain kicks up." He winked. "Probably wants to see how tough you are."

Judd replaced the last spark plug and wiped his hands on a rag. He grinned. "A corner of a hurricane might not be too bad. Give me something to write home about."

"They surely are something to see. We ever get a good one you'll wish you were back in one of those mines, fifty feet underground where the storm can't get you."

Judd forced a smile, but he was pretty sure no storm could ever be big enough to make him want to go back inside a mine.

◊ ◊ ◊

It took Larkin days of thinking, writing, and revising, but she finally had a letter ready to go in the mailbox on Friday, October fourteenth. She carried it in her pinafore pocket while she tended to her duties.

She was on her way out, heart light at the thought of how her brother would get her letter and immediately send for her to join him, when she heard Lill call out.

"Larkin."

She backed up a few feet and stuck her head in Lill's room. "I'm here."

Lill patted the bed, grimacing as she did so. Larkin knew she was in pretty constant pain these days. "Come sit a minute."

Larkin stuck one hand in her pocket and crinkled the envelope. She was itching to get it in the day's mail, but Lill was more important. Another few minutes wouldn't matter. She went in the room and settled on the edge of the bed.

Lill sighed, and the sound was so soft, like the flutter of a bird's wings. "I'm not long for this world."

"Oh, Lill, don't talk that way. You're doing really well and—"

Lill held up a hand. "No. No. It's a good thing. I've made peace with the past and, thanks to Mother force-feeding me the Bible all those years, I'm not worried about what comes next." She got a faraway look in her eyes, and Larkin could almost imagine she was peering through one of heaven's windows at that moment. She refocused. "It's you I'm worried about."

Larkin raised her eyebrows. "Me? Why in the world?"

"You have a gift for life and it's wasted on those who don't even know they're dying."

Larkin wanted to protest, but Lill silenced her with a look. "You positively bubble over with the joy of living. It's been a pleasure to see, but I have this notion I can't shake that God has bigger plans for you."

Larkin couldn't think what to say. She considered that she, too, had the feeling she was supposed to do something great. She touched the letter again, hoping it was the first step toward her destiny.

Smiling, Larkin straightened Lill's bedclothes and patted her bony hand. "Thank you, Lill. I hope you'll stay here with us a long time yet, but I'm glad you told me all the same."

Lill's smile was angelic. "Oh, honey. I hope I'm not here but another minute or two. I'm tired and there's too much sorrow in this world for me anymore. But you—you have a gift that's yet to be used up. You go on out there and do what the Lord tells you to."

Larkin stood and leaned over to kiss the cheek of this woman who had become so precious to her. "I'll do it, Lill. I promise."

Lill cupped her face and smiled into her eyes. "That's good enough for me," she said.

Larkin left the room and tidied up the cleaning closet on her way out. It wasn't really her job, but one of the other girls had left it in disarray and the mindless work gave her a few moments to mull over what Lill said. Her words felt almost prophetic, which was something Larkin had never thought much about. Did God really have a specific plan for her? And if He did, surely it was the work she wanted to do in Appalachia. Learning about Ben was like a message from God that she was on the right track. Yes. That was it. Everything fit together just so.

"Larkin."

She turned to see Nurse Enright standing in the doorway. She stood up a little straighter. "Yes, ma'am, just finishing up here."

The head nurse stepped into the closet and eased the door shut behind her. Larkin felt all her senses go on alert.

"Lill just passed."

Larkin felt confused. "She . . . what?"

"She's gone." Nurse Enright gave her head a little shake. "Just like that. Just like she'd made up her mind to walk through an open door."

Larkin swallowed hard. Nurse Enright wasn't usually nice like this. She thought she could stand the news better if she weren't being so nice.

The older woman reached out and patted Larkin on the shoulder. "She doesn't have any family that we know of. I thought you might want to say goodbye since the two of you had gotten close."

Larkin nodded as tears spilled onto her pinafore. She had the wherewithal to be surprised that Nurse Enright had noticed her relationship with Lill. Maybe the head nurse wasn't so tough after all. She decided to go back to the little room and kiss Lill's cheek one more time. Although she supposed they'd already said their goodbyes even if Larkin hadn't realized it at the time.

◆ ◆ ◆

Larkin dragged home around six that evening. The perfect Friday afternoon had given way to darkening clouds, and the sky had the strange glow it got when a hurricane was off the coast. There had been a hurricane warning issued that morning for a storm that killed hundreds in Haiti a few days ago. But the weather forecasters were saying it would be a glancing blow at most. Larkin gazed out at the horizon, trying to picture the swirling maelstrom out over the ocean somewhere. She almost wished it would come ashore and strip all her sadness away.

Although she knew Lill had been ready to die even at her young age, the loss left her feeling like she was wasting time living in her parents' house and doing halfhearted volunteer work. Life was short and she had much to accomplish. Lill had said so.

Larkin walked inside and found her mother putting dinner on the table. Daddy sat in his usual spot, newspaper folded beside his plate.

"George, put that paper away. Larkin's home, so now we can all sit down and have dinner as a family."

Daddy sighed and pushed the paper aside. He smiled at Larkin, but she had the notion he wasn't really seeing her. She debated telling her parents about Lill but decided not to. What would they care that a woman they'd never met was gone? She probably shouldn't care so much either, but she did.

After a short blessing, they dug into their pork chops with wild rice and green beans. Mother was getting fancy again, but Larkin was pretty sure Daddy didn't appreciate it. He just ate, casting longing glances at the newspaper.

"Daddy, do you know what happened to Ben?"

Larkin's mother froze with her fork halfway to her mouth. After a moment she took the bite and forced it down. Daddy kept eating, but he looked hard at Larkin.

"Ben who?" he said at last.

"My brother. Your son. You know who I mean. We're all adults here." She darted a look around the table. Mother was pale and sipping her water. "I don't understand why we can't talk about him." Then in a smaller voice: "I miss him."

"Your brother was as good as dead the day he chose to follow in my father's footsteps and sacrifice his family on the altar of the church." Daddy folded his napkin, picked up his newspaper, and left the room.

Larkin stared at her plate, not daring to meet her mother's eyes. Lill died. Ben did not. She couldn't begin to fathom why her father would choose to behave as though he had. And what did he mean about sacrifice?

"Larkin."

She raised her head and met her mother's eyes. Her sad eyes.

"I don't quite understand it either, but I've had more time to think about how your father's past has influenced him." She sighed and took a sip of water. "His own father—you probably don't remember him since you were so young when he died—was a very religious man. He worked in turpentine, barely making enough to keep the family fed, but even so he gave every penny he could to the church. George doesn't talk about it much, but I think he sometimes went without so your grandfather could help pay for a new organ or the pastor's salary." She began clearing dishes as though it was easier to talk with her hands occupied.

"You might say your father pulled himself up by his bootstraps and went to work for Waccamaw Timber's biggest competitor. I didn't really know him then." Her hands stilled and she got a faraway look on her face. "But I'd seen him around and he was so handsome, so commanding." She gave her head

90

a little shake. "Something I've never been privy to transpired between George and my father, and suddenly he was my father's right-hand man at Waccamaw and that other company went out of business within the year. We began seeing one another, and when we married, Father made it clear George would be his successor at the company. When his own father died, he left every penny to the church."

She stood, gathering an armload of dishes. "I think your father feels like he's been fighting the church all his life, and your brother, well, it's as though he's gone over to the enemy's side."

Larkin felt the tears she'd held back at Lill's bedside begin to well. "Why can't he just love Ben, anyway? Why can't he let us make our own choices?"

Her mother bowed her head. "Pride, I suppose. We all have it, it's just some of us let it have more say in our lives than we ought."

Larkin sighed and began piling up dishes, as well. "Well, he can't make me stop thinking about my brother."

"No. He can't do that. And I hope you will always remember him. And maybe one day . . ." She paused, and Larkin felt hope swell. "Well, never mind."

Feeling dejected, Larkin was halfway to the kitchen when she remembered the letter in the pocket of her pinafore hanging on a hook near the door. She gasped. With Lill dying, she'd forgotten to put it in the mailbox. She glanced out the window. The rain had begun falling after they sat down to eat and now it was coming in waves—heavy, then gentle, then heavy again. It was pouring at the moment but would likely ease up and even stop shortly. Larkin deposited the dishes in the sink and opened the back door, snagging her letter as she did.

"Larkin, get back in here. They're saying that hurricane will pass us by, but it's still not fit to be outside." Mother began running water in the sink.

"I just need to . . ."

"What could you possibly need to do this evening?"

Larkin fingered the envelope, then tucked it inside her blouse. She could mail it in the morning. It wasn't going to be picked up tonight anyway. She went to help her mother with the dishes, then wandered into the den, where her father was listening to the radio.

"Reports out of Charleston say the seas are getting pretty bad down that way. Seems like Hazel is swinging a little closer than they thought."

"Should we do anything?" Larkin peered out at the forbidding sky. The rain had stopped, just as she'd expected, but there was an eerie stillness. Approaching hurricanes could be fickle—stormy one moment and quiet the next. They wouldn't know Hazel's true intent until she got a lot closer—or turned out to sea.

"I'm going to get Hank on the phone, make sure he's secured the jobsites." Daddy glanced out the window, too. "We're far enough off the beach, we should be fine." He turned to go pick up the hall phone, but Larkin touched his arm.

"Daddy, I . . ."

"What is it?" He sounded impatient, in a hurry to make his phone call.

Larkin stiffened her spine. "I want to get in touch with Ben. I want to know what he's doing, where he is. Maybe even go see him." She felt a tingle of adrenaline laced with fear. She raised her chin.

Her father drew himself to his full height and glared at Larkin. "I am willing to tolerate a great deal of nonsense from you, young lady. But there will be no further discussion of your brother. Ever."

He spun on his heel and left the room. Larkin stood, hand still extended where she'd reached out to touch his arm. Tears rose, but she dashed them away. Fine. She'd do this without his blessing. It was high time she stretched her wings.

Larkin moved to the front sitting room where they hardly ever went. The furniture was perfect, the art matched the drapes, and there wasn't a speck of dust. A break in the clouds let the last rays of the sun shine through with that eerie, hurricane light—like throwing a yellow scarf over a lampshade. Larkin went to the front door and eased it open, holding her breath as it creaked slightly. She slipped outside. She would mail her letter tonight. If only because she needed the fresh air.

CHAPTER

12

Judd felt restless. Maybe it was the storm brewing. Everyone seemed to think the hurricane would stay well out to sea, but he wasn't so sure. He'd seen enough storms roll up in the mountains to have the feeling this one was coming straight for them. Rain had fallen off and on all evening, and he'd never seen a sky quite like the one out there tonight. Wind whipped the palmetto trees in fits, like it couldn't make up its mind whether to stay or go. Judd hoped it would go.

He was supposed to meet Carlton at the timber company office at nine the next morning. He'd packed a knapsack with a few items he thought he'd need. Carlton had promised him the use of a rifle and fishing equipment "should the need arise." Judd checked his pack again, the uneasy feeling translating itself to everything around him, making the room, the house, and the yard look like alien territory. It reminded him of Korea and how danger often lurked in the least likely places.

Judd could hear the radio playing in the sitting room, so he stepped down the hall and lounged in a doorway. His landlady and the older man who stayed in the back room were seated, leaning toward the voice emanating from the speaker.

". . . a high-level northeasterly wind was expected to push the storm out to sea," the announcer said. Then there was a pause that lasted a beat too long. "But reports from down around Charleston, South Carolina, suggest the seas are getting rough. The last report from a hurricane-hunter airplane indicated that Hazel has reached one hundred fifty miles per hour and has shifted to the northwest moving at thirty miles per hour." There was another too-long pause. "Batten down the hatches, folks. This one could hit."

His landlady snapped off the radio and looked at Judd, who stood up straighter. "You ever seen a hurricane before?"

"No, ma'am."

She shrugged. "May not see one tonight, but my bones tell me you will." She glanced out the front window. "I'm going to my son's place inland a ways. You and him"—she pointed with her thumb—"are the only ones still here. Don't do anything foolish."

Judd wasn't sure if she was cautioning them to behave in her house while she was gone or was offering a warning about the coming storm. He decided to walk the few blocks to the beach. He had the feeling something was happening down there and he wanted to see it for himself.

On his way to the beach, Judd didn't see another soul. No cars were out, and people—if they were still around—stayed indoors. He'd always liked storms—they made his spirit lift inside him as though responding to the wildness without. But this evening his spirit cowered and he had to force himself to keep going. Surely he'd see the danger before it arrived. A storm couldn't drop on a man from nowhere. He glanced at the sky and suppressed a shiver.

He wished Joe could see this. He wished his brother were there with him experiencing the wonder and thrill of the coming storm. He glanced to his right and saw the carousel in front of the Pavilion sitting quiet. The animals seemed to be frozen in the very act of fleeing the hurricane. Judd had an urge to turn them loose.

A few steps more and Judd finally saw the ocean beyond the Pavilion. He hadn't planned to come here, but it was a good spot. He moved around the building to the boardwalk, and his stomach clenched. He'd seen the ocean in several moods by now, but he'd had no idea it could stand up, five times taller than a man, and crash to the shore as though it meant to consume the very earth in its path. It was horrifying and wonderful at the same time. And it looked like it had already exceeded its limits—creeping up the steps toward the Pavilion itself.

"Joe, what you make of that?" he whispered.

And it was as though he could hear Joe laughing inside his head. "Ma would tell us to get our hind ends up on top of a mountain and right quick."

Judd laughed, too. That was what Ma would say, but Joe, he'd stick right here and watch the storm roll in. He always liked to be where the action was. Judd let the tears come then. Rain had begun falling again like someone flipped a switch, and the wind lashed at his clothes like it wanted to strip him bare. And maybe he was laid bare standing there with nature roaring around him and grief washing over him. But this time he felt the grief pass through and come out the other side. It had been stuck in his craw for too long. The storm and the image of Joe laughing finally knocked something loose and Judd took a deep breath, opening his arms wide to the roar and crash of the weather.

This storm could kill him if he wasn't careful, but if it didn't he thought he just might decide to live again. It's what Joe would've wanted. He might even start making plans of his own instead of just trying to live out Joe's dream. He'd come a long way at Waccamaw Timber, mostly by luck, but if he was intentional about his future—well, he just might have one here in South Carolina.

Judd stood and let the wind and rain pummel him and scrub

his soul clean for a good long while. If he closed his eyes, the storm sounded like a waterfall he and Joe had once found while hunting. There'd been heavy rains that spring, and the small creek had been transformed into a rushing torrent. Joe dared him to stand under the pounding cascade, then jumped in there himself, laughing and hollering at how cold it was. Judd only stuck a foot in after him before changing his mind and then they sat in the sun, talking. Judd wished he could remember what all they talked about, but he didn't suppose it mattered so long as he remembered it was good.

He felt like he was getting used to the storm and he was pretty sure it wasn't getting any worse. Surely if it were going to get worse, he'd know it by now. Soaked and chilled, he finally turned to begin the walk back to the boardinghouse. He saw movement at the corner of the building and let the wind push him that way.

The open-air section of the Pavilion was dark with rain and utterly empty. Except for a girl with a ponytail. And she was . . . dancing. Judd crept closer, hid behind a post, and watched. Sure enough, it was Larkin. Her wet dress clung to her, and she did what he guessed was that shag dance everyone seemed to love so much. She was good at it, and it occurred to him that even wet, she was the prettiest girl he'd ever seen. He swallowed hard. Maybe especially wet.

She turned, and he stepped out from behind the post, clearing his throat, which didn't seem like much noise in the midst of a tempest. She squawked and clutched at her chest.

"Where in the world did you come from?"

Judd angled his head back toward the ocean. "Been watching this here storm roll in. Can't say as I've ever seen anything quite like it."

Larkin stood perfectly still in the midst of chaos, the wind playing havoc with her hair. "I don't suppose you would have in a landlocked place like West Virginia."

Judd thought he heard a tension in her voice that wasn't necessarily due to the storm bearing down on them. Just then the wind abated and the rain stopped. He looked up to see a clear spot in the sky where a full moon showed through.

"Folks might excuse me for being out here since a hillbilly like me doesn't know any better, but what are you doing out on a night like this?"

Larkin sighed and glanced at the moon as a cloud scudded across it, hiding it once again. "High tide tomorrow morning. Extra high with the full moon." She glanced toward the ocean where the waves were like barely contained animals straining at their tethers. The roar was deafening, and for a moment Judd felt as though the sea were a lion seeking to devour him. "I don't suppose either of us ought to be out here even though it's not too bad yet. Still, once I set foot outside the house, I just felt so . . . free. Then I decided to come see if the Pavilion would be alright. Might be my last summer to dance here."

Judd wrinkled his forehead and tried to put a lightness in his voice. "You going somewhere?"

She shot him a look he almost might call mean, except he was pretty sure she couldn't look mean. "No thanks to you. But if I have my way, the letter I just mailed means I'll get to live out my dreams yet."

He raised his eyebrows. Dang, she was pretty when she was worked up. "That right? Would this be the dream to rescue all those poor mountain children?" He sounded more derisive than he meant to, but she'd apparently already dismissed him from her world.

"Yes, sir. Just as soon as Ben tells me I can come—" She stopped abruptly and darted a look at him. "What I mean to say is just as soon as I get word back from Kentucky, I'll pack my bags and head north."

Ben. There was that name again. He wanted to ask who this man was that George Heyward was hunting and Larkin was apparently running off to be with. Well now, that right there might explain a few things. If Larkin was in love with someone Mr. Heyward had sent packing, that would explain her interest in the mountains and this silly notion that she was going to go be a help there. She was looking at the situation through rose-colored glasses.

The wind picked back up as if suddenly remembering what it had been doing. Rain began pelting them, stinging and tasting of salt. Judd squinted at Larkin, who hunched her shoulders and glared at the sky like she was daring it to do its worst. He took a step toward her and saw most of the tin roof from a building across the street lift into the air, turn like it was finding just the right angle, and fly toward them.

Judd tackled Larkin, covering her body with his own. The roofing slammed into bleachers near where they lay and rattled like it wanted nothing more than to fly once again. Judd gathered Larkin into his arms and bolted for the main building. Her feet hit the ground now and again, but he was mostly carrying her. He burst through a door wondering why in the world it was unlocked and stopped inside to catch his breath. His leg throbbed unmercifully, and Larkin panted beside him.

"What are you kids doing over there?" The voice boomed through the empty building. A burly man with shirtsleeves rolled up past his elbows approached them at a trot. "Storm watching, were you? Y'all must not be from around here." He glared at them, hands on his hips. "Fools like you are why storms like this kill people."

Larkin was shaking now. Judd wrapped an arm around her shoulders. "Yes, sir. It was foolhardy for sure."

The man threw his hands in the air and shook his head. "Way I see it, that storm's going to put high tide right where we're standing even if they are right about old Hazel pushing out to sea. Came down here to open the doors so it can wash through and maybe leave this old gal standing."

He squinted at Larkin. "Aren't you George Heyward's girl?"

"Y-yes, sir."

"George know you're out?" He eyed Judd as though he might feed him to the ocean.

"No. I just had to come see if the Pavilion was alright and . . . and this man"—she glanced at Judd as she moved out of the circle of his arm—"was kind enough to rescue me."

The man blew a huff of breath through his nose. "Fine, fine. I don't have time to sort out your mess. Young man, you help me get this building ready and then I'll run you both home." He rolled his eyes toward Larkin. "Quiet-like."

"Thank you," she said.

Judd helped open doors and move anything loose to a more secure location. When they were done, the storm had quieted again—Judd was beginning to understand that it came in fits and starts—and he assured the big man he could make it to his boardinghouse on his own.

"Son, if this storm keeps coming, you'd best be skedaddling back over the causeway. A storm surge can climb higher than you'd ever dream if it hits just right."

Judd nodded his head, looked at Larkin one last time, and ducked out into the stormy night.

◊◊◊

Larkin couldn't get her teeth to stop chattering. She clenched her jaw as the man from the Pavilion who knew her daddy drove her home through streets awash in rain while wind lashed at the palmettos and flung debris clattering against the windshield. She tried not to think about that moment when she lay flat on the ground with Judd Markley stretched out over her, protecting her from whatever the storm might bring. It was the safest she'd ever felt.

As soon as the car stopped in front of her house, she jumped out with hurried thanks and scooted inside the same front door she'd slipped out of earlier. She pushed it shut behind her and held her breath, listening. The television was on in the den, and she could see her mother's slipper-shod foot where she sat in her usual high-backed chair. If tradition held true, Daddy would be stretched out on the sofa with papers stacked on the end table at his elbow, bourbon glass close at hand.

Larkin waited for the noise on the television to reach a crescendo and tiptoed past the door on the far side of the hall where the light was dim. She assumed she'd made it when no one spoke from inside the den. She darted up the stairs and shut herself in the hall bathroom, where she turned on the shower and soon stepped under the warm spray. She finally felt as though her pulse was slowing, as though she could get a deep breath. Her left arm stung, and she craned her neck to see a cut just below her shoulder. It wasn't bad, but it reminded her of how close she'd come to—what? Serious injury at the very least.

It had been silly, her notion to walk the dozen blocks to the Pavilion on a night when a hurricane brewed off the coast. It had been four blocks to the nearest mailbox, and at that point she'd felt an undeniable tug to see if her beloved dance floor was intact. Her thought had been that if she really were going to go off and be a missionary alongside Ben, she might not dance there again. At least not anytime soon.

Being alone with the storm thrilling the air around her, she'd felt . . . more alive than she knew was possible. She couldn't have turned around and just gone home at that point. Who knew Judd Markley would be out in the storm, too?

She toweled herself dry and slipped into a fluffy terry-cloth robe.

"Larkin." There was a tap at the door.

"Yes, Mama?"

"We're calling it a night. You aren't afraid of the storm, are you? We could all camp out in the den like we did when you and . . . when you were small."

Larkin opened the door as she ran a comb through her wet hair. Her mother looked uncertain—maybe a little vulnerable. She gave her a quick hug.

"I'm not afraid. Are they still saying it's going to blow out to sea?"

Her mother glanced over her shoulder to where a streetlight shone through the bedroom window, illuminating the tossing trees outside.

"They're talking about it hitting a glancing blow now, but I'm not so sure."

Larkin felt an unexpected lightness remembering her close call, the letter that Ben would receive soon, and the way Judd looked at her after he'd pulled her inside the Pavilion. She smiled.

"Oh well, I guess we'll be fine either way."

She reached for the light switch, but before she could flip it, the power flickered once, twice, and plunged them into darkness.

CHAPTER
13

Judd tried to go to sleep and must have drifted off when the dying whir of his fan woke him. He glanced out the window into an eerie darkness—no streetlights, no windows aglow, nothing. Power must be out. He was only thankful it wasn't quite so dark as the bottom of a mine.

He heard a thump and found his way to the door. A voice came from the hallway.

"Got a candle or a lamp or anything?"

"Nope. Seems like Mrs. Hardee had some candles on that side table in the dining room."

The two men fumbled their way to the dining room, located the candles, produced a box of matches, and finally lit the room. Somewhat.

Judd squinted at the older fellow he'd seen around the place. They'd been introduced early on but hadn't had much cause to socialize. Judd thought he remembered the man's name was Floyd. Floyd Bellamy. He rarely had much to say, just ate and returned to his room. Nodded when they passed in the hall. Judd had no idea what he did with his days. He supposed this was his chance to get to know his neighbor.

"You from around here?" Judd asked.

Floyd nodded his head and slid down the wall to sit on the floor. "All my life. Ain't seen too many hurricanes, though. Had a brush with one in forty-four, but that was mostly just rain." He glanced toward the rain-lashed window. "Not like this."

"Reckon we're safe?"

Floyd shrugged. "One thing I've learned in this life—there's no such thing as safe. My wife got took when a bad tooth poisoned her blood. She wasn't safe just sitting in the parlor on a Sunday afternoon."

Judd slid down beside him. They were in the corner of an inside wall, and he figured if a tree fell they'd be in a fair spot to survive.

As though he could read Judd's thoughts, Floyd tapped the floor next to them. "'Course, the main worry is that there full-moon tide. If this storm really does come ashore, it's going to hit pretty close to high tide and I've seen water shoot so far inland you'd think the beach would never show again."

Judd pictured the distance between them and the ocean. "Surely it wouldn't come this far."

Floyd sighed and hunched his shoulders. "Hope not." He sat in silence a moment. "You going back to bed?"

Judd shifted, trying to stretch his leg out into a more comfortable position. "I'm thinking I'll just sit here and wait her out. How about you?"

"I was thinking the same. Tilt your head on back there and get some shut-eye if'n you can. Gonna be a long night."

Judd nodded, thinking there was no way he'd ever sleep sitting up against the wall in a strange house while a storm raged outside. But he must have drifted off, because the next thing he knew, Floyd was shaking his arm.

"We're in the thick of it now," Floyd said. "It's morning, and if I judge right, the eye will pass before too much longer. That means ole Hazel has hit the high tide right on the nose."

Judd swallowed hard and wiped sleep from his eyes. The air in the room felt thick and stale. It reminded him of the air in the mine after the cave-in. Too still, too heavy with the storm raging outside the walls. He wanted to run out into the open so bad he could barely stand it. Floyd laid a hand on his arm as if he understood. He looked at the old man, grateful he wasn't alone. He wondered where Larkin was and hoped she was safe. And he wished, just a little, that he could go on back home now.

"How'd you come to live in a boardinghouse?"

Floyd stood and stretched his limbs, then settled back into place. "After my wife died, I made do on my own for a while. My daughter came by and redded the place up when she could. Got two boys, but they moved up north to work in factories." He sighed and ran a wrinkled hand over his face. "The older I got, the shakier I got, and sometimes I'd forget things, so I moved on in here before my daughter could put me in one of them homes." He stretched his hands out in front of him, and Judd could see that they did shake.

"Had me a nice tobacco allotment. Sold it and put enough in the bank to keep me here for a good, long while." He hung his head. "Hopefully long enough."

Judd wanted to ask what he did with himself all day long, but didn't. Maybe because he was afraid of the answer. What did a man do with himself when he couldn't work anymore?

He looked toward the window, saw a hint of morning light and nothing moving. "Looks like the storm's passed."

"Nope. It's just the eye. We'll get the backside of Hazel here shortly." Floyd stood up again. "Won't hurt nothing to take a quick look outside, though." He looked sharply at Judd. "Just don't go wandering off."

They opened the door and stepped out into an eerie stillness. The air was thick—almost yellow. Debris was scattered everywhere, and when Judd looked to the street, he saw . . .

water. It lapped at the bottom step, bumping bits of wood and who knew what else against the concrete. He looked back at Floyd, hoping the old man could help him make sense of what he was seeing.

"Yup, looks like Hazel flung the water way on up here. Houses down at the water will either be flooded or gone. Lucky we didn't get our toes wet."

"But it's blocks to the ocean," Judd protested. "High tide doesn't come any farther than the beach."

Floyd squinted up at the sky. "Backside of the storm'll pull a lot of this water on out. We may get killed by a falling tree, but we're not likely to drown." He nodded his head once, as though he'd found everything to be satisfactory, and then went back inside. "Don't you linger now. This storm ain't over."

Judd stood, feeling like he'd missed the lesson leading up to this test. He leaned to the side and tried to look past the flooded houses on the other side of the street. He couldn't say for sure, but it seemed like there was a whole lot more open country than before. Maybe it was just all that water. He felt a tickle of wind and hurried back inside.

🌢🌢🌢

Larkin huddled in the dark hallway beside her mother. She'd dragged out a pillow and blankets to try and sleep, but it was mostly too hot and too frightening to rest. Daddy kept getting up to check things, which was just silly since he couldn't do anything about anything. She couldn't stop thinking about Judd. Her latest fantasy was that Ben would want her to join him immediately and Judd would escort her to Kentucky, just to make sure she was safe, and then be so touched by her dedication that he'd stay and . . . Oh, what was she thinking?

Daddy would never let her go by herself, much less with a timberman. She was going to have to plan her escape. Just as soon as she heard back from Ben. . . . A sudden thought struck her and she half rose. Her mother gave her a questioning look, and Larkin settled back into place with a sheepish smile.

Her letter was in a mailbox that might very well be washed out to sea by now.

Daddy came back into the hall and slid down the wall opposite them.

"What's happening out there, George?"

He puffed his cheeks and blew air. "Two live oaks I can see are down out front. A piece of Harold Williams's roof has blown off, and Mrs. Enright is going to need a whole lot of work done on her porch. Palmetto tree has taken out the side closest to us. Can't see as the water has made it this far inland, though."

Larkin felt her mother shudder. "If it did, we'd need Noah's Ark."

"How much longer do you think it'll last?" Larkin asked.

"The eye is passing and the storm seems to be moving fast. Not too much longer, I think."

Larkin clutched a pillow to her chest and listened for the wind to start again. She'd begin making plans as soon as they were in the clear. And Judd Markley needn't figure into her future at all.

Judd and Floyd stepped out of the house after the worst of the storm had passed. Wind still whipped, but it was nothing compared to the power of the hurricane at its height. A few other folks were out in the neighborhood, looking over the damage and marveling at the chaos. A wooden beach chair sat in the middle of the street, and part of what looked like an Esso sign rested on top of a car next door.

Floyd kicked at some bits of wood and metal that found their way into the lee of the front porch. "Gonna take some work to get this all sorted out," he said.

"Will it be worse down toward the beach?"

"Sure as shootin'. 'Course, that's more likely the kind of work you'd need a dozer for. Probably won't be a whole lot left to fix up."

Judd looked that direction. "I might walk down there and see for myself."

Floyd waved him on, seemingly content to poke around the boardinghouse.

"You be alright here on your own?"

Floyd's laugh sounded dry. "Safest I've been all day."

Judd grinned and started toward the ocean at a trot. The closer he got, the slower he moved. It was as though a giant hand had reached down to sweep away anything within two blocks of the ocean. And it hadn't been tidy about it, either. Houses had been lifted from their foundations and set into the street. Cars were piled up in a heap like so many bathtub toys, and there was sand everywhere. Judd had simply never seen anything like it. He finally made it to the Pavilion and found the building still standing, although it was the only thing solid in the midst of destruction. The beach looked like a lumberyard. Surrounding buildings were collapsed with shards of broken boards and metal jutting out at odd angles. He'd never seen such devastation and it unnerved him that chaos like this could come from the sky. He'd thought having a mountain hanging over his head was worrisome, but this . . . this came from the very air around him.

He looked up the beach toward the pier, but there was just blue sky and rubble where it used to sit. Judd listened to the surf, still rough, but back in the sea where it belonged. He noticed a refrigerator sitting at an angle in the sand and, overcome with curiosity, picked his way to it. He opened the door and found food still inside. He jumped when a twisted piece of metal broke loose and clattered to the ground. No one else had ventured this close to the ocean yet, maybe for good reason. He suddenly felt very alone and exposed. He turned and hurried back to the boardinghouse. He guessed maybe there was just as much to fear above ground as beneath it.

◆ ◆ ◆

Back at the house, he didn't see Floyd right off, so he circled around back looking for him. As he walked around the side he saw the vine he'd taken from Larkin had finally burst into full bloom. It twined happily on the string Judd tied for it to cling to. Apparently a little wind and rain had been just the thing. He touched a vibrant petal and then remembered his task. He walked on around back and found Floyd sitting on the steps, looking pale. He noticed a handkerchief wrapped around the old man's left hand.

"You alright?"

"Aw, I was poking around back there and cut my hand on a piece of tin roof. Durn foolish thing, trying to lift that bit of rubbish." He grimaced. "I don't suppose it'll kill me."

Judd sat beside him and looked a question at his hand. Floyd extended it, turning his head the opposite direction.

"Never have much liked to see my own blood."

Judd peeled back a layer of saturated fabric and found a deep gash in the piece of flesh connecting thumb and index finger. Looked like he'd tried to slice the thumb off and didn't quite get the job done.

Judd rewrapped the hand and then added his own bandanna. "It's a beaut. I'm thinking it might not be a bad idea to get you on over to the hospital so a doctor can take a look at that."

Floyd's Adam's apple bobbed. "They most likely have their hands full without having to mess with a foolish old man who ain't got the sense to leave all this trash to somebody younger."

"You're probably right. Might be we could give them some help. Carry fresh water, direct traffic—something."

"How we gonna git there?"

Judd looked up and down the street. "It's not too awful far. Maybe if we start walking, somebody'll give us a ride."

Floyd shook his head. "I dunno. Can't walk so far as I used to."

Judd looked around and spotted a child's wagon jammed under the sagging porch next door. He retrieved it with a mighty tug and trundled it over to Floyd. "All aboard," he said with a grin.

Floyd tried to laugh. "This here cut does hurt something fierce. Might be some nurse could bandage it up proper and then we can tote supplies for them as are really sick." He stood, wobbling a little. "Let's give her a shot."

He climbed into the wagon, knees at odd angles. Judd gave him what he hoped was a reassuring smile and started the long haul to the hospital.

CHAPTER
14

As soon as the storm abated, Larkin's father set out, determined to get to his office and learn what damage had been done to the various timber sites. Larkin couldn't think what good it would do since the phone lines were almost certainly out everywhere, but decided it wasn't her concern. She and her mother went out to see what had happened in their neighborhood.

A police car wound its way onto the street, and Mother waved it down to ask what was happening throughout the area.

"It's an awful mess, ma'am. Y'all are pretty lucky here— looks like your houses are still standing and not too many trees down. Some places have been wiped clean. Houses gone or broken up like kindling." He looked them up and down. "There's a shelter at the high school, and the hospital could use a hand if y'all feel like helping out."

Larkin surged forward. "I'm a candy striper at the hospital. I'd be glad to go help."

"Hop in. I'll get you there."

"Larkin, your father might prefer you stay at home." Mother placed a restraining hand on her arm.

Larkin squeezed Mother's fingers and then opened the door

of the police car. "I know, but this is the right thing to do." She didn't even glance back as the young officer began driving away, steering through the debris.

At the hospital, Nurse Enright immediately set Larkin to the task of talking to anyone who came in who didn't appear to be hurt. She had a clipboard with a hastily scrawled list of places people could go for help. She also handed out cups of drinking water, and someone stuck several crates of bananas in the corner, so she handed those out, too. Everyone who came in had a sort of stunned expression and seemed grateful just to have someone to talk to. They poured out stories of being carried away by the storm surge or crouching on top of furniture as water licked at their toes. Some had been trapped in the tops of trees until the water subsided. Larkin felt exhausted just listening to what had happened to folks.

"You look like you could use a break."

Larkin had just finished talking to a mother with two children whom she'd told to wait in a specific spot outside. A Salvation Army truck would be along to take them to the shelter at the high school. She turned to see who had spoken.

"Judd." She dredged up a weak smile. "Looks like we both survived." Then it occurred to her he'd come to the hospital. "Are you alright? You're not hurt, are you?"

He smiled. "Nope. Fine as frog's hair. Just brought a friend in with a nasty gash on his hand." He laughed softly. "Tried to haul him here in a wagon, but thank the Lord a truck picked us up and brought us on in."

"Will he be alright?" Larkin let Judd lead her to some chairs behind a screen where they both sat. There had been a lull in the people coming in, so she supposed it wouldn't hurt to rest a bit. And oh, her feet did ache.

"I think he'll be fine. 'Course, it'll be a while before they get him seen. Lots of folks worse off, waiting back there for some doctoring."

Larkin rubbed her gritty eyes. She must look a mess, but she was too tired to care. "So what did you think of your first hurricane?"

Judd grinned. "I think I'd like for it to be my last."

She laughed. "Going back to your mountains, then?" She asked the question lightly, but it occurred to her she liked having Judd around and would miss him if he did go.

His smile fell away and he rubbed his hands on his pant legs. "I might go back there one of these days." He wrinkled his forehead. "Seemed awful important to leave when I did, but now . . . well, I guess I've changed some."

"Me too."

He raised his eyebrows, and Larkin couldn't resist what felt like an invitation to share her heart. "I'd already decided I was going to go work in the mission field as soon as I hear back from . . . well, as soon as someone I know tells me where to come. Of course, my letter might be lost in the storm, so I suppose I'll have to write to him all over again." She glanced back at the waiting room where some more people had entered. "And now, after being here all afternoon helping people, I just know it's what I'm meant to do." She stood and refastened her ponytail. "I know you don't think much of my going to help people in your mountains, but I feel more determined than ever to go. This"—she swept her arm to indicate the room and the people waiting—"has made up my mind. Letter or no letter."

She touched Judd's shoulder, smiled, and headed back to her post with a lightness of heart. Yes, she was tired, but she had a purpose and it was good.

◌ ◌ ◌

Judd watched Larkin go talk to the newcomers and saw how her smile soothed them. He had scoffed at her plans, but watching her now made him think she might be made of sterner stuff than he'd imagined.

He rested his elbows on his knees and stared at the floor between his boots, thinking about how Larkin had a dream, an ambition to change the world. What did he want? All he'd been doing since he woke that day in the hospital, leg encased in plaster, was run away from losing Joe. But had he wanted anything even before that day?

He remembered a time when he was nine or ten years old. Dad had taken the whole family to a tent revival, and even now he could remember that young preacher. Tall and thin as a rail, he'd towered over the makeshift pulpit. He'd leaned into the crowd, talking about eternal life and . . . how had he put it, "the quickening of the Holy Spirit"? Judd had heard plenty of hellfire and brimstone, but that was the first—and maybe the only—time he'd heard that God loved him and wanted to lead him through life. Judd remembered wanting that, too.

On the last night, when the preacher called anyone who wanted to be indwelt by the Spirit to come on down to the altar, Judd had stood and taken two steps. That's when his father caught him by the collar and jerked him back.

"You ain't old enough to understand, and no son of mine is going to make a false profession of faith." His father glared at him. "Sit on down and we'll talk when you're old enough not to be taken in by pretty words."

Until that moment, Judd had felt a growing conviction that he had a purpose—a reason for being that was about to be revealed. But his father said he was too young to know what life held for him, and Judd believed him. He guessed he'd never bothered to wonder what plans God had for him after that night.

Judd raised his head and watched Larkin. There was something about her, a kindness that went deeper than her lovely face and charming ways. It was like she somehow had more life in her than anyone else around.

Judd suddenly wanted to tell her he'd take her to West Virginia or anywhere else she wanted to go. But then he remembered that she was waiting to hear from someone—this Ben fellow. Probably a beau. Probably a man who was smart enough to run right on down here and snap Miss Larkin Heyward right up the minute she said she was willing.

Getting to his feet, Judd started for the door. He'd leave Larkin to her overflow of life and go see if Floyd had been tended to yet. Then he'd best see how he could help folks clean up all that mess out there. He didn't know what he was made for, but he did know he could work as hard as any man.

Halfway across the room, Judd stopped and jogged back to Larkin, who turned from her latest customer to turn that smile on him. He swallowed hard.

"I went on down to look at the Pavilion once the storm was over."

Hope lit her face. "Is it still there?"

"Sure thing. Wet and dirty and maybe a little rough around the edges, but it's standing."

Larkin reached up and hugged him. "Thank you for telling me. I don't know when I'll ever dance there again, but the Pavilion will always have a special place in my heart. It's a comfort to me knowing it's there if I ever decide to come back."

Judd rubbed the back of his neck where it felt as though her fingers had seared his skin. "Thought you'd want to know." He nodded once and turned to leave again. This time he couldn't think of a reason good enough to turn around.

CHAPTER
15

Judd had to admit, he liked driving this car. Especially on the brand-new turnpike into his home state. They were calling this stretch of highway "the engineering marvel that beat the mountains." Judd didn't think the mountains were beaten exactly, just tamed a touch.

Larkin's convertible looked like an exotic bird blown off course, but he didn't care. The deeper they got into the mountains, the more suspicious folks were when they stopped, but as soon as they got a good look at Judd and heard him speak, they eased up a mite. Of course, even his mountain twang couldn't quite convince locals that he and Larkin belonged there. Folks could tell there was a story brewing and no one liked to be left out of a good story. Judd figured it wasn't his story to tell.

As they approached Beckley and the last of the highway that had been opened, Judd glanced at Larkin where she'd fallen asleep against the window. He still wasn't sure this was a good idea, but he couldn't pass up a chance to give Abram a hand. As glad as he'd been to get away from the home place, seeing the mountains rise in front of him felt right. Larkin stirred and sat up with a yawn.

"I didn't mean to fall asleep. Where are we?"

"Been in West Virginia for a little while. Probably take us another couple of hours to get to Bethel." He turned off the highway onto a two-lane. The roads would get steadily narrower from here on out. "You sure you don't want me to take you to this place in Kentucky? I can hitch a ride back home from there."

Larkin was quick to answer. "No, someone will come fetch me. Or more likely I'll drive myself on over. You've already done enough bringing me all this way."

Judd downshifted into a turn. "Couldn't hardly keep away after getting that letter from Abram. Hurricane Hazel didn't stop to catch her breath after wiping half the coast off the map. They say it made it all the way to Canada where it was almost as bad as in the Carolinas."

Larkin looked out the window. "We're lucky no one died in Myrtle Beach. The death toll other places just keeps climbing."

Judd hated to see Larkin looking sad. "Well, everybody's fine at home—just trying to clean up from all that wind and water. Thank goodness Abram and Lydia got the garden put up before the rain came. But there's a bridge out, and the church down on the river was pretty much washed off its foundation." He felt like he was babbling, but he wanted to talk to Larkin and couldn't think of what else to talk about. "Barn roof's half gone. I'm thinking that's where Abram and I'll get started."

Larkin nodded but didn't look like she was paying close attention.

"So when will—Ben, is it?—when will he come fetch you?"

Larkin narrowed her eyes. "What makes you think it's Ben who's coming for me?"

"You mentioned him once or twice. Figured that's who it would be."

She tossed her ponytail over her shoulder. "I don't suppose

it matters now that you aren't likely to see Daddy. Yes, Ben's who I expect, but I'm not exactly sure . . . I mean, the date isn't definite . . . well, I don't quite know when he'll come." She twirled her hair around a finger. "Probably I'll just go to him."

Judd slowed for the winding road and tried to ignore the uneasy feeling curling in his belly. "Larkin, all of this has been arranged, hasn't it? Your father wanting me to take you as far as West Virginia so you can go on to Kentucky?" He fished a piece of paper out of his breast pocket. "This is the letter on company stationery saying I have two weeks' leave to go home and look after my family. Asking me to take you as long as I'm going." He glanced at her, suspicion taking root. "You wouldn't have anything to do with this, would you?"

Larkin twirled her hair faster and looked out the window as though the whirling scenery was the most fascinating thing she'd ever laid eyes on. "Why would you ask that?"

Judd pulled over at a farm gate, shut off the engine, and turned to look at Larkin. "What's going on here?"

She threw up her hands and blew out a puff of air. "Oh, fine. I just had to get to Kentucky, and when you mentioned that your family needed help, it all seemed so perfect. You could go home and I'd have someone to help me get to Kentucky." She looked at him sideways, then turned her attention to the cows in the pasture beyond the fence. "I just knew Daddy would give you the time off, but I thought he might contrive a way to keep me from traveling with you." She looked at him with wide blue eyes. "So I wrote that letter you have." She must have seen the thunder in his face. "And I left a letter of explanation for Daddy, too. You should be fine when you go back, and I'll be in Kentucky with Ben by then, so everything will be alright."

Judd gripped the steering wheel hard. He wanted to explode, wanted to blow up and maybe give this silly female a thing or two to think about. He breathed in through his nose and out through his mouth. What had he gotten himself into?

"I have a feeling your father will not be pleased to see me when he realizes I'm responsible for helping you run away to the wilds of Kentucky. Never mind how he'll feel about me abandoning my job."

Larkin flipped her hand in the air. "I'm not running away. I'm running *to*. It's my calling. It's what I'm meant for. If Daddy had his way, I'd marry some attorney or doctor and join the garden club. He *might* approve of me volunteering at a nursing home or something like that." She smiled, looking like a child who'd just been promised a trip to the fair. "Once I start making a difference in people's lives, he'll change his tune."

Judd let his head fall forward against the steering wheel. He closed his eyes. "And what am I supposed to do in the meantime?"

"Go help your family. I'll call Daddy and explain everything." She sighed as though it were a huge concession. "Even though the letter already explained it all."

Judd looked at her, pretty as ever, but maybe more naïve than he'd realized. He started the car and continued driving. He was tempted to turn around and run her right on back to South Carolina, but they'd have to drive through the night and he was tired. He guessed he wouldn't be in any more trouble if he took her home in the morning. Whether she wanted to go or not. In the meantime, he'd be the one calling George Heyward to take responsibility for the mess they were in.

◊◊◊

It was dusk when Judd pulled the Roadmaster into the front yard at his brother's house. They'd stopped twice to use pay phones to try and reach Mr. Heyward. The first time the phone was out of order, and the second time Judd had reached the Heyward home only to have the housekeeper tell him Mr. Heyward was out of town on business and Mrs. Heyward was out for the evening. He hated to think what business Mr. Heyward might be on, considering that he'd practically kidnapped his daughter. Each time Judd failed to connect with her family, Larkin seemed to relax a little bit more. He guessed every ounce of tension she shed fell directly on his shoulders.

Judd stood from the car and peered into the gloaming to see how badly the farm had been hit. There was a gap in the roof on the barn and quite a few trees down behind the house. At least they'd have plenty of firewood for the winter.

Larkin got out of the car and wrapped her arms around herself. "It's freezing," she said.

Judd smirked. "Been known to have snow in November."

She made a face at him. "I've seen snow. One year it snowed on the beach in January." She got a dreamy look on her face. "It was so pretty—the surf lapping at the flakes on the sand."

Judd laughed. "And how long did that last?"

"I suppose it was gone later that afternoon, but it was still snow." She tossed her ponytail. Judd was beginning to realize that's what she did when she was put out over something.

"What do we have here?"

Judd turned to see Abram on the porch, thumbs hooked in the galluses of his overalls. It occurred to him that he hadn't really considered how to explain Larkin.

"Thought I'd better come help put things back together after the storm."

Abram looked at Larkin but spoke to Judd. "Thought you'd be busy setting that timber company to rights. You quit your job?"

Judd glared at Larkin. "I didn't quit. Plan to go back shortly."

"Hunh. That boss of yours must be an awful good Christian to let you come home like this." He finally looked at Judd. "You gonna introduce me to your lady friend?"

Judd schooled his expression. "This is Larkin Heyward. She's on her way to Kentucky to meet . . . a feller and was good enough to let me come along for the ride."

"That so, miss?"

Larkin glided up to the porch and extended her hand. She looked like a queen—and almost as out of place. "That's so. Your brother has been most kind to escort me this far. I plan to do mission work in the coalfields of Kentucky." She batted her eyelashes and glanced back at Judd. "I'm in your brother's debt."

Abram took the extended hand like she was giving him a frog and he was too polite to turn it down. He smiled and looked confused. "You needing a place to put up for the night?"

"I surely am. If there's a guesthouse in the area, I'd be happy to go see if they have accommodations."

Judd snorted and began hauling bags out of the trunk. All he had was his duffel, but Larkin appeared to have packed up all her earthly belongings. He was curious to hear what Abram would have to say. Before his brother could open his mouth, Lydia—who must've been just inside the door—stepped out onto the porch.

"We'd be proud to have you stay with us," she said, tucking her hands under her apron.

"Oh, I hate to impose."

Judd didn't think all Larkin's syrup was necessary, but it surely seemed to be working on his family.

"It's no bother. You can sleep in Judd's old room. We're about to sit down to dinner. You'uns come on in and eat a bite."

Judd opened his mouth to ask where he'd be sleeping, but then snapped it shut when he saw Larkin hook her arm through Lydia's and sashay on into the house. Abram raised his eyebrows at his brother and followed the ladies inside. Judd left Larkin's things on the ground, hefted his own bag onto his shoulder, and followed. That woman seemed to have everything figured out. Let her tote her own stuff.

◊ ◊ ◊

Larkin was so nervous she was shaking. She'd made it this far half expecting her father to catch up to them at any moment. She'd written Ben a second letter and mailed it from an inland post office where the storm had wreaked less havoc, but she hadn't heard back. Maybe she should have given Ben more time to respond, but every day made her feel a little more trapped. She continued to do volunteer work, but after a week or so the urgency died down and folks were settling into what she thought of as rebuilding mode. And she wasn't so desperately needed anymore. She wanted to be needed.

"Who are you?"

A little boy with red hair and adorable freckles stood his ground like a fierce lion cub. Lydia had gone on into the kitchen while Abram and Judd were hanging back at the door, talking too softly for her to hear them. Looked like she'd have to face this latest challenge on her own.

"I'm Larkin."

He seemed to consider this, and Larkin noticed a second little head peering at her from around a corner. This child couldn't be more than five, with strawberry curls and huge blue eyes. She watched them both intently.

"Like the bird?"

Larkin turned her attention back to the boy. "Kind of, but with an *i* and *n* added on."

He nodded. "You look kind of like a bird, but not a lark. They're too plain. You're more like a rufous-sided towhee with your pretty hair." He turned toward the hall. "Hey, Gracie, ain't she like a towhee?"

The little girl eased out from her hiding place. "She's a pretty lady, not a bird."

"That she is, my little Grace from God." Abram stepped into the room and swooped the child into the air. "But not near as pretty as you." He winked at Larkin. "Have these young'uns introduced themselves properly?"

"Well, I gather that's Grace in your arms, but I have yet to learn the name of this brave fellow."

"Yes sir, brave's the word." He set Grace down and placed a hand on his son's head. "But James is prone to dreaming overmuch."

"He'd likely make a fine poet," Larkin said and then wondered if the child would even know what a poet was.

James grinned and squared his shoulders. He began reciting with, "'I wander'd lonely as a cloud that floats on high o'er vales and hills, when all at once I saw a crowd, a host, of golden daffodils.'" He continued apace until he reached the end and recited with a flourish, "'. . . and then my heart with pleasure fills, and dances with the daffodils.'"

Larkin clapped her hands in delight and astonishment as James gave a little bow.

"Oh, now you've done it," said Judd, dropping his duffel with a thump. "That young'un knows more poetry than I've ever read. If we don't catch him now, we'll not get a word in edgewise all evening."

James launched himself at his uncle, and they rolled onto a sofa in a laughing mass of arms and legs. Grace wiggled and clapped her hands, crying, "Me too. Me too." Judd stood, caught the little girl up in his arms, and tossed her in the air. Larkin thought she saw him wince, and he rubbed his leg after he set the child down.

"Get on in here before this food gets cold," Lydia called.

Larkin meant to offer to help with the meal but had been too caught up with the children.

They filed into the kitchen where a plank table stood off to one side weighted down with dishes. Judd sat between the children on one bench, while Lydia patted the opposite bench inviting Larkin to sit beside her. Abram sat in a chair at the head of the table.

"Let us pray," he said, and all traces of the earlier levity disappeared. "Dear Father in Heaven, thank you for the bounty of thy blessings set before us on this table. Thank you for the hands that prepared this food for our nourishment. Thank you for bringing Judd home to us, and bless Miss Larkin as she strives to do your work in Kentucky. In Jesus' name, amen."

Hands unclasped and heads lifted as they began passing dishes around the table. Larkin accepted each bowl or platter and helped herself to at least a taste. They certainly seemed to eat well. There was a roast, mashed turnips with butter, green beans stewed with pork fat, fluffy biscuits, and a bowl of applesauce.

Larkin tasted the meat and found it had a unique flavor—tasty but not what she'd expected. "This is the leanest beef I think I've ever eaten." She hurried to add, "And it's delicious."

Judd and Abram exchanged a look.

"It's deer meat," James offered with a confused look on his face. "Don't you know the difference?"

Larkin paled and swallowed. She knew lots of folks who ate venison but hadn't tasted it herself. Her mother said it was for people who couldn't afford proper meat. She pasted on a smile.

"Seems I do now," she said brightly. Lydia looked concerned, so Larkin took another bite and fought it down. "Delicious. Truly."

"You'll likely be eating lots of wild game once you get to Kentucky," Judd said with a gleam in his eye. "Squirrel, rabbit, deer, maybe even possum."

Larkin split open her biscuit and ignored him. She'd been meaning to lose a few pounds. Perhaps this was her opportunity.

CHAPTER

16

Larkin folded the thin pillow in half and jammed it under her head. How in the world was she going to track her brother down? And apparently she was going to have to do it before Judd tossed her in the car and drove her back to South Carolina. She had the name of the town where Ben collected his mail but had no way of knowing how to find him beyond that. Her only hope was that someone at the post office in Logan would know. He must come for his mail—surely they could give her directions. Or, worst-case scenario, she could just wait at the post office until he showed up.

She remembered the last time she'd seen him the evening of his graduation party. She'd watched him out the window after Daddy slammed the door in his face. He'd stood in the driveway for a long time, looking at the house as though memorizing it. Eventually, Mother stepped out, suitcase in hand, and glanced around like she was afraid she was going to get caught. She handed the bag over to Ben, kissed him on the cheek, and darted back inside. After that, Ben climbed into his car and drove slowly away. Larkin watched until his taillights disappeared.

◆◆◆

Judd woke on the sofa with a crick in his neck and a little girl staring at him with big blue eyes. He winked at her, and she giggled, then clambered up over him and nestled between the back of the sofa and his knees.

"Did you come back to dig more coal?" she asked.

Judd rose up on one arm and considered his niece. "No. I came back to help your pa put the roof back on the barn."

"Good. Uncle Joe went down in the mine and didn't come back."

Judd swung his feet to the floor and tucked Grace close to his side. "That's so," he said, swallowing past a lump in his throat. "That's surely so."

He sat quiet for a few moments, getting his bearings, missing Joe and giving thanks for the child tucked in next to him.

"Your ma up yet?"

"No. Daddy went to do the milking. He said to leave Mommy alone until he got back."

"Guess he didn't mention me," Judd said with a grunt as he stood and stretched. "Give me a minute in the privy and then we'll get some coffee going."

Grace bounced with excitement but stayed put on the sofa. She was still there when Judd came back in. He scooped her up and carried her, giggling, into the kitchen where he pumped water into a basin so they could both wash their hands and faces. Then he stoked the wood stove and set the coffee to percolating.

"Lawsy, Judd, are you in here making breakfast?" Lydia appeared, pushing the last pin into her hair.

"No, ma'am. And if you were to eat my cooking, you'd agree it's for the best."

She patted him on the arm and began pulling out eggs, ham, and ingredients for another pan of biscuits. Judd remembered at least one thing he'd always appreciated about living with his brother's family.

As Lydia began cutting lard into the flour she'd spooned into

126

a large wooden bowl, Larkin eased into the room like she was afraid she might step on a snake. "Good morning," she said a little too brightly. She glanced at Judd, giving him the distinct impression she wished he weren't there. "Um, Lydia, can you point me to the, uh, facilities?"

"The what? Oh, you mean the privy. Grace, take Larkin out so she can do her business."

Judd probably shouldn't have enjoyed Larkin's discomfort so much, but she did flush the prettiest shade of pink. He stared at the ceiling and whistled so he wouldn't laugh at the shocked look on Larkin's face.

"Out? The bathroom is outside?"

Lydia paused in her mixing. "Oh, honey, they's some houses in town with indoor plumbing, but it'll be a long time before it gets all the way out here." Now Lydia flushed. "I hope you don't mind."

Larkin seemed to be dancing just a little. Judd imagined if she'd avoided learning about the "facilities" last night, she must be fair to pop. Grace grabbed Larkin's hand and tugged her toward the door. Larkin shot him a desperate look but allowed herself to be led away.

Thankfully, Abram came in from the barn just then and Judd was saved from doubling over in laughter by taking the milk and offering to strain it off for Lydia.

A few minutes later, Larkin came back in, found the wash-basin and scrubbed her cheeks until they were almost as rosy as before. "Breakfast sure does smell good. Is there anything I can do to help?"

"No, no, you just sit down over there and keep me company while I cook. Tell me about the ocean and all this business Judd's been writing us about dance halls and amusement parks." She shot him a teasing look. "Sounded to me like he run off to join the circus."

Larkin sat at the table, and the rest of the family followed suit, listening as she told them about the Pavilion and collecting seashells and how it was warm almost all year. She even told them about volunteering at the hospital. They listened with rapt attention until every last bite of breakfast had been eaten and the dishes cleared. Larkin insisted on helping wash up, which pleased and amused Judd at the same time. Watching her wrestle with the pump handle and heat water on the stove was enough to entertain him the rest of the day. She was game, he'd give her that.

After breakfast, Abram and James headed out to the barn to start work on the roof. Judd hated that he wouldn't be able to follow them, but he didn't see how he had any choice but to take Larkin back home. He invited her out onto the porch with a look, and she followed slowly as though she'd rather stay and help Lydia and Grace with the rag rug they were making.

Outside, she wrapped her arms around herself and shivered. "Is it always this cold?"

"It's not cold yet. Haven't even had the first hard frost." He scuffed his boot, sighed, and removed the lightweight jacket he'd put on to go out and work. It nearly swallowed Larkin, but she pulled it around her throat and smiled and somehow it looked good on her.

Judd cleared his throat. "I don't see as we have much choice but to go straight back to Myrtle Beach and try to make amends with your father."

"Pardon?"

"You've strung together enough lies and half-truths that your only way out is to own up to them and ask for forgiveness. I'll have a fair amount of apologizing to do myself considering I was so easily taken in by you."

The rosy cheeks were back, but Judd didn't think it was the cold this time. "If you'd rather not tell the whole story to Abram and Lydia, I guess you could say you got cold feet

128

and want to go home—something like that. Although seems to me trying your hand at some solid honesty might not be a bad idea."

"Are you lecturing me?"

Judd rubbed the back of his neck. Now he was starting to feel the morning chill. "Sounds that way, doesn't it?" He was surprised he couldn't see steam coming out of Larkin's ears.

She removed his jacket and held it out to him. He took it and slipped it on again. "Very well. Why don't you go give your brother a hand while I explain the situation to Lydia and gather my things."

It wasn't a question, and Judd decided it wouldn't hurt to give her a little space to smooth her feathers back down. "One hour," he said. "We're pulling out of here in one hour."

"Fine."

Judd ambled on out to the barn, feeling almost satisfied. He hated to leave without helping Abram, but neither did he want to put off facing up to his mistake even one more day. He smiled thinking he really did like Larkin and maybe, once she owned up to the error of her ways, she might even learn a valuable lesson. He ducked his chin into the warmth of his collar and smiled when he realized he could smell her perfume.

◊ ◊ ◊

Larkin explained her situation to Lydia, telling her how sorry she was to be leaving again so soon. Grace in particular looked deeply disappointed, and Larkin wished she could stay with these sweet, kind people. But she had a duty to fulfill and she couldn't let her emotions get the best of her.

She loaded her things in the trunk, darting looks at the barn. Judd was standing on a ladder or something so that he was sticking halfway out of the damaged roof, but he was facing away from her. She went back inside and hugged her new friends as though her life depended on it.

"I think you'd do well to wait," Lydia said. "I've learned the hard way it never pays to be in a hurry."

"I'm sure you're right," Larkin said. "But sometimes you feel like you have no choice."

She walked back outside and looked toward the barn as Judd ducked inside and hollered something down to James where he stood below.

◦ ◦ ◦

Judd asked Abram what time it was.

"Getting on toward ten. You ain't hungry again already?"

"No, just figuring it's time I checked on Larkin. Seems we might have to head on back to South Carolina this morning."

Abram looked puzzled. "Is she fickle?"

Judd guffawed. "That's one word for it. Come on to the house and we'll let her explain."

They stowed their tools and made their way to the house. Lydia and Grace were on the porch plucking a bird.

"This ole rooster wasn't good for anything but making noise and aggravating the hens," Lydia said. "Thought we'd have chicken and dumplings for supper."

"That would be a relief to Larkin if we were staying," Judd said. "'Course, if she was around when you wrung that bird's neck, she might not have the stomach to eat it."

"Oh no, she was long gone by the time we dispatched this fellow."

Judd had to replay that last comment. "Gone. Where'd she go?"

"On to Kentucky to meet up with that Ben fellow. Said she felt God's call on her, and as much as she wished she could stay for a few days, she'd best be getting on." Lydia grinned. "I think she might be sweet on you, Judd. Said she couldn't bear to tell you goodbye."

Judd suddenly understood what people meant when they said

something made them want to tear their hair out. He drove his fingers through his hair, making it stand on end.

"I was supposed to drive her back to South Carolina."

Lydia used a candle to singe some pinfeathers. "Guess she changed her mind."

Judd groaned. Changed her mind indeed.

CHAPTER
17

As Larkin drove the worst roads she'd ever seen, she tried to figure out how she was going to find Logan, Kentucky, so she could find Ben. The map splayed across the passenger seat looked so clear, but surely none of the roads marked out on paper were as curvy as the one she was traveling. She had a headache from trying to peer around bends in the road, and it had been far too long since she'd seen a house. Getting lost hadn't occurred to her as she sped away from the Markley family farm that morning, but now she realized it was a real possibility.

She'd read about the feud between the Hatfields and McCoys. If she wasn't mistaken, she was driving through their part of the country even now. Of course, that feud had ended in the previous century, but what if there were other feuds going on? What if she got caught up in some battle between mountain men with rifles? She suppressed a shiver.

The road seemed to be dropping down into some sort of valley or maybe even a ravine. Rounding another curve, Larkin saw a river and railroad tracks. A train was passing, long and black. She could see coal piled high in each car and could smell something like sulphur hanging in the air. She realized she had a choice of following the river or turning left to cross a bridge beyond the tracks. She pulled over as far off the road as she could get to check the map, although it had been an hour since she'd seen a car. She'd probably do fine to stop in the middle of the road.

Larkin squinted at the map as the train clattered on by. She traced the line she thought she was traveling—yes, there was a blue line next to it for the river. And crossing the bridge did appear to be the correct route. Folding the map, she put the car into gear and began to ease out onto the rough road. But the car wouldn't go, as though a giant hand held on to one of the rear tires. She gunned the motor and stalled the engine. Restarting it, she had even less luck. The weight of the car settled low in the back.

Getting out, Larkin picked her way to the rear of the vehicle and saw the tire was mired in mud. She leaned heavily on the trunk and looked around at the expanse of water and road and trees around her. Nothing and no one. She heard the train whistle in the distance and wondered how long it would be until another one came by. Would a train stop to help someone out of the ditch? She climbed back inside the car and examined the map again. It looked like there was something of a town a few miles beyond the bridge. Maybe she could walk there. She'd just have to dig her most sensible shoes out of her luggage and see what she could find. Thank goodness it was still early in the day, and the sun was doing its best to warm the air. Sighing, Larkin told herself this was just the sort of adventure she'd had in mind when she set out for Appalachia.

◆◆◆

Judd had a fair idea of how to get from Bethel to Logan, Kentucky—he just wondered if Larkin did. Fool woman. Abram had given up the day's work to ride with Judd as he searched for what he thought of as an exotic southern flower about to face its first hard frost. He could think of at least a dozen terrible things that could happen to Larkin, and as mad as he was at her, he couldn't stand imagining any of them.

"Bullheaded, that's what she is."

Abram nodded and stroked his beard. "Awful purty, though."

Judd glared at his brother. "Don't see as that matters a hill of beans."

"If I ain't mistaken, you're sweet on her."

Judd grunted. "You're mistaken. How could I be sweet on someone who'd lie to me, then run off and risk who knows what in country she has no clue about navigating?"

"Sounds like she has the courage of her convictions. Willing to risk her reputation and maybe more to do something she believes in. Reminds me of . . . Joe."

Judd sagged behind the steering wheel. "That doesn't mean I'm sweet on her."

"If you say so." Abram went back to watching the country slide by. "How you reckon to run her to ground?"

"If anyone's seen her in that mint-colored convertible, they'll surely remember. We'll just have to do some asking around."

Two hours later, after talking to some kids cutting cornstalks for fodder and then a preacher out traveling the circuit on horseback, they felt like they were pretty well on Larkin's trail.

"If this is the way she come, she's right fair turned around," Abram said.

"About what I expected," Judd answered. "Probably find her in a ditch somewhere crying her eyes out." He softened at the idea. "Not that I'd wish that on her."

"'Course not." Abram squinted through the cracked windshield of his truck. "You see something a shade of green that don't appear quite natural up there ahead?"

Judd did. It was the Buick, and it was stuck in a ditch just like he'd imagined. He felt a surge of hope that swamped his anger and washed it a little farther out to sea. He pulled in behind the car, careful not to get into the swampy spot that trapped Larkin. He expected her to pop out of the car and run to greet them, but there was no movement.

"She's probably embarrassed. Or asleep."

He got out to investigate, only to find the car empty. Hope was replaced by a wave of fear that made his earlier emotions seem like morning mist. What he felt now was a heavy fog settling over his heart. He glanced around. While there were good folks in the mountains, there were bad ones, too. Just like everywhere. He gnawed his lip and considered what to do. Glancing inside the car, he saw her map. The door was unlocked and nothing looked disturbed. Maybe she decided to walk somewhere. He examined the map and saw it was folded to a road—not this road—that ran along a river and crossed a bridge. Beyond the bridge was a town. Larkin likely thought she could walk there. Of course, since she was in another place entirely, she had a lot of walking ahead of her. Judd raced back to the truck and headed for the bridge. They had to catch up to her before someone else—someone unsavory—did.

▲▲

Judd thought he could feel his heart pounding in his ears as the truck bounced across the bridge and began climbing a hill. There was an occasional house or barn, and once a truck squeezed past them on the narrow road, but there was little that seemed likely to attract Larkin.

"She might've stopped to ask for help," Abram said.

"Or she might've kept walking, thinking she'd come to a town with a telephone so she could call that Ben she keeps talking about," Judd said.

"Oh, I see."

"What do you see?"

"You're worried she's in love with this Ben feller. I thought he was just a missionary or something."

"I don't rightly know what he is, but it doesn't matter." Judd could feel the tension driving his shoulders up around his ears. "I just want to find her before she gets into any more trouble."

Abram nodded like he knew the true story. Judd fought down the urge to kick his brother out of the truck. That wouldn't help the situation at all.

They rounded a bend and saw a hand-lettered sign that read, *For Sale—Rabbits.*

"Let's ask these folks if they've seen her," Judd said, turning down the rutted drive.

"She partial to rabbits?"

"I don't know, but she might see that sign as a sort of invitation." Judd thought it was a weak idea, but he was grasping at straws now.

They pulled up in front of a small brick house with a concrete porch out front. Wrought-iron posts held up the neatly patched porch roof, and the trim was crisp and white. Judd could see a grape arbor off to one side, and a hedge was trimmed into a uniform rectangle. The door creaked open, and a woman with cottony white hair peered out at them.

"If you've come about the rabbits, we're plumb out. Last one went just today."

Judd approached the porch and propped one booted foot on the edge. "No, ma'am. We're actually hoping you might know if a friend of ours passed this way. Young woman with reddish-brown hair. She got her car stuck back there a ways, and I thought she might have stopped to ask for help."

"Oh, you mean Larkin. Ain't she the purtiest thing you ever seen?" The woman laid a hand against her breast and stepped out onto the porch. "I'd have been glad to just sit and talk with her all day, but she was all fired up about getting on to Kentucky."

"Where is she now?" Judd tried to appear calm, but it was all he could do not to grab the woman by the arms and insist she produce Larkin right there and then.

"William run her on back to her car. He figured he could pull it out of there with his truck and point her in the right direction. Land sakes, but she got turned around somewhere. William will give her the right of it, though. He knows a shortcut over to Highway 52. Once that runs into 119, she'll be fine—take her right on into Kentucky."

Judd thought he might have to sit down. "When did they leave?"

"Oh, must have been an hour or so ago." She looked beyond Judd's shoulder. "Here comes William now. Must've got her going just fine."

An older man in green dungarees with a crease ironed down the front hopped out of his truck with the spring of a man half his age. "Howdy. If you come about the rabbits, we're plumb out."

"No, William, they come about the girl, not the rabbits."

"Well that's good, then. You kin of hers?"

"Not exactly," Judd said. "But her father will expect me to get her home again safely."

William nodded like he knew just what Judd meant. "Reckon she's halfway there by now. She was awful eager to get back to that mission work." He got misty-eyed. "Awful good to see the younger generation on fire for the Lord like that. You a preacher?"

Judd opened his mouth, then snapped it shut again. "I'm not. Just a friend trying to look after Larkin."

The old man's eyes gleamed. "She needs lookin' after. You catch on up to her and she just might let you do it." Then he laughed and stepped up on the porch where he wrapped an arm around the waist of his wife. "Get you a good 'un the first time and you won't have to look ever again."

His wife swatted at him. "William, quit acting the fool and tell these boys how to get over to Highway 52 so they can catch up with that girl."

Three hours later, Judd poked Abram who was snoring softly on the passenger side of the truck. "We're here."

Abram snorted, rubbed his eyes, and pulled out a handkerchief to blow his nose. "Where's here?"

"Logan, Kentucky." He nodded out the window. "And there's Larkin's car out front of that store.

"Reckon she's inside?"

"I aim to find out."

Judd climbed out of the truck, stretched, and took a deep breath. What, exactly, was he going to say? He rubbed his hands down his shirtfront, smoothing it and drying his suddenly sweaty palms at the same time. He guessed he'd know what to say once he said it.

♦♦♦

Larkin stood inside what she supposed was meant to be a store. There looked to be a little bit of everything jammed inside without much rhyme or reason. Brooms stacked next to shoes, canned goods beside penny nails, and bolts of fabric stacked beside tin pails. She didn't see anyone right away and was grateful for a few moments to orient herself. She could smell oil and dust, which turned out to be a surprisingly pleasant combination.

Feeling her confidence returning, Larkin moved further inside. A pear-shaped man wearing a long apron stepped out of the back room. "Can I help you?"

"I certainly hope you can," she said with as much charm as she could muster. The man smiled and stepped behind a counter where he braced both hands.

"If I don't have it, you don't need it. What can I get you?"

Before Larkin could ask him about Ben, she heard the door open and glanced behind her. She choked on her words as Judd Markley stepped inside. He didn't speak, just nodded and moved to a shelf as though examining the soap powders displayed there.

"I, uh, well you see . . ." Larkin took a steadying breath. "Actually, I was hoping you could help me find—"

This time the door didn't creak on its hinges. It flew open, slamming against the wall. "Larkin Matilda Heyward."

She froze and looked toward the front of the store. She'd never liked her middle name, and the only one who used it like that was . . . "Daddy."

CHAPTER

18

Either Judd was out of Mr. Heyward's direct line of sight or he only had eyes for his daughter. Even as Judd fought what he knew was an unreasonable urge to turn coward and run, Larkin spoke.

"Judd." Larkin's voice wavered. "Look. Daddy's here."

"I've been here for almost twenty-four hours now. Your mother told me all about your plans to join . . . Ben when you disappeared. What I want to know is where you've been in the meantime."

He addressed Larkin but had shifted his position so he could look at Judd, who felt he was being accused of something he wasn't sure how to defend himself against. He had a whole lot of questions, but none rose to the surface. He was trying to formulate an explanation when Larkin stepped forward.

She moved closer to her father but didn't touch him. "We've been helping Judd's family. It was on the way and they had hurricane damage, too." She laughed softly. "Can you imagine? That hurricane made it all the way to West Virginia."

Mr. Heyward's look wiped the smile from her face. "Anyway, I left Judd with his family and came on to Logan so I could join

Ben and help him with his mission work. Judd thought I had permission." She cast a nervous glance at him. "But I guess he was worried and followed me." She laid a hand on her father's sleeve. "I told him I explained it all to you in a letter. Surely you found it." She fluttered her eyelashes and smiled again.

"Now," she said, putting her hands on her hips, "we're all here and this is the perfect opportunity for you and Ben to make amends." She looked at the storekeeper. "Can you direct us to his residence?"

"Stop."

Judd had no idea so much force could be packed into a single word. Mr. Heyward was a shade of scarlet that would rival the brightest redbird. He closed his eyes and seemed to be doing some sort of breathing exercise.

"Young lady, you are coming home with me. Now." He turned to Judd. "As for you, I'll need to discuss this with you further, but I'm aware of how"—he glanced at Larkin—"determined my daughter can be." She gasped, and Judd thought she might stomp her foot. "If you'll drive her car back to South Carolina for me, there will be appropriate remuneration." He took a breath. "And you can keep your job just as long as this story she's spinning holds true."

"But Daddy—"

He held up a hand. "No buts. If we start now, we can be halfway home by dark. We'll stay in a hotel tonight and be back in Myrtle Beach by lunchtime tomorrow."

Larkin stared at her father. Then she walked over to one of two rocking chairs, sat and crossed her arms. "I'm not going." She glared at George Heyward. "And you can't make me."

◊ ◊ ◊

Larkin sat not so much because she was immovable as because her legs wouldn't hold her up anymore. She had to sit or collapse. She'd gone around her father before. Perhaps she had even manipulated him—but she'd never openly defied him, and it set her to trembling to do so now.

She'd certainly seen her father angry, but never had so much ire been directed her way. The storekeeper looked like he wanted to run them all off, and Judd mostly looked confused. Oh, what he must think of her.

Daddy took two steps in Larkin's direction, and for the first time in her life she felt a touch of fear as he approached. He'd never struck her, not even when she was a naughty child. At this moment, though, she thought he just might lash out. Judd took a step forward too, as though he would intervene.

Larkin braced herself, but her father stopped. And then he staggered and thumped into the chair beside her, clutching his chest.

"Daddy, what is it?" Larkin knelt beside him and grabbed his free hand. He tried to shake her off.

"Nothing. It's nothing. Just some indigestion."

The storekeeper stayed behind the counter, looking worried. "Do I need to send for the doc?"

"Yes," Larkin said at the same time her father said, "No."

"I'll go—where is he?" Judd offered.

Larkin ignored the hurried conversation, focusing on her father. While she was upset that he was trying to ruin her plans, she was also terrified that he might be seriously ill. She loved him. And she knew that he, in his way, loved her.

Judd shot out the door. Larkin used a handkerchief to pat at the perspiration beading her father's forehead, even in the cool of the November afternoon. A handful of customers came in and exchanged whispers with the storekeeper. By the time Judd returned, five or six newcomers were clustered near the front counter, trying to look like they weren't sticking around to watch the drama unfold. Larkin had to clench her teeth to keep herself from telling them all to go away. Daddy sat now, eyes closed, but he no longer tried to pull free from her touch.

As a matter of fact, he clutched her hand with a fierceness she'd never known before.

Judd took stock of the situation and spoke to the group that had gathered. They nodded their heads, glanced toward Larkin and her father, and finally began to make their way to the door. One older woman paused and then hurried over to Larkin.

"If you'uns need a place to stay or a good meal, get Carl there to send you on over to the church. I'm Maude Tenney and I'd be proud if you'd call on me should the need arise." She patted Larkin's shoulder and headed on out the door.

Larkin felt tears rise at the unexpected kindness. She looked to Judd and had the notion he was touched, as well. He walked over and knelt down beside them.

"Doc Baldwin's on his way. He was in the middle of cutting a rusty nail out of some little feller's foot, but he was nearly done. Said he'd be here quick as he could."

Larkin shuddered at the image but was thankful the doctor would be there soon. She patted her father's arm, and he squeezed her hand again.

"You feel any better, Daddy?"

He blew out a slow breath. "You know, I think it has eased some. Probably won't need that doctor by the time he gets here."

Larkin fought tears. If her father died of a heart attack in the middle of the Appalachian Mountains, it would be all her fault. She'd wanted to come here and help people, not cause trouble for her family. If Daddy died, he'd never make up with Ben.

The doctor bustled in, shooed Larkin and Judd away from his patient, and began examining George Heyward.

"Let's get a breath of fresh air," Judd said and led her out front.

Larkin stood on the wide top step and drew in a deep breath, but when she exhaled, it came out as a sob. And Judd was right there, so she turned to him, and he opened his arms wide. Larkin sank into him, crying all over his rough work shirt. His arms felt awkward at first, but as she cried, he seemed to get his bearings, and by the time her tears had run their course, she felt like she could stay right there, safe, forever.

But then Judd eased away and looked down into her face. He handed her a simple white handkerchief, and she dabbed at her eyes with it.

"You going to be okay?" he asked.

The worried look on his face tickled Larkin. He'd been so aggravated with her and now he looked like he was afraid she'd fall to bits right there at his feet and he'd have to pick up the pieces. She giggled, then clapped a hand over her mouth.

"Oh my. I'm afraid this is all a bit much for me." She blinked back new tears. "If anything happens to Daddy, it'll be my fault."

Judd glanced in through a window. "You haven't helped matters, but I have a feeling your father worries more about his business than his health."

He glanced back and brushed a tear from her cheek. Larkin's breath hitched and she leaned toward him as though he'd tugged on a string. Then he grinned. "I guess this situation isn't *entirely* your fault."

Her eyes widened and she swatted him. "You're just trying to distract me," she said. "I'm going back inside to see how Daddy is."

∙◢◢∙

Judd filled Abram in on all the hubbub and suggested he head on home before it got dark. Abram was reluctant to go, but Judd felt pretty confident he'd soon be driving Larkin's car back to South Carolina for her. He knew his brother almost never spent the night away from his family and he didn't want to be the cause of it happening this time.

Abram finally shook his head. "You sure can pick 'em, brother. Write us a long letter with the rest of the tale."

Judd said he would, then followed Larkin inside. He'd only teased her because he'd seen George Heyward standing up and moving around as though all were well. Larkin had accused him of trying to distract her, but he was the one who was distracted. By the softness of her in his arms. By the smell of her hair under his chin. By the vulnerability she'd shown him and the need she'd expressed without words. He'd wanted nothing more than to lean down and kiss those tears away, which left him feeling off-balance. He'd been so angry about her deception, he was unprepared for the feelings of compassion and forgiveness welling up in him now.

He wondered what Joe would have sacrificed to follow his dreams. And now that he was beginning to lay out some plans of his own, he wondered what he might be asked to trade for them. Larkin was ready to do whatever it took to make her own dreams come true. And while that didn't make her manipulating people right, he guessed he could extend some grace for good intentions. A smile traced his lips and he went back in the store.

Larkin knelt at her father's side. "Should you be sitting up?" She looked at Dr. Baldwin. "Shouldn't we put him to bed or something?"

"I've advised your father to see his own physician as soon as he returns home, but I'm optimistic this is nothing more than a severe bout of dyspepsia brought on by stress." He glanced at Mr. Heyward. "Your father has confessed that he has been under undue stress lately. I've advised him to take his ease—that's the best medicine for him at the moment."

Larkin wrapped her arms around her father. The older man stiffened, then let himself be embraced. "I'm fine, Lark, really I am. I just wish you hadn't . . . well, it's done now." He stroked Larkin's hair. "And if you'll just come on home with me, this can all be over and done with."

Now it was Larkin's turn to stiffen. She eased back and looked into her father's eyes. She glanced back at Judd, and he could see the battle waging in her heart. She gave her father another hug.

"Alright. I'll come home with you for now, but I still hope I can come back here one day."

"There are more than enough people for you to help back home," Mr. Heyward said. "And maybe your mother and I will come with you to the Pavilion next summer. Sounds like a little frivolity is just what the doctor ordered."

Judd saw the light that always seemed to shine from Larkin's eyes dim a notch and it near about broke his heart.

"Yes, Daddy."

Mr. Heyward settled back into a chair and blew out a breath. "Now, it's getting late for us to be heading back." He looked to the doctor. "Is there a place we can put up for the night and get an early start tomorrow?"

Dr. Baldwin, who'd finished packing up his bag, pursed his lips and looked to the storekeeper. "Whatcha think, Carl?" Where can these folks lodge? I'd offer them the infirmary, but I've got Bart Linger laid up in there."

Carl scratched his chin. "I heard Maude offer 'em a meal and a place to stay."

The doctor clapped his hands. "That'll do—Maude keeps house for the preacher over at the church and it won't be the first time she's helped somebody out of a tight spot."

He gave them directions to the church, clapped a hat on his head, and left. Judd had a notion of the type of accommodations someone who "helped at the church" might offer, but he decided not to enlighten Mr. Heyward or Larkin. Better to spring it on them once it was too late to go anywhere else.

Larkin rode with her father while Judd drove Larkin's convertible the short distance to the church. He was grateful he'd thought to bring his bag and of course Larkin had all her luggage. Mr. Heyward appeared to be traveling light.

They pulled up at the church as dusk began to fall. Judd

walked around and saw that there was a sort of hall built onto the back. He knocked, and Maude Tenney answered the door. She brightened like he was a long-lost family member come home at last.

"I could feel in my bones that you'uns would be along. Put a big pot of soup beans on this afternoon, thinking there weren't no need to make that much food, but I've learned to listen when the good Lord gives me a holy nudge." She opened the door wider and waved them all in. "Come on in here and put your feet under the table."

Judd motioned for father and daughter to follow him inside. Larkin pranced in like he'd just invited her into a high-class hotel while her father came more slowly, taking in the surroundings with caution. Of course, there wasn't much to the place. It was one large, open room with a makeshift kitchen at one end and several cots at the other. In between were two trestle tables with eight chairs around each. One corner in the back was curtained off, and Judd thought he saw movement back there but couldn't be sure.

Maude pulled out a chair, inviting them to sit. Judd had to admit the smell of supper was a mighty fine thing. They all three sat at the closest table and waited as Maude dished up bowls of soup beans with ham and slid a plate with a cake of corn bread into the middle of the table. She added a dish of butter, some apple butter, and a bowl of chopped onions. Judd's stomach gurgled, and everyone looked at him. Maude laughed and clapped him on the back.

"Ain't nothing better than a strappin' feller with an appetite. Let's have us a word of prayer and then we'll make short work of these vittles." She looked toward the curtained corner. "Reverend? You gonna come pray over this food afore it gets cold?"

The curtains shifted, and a man pushed a corner back, letting it fall again before Judd could get a good look at what else was back there. But he could have sworn he saw a slight form lying in the bed behind the curtain.

"Well now, company is a real treat. Who have you rounded up to feed tonight?" The man's voice was full and round, like he was used to speaking to crowds. He took several steps toward the table and froze with a look of shock on his face.

Judd heard a chair hit the floor and looked to see George Heyward standing, staring as though he'd seen a ghost. He pointed a finger in the man's direction and made a strangled sound before toppling to the floor.

CHAPTER
19

Well, this is surely a surprise." The preacher, once he'd gotten Mr. Heyward into a chair and lucid, tried to smile, but it fell flat. "I'd always hoped to see you again, but I assumed I'd have to come to South Carolina to do it."

Larkin clung to the man's arm like she was afraid he'd run away if she loosened her grip. As soon as she knew her father was all right, she'd flung herself into the preacher's arms, crying "Ben!" over and over again. Judd supposed this was the long-lost fellow she'd been hoping to join. He hadn't expected him to be a preacher.

Mr. Heyward looked worse than he had back in the store. Ben knelt beside his chair and grasped the older man's hand. Mr. Heyward tried to tug it away at first, then just sat, looking anywhere but toward the man beside him. Larkin, on the other hand, only had eyes for the sandy-haired man with broad shoulders. He wasn't as tall as Judd, but he was broader, probably stronger. Judd flexed his muscles, then stilled. Going by the look on her face, he'd never had a chance with her anyway.

"You act like you know these folks," Maude said.

Ben looked up, then stood and made a little bow. "Maude

Tenney, allow me to properly introduce you to George and Larkin Heyward. My father and sister from South Carolina." He turned toward Judd, who couldn't seem to pick his jaw up off the floor. "This fellow is new to me, but I feel we're likely to be excellent friends before long."

Judd snapped his mouth shut. "Judd. Judd Markley from over in Bethel, West Virginia."

Ben stuck out a hand, and Judd shook it, still feeling slightly dazed. "I'm guessing by the look on your face this is more family drama than you knew you were stepping into."

"I . . . yes. You could say that."

Judd realized Larkin was having a hushed conversation with her father, whose color had returned. Now his expression was an odd mixture of anger and resignation.

Maude clapped her hands. "No matter. It's time to eat and this food's getting cold. Come on then. Everyone gather 'round, and Brother Ben will say the blessing." She flicked a look at Mr. Heyward. "Unless you want to as his elder."

Mr. Heyward shook his head and shuffled to the table as though he were suddenly a hundred years old. He glared at Ben. "No, let the preacher do it." He said the word *preacher* like it was a curse.

Ben nodded, bowed his head, lifted his hands and began praying. "Holy Father in Heaven, thank you for reuniting this family. Thank you for preserving us until this day and for bringing us together to break bread under your roof. Show us the way to go from here. Amen."

Judd realized he'd forgotten to close his eyes. He was too fascinated by the scene unfolding in front of him. So Ben wasn't Larkin's beau, but her brother. The one who ran off to be a missionary. He finally remembered her mentioning something about that the night she told him about her dreams down at the Pavilion. His failure to put two and two together had cost him a lot of aggravation. He had a hundred ques-

150

tions but decided the best course of action for now was to watch and listen.

Maude handed him a bowl of soup beans with a chunk of corn bread bigger than his fist. At least he was eating well. He looked at Larkin, who continued to gaze with love at her brother even as she ate. It was good to see someone reunited with a beloved family member. Judd would surely give his good leg to see Joe just one more time. Mr. Heyward was a fool to throw away his son.

◊ ◊ ◊

Larkin felt giddy, light-headed, like she might float away. She wished she could dance but it didn't seem appropriate. Instead, she simply tried to take her brother in. Of course, he looked older than she remembered—that was natural. But at the same time there was a lightness to him that seemed new. Even as Daddy continued to shoot darts with his eyes, not speaking, barely eating, Ben managed to have a peace about him. It was mesmerizing.

She'd argued with Daddy that he needed to behave himself, to let bygones be bygones, to take this unexpected opportunity to mend what was broken. She took her eyes off Ben long enough to examine her father's tight expression. Nope, no bending there. It was as though he'd slipped a mask over his face and was refusing to take it off. She sighed and beamed at Ben. No matter. She'd found her brother and she wasn't going to let him slip away again.

"So, little sister, how in the world did y'all end up in Logan?" Ben crumbled some corn bread into a glass of buttermilk and began eating it with a spoon.

"I came to find you."

He glanced around the table. "And brought your entourage?"

She giggled. "That wasn't part of the original plan." She saw the look of thunder on her father's face and sobered. "Seriously.

151

I wanted to come work in the mission field with you. Didn't you get my letter?"

Ben looked uncomfortable. "I did, but I didn't think you'd really pack your bags and drive north." He glanced at their father. "And I certainly didn't think George Heyward would come with you."

Daddy's jaw tightened. He didn't like for his children to call him by his name. Larkin patted his knee.

"But now we're all here and we can begin to make amends for what's driven the two of you apart." She gave them both a mock stern look. "Isn't it about time you boys made up with each other?"

Her father pushed his bowl back and addressed Maude, who was watching the exchange wide-eyed. "Madam, can you point me toward my overnight accommodations?"

Maude looked confused, then her brow smoothed. "Oh, you mean your bed." She tossed her chin toward the cots in the back. "You'uns are welcome to sleep here. I usually go home of an evening. We keep them cots for helpers or for folks in the community who get down and out." She began to get comfortable with her topic. "Just last month we kept the Childers family for three weeks after their kitchen caught fire. They had some little ones and it was a pure pleasure having them underfoot all the day long." She smiled, and Larkin realized she was missing several teeth.

Daddy stood with great dignity and made his way toward the cots. He paused, then reached to pull back the curtain, perhaps hoping to find a cot with a little more privacy.

"Not there." Ben's voice thundered, and Larkin had her first notion that he might be a powerful preacher.

Daddy's hand froze and then he pivoted, glared at Ben, and took the cot just outside the curtained area. He sat, then reclined fully clothed and stared at the ceiling.

Maude leaned in. "Reckon he's alright?"

"He's just a bit out of sorts, what with his earlier illness and unexpectedly seeing Ben for the first time in—how long has it been?"

Ben leaned back in his chair. "Coming up on four years."

"Too long," Larkin whispered.

She'd been determined to keep any sadness at bay, but it was beginning to creep in. She felt like they'd wasted so much time, and when she saw Ben she'd just known God was finally answering her prayers and was about to heal her broken family. She glanced toward the cots and saw that Daddy had turned his back to them. Why wasn't this working out? It had seemed fated there for the briefest of moments.

"Ben, I'm gonna clean up and get myself on home," Maude said. "I'll be back tomorrow to fix breakfast for you and—" her eyes darted to the curtain, then back to Ben—"your company."

Ben nodded absently. "You're more than I deserve, Maude."

"Oh, go on with you. God made me for this. I'm just doing what I'm supposed to."

Larkin helped the older woman tidy up while Judd and Ben sat in chairs near a potbellied stove. Larkin realized it was getting cold around the edges of the room and she began to wonder if she'd brought enough clothes to keep her warm. December was right around the corner, and she meant to fight with everything she possessed to stay and help her brother.

After waving Maude off into the night, Larkin joined Judd and Ben. She smelled a sharp sulfurous odor that reminded her of trains and inky darkness.

"What's that smell?" she asked.

"Coal," Ben said, opening the little door in the side of the stove and scooping some of the black stuff inside.

"Money," Judd said and grinned.

Ben laughed and then took Larkin's hand. "Seriously, little sister. Why did you come?"

"I want to help you. I want to help the people in these

mountains. I've been volunteering at a hospital in South Carolina, and helping people makes me feel . . . alive."

Ben blew out a breath. "I take it you and Dad didn't discuss this ahead of time."

"No, he thinks I should marry someone rich, and so does Mother."

"That would make your life quite a bit easier."

She tugged her hand away. "I don't want easy. I want good."

Ben laughed and slapped his leg. "Now that'll preach." He scrutinized Judd. "What about you?"

"I'm just along for the ride. I've got family just over in West Virginia who were hit pretty hard by all that rain and wind a few weeks ago. I've been working for your father, but I—uh—got some time off to come lend a hand." He skewered Larkin with a look that Ben was kind enough to ignore.

"You'll be heading back there, then?"

"Soon enough," Judd said, and it made Larkin feel inexplicably sad. "Unless I agree to drive Larkin's car back to South Carolina. Haven't quite made up my mind yet."

"It's good not to make snap decisions." Ben spoke to Judd but looked to Larkin.

"This wasn't any snap decision. I've been thinking about it for months and months."

"That long?" Ben asked in a way only an older brother could.

Larkin folded her arms across her chest. "You'd better give me a chance." She realized she sounded like she had when they were little and Ben wouldn't cooperate.

Ben grinned. "Or what? You'll tell Daddy?" As soon as he said it, he sobered. "Look, I appreciate you coming all this way and I'll admit I could use your help, but it's more complicated than that."

"Why?" Larkin asked. "Why does it have to be complicated?"

Ben didn't answer. Instead, he looked toward their father's still form with sorrow-filled eyes.

CHAPTER

20

Judd had rarely spent so restless a night. When dawn finally softened the windows on the eastern end of the building, he sat up on his cot and tried not to look toward Larkin's head cradled on a pillow twenty feet away. Never mind that her father and brother were closer by than that. He'd heard every soft sigh and rustle from her cot all the night through.

But now morning crept ever closer and the room had grown cold. Ben banked the fire in the stove before he crawled into his own cot, and the last of the heat had dissipated hours ago. Frost rimed the windows, and even in her sleep, Larkin burrowed deeper under her quilts.

Judd was about to get up and see about the fire when Ben slipped out from behind the curtain in the corner. He held a finger to his lips and nodded toward the door. Judd—who'd slept in his clothes—slipped on his unlaced boots and shrugged into the jacket he'd left draped over his feet during the night. He followed Ben out into the frosty November morning.

Outside, Ben breathed deep, throwing his arms wide. "This is the day the Lord has made," he said in his pulpit voice.

"Let us rejoice and be glad in it." Judd answered without thinking, and Ben shot him a look of amusement.

"Well, you were raised in the church." He raised one eyebrow. "Did it take?"

Judd bent down to tie his boots. "Opinions on that vary."

"Mm-hmmm. I see."

Judd wasn't sure what he saw, and the fear of what it might be kept him from asking. "What's the trouble between you and your father?"

Ben's shoulders sagged. "There's no love lost between my father and the church. His own father's zeal turned him against the trappings of God. Even so, we turned up in the second pew of First Presbyterian Church every Sunday morning." He flashed a grin. "Guess Dad didn't expect it to take." He sobered. "I didn't tell him about the call I felt on my life and I should have. Then, when he made it abundantly clear he expected me to take over the timber company, my decision not to follow in his footsteps probably felt like treason. We haven't spoken since, although I've written many a letter that's gone unanswered."

Judd scratched his stubbly chin. "What'll happen to Waccamaw Timber when he's gone?"

Ben shrugged. "I don't quite know. He took the company over from my maternal grandfather, and I think the idea of it passing out of the family is just about the worst thing he can think of." He glanced toward the hall. "I thought maybe Larkin would somehow take it on, but now that she's here it would appear that's less likely than ever. Dad must be just about at the end of his rope."

Judd nodded and shoved his hands deep in his pockets. He could smell coal smoke in the air—it reminded him of how much he'd missed these mountains in the few months he'd been gone. It also made him miss Joe, but that pain was less sharp here in this place that was familiar and yet not.

Ben chewed on the inside of his cheek. "From the look of

things, we're leaving the old man out to dry." He chewed some more, then rubbed his hands together and grabbed an empty coal scuttle.

"I'll fill this up—how about you go back in there and stoke what fire's left? We'll get some coffee on lickety-split and rouse those sleepyheads."

Judd gripped the other man's arm—gentle but firm. "Who's behind the curtain?"

Ben snapped his head around. He searched Judd's face. "A boy—ten years old. He's got polio, and his family won't have anything to do with him."

Judd recoiled and caught himself. There'd been a polio outbreak back home two years earlier with several children dying and one left paralyzed. He hadn't known any of them well, but the fear permeated the community.

"Is it safe to have him here?"

Ben tilted his head and looked toward the sky. "None of us are safe this side of heaven, but I'm not worried about catching it if that's what you mean." He rubbed his face and looked weary. "He's through the worst of it and needs physical therapy now. His right leg got hit the hardest—thank God it didn't affect his diaphragm. If I could just get his parents to bring him home, but they have six others and I understand how afraid they are."

Judd quelled the urge to go inside and insist Larkin leave with him right then and there. He stretched his neck. Maybe he understood a little of those parents' fear himself. "Is there anything I can do?"

"Start the coffee as soon as you get the fire going." Ben smiled. "I have this feeling I'm going to need it."

Judd nodded and tiptoed back inside so as not to wake anyone. He stoked the fire as quietly as he could and then rummaged around until he found the coffeepot and some beans. Shoot. Grinding these was going to make some noise. He glanced toward the sleeping figures on the cots and felt a jolt. George

Heyward lay there, a lump under a mound of blankets, but Larkin's cot was empty. He hurried over and realized he could hear soft voices behind the curtain. He jerked a panel aside and saw Larkin seated on the side of a proper bed with a boy tucked up under her arm.

🌢🌢🌢

Larkin looked up when Judd pulled the curtain aside. She gave him her biggest and brightest smile. She'd rarely felt this content in the whole of her life and she longed to share the good feeling with everyone around her.

"Judd, this is Kyle. He's been sick, but he tells me he's feeling better now." She looked down at the little boy and squeezed him tighter. "We've made plans to look at some books and maybe walk around the room a bit today. Of course, that's only if Pastor Ben says it's alright."

"Pastor Ben says it's more than alright." Ben stood beaming at them like he'd never seen anything more wonderful in his life.

Daddy stirred and sat up. "If there's going to be this much noise, there'd better be coffee."

Ben gave Judd an expectant look, and Larkin had to hide her amusement. Apparently, Judd was falling down on his assigned tasks. He flashed a look she couldn't interpret and then went back to the kitchen area to make coffee.

Ben pinned the curtain back and settled into a chair near Kyle's bed. "You're looking strong this morning."

Kyle smiled and raised one skinny arm to flex his muscle. There wasn't much to it.

"No more hot compresses for you," Ben said. "Now we need to get those legs strong again. I think Larkin's just the one to help you with your exercises this morning."

Kyle looked up at Larkin with such joy in his eyes it took her breath away. She swallowed past a lump. "I'd be delighted."

Ben showed her how to work with Kyle to do some simple

exercises while Daddy watched, arms folded across his chest and eyes hooded. "Is it safe for her to be doing that?"

"I can't think why it wouldn't," Ben said, but there was tension in his voice.

Daddy finally stood and went to the table where Judd was setting out stout mugs. The smell of the brewing coffee permeated the air and made Larkin realize how hungry she was. Her stomach gurgled and Kyle giggled.

"Are you laughing at the way my tummy's talking?"

He nodded.

"Well I'm going to see if I can get yours to talk back." She started to tickle the boy, who giggled louder and rolled around on his bed trying to get away, though not very hard.

Ben interrupted them to ask how many eggs they thought they could eat.

"Oh, I can eat at least six," said Larkin, watching Kyle.

His eyes got big. He sat up and puffed his chest out. "Me too."

Ben laughed. "I'll be surprised if you can eat six between the both of you. How about I start you off with two each and we'll go from there?"

Kyle nodded, looking relieved, and Larkin laughed from pure joy. How in the world could this moment with a sick child, an angry father, a long-lost brother, and an annoyed former coal miner bring such happiness into her life? She wasn't sure, but she knew she wanted more of it. She gave Kyle a piggyback ride to the table, more determined than ever to remain here, no matter what her father had in mind.

◊ ▲ ◊

Judd looked around the table and marveled at the varied expressions. Ben seemed bemused—maybe uncertain about what he was going to do with his unexpected visitors beyond breakfast. Mr. Heyward was sour—mouth tight, barely speaking, anger radiating off him. And then there was Larkin, who seemed to pour pure light out into the room where Kyle—who wasn't nearly big enough to be ten—soaked it up like sunshine.

It occurred to Judd that he'd be willing to do just about anything to keep that look on Larkin's face. He didn't know if there was a thing he could do to help the situation, but right then and there he determined to try. He'd never been one for meddling, yet Larkin made him want to stick his oar in—welcome or not.

Judd was trying to think how to get everyone to put their cards on the table as Ben dished up eggs and ham all around. He sat and bowed his head, so Judd did likewise. After a short prayer, there was little sound beyond forks clicking against plates.

"Seems like we've all got some decisions to make," Judd said.

Ben laid down his fork. "That we do. And Dad, I've been thinking about how you must feel like I'm letting you down, not carrying on the family business."

Mr. Heyward's eyes opened a little wider and he leaned in. "Have you now?"

"I have. And I want you to know how sorry I am. I realize this"—he indicated the room and whatever was beyond it with a wave of his hand—"isn't what you had in mind for me."

Hope dawned on Mr. Heyward's face. "Son, if you'd just realize how important it is that you—"

Ben held up a hand. "Dad, recognizing the pain I've caused you doesn't change anything. I don't want to give you the wrong idea. I'll always choose to serve my heavenly Father first. I just want you to know seeing you here like this has made me appreciate how hard this must be for you and I'm sorry for that."

Mr. Heyward stood, grating the legs of his chair over the wood floor. "You're sorry for that? And I'm supposed to be satisfied?" His face began to turn red, and Judd feared a repeat of the day before.

"Mr. Heyward, the doctor said you should try to stay calm." Judd felt pretty certain he was overstepping his bounds, but he felt like he had to do something.

The older man sank back into his chair, much to Judd's surprise. "Calm? How can I stay calm when the future of Waccamaw Timber Company is disintegrating before my eyes?"

"Oh, Daddy, surely it's not as bad as all that." Larkin tried sharing a little sunshine with her father. "You've got years and years ahead of you to run the company, and if Ben doesn't want to take it on, maybe one of us will have a grandchild you can train up." She blushed and looked at the floor as she spoke. "Or maybe Hank could take the company over one of these days. You trust him like family."

Mr. Heyward hung his head and swung it side to side. "After all I've done." He looked toward the ceiling. "I'm the one who got the goods on Waccamaw's biggest competitor and made sure they'd go under. I worked long hours and sacrificed so much to become indispensable to your grandfather. He didn't think I was good enough for Augusta, but I proved myself to him over and over again. I made something of myself so that I could give my children all the advantages my own father denied me." He finally met Ben's gaze. "And now you've thrown it all right back in my face. Both of you."

Ben opened his mouth to speak, but his father held up a hand. "If neither you nor Larkin are able—or willing—to take over the company, then after I'm gone it will go to a cousin who could be dead for all I know. Your grandfather Victor's sister married poorly, but I understand there was a child who may yet be found."

Ben waited a few moments, then spoke. "Which I presume would be highly unsatisfactory. So the question is, what do you propose we do now?"

The older man drummed his fingers on the table. "It's not too late for you to come back and step into your rightful place." He ducked his head and the drumming stopped. "It's what I've always wanted."

Ben puffed out some air. "I know. I know. But God has other

plans and I've long been determined to be obedient to Him. Maybe we should look for this cousin."

Mr. Heyward stood, sending his chair toppling backward. "You would give the company away to a stranger?" His hands shook. "If you choose to let Waccamaw Timber Company atrophy or slip away, I can't stop you." He turned toward the door. "If nothing else, you've confirmed the decision I made to turn my back on you." At the door he stopped and looked toward the group still sitting at the breakfast table. "Larkin, you go ahead and do whatever you want. Why should any of my children honor or obey me?" Then he slipped out the door, and moments later they heard an engine start and tires crunch over dirt and stone as George Heyward headed south once again.

CHAPTER

21

Judd was beginning to find the silence uncomfortable when Maude burst in, hair frazzled and eyes wild. "Oh, my stars. Preacher, you'd better come quick."

Ben leapt to his feet and hurried to take Maude's hands in his. "What is it? What's the matter?"

Tears pooled in the older woman's eyes. "Granny Jane sent for me this morning, which is why I wasn't here to make your breakfast." She cast a glance at the table and seemed relieved to see the remains of the meal Ben prepared. "I went quick as I could, and she's pitiful to see. Says she ain't much longer for this world."

Ben's brow furrowed. "I saw her two days ago and she was spry as I've seen her in a long time."

Maude hung her head. "They say some folks take a fit of good health right before the end. Anyhow, she says she wants to see you quick. Oh, and she said to bring that sister of your'n. She reckons this might be her last chance to lay eyes on her."

Ben squinted at Maude. "Uh-huh." He clasped the older woman in a quick embrace. "Well, we'd best head on over there then. Judd, you come too. I have a feeling you'll be wanted."

Judd felt his eyebrows climb his forehead. Why would an old woman he'd never met want him to see her on her deathbed? He shrugged at Larkin and grabbed his jacket. He didn't quite know what else to do.

"Maude, will you watch Kyle?" Ben asked. Then he bent to the boy's eye level. "Soon as we get back, Larkin will take you for a walk in the sunshine." Kyle's eyes lit and Ben tousled his hair. "Alright then, let's load up. Granny's house isn't but fifteen minutes away."

As soon as the threesome walked into the front room of the cabin clinging tenaciously to the side of a mountain, Judd felt right at home. He'd known a dozen houses like this one over the course of his life. It was exactly right, from the tilted porch to the smell of smoked meat clinging to the rafters. He looked around and saw three jobs he'd like to tackle, but supposed it didn't matter if the owner was indeed dying. Still, he longed to nail down that top step that rattled as they crossed it.

The cabin was little more than one big room with blankets for partitions. An old woman lay in a bed in the far corner, a quilt tucked snug around her solid form. Judd eyed her neatly braided hair coiled on her head like a crown. Her veined hands were folded over the covers, and her eyes were bright. Somehow he thought someone who was dying would look worse off.

"Granny," Ben said and stepped lightly to her side. He pulled a wooden chair around and sat, taking one of the old woman's hands in his. "What's this Maude tells me about you dying?"

Granny Jane half smiled. "Is that what she told you? Law, I don't know where she got that idee. I may not be as good as I once was, but I might be around another day or two yet."

"Un-huh. You probably thought I wouldn't come if you just sent for me to bring my unexpected guests over to parade in front of you."

Granny gave Ben a stern look. "Don't sass me, young man. I'm not too old to whop your behind."

Ben laughed and shook his head. "Granny, what have I told you about gossip?"

"You've told me to keep shy of it. Which is why I wanted you'uns to come over here and let me get the truth firsthand. Them folks down at the store had six different tales to tell and probably ain't none of 'em true." She looked over Ben's shoulder. "Now, is she your sister or not?"

Ben gave up. "Yes, ma'am. This is my sister Larkin, all the way from South Carolina."

Granny motioned for Larkin to come closer and grabbed her hand as soon as she could reach it. Then she tugged until Larkin had no choice but to perch on the side of her bed. "Lean on in here, girl. I cain't see as good as I once did." She reached up and grasped Larkin's chin, turning her head one way and then the other. "I see the resemblance. 'Course, she's a sight prettier than you."

Laughter burbled out of Larkin, Granny cackling along with her. Judd found himself smiling and noticed that Ben was, too. Soon they were all laughing, which felt like sunshine in the dark of winter.

Larkin wiped her eyes and took Granny Jane's hands in her own. "I'm so glad to meet you. Ben wrote home about you and I just knew I'd love you the minute we met."

"Oh, child. It's good to see someone who doesn't hoard their love like so much gold. It weren't quite right of me to trick you'uns into coming over here, but I'm surely glad I done it." She shifted her gaze to Judd. "Now, who's that good-lookin' feller? I heard your pa was here, but that can't be him."

Larkin grinned. "Good-looking? I thought you didn't see so well."

"I can still spot a fine specimen of a man, and he's too dark to be kin to the pair of you fair ones."

Ben chimed in before Judd could get any more embarrassed.

"That's Judd Markley. He's from over in West Virginia, and Larkin here has tricked him almost as good as you tricked us."

Granny nodded and tapped the back of Larkin's hand. "Be careful, girl. Sometimes getting what you think you want makes you realize what it was you really wanted all along."

Larkin glanced at Judd, a confused look on her face. "Yes, ma'am. I won't ever try to trick him again."

Granny Jane nodded and turned her attention back to Ben. "So where'd your pa go? I heard he stayed the night. Is he back at the church afraid to come see a dying woman?"

"He went back to South Carolina this morning," Ben said. "I guess things haven't worked out the way he hoped."

"Mmm-hmmm. That'll frustrate your average man and right quick. Of course, they's only one way for things to work out and that's the Lord's way." She grabbed Larkin's hand. "Is your father a believer, girl?"

Larkin's face went blank. "I . . . well, I think so."

"If you only think so, then he probably ain't. We'll pray for him, though. Won't we, Ben?"

"Yes, we will. We will indeed."

"All right then. You children go on now and let a tired old woman rest. I may not be dying today, but all this excitement has plumb wore me out."

Ben stood and took Larkin's hand, drawing her toward the door. "Granny, you know this visit has been pure tonic for you."

Granny cackled. "You're smarter than you look, preacher. Now, send them two back by here at dinnertime. That purty sister of yours can make me dinner while her feller does a few of those chores you've been after me about."

Ben grinned. "Is that what it takes? Well then, if it's all right with Judd and Larkin, they'll be back around in a few hours." He looked a question at Judd, who shrugged. He ought to be getting on back to Abram's, but he'd be glad to fix this place

166

up a bit before he went. Larkin practically bounced with excitement, so he guessed it was fine with her, too.

◆ ◆ ◆

Back at the church, Larkin prepared to take Kyle out for his promised walk. Kyle picked up a coal hod on his way to the door.

"I'll show you the old mines and we can fill this here bucket for Pastor Ben."

Judd's ears perked up. "What old mines?"

"It's alright," Kyle said. "My ma sends me there sometimes when we're short of coal. Anybody can take it if they don't mind it not burning clean. 'Course, it's getting kind of scarce." He puffed out his chest. "Might have to go inside a little ways to find anything good."

Judd took the bucket from Kyle. "It's not the coal I'm thinking of," he said. "Abandoned mines are dangerous places. I don't want you or Larkin anywhere near one."

Kyle deflated, and Judd felt a little bit bad about spoiling his fun, but the notion of those two anywhere near the overwhelming blackness of a mine—especially one that was abandoned and likely unstable—made his hands shake and his knees go weak. "Larkin, promise me you won't go near those mines."

She wrinkled her brow but nodded. "We won't, I promise." She turned to Kyle. "Besides, there are probably lots of other good things to see, right?"

Kyle perked back up. "Sure thing. We can go down to the creek and see if the high water washed anything good up on the bank. I found an inner tube one time that we patched up and used for a sled."

Judd watched the pair amble off through a pasture, worry needling his mind. "Which direction are those mines?" he asked Ben.

"Other way entirely. Don't worry. Kyle's a smart kid. Now

come help me stack this firewood before I let Granny work you to death."

The men worked in silence for a while, Judd lost in his own thoughts and wishing he could keep the people he cared about safe from harm.

Ben finally spoke. "I've been trying to get Granny to let me fix her place up since we met," Ben said. "She'll convince other folks to let me step in but won't have any of it herself. Says she's old and it doesn't matter if her place falls down around her ears. Of course, she's been threatening to die for as long as I've known her, and as you can see, she's healthier and sharper than some women half her age."

"I've run into one or two like her," Judd said.

"Sure as shootin', she's playing matchmaker between you and Larkin." Ben paused and stretched out his lower back. "How do you feel about that?"

Judd flushed but kept working. "I'm pretty sure your father wouldn't approve, so I'm not sure it matters how I feel."

Ben laid a hand on his arm. "Judd, my father is a determined man who often loses sight of important details in the pursuit of what he wants. As far as I'm concerned, the only thing that matters is how you and Larkin feel. I don't suppose you've driven her all this way and then stuck around just because you're a gentleman."

Judd straightened and watched a crow fly across the cloudless expanse of sky. "I've never met anyone like her. She's brimming over with joy and light. Sometimes I think I could stand a dose of that every day for the rest of my life, and other times I think I'll go blind if I look at her too long." He scrubbed his hair, which was getting too long and starting to curl over his ears. "Guess what I'm saying is, I don't quite know how I feel."

Ben laughed. It was a bass note of delight that startled a rabbit and sent it leaping for the edge of the woods. Judd looked at his new friend blankly. Laugher didn't seem the right response.

Ben slapped him on the shoulder. "I think that's the best answer I could hope for as Larkin's big brother. Sounds to me like your intentions are good, and from what I've seen and heard, you're a man to be trusted. My mother may have her heart set on a doctor or a lawyer, but I say Larkin couldn't do much better than you." He bent to pick up more wood. "So you have my blessing to try and figure out how you feel."

Judd blew out a breath. This whole family left him feeling like he was skating across a frozen pond in his stocking feet.

◦ ◦ ◦

"Nail that top porch step down for starters, then you can climb up onto the roof and see if you can't get that corner over there to stop leaking." Granny Jane was sitting in a rocking chair near the cookstove, quilts tucked all around her. She hardly gave Judd a moment to get his bearings before she set him to work. "Girl, you know how to make biscuits?"

Larkin's eyes went wide as she looked from Granny to the wood-burning stove. "Um, not really."

"Well then, I'll teach you. If'n you're gonna catch that man or any other, you'd best learn how to cook. We'll fry up some fatback, too. Both of you need some meat on them bones."

Judd hid his smile as he headed out to the porch with tools he'd borrowed from Ben. Larkin was in for an education and he wished he could just sit and watch. Maybe he'd get clearer on his own feelings if he could see how this Southern flower handled mountain life as taught by an old woman born to rough ways.

◦ ◦ ◦

Larkin stared at the monster of a stove. It was hot and black and there were no knobs to tweak. She hadn't the least notion what she was supposed to do. Neither Mother nor their some-times housekeeper Liza let her help with the cooking, and she hadn't paid nearly enough attention when she had the chance. Judd was already out front, hammering away, so he wouldn't be any help right now. She cast a nervous glance Granny's way.

"Never used one of them before, have you?"

"No, ma'am."

"Likely you've used one of them fancy gas stoves."

Larkin nodded, not wanting to admit she hadn't much used the modern stove in the kitchen back home, either.

"See that bowl on the table with the cloth over it?" Granny pointed. "Spoon those greens into a pot and set it over on the right corner of the stove—they'll warm slow there."

Larkin did as she was told, appreciating the warmth radiat-ing from the already-fired stove. She wasn't sure she liked the look of the grease congealed on the top of the greens but told herself it would be more appetizing once it was warm.

"Now open the oven door and stick your hand inside. Count slow until it gets too hot to stand."

This procedure made Larkin nervous, but again, she did as she was told. She grasped the handle and screeched as it seared her delicate skin.

Granny shook her head. "Don't you know to use a rag? If'n you had an apron on, that'd be just the ticket. Get that cloth over there and use that."

Larkin blinked back tears and stuck her blistered finger in her mouth. She used her left hand to open the door, likely frus-trating Granny when she had to try twice before growing bold enough to touch the metal, even with a cloth over her hand. She tucked the rag under her arm and held her uninjured hand inside the cavity.

"I counted to thirty and maybe I could have stood it a little longer." She wondered if this was a test to see how tough she was. She didn't feel very tough.

"Not hot enough. Grab them dry logs on top of the pile and throw 'em in."

Larkin wrapped the cloth around her burnt hand and picked up a stick of firewood. She considered where she was meant to throw it in. Surely not inside the oven compartment?

Granny cackled and handed Larkin a sort of metal stick. "Pick up that eye there and toss the wood in on the fire."

Larkin fit the bit of metal into a notch in one of the circles set in the top of the stove and found she could lift it up. Flames crackled inside. She added wood, jumping when the fire flared up. She clapped the eye back into place wishing she could quit this nonsense and nurse her hand.

"It'll take more than that. Add two more and we'll get to mixing."

Larkin repeated the process, flinching each time she put pressure on her burn. Then she fetched out a bowl, a blackened pan, flour, baking soda, salt, and a crock of lard. Granny sent her out to the springhouse for some buttermilk and finally walked her through the process of making biscuits.

"Now, don't knead that dough overmuch. Makes your biscuits tough." She pointed out a jelly jar and told Larkin to use it to cut out rounds of dough to tuck into the pan. "Stick your hand back in that oven and count some more."

Larkin stuck her burnt hand in and yelped, then switched to her left hand. "Twenty and that's all I can stand."

"Oughta be right. Stick that pan in there and wait seven or eight minutes, then we'll turn it around so's it doesn't get too done on one side. Now, go on out there to the smokehouse and cut us some fatback."

Larkin walked outside and looked around. She didn't see Judd and she didn't quite know where to find the smokehouse. There were several outbuildings, so she started trying doors. The first one was the privy, but the second had to be right since there was what appeared to be a big hunk of meat hanging from the rafters. Larkin stared. What in the world was she supposed to do with that?

"Need a hand?"

Larkin jumped a foot and whirled around to see Judd, a lazy grin making a dimple show to the right of his mouth. "Granny said to bring in some fatback and I don't quite know . . ."

Judd smiled bigger and a second dimple appeared. "I'll fetch you down some."

He lifted a squared-off piece of what looked mostly like fat and cut several long slices with a knife that must be for that express purpose. He handed the meat to Larkin, who wished desperately for a platter or a bowl. Although the cool fat was soothing against her burnt finger.

His touch lingered and she became aware of how close he was, how tall and how solid. He reached around her to hold the door open, and his nearness left her breathless. She was afraid she was staring but couldn't seem to tear her eyes from his.

"Larkin, I . . ."

Whatever he meant to say died on his lips as she stood on tiptoe to press her mouth to his. As soon as she did, she felt shocked at her boldness. This was a world away from the casual kiss she'd shared with Wayne on the dance floor. She drew back, ready to run, but Judd caught her with two fingers laid along her cheek.

"I was about to say I'm glad you're here." His eyes darkened, and Larkin thought she could gaze into them forever. He leaned toward her again just as Granny Jane hollered for her to hurry up.

She whirled around, turning back long enough to say, "Dinner'll be ready shortly."

Judd nodded, and the look in his eyes made Larkin feel like she could melt into a puddle right there in the smoke-heavy, none-too-clean shed. She turned and scurried back inside.

"What in the world took you so long? Check them biscuits."

Larkin almost touched the stove again before remembering. She used the hem of her skirt to flip open the compartment and saw the biscuits blackened on one side.

"Turn the pan so they brown evenly," Granny said.

Larkin did, pushing the pan as far away from the fire as it would go in hopes it wouldn't burn both sides. Then Granny directed her in how to fry the meat in a cast-iron skillet. The fat popped, burning her again and leaving grease spots on her blouse.

Finally, the time came to dish everything up. Larkin reached for the pan of greens and found them stuck to the bottom. She scraped them out the best she could and poured water in the pan to soak. She turned the biscuits out onto a plate, half burned and half doughy. The fatback seemed okay, although she thought it limper than meat should be. Granny harrumphed and crossed her arms.

With the simple yet somehow incredibly complicated meal ready, Larkin called Judd in to eat. He climbed down from the roof and joined them at the wooden table, helping Granny from her rocker to one of the side chairs.

"Will you say grace?" Granny asked Judd. "I always did prefer to hear a man bless the food."

Judd folded his hands and bowed his head. "Dear Lord, thank you for this food and for the hands that prepared it." His voice deepened and roughened. "May your blessings ever shower on us as they have today. Amen."

Larkin felt her damaged hands—the ones Judd just blessed—quiver as she passed him the bowl of greens. This meal could hardly be counted a blessing. She put the blackest biscuit on her own plate, splitting it open to hide the ruined crust. Judd's hand hesitated over the plate as though trying to find a safe place to land. He finally selected a piece of bread that was only half burnt and passed the food on. Larkin tried not to stare as he took a bite of greens and worked them around. He swallowed and bit into a biscuit, chewing, chewing—how long did it take to chew a piece of bread?—and then forking in a piece of fatback that he'd been working to cut for too long.

Larkin couldn't stand it anymore. She lowered her head and picked at the food on her own plate. Somehow it all tasted the same—like smoke and grease. Maybe she wasn't quite as ready to tackle this way of life as she'd imagined.

CHAPTER

22

Judd needed to get himself back to Abram's farm and from there back to South Carolina, but he couldn't bring himself to want to be anywhere Larkin wasn't. After one of the worst dinners he'd ever made himself swallow, they'd gone back to the church and were now preparing to stay their second night. Judd knew he should be making plans to get on the road at first light, but other plans—dreams really—kept swirling through his head.

"Fine day's work," Ben said, leaning his chair back on two legs. "Sure could use a man like you around here. Seems like folks trust you more than a Lowcountry boy like me."

"I might've run across the same thing down there in South Carolina," Judd said. He kicked off his boots and stretched his stocking feet toward the stove.

"Dad been treating you right on the job?"

Judd laced his fingers across his belly. "He has. Seems like a fair man with a knack for business. I'm just hoping he won't hold all this folderol against me when I get back."

"I doubt he will. He values his workers, I'll give him that."

Judd glanced toward the door where Larkin had disappeared

a few moments earlier to conduct her "evening constitutional" as she put it. "But maybe he values his daughter more."

Ben sighed heavily. "He probably does—in some ways. I think he's still trying to win his father-in-law's approval, even though the old man has been gone a long time. Dad puts a great deal of stock in being successful."

Judd tilted his head back and stared at the ceiling. "What do you see as success?"

Ben let his chair thump back down on all four legs. "Now, that is a mighty fine question." He rubbed his chin. "Improving people's lives. Giving them a raft to hold on to when they're adrift in a sea of pain."

Judd considered the ceiling some more. "Not much money in that."

Ben laughed long and deep. "No, indeed, but there is a great deal of satisfaction and, for whatever reason, that seems to be enough for me. Jesus sent His disciples out to preach and heal people and He told them, 'Take nothing for your journey, neither staves, nor scrip, neither bread, neither money; neither have two coats apiece.'" Ben smiled and it lit his face, so that Judd saw the resemblance between him and Larkin. "There's making money and then there's making a living. I prefer life."

Larkin pranced into the room then, arms tight around her and the cold clinging to her skirt. "Please tell me this is as cold as it gets."

Judd laughed. "January and February are the real test. This is just playing at cold."

She gave an exaggerated shiver and held her hands out to the fire. "I suppose I can bear it so long as Granny keeps my body warm slaving over her cookstove—goodness knows I need the practice—and Kyle keeps my heart warm by getting better."

Judd looked at Larkin and felt a lump rise in his throat. These people were good. They were light in a dark and even dangerous place. Larkin almost glowed with the joy of helping others, even though he suspected she'd been more hindrance to Granny Jane. He'd only ever helped anyone when it served his own purposes, and the one time Joe needed his help more than anything, he'd failed. How could he leave her here? How could he risk his heart by staying?

"I'm going to hit the hay. Probably should get an early start in the morning." Judd stood and headed for his cot.

He could feel Larkin's eyes on his back. "You're leaving? After all you did for Granny today, I hoped . . ."

"Gotta get back to the farm and then head south." He glanced at Larkin and steeled himself against the October sky of her eyes. "Of course, that's assuming your father still wants me to work for him. It'll be a long bus ride for nothing if he doesn't."

Larkin looked at him like he'd just spit on the floor. She blinked and her mouth worked, then she turned back to the stove, but the light seemed to have dimmed inside her.

Judd slid under his blankets and turned his back to brother and sister. Yes sir. He'd get up at first light and walk until he could hitch a ride. Hopefully he'd be back at the family farm before sunset the following day. He wanted to make Larkin come with him, to tuck her snug under his arm and keep her safe always. But he knew that even then something bad could happen. The way it had with Joe. And that he could never bear.

◆ ◆ ◆

"I want you to take my car." Larkin slid a bowl of lumpy porridge with burnt bits in front of Judd and set a pitcher of cream within easy reach. "It's not suited to the rough roads around here and it would be best if you took it back to South Carolina."

Judd had meant to be gone before anyone else was up, but somehow he'd slept deep and long, only awakening when the smell of coffee tickled his nose. He poured cream over his cereal as a way to stall.

"You might need it."

Larkin shrugged one pretty shoulder. "Ben has the truck and that rattletrap bus out back. Can't think why we'd need a convertible."

Ben settled in the chair opposite. "I think she's right, Judd. Folks around here will think we're showing off with a car like that. Doesn't exactly help us fit in."

"You're letting her stay, then?" Judd pushed his bowl back a notch. He'd hoped Ben might come to his senses and save Judd the trouble of leaving Larkin behind.

Ben looked at his sister, whose eyes shone. "If she still wants to stick around after a cooking lesson from Granny Jane, then she might could be a help." He stirred his own porridge, tilting his head as though looking at it from another angle would improve it. "So, yes, she's more than welcome to stay for as long as she likes."

Larkin squealed and clapped her hands. She did a little dance step over to the stove and tossed a stick of firewood in like she'd been doing it all her life.

Judd watched her and wondered if maybe he should stay, too . . . but no. He had a duty to his family, not to mention his employer, and that kiss was probably just her being nice—making up for all the trouble she'd caused him. He needed to finish up back at the farm, then go face Mr. Heyward. And driving Larkin's car was the quickest way to get it all done. He'd say his goodbyes and get on the road. He looked at Larkin once more, telling himself he could always come back, but doubting he ever would.

◆▲◆

Even before Abram's farm was shipshape again, Judd pointed the Buick south for the long drive back to Myrtle Beach. The miles of road gradually flattening and straightening out gave him way more time to think than he wanted. He tried not to think about Larkin—which was impossible since he could smell her perfume and see one of her scarves peeking out of the glove box. He tried to think about exactly what he'd say to Mr. Heyward instead.

He was still thinking when he pulled up at the Waccamaw Timber Company building on a Monday afternoon in mid-November. He parked and went inside, imagining this was what it would feel like to brace a bear in its den.

Mr. Heyward sat behind his desk, staring at some papers and tapping a pen on his blotter. He looked up, and his brow lowered and then cleared. He leaned back in his chair, laced his fingers across his belly, and looked expectant.

"I brought Lar . . . Ms. Heyward's car back. I hope—"

George Heyward waved his hand. "Save your breath. I know my daughter, and between Hank and me, I think we have a pretty good idea about what kind of man you are. No one would blame me if I fired you on the spot, but I'm prepared to scratch this little adventure up to poor judgment and the influence of a pretty girl determined to get her way. Plus, with all the hurricane damage, we need every hand we can get." He stood and braced his hands on his desk. "Next time, though, I'd advise you to examine what you're offered a little more closely. I can't see letting something like this pass a second time."

"Yes, sir." Judd felt the silence bloom. "Guess I'll just head on back to the boardinghouse and get ready for work tomorrow."

Mr. Heyward nodded and resumed his seat. Judd turned to go. As he was about to pass through the door, his employer cleared his throat.

"Did she settle in alright? Was my . . . was Ben seeing to her?"

"Yes, sir. Like two peas in a pod."

Mr. Heyward nodded once and spoke as though to himself. "They were always like that. From the day Larkin was born."

Judd exhaled long and slow and set out the few blocks to his old room in the boardinghouse.

◢◢◢

While Judd was grateful to fall back into the routine of work, especially during mild November days that would have been frosty back home, he felt an odd lack that bit deep. He tried to blame it on missing Joe, but that pain had blunted. Something he once doubted could ever happen.

Judd grabbed his sack lunch and thermos on the Monday before Thanksgiving and headed out the door. He'd managed to get his hands on a cheap 1946 Ford truck that had just about been run into the ground. After spending all weekend working on it, he had it running and would be driving himself to work from now on.

He slid behind the steering wheel and started the truck on the second try. He put it into gear, thinking about how he'd rather be deer hunting back home. He remembered two years earlier when he and Joe laid off work to head for the woods. They'd hunted all morning without getting anything, then sat down in the sun around noon to eat leftover biscuits with jelly and hard-boiled eggs.

Judd remembered leaning back against a tree trunk and looking up at the blue, blue sky. Joe tossed him an egg. "Boiled that one especially for you," he said. Judd should have suspected something, but he fell for it. He'd cracked the egg and found it raw inside, making a mess of his hands and his britches. He acted like he was mad, but mostly he was tickled. It had been a good day, even though they didn't get a deer. Judd thought about that egg and how you couldn't always tell the truth of a thing by looking at it from the outside.

Judd's days with the forest service had been cut back since so many stands of trees had been laid over like toothpicks by the storm. They were trying to salvage as much downed timber as possible before it started rotting or became infested with insects. Although there was plenty of work to keep everyone busy, the surplus was driving prices down. Judd tried to tell himself that wasn't his worry, but he somehow felt more invested in the company now that he knew more of its history.

With the increased pace of work, Judd was mostly doing mechanic work and this morning he'd be rotating back to the landing he'd worked that first day in August. When he pulled up, the other men came over to examine his truck, giving him a hard time about the rust spots and skinned places. Judd eased into the camaraderie like a warm tub of water but still felt that strange lack prickling him underneath it all.

Pete sidled over. He wouldn't hardly leave Judd alone about Larkin and their trip north. Judd supposed everyone knew about it, but Pete was the only one with the nerve to ask questions.

"Guess now you can run on back to them mountains any time you feel like it," he said. "Now, who is it she's staying with again? Kin of yours?"

Judd sighed. "You're looking fit this morning, Pete. Looks like that leg's healed up real good."

Pete thumped the leg in question. "Gives me fits any time it's fixing to rain, but other than that seems like I ain't no gimp after all." His eyes flicked to Judd's leg. "Could've been worse."

"That's the spirit," Judd said, slapping his friend on the back. He started over to Chuck to see which needs were most pressing this morning, but Pete spoke up again.

"Wife said I oughta ask you to join us for dinner on Thursday. You probably got plans already, but I said I'd ask just to make her happy."

Judd hadn't really given any thought to what he'd do on Thanksgiving. He certainly didn't have any plans or expect anyone else to ask him. "That'd be fine. Tell Sally I'm grateful for the invitation."

Pete came as close to smiling as he ever did and trotted off to get his own day's work started.

◊ ◊ ◊

Thursday morning Judd woke thankful that he did, after all, have someone to spend the day with. Pete might not be his first choice, but Sally helped make up for her husband's cantankerous ways. He walked out of his room, whistling, a brown paper sack under his arm. Floyd sat in the sun on the front stoop. His hand had healed well, and Judd had gotten into the habit of listening to *Amos 'n' Andy* on the radio with the old fellow every Sunday afternoon.

"Happy Thanksgiving, Floyd. You waiting on your daughter?"

Floyd sighed and turned his face up toward the sun. "Seems like I'll be waiting a long while. She called this morning to tell me she can't come get me after all. Both her young'uns got the flu." He dropped his head back down. "Guess I'll make do around here."

"Come go with me," Judd said, then wondered how Pete would take it if he showed up with an uninvited guest.

Floyd perked up. "Where you headed?"

"Friend's house. Not sure who all will be there, but if there ain't enough to go around, you can have mine."

Floyd slapped his knees and stood. "I'm in, and I thank ya for asking."

They piled into Judd's truck, which started immediately as though it, too, were pleased with the outing. Judd learned more about Floyd's grandchildren as they traveled. The older man had high hopes for his youngest grandson who was eight and loved trains, but wasn't so sure about the oldest girl who was fourteen and wanted to be an actress. In turn, Judd talked about James and Grace, finding that he missed them extra on this Thanksgiving Day. He'd normally take James squirrel hunting to keep him out from under his mother's feet, and when they got home he'd entertain both children with Paul Bunyan stories while the smell of wild turkey and dressing permeated the house.

Judd remembered to worry how Pete would take to his unexpected guest as they crossed the bare yard littered with magnolia seedpods. As they stepped up on the porch, he could smell ham baking through the open door. An open door at Thanksgiving. Now that was a wonder.

Pete banged the screen door and grabbed Judd's hand. "Glad you could make it, pal." He eyed Floyd with his neatly trimmed beard and web of wrinkles. "You a friend of Judd's?" he asked, extending his hand in Floyd's direction.

"Proud to be counted as such," Floyd said, pumping Pete's hand in a firm grip.

"Then you're a friend of this house, too. Come on in. Sally's in there fussing over dinner with her mother and sister. Her dad died not long after we married, and I swan I needed to get some menfolk in here this year to keep the women at bay." He slapped Floyd on the back. "Glad you came to even up the numbers." Sally came out to greet them as Pete noticed the paper sack Judd was carrying. "What's in the poke?"

Judd reached inside and pulled out a stack of small squares of wood bound with ribbon. He grasped the top block and held it up so the others hung down. Then he tilted the top piece of wood until it touched the block beneath it and appeared to come loose and cascade down the strand. He tilted the block the other direction to repeat the effect.

Sally clapped her hands. "A Jacob's Ladder. I haven't seen one of those since I was a girl. Mother, come see what Judd brought us."

An older woman with gray hair in waves came out of the kitchen wiping her hands on her apron. "Well, I'll be. Seems like your daddy knew how to make them things. She reached for the toy and made it cascade back and forth. "Now that takes me back." She looked at Judd, eyes shining. "What a treat."

Judd ducked his head. "Sometimes I run out of things to do of an evening and I like to keep busy. Glad you don't think it's silly, me bringing you a toy." He cleared his throat, feeling moisture rise to his own eyes. "My brother Joe could do all kinds of tricks with one of them things. Lost him in a mining accident last spring and it brought him back to me a little to make a Jacob's Ladder."

Sally gave Judd a hug and rested her soft head against his shoulder for just a moment. "I think your present has brought us all some joy today. Now y'all get comfortable in here and we'll have dinner dished up and on the table lickety-split."

Judd settled on the sofa next to Floyd and started talking politics with Pete. He was glad his gift had been appreciated. Between that and all the good smells coming from the kitchen, he could almost keep his homesickness at bay. An image of Larkin at Granny Jane's table flashed through his mind and he wondered how she was faring so far from home. At least as well as him, he hoped.

CHAPTER
23

Larkin had never given much thought to where her food came from, but this Thanksgiving she was all too aware. They'd held a community hog killing the previous week, and after losing her breakfast in the bushes, she wasn't certain she could eat pork ever again. Which is exactly what was in the oven as she helped Maude cook a feast in the church hall for folks who didn't have families or couldn't be with them.

Granny Jane was coming, as was Maude's unmarried son, Paul. Then there was Darlene, a mother of two whose husband had run off back in September. They'd round out the party with Ben, Larkin, and Kyle, who was well enough that folks weren't afraid of him anymore. Larkin had asked when he'd return to his family, and Ben got a grim look.

"Kyle has six brothers and sisters, and his parents seem willing to leave their second-to-youngest child in the care of the church for as long as we're willing to keep him." He rubbed a hand over tired eyes. "I'm not sure they can afford to give him the food and rest he needs, so I hate to send him back."

Larkin wrapped an arm around her brother's waist. "Well, I'm head over heels for him, so I'm glad he's still here."

Ben squeezed her in return. "He's pretty smitten with you, too."

Larkin smiled, feeling content in spite of the challenges she'd faced since coming. Other than Granny Jane, the locals didn't seem to want her help. Every time she knocked on a door with a basket of inferior baked goods over her arm, she was met with little more than polite distance. She'd even offered to watch Darlene's children for her while she looked for work. The woman, who couldn't be much older than Larkin, stiffened and said she didn't need any handouts. Larkin assured her it wasn't a handout but rather a helping hand, until Darlene finally blurted, "You need to go now." Larkin had never been so humiliated. She blushed even now just thinking of it.

"Larkin, will you stir the creamed corn and push it back to a cooler part of the stove?" Maude was bent over the oven, turning and basting the pork roast that somehow smelled sharp and metallic since Larkin had seen it walking around less than a week ago. She pushed down a wave of nausea and told herself it was the same as the Sunday roasts her mother had made time and again.

Granny Jane had promised to bring several pickled items, and Darlene was in charge of biscuits since it was hard to roast meat and bake bread all in the same oven. Sweet potatoes cooked in the same pan as the pork, and Larkin had cubed turnips into a pot of greens just a little while ago. She was probably over-stirring everything, but she was terrified that something might burn. Surveying the feast, Larkin couldn't help but compare it to what she was used to.

Back home there would be a turkey stuffed with dressing on a Johnson Brothers platter. There would be fresh oysters and wild rice along with collard greens and macaroni and cheese. And Mother would spoon jellies and sweet pickles into crystal dishes for the center of the table, which would be graced with a big bouquet of camellias.

Larkin smiled at the bowl of russet leaves and acorns she'd placed in the middle of the table. Maude had given them a funny look but didn't comment. Larkin supposed dressing the table wasn't a priority around here, yet she felt like it was her special contribution. It occurred to her that maybe Judd would appreciate that sort of thing.

Now, where did that thought come from? Larkin stirred the corn and shifted pots to make sure everything was at the right temperature. Judd was probably having a fine time down south and not even thinking about her. Most likely she'd run him off with that kiss in the smokehouse—too forward and too fast. He wasn't like the boys she'd known in South Carolina. No, Judd was a man and probably hadn't appreciated the way she put herself forward.

Granny entered with a burst of cold air and the tobacco smell of fall just in time to distract Larkin from her thoughts. She carried a basket clanking with canned stuff. Larkin hurried over and relieved her new friend of her burden.

"They's an apple stack cake in there, too. Been baking it a layer at a time since last Friday. I figured to go another layer or two, but I give out."

Larkin lifted the tea towel laid over the top of the basket and found a spice-laden cake, rich with stewed apples along with three jars of various pickles. Kyle hung against her arm, eyeing the cake. "Shoo now. No dessert until you've had your dinner."

Kyle grinned and scooted over to the table where he used every bit of his strength to pull out a chair for Granny to sit.

"Is that one of them Dandridge young'uns?" Granny asked. "He looks like his pa, but he acts a whole lot better."

"Now, Granny," Ben said. "Love thy neighbor."

"Oh, I love 'em alright, I just don't always like 'em much."

Larkin smiled and felt her worries over Judd and the meal dissipate. What was done was done and it didn't bear thinking about anymore. She began helping Maude dish up the food and transfer it to the table with its odd assortment of chairs and mismatched plates. As they all settled down to bless the feast, she told herself it was the loveliest table setting she'd ever seen.

◆◆◆

Judd, Floyd, and Pete retired to the backyard after dinner. Judd had enjoyed most everything, even if some of the food wasn't quite what he was used to. When he'd taken a big ole bite of dressing, he'd wanted to spit it out into his napkin, but swallowed to be polite. At first he thought it had spoiled, but then came to learn it was oyster dressing, which was a bad idea if he ever heard one. Still, the rest of the meal was tasty, and he supposed everyone had their oddities.

Pete leaned back in his chair and crossed his feet at the ankles. He laced his fingers across his belly and squinted at Judd. "I ain't beating around the bush anymore. I'm going to come right out and ask. Did you leave Heyward's daughter with that prodigal son of his?"

Judd remembered the night Pete drank too much moonshine. He'd mentioned Ben that night—called him a prodigal then, but Judd hadn't put that comment together to figure out Ben was Larkin's brother. Even now, he wasn't sure he should discuss any of this with Pete, who seemed to have a chip on his shoulder where Mr. Heyward was concerned.

"Why you asking?"

"Oh, well, I like to know the lay of the land. Might be a rumor that Ben's refusing to take over the family business. That'd leave the future of Waccamaw Timber wide open." Pete dug out a ready-made cigarette and lit it. "So, you run him to ground? Does it look like he'll be coming on home anytime soon?"

Judd shifted and kneaded his leg more out of habit than because it hurt. "I gotta tell ya, Pete, I don't think any of this is my business or yours. Might be we should leave Mr. Heyward's family to him to sort out."

Pete grunted. "Might be my business more than you know. You keep your cards tight to your chest if you want, but I'm gonna find out what I can before it's too late." He got a cagey look. "You ever decide you want to throw in with me and maybe we'll go see can't we dig up some treasure that'll make George Heyward sing a different tune."

This was the second time Pete had mentioned treasure. Judd's curiosity was aroused, but he figured he'd better let the conversation go. His mother always said curiosity killed the cat, and he was beginning to suspect she was right.

Floyd, as though sensing a distraction was needed, drew out a pocketknife and began cleaning his nails. "That mother-in-law of yours is a widow, right?"

Pete sat up straighter and looked at the older man hard. "She is. You looking for someone to spark?"

"She's a handsome woman and a mighty fine cook. I'm not thinking to get married again, but maybe she'd like to drink some coffee and talk about old times."

Pete snorted. "She probably would. Don't look at me to do anything about it, though. I'm not playing cupid for an old codger."

"Fair enough," Floyd said. "Judd, what say we go see if the ladies need us to stack dishes on the high shelves for 'em? In my experience, they like that sort of thing."

Judd stood and stretched out his back. "Sure thing. Then we'd best be getting on back. Pete and I still have to work tomorrow."

They shook hands all around and then Judd trailed into the house after Floyd, who did seem to have a little extra pep in his step. Thinking of Larkin once again, he guessed a pretty girl could do that to a fellow.

◊ ◊ ◊

Judd had his head under the hood of a truck when Chuck found him the next day.

"Got the crew shutting down the site," he said. "Come Monday we're moving to a new location. Supposed to be one of the best stands of timber in this part of the state and far enough inland that the storm didn't knock it flat. You ready for some new scenery?"

Judd straightened and looked around. "I've been on several jobsites and I can't say as there appears to be much difference in the scenery."

Chuck laughed and slapped Judd on the shoulder. "That's the gospel truth. From what I hear, Mr. Heyward's been sitting on this one for a while and it's not just pine but some real pretty hardwood. Hank said parts of it could've been harvested four or five years ago and it's been on the books for thirty years." He lowered his voice. "Kind of makes me wonder if the old man's in a pinch for some extra cash. With the market flooded by storm timber, prices have been low. Maybe he's been saving this one back for an emergency."

Judd had nothing to say to that. He tried to avoid speculation—especially when it concerned his employer.

Chuck saw a worker taking his ease, hollered at him, and darted off in that direction before the silence became awkward. Judd watched the foreman go, trying not to think overmuch about what he'd said. Mr. Heyward could do as he pleased with his property, and Judd didn't need to have an opinion one way or the other.

◆ ◆ ◆

When Judd arrived at the new jobsite on Monday morning, there seemed to be something of a commotion going on. He worked his way through a gaggle of workers to see Pete standing on his skidder with a trimming saw in his hand, waving it around and hollering.

190

". . . no right to cut this timber. Land and the trees on it are as good as stolen. It's time we stopped taking this lying down and stood up to George Heyward and his kind." He reached down and lifted the floor panel of the skidder and jammed the saw inside. He rammed it up and down several times before some men reached him and hauled him down.

Chuck grabbed Pete by the collar. Both men were red in the face, but now Pete was mostly still as men held him on each side.

"What in tarnation are you carrying on about?" demanded Chuck. He loosened his grip and took a deep breath. "It's just another job. Nothing different about this one. Now, what's got you so riled up?"

Pete's lip curled, and for a minute Judd thought he might spit on the foreman. Then some of the fire went out of him and the men holding him relaxed their grips. "Don't matter," Pete said. "Not like I can prove anything." He hung his head and sagged. "But I can't work here, either."

"Not after fouling the machinery up, you can't," Chuck said. He caught a glimpse of Judd, who'd eased on up to the front of the crowd. "Unless Judd there can fix it. Then I might get by with docking you a day's pay." He reached out and gripped Pete's shoulder. "You got ahold of yourself now?"

Pete shrugged away from the men holding him and took several steps toward his truck. "That I do. And what I meant was, I ain't going to work here. I quit. Find yourself some other skidder operator."

He walked to his truck, got in, and drove away without looking back. Chuck watched him go, face blank and eyes wide.

"What do you make of that?" he said to no one in particular. Then he turned and headed for Judd. "You can fix machines. Can you run 'em? These boys can cut awhile before we need the skidder anyhow."

191

Judd rubbed his chin. "Probably, but let me get in there and see what Pete's done before we get ahead of ourselves."

Chuck nodded, then shooed the rest of the men off to work. Judd approached the skidder wondering what in the world had set Pete off like that.

CHAPTER
24

Larkin crumpled the sheet of paper and threw it into the stove where it flared then died. No matter how hard she tried, she couldn't find the words to reconnect with her father. Which made her wonder if they'd ever really had a connection in the first place.

Ben came in from visiting in the community, which Larkin had learned meant pitching in with odd jobs wherever anyone would allow. She'd tried to go with him, but everyone treated her like a porcelain doll. Too fragile and pretty to be good for anything but looking at. From the looks of Ben today, he'd been filling someone's coal bin. An image of Judd flashed across Larkin's mind. He must have been even blacker after actually working in a coal mine.

"What're you up to there, little sister? I thought Granny Jane was going to teach you to make a dried apple pie this afternoon."

"She sent word that her niece had come to visit and asked me to come tomorrow instead. Not that I'd be any better at making a pie than biscuits, chicken, or anything else Granny's tried to teach me." Larkin looked at the blank sheet of note paper in front of her. "So I thought I'd write to Daddy, but I can't think what to say. Telling him I'm an utter failure around here would only give him satisfaction."

Ben rinsed the worst of the grime off his hands in a wash-basin and sat down next to Larkin. "I've had that problem myself from time to time."

"Which problem? Being a failure or not knowing what to write?"

"Both, actually. Dad sees me as a failure, and I struggle to know what to say to him."

"But you only wrote to Mother."

"I wrote Dad every few months. Probably both of them were keeping the letters from each other." Ben pinched the bridge of his nose. "Or maybe he threw them away without opening them. I don't really know. He never wrote back, so . . ." He shrugged.

"What did you write?" Larkin leaned on her elbows and cradled her chin.

"Mostly I wrote about what I was doing. I'd describe the people I encountered, talk about the problems they were facing, how hard it was for me to get them to trust anything I offered. I hoped he'd see how important my work is and forgive me for not sticking around to take over the timber company."

Larkin pondered that a moment. "Maybe he was hoping in turn that you'd see how important his work is."

Ben laughed, then wrinkled his brow when Larkin didn't laugh with him. "You're serious. Do you really think making money by stripping the land of its resources is as important as sharing the gospel with these people?"

"No. Not that. But Hank's told me about some of the men who work for Daddy and how much they need good-paying jobs so they can take care of their families. And Judd, he did more than just work with those men. He's the one who helped another worker when he got hurt on the job, and he visited him until he was well again. I think they're still friends."

She took a breath and leaned back in her chair. "And I always kind of thought I wasn't doing much at the hospital, but seems like what those people needed most is the same as the people around here. They just want someone to listen to them and care about them." She sighed. "Not that they talk to me, but I hear what they say to you—how they trust you with their troubles."

Ben looked like he was really paying attention now—leaning forward, arms folded on the table between them. Larkin noted the black under his fingernails and wondered how long it had taken Judd to get his clean after he decided not to go into the mines anymore.

"Anyway, as much as I love it here, I'm beginning to think you can do God's work anywhere. All you have to do is look for someone who's hurting and see if you can ease the pain."

Ben laughed softly. "Little sister, you just preached me the best sermon I've heard in a long time. Might have to put you in the pulpit come Sunday."

Larkin felt her cheeks warm. "I don't know about that. I just think maybe Daddy's hurting and I wish I could help him, too."

Ben stood and came around the table to give her a hug. He spoke, but his voice sounded thick. "That's exactly what I want. Thanks for reminding me."

He walked over to the stove and picked up the coffeepot that always sat there keeping warm. He poured a measure into a thick mug and sipped. "I have an idea."

Larkin turned to face him, feeling excitement rise. Something about his expression made her think she was going to like this idea.

"How about you and me go home for Christmas?"

Larkin rose and knelt in her chair to face her brother more fully. "You mean back to South Carolina? With Mother and Daddy?"

"That's exactly what I mean. You write and tell Mom to expect two extra at her table come Christmas Eve. Dad claims I'm not welcome there, but I don't think he'll turn me away at Christmas." Doubt skittered across his face, but then he steeled himself. "Maybe we can figure out what to do about the timber company while we're there."

Larkin clapped her hands. "This will be the best Christmas ever."

After work, Judd drove over to Pete's. He'd gotten the skidder working and operated it all afternoon. He had a new respect for Pete's skill in using the piece of equipment, but he didn't think now was the time to mention it.

As soon as he stepped up onto the porch, he smelled pork chops frying and his mouth started to water. He didn't mean for them to ask him to stay to dinner, but if they did he sure wouldn't turn it down.

Judd rapped on the door and waited. He heard voices inside— one angry, one cajoling. Finally, Sally cracked the door open, then held it wider.

She hollered over her shoulder, "Pete, it's Judd. Surely you don't mind seeing him?"

They heard a grunt from the sitting room, and Sally motioned him on in. She spoke softly. "He still hasn't told me exactly what happened, but he's cranky as an alligator that hasn't eaten in a month."

Judd nodded, figuring it wasn't his place to tell Sally her husband quit his job that day. He stepped into the sitting room, where Pete sat in an armchair staring out the window.

"What d'you want?"

Judd held out a black lunch box. "You left in such a hurry, you forgot this."

"Don't need it no more."

Judd eased down onto the end of the sofa, setting the lunch box on the floor at his feet. "Anything I can do to help?"

Pete turned raw eyes on his friend. "You're the only one who gives a—" he glanced toward the kitchen where Judd suspected Sally was listening—"hoot." He flopped his head back against the chair. "That land belonged to my pappy. He lived there in little more than a shack with my grandmother till she died. Should be mine now, but old man Heyward cheated us." He raised his head, fire in his eyes again. "You saw how good the timber is. You know how much it's worth. He's just rubbing it in, sending me out there to work that stand. Well, I won't do it."

Judd had no idea about the truth of what Pete was telling him, but he could see how there might be hard feelings no matter what had happened. "Sorry to hear that," he said.

Tears welled in Pete's eyes. "Dang if I don't think you are." He shook his head. "I never have seen the like of you, Judd Markley, but I sure am glad you crawled in under that tree to doctor me back in August." He braced his hands on his thighs. "You stick around and eat supper with us. Sally's in there trying to cook something to put me in a better mood and I'm inclined to let her think it's worked."

"Have you thought what you'll do for a job now?" Judd asked.

"Aw, I can probably get hired on with another outfit. I was working for Heyward mostly 'cause I hoped to get something on him." His eyes narrowed. "Seems like you might could help me out with that if you wanted to. I've got a notion to do a little treasure hunting out there on that land. Might turn up something that'll shed a whole new light on this situation."

Judd held up his hands and started to speak, but Pete interrupted him. "Naw, I guess not. That's what I like about you. Don't meddle in other people's messes. C'mon then, let's eat."

◆◆◆

Larkin and Kyle had gotten into the habit of visiting Granny Jane most afternoons since she was the only one who seemed willing to let Larkin do anything.

"I'm glad you're going home to see your kin for Christmas, but I surely will miss having you'uns around." Granny sat in her favorite chair near the stove, a walking stick close at hand.

"We'll miss you too, Granny, but we'll be back to ring in the new year."

Granny eyed Larkin as though she were examining her very soul. Finally satisfied with whatever she saw there, she nodded and thumped her cane. "That's right. You'll be here for Old Christmas and that's the one that matters most." Before Larkin could ask what she meant, Granny added, "Today we'll make molasses candy."

Kyle brightened, and Larkin could feel the excitement vibrating through his fingers where they clasped hers.

"Boy, fetch that jar of molasses down off the shelf." Kyle scurried to do her bidding as Granny directed Larkin to mix the viscous sweetener with water and a little salt in a saucepan. After it boiled a good while, she showed them how to drop a little bit into a cup of water to see if it formed a soft or firm ball. Once it was at the hard-ball stage, Larkin shifted the pan to the table and let it cool.

"Now get some of that butter there and rub it into your hands real good," Granny said.

Larkin was mystified but did as she was told, giggling with Kyle as they slicked up their hands. Granny smiled right along with them.

"Now stick your finger in there and see if you can stand it."

Larkin touched the surface of the candy and found it plenty warm but thought she could stand it. Maybe she was tougher than when she'd first arrived.

"Scoop up a handful and start stretching it out between your hands."

Larkin obeyed, flinching at the heat but finding she could manage if she moved quickly. The string of candy was lustrous and lovely. As she pulled, doubling it back on itself, the color began to lighten and the candy cooled.

"Once it's cool enough, get that boy in there to help," Granny said. "Stretch it out wide and keep going until it gets stiff."

Kyle stepped up and pulled and pulled the sweet stuff until it had gone from brown to a golden yellow and got harder and harder to pull. Granny had Larkin lay it out and cut bite-sized pieces that were meant to be left until they'd fully hardened. But none of them could resist popping a piece of candy into their mouth—not even Granny, who had to gum it.

Granny sat smiling in her rocking chair while Larkin sat with Kyle leaning against her knee. They stayed still for a moment, savoring the sweetness of the candy and listening to the fire pop in the stove.

"Child," Granny said at last, "you have brought more life into this little cabin in the last month than I remember in the last twenty years." She closed her eyes and rocked some more. "I've been on my own since Ellis—that was my husband—died back in '38. But I think a part of me has been dead since my boy passed. He had the rheumatic fever, and I knew he probably wouldn't live long, but the day he turned twelve he sat up in bed and shot a groundhog out the window. He was so proud." Granny stilled and opened her eyes. "You think I'll see him again in Paradise?"

Larkin pulled Kyle a little more snugly to her side. "Yes, ma'am. Ben was telling me something about how King David's baby boy died, and David decided it wasn't any use to grieve since he couldn't bring the child back, but he could go to be with him one day. If a king believed it, we can, too." An image of Lill passed through Larkin's mind. She thought Granny Jane and Lill would get along like a house afire and maybe, one of these days, they'd get to meet. She smiled. "Yes, I surely do think you'll see Ellis and your son again."

"That will be fine," Granny said. "Now you and that boy git on home before dark falls. And take most of that candy with you." She grinned. "Although you might leave me a piece or two." Her smile spread. "In case company comes."

Chuck motioned Judd over as he climbed down from the skidder. He'd been on it a week and was just beginning to feel like he wasn't slowing the guys down. He hoped the foreman wasn't going to take him off it.

"Hank said to send you on back to the main office toward quitting time today. Don't know what for, but maybe you're gonna get a raise."

The way Chuck spoke the words made Judd think he was just trying to sound positive. Judd wondered if he was in trouble. Maybe Mr. Heyward hadn't forgiven him for carting Larkin off to the mountains after all. He guessed if he had a daughter, he wouldn't think much of it himself.

He drove over to the office, remembering that hot summer day when he'd first laid eyes on Larkin in her pretty sundress. He'd learned there was more to her than he first suspected. Maybe her father had, too.

Hank was sitting in his truck in the parking lot. He got out and waited for Judd. "Mr. Heyward's got someone in there right now. Should be done in a few minutes."

"You know what he wants?" Judd asked.

Hank shrugged. "Even when I think I know, I'm wrong half the time. It's probably better to wait and see what he has to say."

Judd nodded, thinking that sounded like something Abram might tell him. He looked off toward the ocean, imagining he could hear it now that there wasn't much traffic and only half so many buildings between here and there. He could smell it sure enough and, even though it was mid-December, there was still a softness to the air that reminded him of early spring.

"Say, you know anything about Mr. Heyward getting that tract we're working on from Pete's dad?"

Hank leaned against Judd's truck and crossed his arms, one eye on the front door of the office building. "Is that why he walked off the job?"

"Seems like."

"Yeah, from what I hear, Pete's dad—Wade Dixon was his name—was bad to drink and maybe played cards with the wrong people. You know, the sort who don't take kindly to being owed money. I don't know the details, but I think maybe he needed cash pretty bad. Seems like he'd been knowing Mr. Heyward all his life, and Heyward saw his chance to get a prime piece of land." He straightened as a man in a suit and tie exited the building. "If I had to guess, I'd say they both got what they wanted at the time. I can see how Wade might have come to regret it, though."

Judd nodded without commenting and followed Hank toward the building. One mystery was solved, and now he was about to dig into another.

♦ ♦ ♦

"Judd, come on in here, son, and make yourself comfortable."

George Heyward was downright effusive in his welcome. It made Judd nervous. He eased into the padded chair Mr. Heyward indicated and crossed his legs. He hoped this wouldn't take long. He'd developed a hankering to set his feet in the sand and watch the waves roll in before it got dark.

Mr. Heyward hitched one leg up on the front edge of his desk and angled toward Judd. Hank lurked in a far corner. "I just wanted to thank you for taking such good care of my daughter when she . . . hornswaggled you into taking her to Kentucky. I appreciate how your family took her in and the way you treated her with respect."

Judd didn't know what to say to that, so he remained silent.

Mr. Heyward waited a beat, then went on. "She and"—he flinched, but Judd didn't think he was supposed to notice—"her brother are apparently coming south for Christmas." He chuckled, but it sounded forced. "As you can imagine, Augusta is very excited."

Judd still had no idea what it was Mr. Heyward wanted with him. He sat quietly, hands folded, and waited to find out.

Mr. Heyward cleared his throat. "They likely won't be here long, but I . . . ah . . . had the impression you might . . . ah . . . admire my daughter."

Judd fought to keep his astonishment at bay. Mr. Heyward stood and paced a little.

"And so I thought I'd let you know that you have my . . . permission to call on Larkin while she's back in town." He perched on his desk again. "You're a good man, and if you could, oh, I don't know, give her incentive to return to South Carolina, well, that would suit me fine."

Judd didn't know that he or anyone else had the power to get Larkin to do anything she didn't want to, but at the same time he would surely welcome a chance to spend more time with her. She could be strong-willed and uncooperative, but he'd missed her far more than he would have guessed. And he wouldn't have supposed in a hundred years that her father would approve of his sparking her.

"That's quite a compliment, sir."

Mr. Heyward looked relieved. "Then you'd like to see her?"

"I reckon I would."

"Excellent. We'll expect you for Christmas dinner then. I'm assuming you don't have other plans?"

Judd shook his head, struck dumb by the invitation.

"Excellent. Come at two in the afternoon. For some reason Augusta thinks we have to eat at an odd hour."

Mr. Heyward circled behind his desk, sat, and picked up a pen. He glanced at Judd, who still sat, unmoving. Judd got the message and leapt to his feet, exiting the office with a look at Hank, who offered nothing more than a slight shrug before closing the door.

CHAPTER
25

Larkin paced her room. She was torn between sinking into what she now recognized as luxury and feeling guilty that the people she'd met back in Logan probably wouldn't ever experience anything half as nice. Her four-poster bed was piled high with pillows, china dolls from her youth stared at her from a shelf, and the sheer quantity of beauty products on her dresser took her by surprise. She wished she could take one of the dolls to Judd's niece Grace, maybe a pot of moisturizer to Lydia, and some perfume for Granny Jane. She giggled at the image of the old woman dabbing "Joy" behind her ears.

Flopping on the bed, Larkin stared at the light fixture. She'd barely seen her father since they'd arrived that afternoon. Mother insisted she have a bath and lie down before they went to Christmas Eve services at First Presbyterian Church. She'd carted Ben off to the sunroom to get "reacquainted." Well, of course she had—she hadn't seen him in years.

Larkin wondered if Judd knew she'd come home. Which led to wondering if he'd even care, which led to misery, so she stopped thinking that way. Instead, she went across the hall to the bathroom, where she took a long, hot shower. It was probably the first time in her life she'd fully appreciated indoor plumbing, and all she could think was how much Kyle would love to splash in the bathtub. Maybe with a toy boat.

Larkin toweled off thinking about the people of Logan, Kentucky. They hadn't exactly welcomed her with open arms and she didn't think she'd done anything much to help them, but somehow she missed the place just the same. She missed the smell of coal burning and the taste of beans, the solemn-faced children who were serious even in play, the women with their lined faces and worn hands. She even missed the stoic men, who sat so straight in church and were always ready to help one another. She was beginning to wonder if it was even possible for her to really and truly be a help to those people who seemed so proud and self-sufficient. Still, Ben had found a way and maybe she would, too. She just had to stick with it.

Wrapping herself in a fluffy robe, Larkin considered that she did not miss the cold. If only there were a way to combine the two places and all the people she wanted in her life. That was the sacrifice, she supposed.

Dinner was a mostly silent affair. Ben took a stab at conversation, but Daddy glared at him like he'd just broken out of jail, and they soon subsided into silence.

Back in her room, Larkin pulled out a midnight-blue velvet dress to wear to church. She hadn't worn it since the previous holiday season. Normally, she and Mother would have gone shopping for something new, but there'd been no time, and now that she thought about it, Larkin had to admit there wasn't any reason, either. The price of a new dress would feed most of Logan for a week.

Sliding the frock over her head, Larkin found it a bit looser than she remembered. She held her hands out in front of her and examined the short nails, the chapped skin. She felt her arm and thought she might even have some new muscles from hauling firewood and water. Skipping makeup, she slid a brush through her hair and tied it back with a ribbon that matched the dress. She looked at herself in the mirror and wasn't sure she recognized the woman looking back at her. It certainly wasn't the girl who'd first laid eyes on Judd Markley on a steamy August afternoon. She wondered if he'd notice a difference if he saw her.

"Larkin, hurry up, sweetheart." That was Mother.

Larkin scurried down the stairs to where the rest of the family waited. Daddy was pretending to admire a Currier and Ives print in the entry hall. Mother's arm was linked through Ben's, and they both glowed with pleasure. Larkin slid her own arm through Daddy's in a fit of holiday spirit, and although he looked surprised, he patted her hand and walked her out to the car.

The drive to church was quiet, only now it felt more reverent than awkward. Christmas lights twinkled, with more than one house having a candle shining in the window. Larkin hadn't paid much attention in the past, but Granny had told her how she always put a candle in her window on Christmas Eve to welcome Mary, Joseph, and the baby Jesus. Larkin laughed, because of course they weren't really coming, but Granny had stilled her with a touch and said, "Oh, but they are coming." She tapped her chest. "And there's always room in my heart."

They pulled up at the brightly lit church and were greeted by businessmen, politicians, socialites, and anyone else who mattered in Myrtle Beach. Patty and Nell rushed up and nearly knocked Larkin to the ground as they hugged and exclaimed over her.

"Oh, we've missed you ever so much. The weekends are an absolute drag without you around," Patty said. She gave Nell a sharp look. "Especially since Nell's started encouraging Leon. I told her he'll take her seriously if she's not careful."

Larkin watched her friend's cheeks pink and eyes glow. "Maybe she wants him to take her seriously," she said.

206

"Humph. While I'd love to have her for my sister, I could never expect her to tolerate my brother long enough to do it."

Nell laid a hand on Patty's arm. "He's not that bad, you know. He's actually really sweet."

Patty rolled her eyes and linked her arm with Larkin's. "Oh, maybe not. I just think you could do better. Now, how about you, Larkin? Have you found a handsome coal baron to sweep you off your feet?" They started toward the front door. "And when are you coming back home? Even if there is someone, I can't imagine living so far north." She said the word *north* like Larkin was living in Siberia.

Thankfully, Larkin was saved from having to answer by her father, who motioned them through the front door like a conductor indicating that the train was about to leave the station. Larkin gave her friends a smile and a shrug and hurried them inside, where they parted to sit with their families.

Pastor Brearley stepped up to the pulpit and began the service. Larkin tried to pay attention but caught herself scanning the crowd over and over. Who was she looking for? It wasn't as though she'd been gone long enough to miss anyone much. She saw Wayne sitting with a pretty girl she didn't know. She might have minded that once, but didn't tonight.

As they finished singing "O Holy Night" and resumed their seats, she twisted to get a look at the back of the church and her breath caught. There, in the far corner, sat Judd Markley, looking like he might bolt for the door any moment. She whirled back around, heart thumping in her chest. She guessed she'd been looking for him all along.

Larkin tried to think how, once the service was over, she could hurry to the exit and catch Judd before he slipped away. She just wanted to say hello—he was probably feeling lonesome at Christmas. She was so distracted, she didn't know what was going on when Ben handed her a candle. The pastor stepped down from the pulpit and approached the Christ candle.

Lights were shut off section by section until they stood in inky darkness. Then Pastor Brearley held the candle in his hand to the flame of the Christ candle. The choir began softly singing "Silent Night," and the pastor moved toward the congregation, where he lit the candles of the people in the first pews. They then turned and lit their neighbors' candles as the congregation began to join in the song.

By the time they finished singing, everyone held a lit candle and the room was glowing with flickering light. Larkin looked around in wonder at the radiant faces illuminated by the joy of Christmas, and for the first time since setting foot back in South Carolina she remembered what Christmas was all about. She caught a glimpse of Judd, who was gazing at his candle as though it were the most precious thing he'd ever seen. She swallowed hard and turned back as the pastor began to speak.

"Now go forth on this most holy of nights and remember the greatest gift the world has ever received. Merry Christmas."

There was a shifting, a shuffling, and candles were extinguished as the lights flickered back on. Larkin squinted and waited a few more moments before she blew her candle out. She longed to see Judd, to squeeze his hand and kiss his cheek. But maybe she shouldn't. It seemed strange, as though they'd traded places with him moving south and her north. And maybe that was how it was supposed to be. She closed her eyes and whispered a quick prayer. When she opened them, Judd stood nearby, talking to her father.

◊ ◊ ◊

Judd didn't like to push in where he wasn't invited, but he'd had a yen to go to church on Christmas Eve, and everyone knew where the Heywards attended—so he took the chance.

Larkin looked like an angel in her blue dress with her hair pulled back. It was all Judd could do to stay in his pew and not march up there and declare himself like the fool he knew he was. Mr. Heyward spotted him almost immediately and gave him a solemn nod that Judd didn't even try to interpret. When Larkin turned around and saw him, he thought for a minute she might come to him, but that was silly.

Then the lights went out. Judd wasn't expecting that. The single candle flickering way up front had been like that first gleam of a lantern on the far side of the cave-in, and Judd held on to it with his eyes. He remembered that hint of rescue and how it flooded him with hope. Of course, he didn't know Joe was already dead then. All he knew in that moment was that he was still alive and might see the light of day again.

By the time the short, round man wearing a bow tie next to him held out a candle to light Judd's, he'd realized something. He was indeed alive. He couldn't do a thing for Joe but keep on living, and that was surely something Joe would be glad to see. The flame of his candle flickering with each exhalation, Judd sang,

> "Silent night, Holy night
> Son of God, love's pure light
> Radiant beams from thy holy face
> With the dawn of redeeming grace,
> Jesus, Lord at thy birth,
> Jesus, Lord at thy birth."

Once the preacher cut them loose, he headed straight for the Heywards, thinking there was no time like the present to get this business of living under way.

After he wished Mr. and Mrs. Heyward a merry Christmas, he shook Ben's hand and turned to Larkin, who looked different somehow. There was an innocence about her face, while her eyes glowed with a knowledge that made her look—grown up, he supposed.

"You still liking Kentucky?" he asked.

"More than Kentucky likes me. I suppose folks are still getting used to the idea of me, but I'm determined." She raised her chin and he believed her. "Seeing Ben reunited with Mother and Daddy was about the only thing that could have persuaded me to leave. Granny Jane said we'd celebrate Old Christmas when we get back." She smiled. "Although I have no idea what that means."

"January sixth," Judd said. "Folks used to celebrate Christmas then—something to do with the calendar changing way back in the day. Some folks are slow to adjust."

"Do you have plans for tomorrow?" Larkin asked.

Judd felt his ears turning red and wished he had a hat to pull down over them. "Maybe your father forgot to mention . . . he invited me to dinner."

Larkin clapped her hands, and for a minute Judd thought she might fling her arms around his neck. "I'm so glad!" she cried. "That's the only thing that could make this Christmas better."

Now it was her turn to flush, but Judd thought it looked way better on her.

"Let's be getting on home," Mrs. Heyward said. She laughed, a sweet, low sound. "Santa won't come until you're asleep."

Larkin giggled, squeezed Judd's arm, and began moving toward the door, although the family was intercepted by half the people they passed along the way. Apparently the return of Ben, the prodigal, was causing a bit of a stir in the congregation. Judd watched his new friend shake hands, press kisses to wrinkled cheeks, and offer brief words of explanation for his long absence. Mr. Heyward just trailed along, looking sour.

Judd slipped over to a side door and eased out. The church was just a few blocks back from the ocean, so he wandered on down to the beach, noting the empty places where houses stood before the hurricane. He sat on a dune and watched the bright curls of foam wash in over and over again. Back home, folks believed animals could speak at midnight on Christmas

Eve. He looked around and supposed, other than a sea gull or a stray dog, he wasn't likely to encounter many critters, talking or otherwise.

One year, he and Joe slipped out to the barn on Christmas Eve. Judd didn't want to go, but Joe argued they had a fair chance of not only hearing what a cow had to say but also of seeing Santa Claus when he swung by in his sleigh. The night had been cold and perfectly still with a dusting of snow. They'd tried to walk in their father's boot prints between the house and the barn so no one would see their tracks. Inside, the milk cow and the mule they used for plowing slept while a barn cat ambled over and curled about their legs.

"I'd rather hear what Jack or Daisy have to say, but I guess the cat'll do in a pinch," Joe said.

They sat in some loose hay and watched the cat until they were sure midnight must have come and gone. She never spoke a word. Judd remembered waking in the warm and fragrant hay as Joe shook his arm.

"I hear something," he hissed, pointing toward the tin roof.

There was a pattering that could have been some old hickory nuts or sticks breaking loose in a sudden breeze. Both boys held their breath and stared at one another wide-eyed.

"What if he sees us?" Joe whispered. "You suppose he'd be mad and take the presents back away with him?"

Judd swallowed hard. He'd never thought of that. "We'd best get on back to bed."

They went to the door and darted across the yard, forgetting to hide their tracks. Back inside, they dove under the covers of the bed they shared. Abram had his own bed in the same room and he'd only snored louder for a moment. They pulled the quilts over their heads and feigned sleep until the real thing overtook them.

The next morning, their father gave them a stern look. "Santa must've landed on the roof of the barn by mistake and sent his elves over to the house from there. Sure was a mess of tracks in the barnyard this morning."

Judd thought his heart might beat out of his chest.

"Must've found everything alright, though. They's a pile of stuff in them stockings this morning."

All three boys hurried into the sitting room—Abram bringing up the rear and trying to act grown. Sure enough, their stockings bulged. There were oranges, nuts, a peppermint stick each, and Judd got a carved slingshot with a leather cup perfect for flinging acorns, stones, and who knew what else?

Later that day, after a big dinner, Joe and Judd went out to try the slingshot. "You know," Joe said, "if that old cat really could talk, she might've told on us."

Judd smiled at his memories. Joe had been on the right track. Even if cats couldn't talk, he'd learned over the years that the truth usually came out one way or another. And the truth was, as much as he wished he could go back and take Joe's place, he couldn't. But there was a sweet girl with laughter in her eyes who just might give him a good enough reason to go on living for as long as he could.

CHAPTER

26

Larkin woke on Christmas morning feeling the way she used to when she was small and still believed in Santa Claus. While she didn't believe in a gift-giving elf from the North Pole anymore, she was beginning to believe in something better—something that required deeper faith but ultimately offered more than a few presents.

She bounced down the stairs to find her father sitting in the den, sipping a cup of coffee and staring at the Christmas tree.

"Merry Christmas, Daddy," she sang.

He sighed and smiled, but it looked like it took quite a bit of effort. "Larkin. Merry Christmas." He patted the cushion beside him. "You've been missed around here."

Larkin snuggled into his side and admired the tree. Mother had really outdone herself this year. "I've missed you too, but there's something about helping people that just makes my heart sing." She bowed her head and curled her feet up onto the couch. "Although they aren't always willing to let me help as much as I'd like."

Her father shifted and looked down at her. "Not everyone

213

wants to be helped. Sometimes people would rather do things themselves."

"But some of those people are so obviously in need. I don't understand what keeps them from accepting what Ben and I are only too glad to offer. Word got out that Burt Linger hadn't chopped enough wood to last the winter before he got sick. He absolutely refused to let Ben do a thing, but then a dozen local men showed up out of the blue and cut and stacked enough wood for the winter and then some. Nobody asked—they just did it." She leaned her head against her father's shoulder. "Why would he let them help but not Ben?"

Daddy turned and looked like he might say something, then sighed again and sipped his coffee. "There's more than one way to help people," he finally said in a low voice.

Larkin started to ask what he meant when Mother and Ben came into the room, laughing and talking a mile a minute. After they opened presents and ate breakfast, Larkin helped clear the dishes and began filling the sink with hot, soapy water.

"Darling, what are you doing?" her mother asked.

"Washing up. I never appreciated how wonderful it is to be able to get hot water out of a tap. Makes doing the dishes a downright pleasure."

Mother just stood there gaping. "I think I can count on one hand the number of times you washed up without being asked."

Larkin flushed, then smiled and laughed. "You'll never have to ask again. Granny Jane has made a kitchen hand out of me."

"I would surely love to meet this Granny Jane. Between the stories Ben tells and the way you've changed . . . well, she must be something to behold."

Larkin laughed louder. "That she is. I'm even going to help you make dinner, and I promise not to burn anything or serve the turkey raw."

Judd wiped his hands on his new slacks for the third time. He thought he could handle any of these people singly, but the fact that he was about to find himself in a roomful of Heywards was giving him palpitations. Granny would prescribe a tablespoon of blackberry brandy, and right about now he'd gladly take it. Twice.

He raised his fist to knock at the door, but before he could make contact, it flew open. Larkin stood there, cheeks pink, apron wrapped around her waist. "Merry Christmas," she sang, grabbing his hand and pulling him inside.

Immediately, Judd was enveloped by the sounds and smells of the season. Bing Crosby sang "White Christmas," and the air was filled with the aroma of roasting turkey, sage, and something sweet. Fresh greenery draped the banister leading up to the second floor, and lights twinkled from a Christmas tree in the den. Judd felt a smile spread across his face in spite of his nerves.

Although he'd shared coffee and a hearty breakfast with Floyd that morning while they reminisced about holidays past, it hadn't really felt like Christmas until this moment. Floyd's daughter had come for him just before Judd left, and he hoped the old man was having a good day with his family.

Mr. Heyward came around the corner wearing a red sweater over his shirt and tie instead of his usual suit coat. Judd smoothed down his own tie, grateful Hank had loaned him one. He stuck out a hand and Mr. Heyward grasped it, pulling Judd close enough to slap him on the shoulder. "Merry Christmas, son. Glad you could join us. Come on in and sit while the ladies finish making dinner."

Larkin grinned and shooed Judd along after her father. He wasn't sure he wanted to sit and make conversation with his boss, but guessed it would be frowned upon if he offered to go in the kitchen and carry dishes to the table.

In the den, Mr. Heyward went over to poke at a small and

completely unnecessary fire crackling in the hearth. Ben sat in a wing chair near the tree, a Bible open in his hand.

"Been reading the Christmas story," he said. "Never gets old, does it?"

A memory popped into Judd's head. "My dad used to read that to us before we went to bed on Christmas Eve. Seems like maybe it stuck with me some." He thought a minute. "I always liked picturing those shepherds camping out at night and getting the shock of their lives when an angel showed up."

Ben smiled. "'Fear not: for, behold, I bring you good tidings of great joy, which shall be to all people. For unto you is born this day in the city of David a Savior, which is Christ the Lord.'"

Judd snapped his fingers. "That's it. And then the sky filled up with angels singing." He closed his eyes. "When I was a kid, I could just picture how that would look out there in the cow pasture."

Ben picked up the verse. "'And suddenly there was with the angel a multitude of the heavenly host praising God, and saying, Glory to God in the highest, and on earth peace, good will toward men.'"

Judd smiled. How had he forgotten that? Sitting near the crackling fire—for heat, not for looks—and listening to his father's rich voice reading out those words. It gave him a chill every year until . . . he couldn't remember when it stopped, only that it had.

"Little more than a fairy tale."

Judd and Ben turned to look at Mr. Heyward where he sat on the sofa, gripping the arm like his life depended on it. The look in his eyes challenged either of them to disagree.

Ben shrugged. "You're not the first to say so and certainly not the last. But fairy tale or not, it's the throbbing heartbeat of my very life." He closed the Bible with his finger tucked inside. "I thank you for taking us to church when we were small. It took a while, but eventually the truth sank in."

Mr. Heyward finally released the arm of the sofa, and Judd thought he could see indentations there. "After my father died, I swore I wouldn't darken the door of a church ever again. But as a businessman in the South . . . well. I should have stuck to my guns."

Ben closed his eyes and held the Bible as though he could read it through his fingertips. "'Not forsaking the assembling of ourselves together, as the manner of some is; but exhorting one another: and so much the more, as ye see the day approaching.'"

Judd watched the exchange with interest. He'd never seen someone stand up to Mr. Heyward. And here was Ben, his own son, doing it without raising his voice or pointing a finger. He just quoted Scripture.

Mr. Heyward stood as though he'd been sprung from the sofa. "No more. Surely it's time to eat and then you can be on your way. Stay another night if you must, but dinner is the last of the time I'll have for you and that only for your mother's sake. I know where my loyalties lie, even if you don't." He turned on his heel and stalked from the room.

Ben watched his father leave, his finger still stuck inside the worn Bible. He turned to Judd. "If you intend to court my sister, you have my blessing and then some. Only be careful. If George Heyward is encouraging you, it's not for your sake or even for Larkin's. I won't go so far as to say what I think he's up to, I just encourage you to step lightly."

Judd stared at the fire, watching the flames dance. He nodded his head, thinking there wasn't any reason to answer that comment aloud. A log, eaten through in the middle, collapsed on itself, sending up a shower of sparks—a last hurrah, thought Judd, before it was consumed entirely.

Larkin dared to have high hopes for Christmas dinner, and while it wasn't quite as perfect as she would have wished, it would do. She was a little mystified as to why her father had included Judd, but hoped it was because her father knew he might be lonesome so far from home during the holidays.

While conversation at dinner wasn't what you'd call lively, they all managed to find something to say. As Daddy sipped his cider, he seemed to relax enough to finally put them all at something like ease. After dessert—a many-layered coconut cake garnished with holly—Daddy pushed his chair back and turned his attention to Larkin.

"Why don't you and Judd go for a walk? Give your mother and brother some time alone."

Normally, Larkin would have found that odd, but her father's smile and the blessings of the day conspired to make her feel as though all was well. She grabbed Judd's hand and tugged him toward the door.

"Leave the dishes, Mother. I'll do them when we get back."

They strolled along the streets, unconsciously heading for the ocean, not speaking at first. Larkin glanced at the tall, lanky man beside her. His skin had darkened with his outdoor work, and she thought maybe his limp was less pronounced than she remembered.

"Do you like timber work better than mining?"

Judd gazed off into the distance. "I suppose so. I certainly expected to when I came south." He shoved his hands in his pockets and walked, head down for a few paces. "There was some good about mining, too. I miss old Harry. We'd break for lunch down there with nothing but mountain over our heads, and Harry'd tell stories to get us laughing so hard our ribs hurt. He was his own kind of sunshine."

"Is Harry still a miner?"

"I reckon so. Don't guess he'd much know how to do anything else. He never married, but he had a widowed sister with four young'uns he helped raise."

Larkin tried to think how to ask her next question. "Do you

. . . ever think about going back? Not to mine necessarily," she hurried to add, "but maybe to work your brother's farm or . . . something."

Judd looked at her and it felt like he could see right through her. "My brother died in that mine cave-in that busted my leg. I haven't had much of a stomach for home since then. He's the one who wanted a job in South Carolina. Seemed like someone should follow that dream." He gave her a lopsided grin, showing one dimple. "And it might be I'm starting to have a few dreams of my own."

Larkin stopped and touched his arm, effectively bringing Judd to a halt, as well. They were about a block from the closed-up Pavilion, and she could hear and smell the ocean beyond. "I didn't know that about your brother."

"It's not something I like to talk about."

"What was he like?" Larkin asked.

Judd wasn't expecting that question. He didn't talk about Joe because people too often asked for the details of how he died, or how old he was at the time, and then they'd say things like it was a shame to lose him so young and he was in a better place. No one had ever asked what Joe was like.

"Like sunshine after a week of rain." Judd didn't know where that'd come from. "They called him 'Sunny' down in the mine because he always made things seem a little brighter when he was around. Between him and Harry we were laughing all the time." Judd looked toward the ocean—he could see waves cresting beyond the buildings—afternoon light catching in the spray. "He was supposed to be working where I was, but he was smaller and . . ." Judd choked on the words he'd never spoken aloud.

Larkin took his hand and tugged him on down to the beach. They stood among the dunes, watching the water wash in and out. After a moment, Larkin said, "Only tell me if you want to."

Judd inhaled the salt air until it filled every bit of his coal-stained lungs.

"Joe said he'd work my seam—it was tighter, hard for even the smallest man." He closed his eyes, wishing for the darkness that almost swallowed him. "I let him go. I was glad of it. Didn't even think twice, just took what was offered. And then . . ." His voice shook and he placed a hand over his closed eyes, trying to make it darker yet. "It was like a cannon going off, and I knew something had given way. I knew something bad had happened. I didn't even think about him then. Only thought about hightailing it out of there. I didn't any more than turn around before the whole mountain . . ." Judd fell to his knees in the soft sand. "It felt like the whole mountain came down on top of me." Now he clamped both hands over his eyes. "The dark. I'd never known such dark, and my lamp was gone."

He felt a hand settle on his shoulder like a bird. "That sounds terrible."

Judd fisted his hands and pressed harder into his eyes until he saw stars dance. "I hardly even wondered if anyone else was alive. All I could do was wonder if I was dead."

He felt Larkin drop to the sand beside him and place an arm around his shoulders.

"But you weren't."

She reached up and pried first one hand and then the other from his face. He dropped back on his heels, eyes still closed. Then he felt a fluttering against his face and eyelids. It felt like . . . he blinked his eyes. She'd kissed his eyes open, and now he was looking deep into the clear blue of hers.

"I'm so sorry Joe died. I think I would have liked him. But I'm awfully glad you're alive, and I think maybe it's time you stopped going back down into the dark."

Judd reached up and touched her cheek, which was just as silken as he'd long imagined. She leaned into his hand, and the sun setting somewhere behind him washed her skin in gold. He reached for her with both hands and kissed her as though, at long last, he'd been given permission.

CHAPTER
27

Judd would have been glad to go back to the house and ask Mr. Heyward for permission to marry his daughter then and there, but he figured he'd better not rush it and scare her off. And anyway, he was still trying to figure out Mr. Heyward's angle. No, the main thing he needed to do right now was figure out how to keep Larkin in South Carolina where he could court her proper.

They stepped through the front door, hand in hand, but as soon as they cleared the threshold Judd felt the air change. Larkin must have felt it too, as she let his hand slip from hers and hurried forward to peer into the den where a fire still crackled.

"Where is everybody?" she called.

"We're here." That was Ben from inside the room. "Y'all come on in. Mom's making spiced cider."

Judd trailed the woman he now knew he loved into the room, where Ben sat alone staring into the fire.

"Mr. Heyward helping with the cider?" he asked.

Ben laughed, but it didn't sound like he was enjoying it. "He's gone upstairs to read the paper. I guess you could say we had a conversation that didn't quite go the way he liked."

Larkin knelt beside her brother's chair. "Oh, Ben, is he still trying to talk you into taking over the company?"

"Yes, and he made some good points. I told him I don't feel called to run the timber company, but that I'd continue praying about it." He shrugged. "God could change my mind yet, but I'm not looking for it to happen."

Larkin patted him on the knee and stood. "Maybe you should stop anticipating what God will do and just see what He does."

Ben stared at his sister, and this time his laughter sounded genuine. "That is a mighty fine piece of advice. When did you get so smart?"

"While you were off gallivanting around Kentucky." She sashayed across the room and settled in next to Judd on the sofa where she scooped up his hand.

Judd felt his neck and then his ears turn red as Ben took in their linked fingers.

"I'm thinking whatever conversation the two of you had, it went better than Dad's and mine."

Judd was saved from answering when Mrs. Heyward appeared carrying a tray with steaming cups. He released Larkin's hand to reach for some cider, but not before a mother's sharp eyes noticed everything. Mrs. Heyward pursed her lips but didn't comment.

After some idle conversation, Judd excused himself, thanked his hostess and headed for the door. Larkin followed him and caught his arm as he reached for the knob. Judd wanted to scoop her in his arms and kiss her again, but hesitated since he was in her father's house.

"I want to call on you—take you out and do this proper," he said laying a hand over her fingers where they warmed his arm.

She giggled. "Do what?"

He looked into her sparkling blue eyes and smiled. He was pretty sure she would always be able to make him smile. "Court you. Woo you." He almost said *Marry you*, but thought it might be too much.

"I'd like that, but we're going back to Kentucky day after tomorrow."

Judd's smile slipped. "I thought you might stay longer." He shifted his weight off his bad leg. "Thought you might even decide to stay here for good."

Larkin touched his cheek. "Back in Kentucky, after that day we spent with Granny Jane, I thought the same thing about you staying there."

Judd felt the desire to push her away and wrap her close in equal parts. He'd thought she understood, really and truly knew how important it was for him to follow the path Joe had laid out before dying. Maybe he'd even thought that kiss meant she cared enough to want to be where he was. He let his hand fall away from hers.

"Guess we both got it wrong," he said and opened the door. He stepped through and turned to see her stricken face one last time. As he did, he caught a glimpse of Mr. Heyward, standing at the top of the stairs, a calculating gleam in his eye.

◆ ◆ ◆

The first day back at work after Christmas was cold. Judd rubbed his hands together and thought this might actually qualify even back home. The humid air made the weather sink into his bones, and his leg ached with a fierceness he hadn't experienced in months. The temperature dampened the men's enthusiasm for working, and the day dragged. When the third man brought Judd a chainsaw that didn't need anything but a little kerosene in the bar oil, he felt like cussing and asking them if they were all fools.

He didn't, though, knowing he was the biggest fool of them all for letting an auburn-haired girl with laughing eyes slip away.

Chuck wandered over, hands shoved deep in his pockets, and shoulders hunched under his jacket. "Cold enough for ya?"

Judd didn't suppose that required an answer.

"You talk to your pal Pete lately?"

"Not since Thanksgiving. Heard he got a job over at Henderson's woodlot."

Chuck nodded. "I don't know how close the two of you are, but seems like you're the only one Pete ever warmed up to. Thought you might want to know he's headed for a world of trouble if he's not careful."

Judd put down the chain he was sharpening. "How's that?"

"Apparently he's found some no-good attorney who's talked him into trying to get his daddy's land back from Mr. Heyward. Pete's been going around talking big about how he's going to take him to court and clean him out. Says he'll end up owning Waccamaw Timber Company before it's all said and done."

Judd sighed. Sure sounded like Pete. "Why're you telling me?"

Chuck shrugged. "Thought you might want to give your friend some advice that's worth more than a plugged nickel." He squinted over to a trash barrel, where some of the men had built a fire and were goofing off around it. "I'd better get over there and break up the sewing circle. Those boys'll stand around and gossip as long as I let 'em."

Judd watched Chuck walk away. He tried not to care what kind of hole Pete had dug for himself this time, but he hated to see the mess it would cause not only Pete but also Larkin's family. He flinched. Life sure would be easier if he could go back to not caring about anyone.

🌢🌢🌢

Larkin and Ben got back to Logan in plenty of time to celebrate Old Christmas, but Larkin felt more keenly than ever the need to help these people—whether they wanted her to or not. In a fit of optimism, she talked Maude into helping her organize a dance in the church hall. Maybe if she could show the locals some hospitality, they'd warm up to her.

The dance was set for Thursday, January sixth—Granny's Old Christmas. Larkin was so nervous she could hardly do anything. She'd made pan after pan of fudge that was only a little grainy, while Maude made divinity with the pecans Ben brought her from South Carolina. Hot apple cider perfumed the air, and the potbellied stove radiated warmth. Larkin agonized over what to wear. She didn't have anything nearly as nice as she would have worn back home, but she worried that even her simpler clothes might make people think she was putting on airs. Plus her hair wouldn't cooperate. She tried it in three different styles but nothing looked right.

"Maude, I can't get my hair to do and I don't know what to wear." Larkin felt like a child throwing a tantrum, but she was at her wit's end. "Not that anyone will even look at me, except what if they do?"

Maude settled the last platter of treats on a long table near the windows and rolled her sleeves down. She was wearing a simple green skirt and a rough blouse with a lily of the valley stickpin near the collar. Larkin halfway wished she could just borrow Maude's outfit.

"Larkin honey, they'll be looking at you most of all. You're like a rose blooming out of season around here."

Larkin flushed, a wave of hopelessness washing over her. This dance was a terrible idea. "I just want to fit in," she mumbled, hanging her head.

"Tell you what. That package over there in the corner is a present Granny Jane done sent you. She wanted you to open it after all the hubbub died down, but if it's what I think it is, you oughta open it now."

Larkin hadn't noticed the package wrapped in the funny papers, lying on her pillow in the corner. She went and picked it up, quickly peeling back the paper. It was a dress. The golden fabric was a sort of rough Swiss dot with pleats at the shoulders and sleeves, and white fabric showing where the collar folded back. It wasn't anything she would have even considered wearing back in South Carolina.

"Granny had that fabric saved for some reason or another. She got Lucille Hardin to make up a dress out of it. Said you needed something practical but pretty to wear around here if you was going to keep sticking your nose into other people's business." Maude took it from Larkin and held it up against her body. "Guess it'll fit alright. It ain't fancy like what you got there," she said and indicated the gauzy dress Larkin had hung on the wardrobe door. "But it's more like what everybody else'll be wearing, if fitting in is your aim."

Larkin held the dress to her body. It was the opposite of everything she'd known, and she decided that made it absolutely perfect. She ducked behind the curtain and slipped it on over her head. It settled in place more or less. It was a little loose, but she found it much more comfortable than the stiff dresses and snug sashes she was used to with party dresses. She pulled her hair into her signature ponytail and twisted that into a loose bun. She glanced in the mirror Ben kept over the washbasin and barely recognized herself. She looked . . . plain. No, not plain, simple. Real. Like for the first time ever, she wasn't pretending to be more than she was. It felt good.

Maude looked her up and down. "That'll give 'em one less thing to talk about."

Larkin giggled. "Am I depriving them?"

Maude huffed. "Most likely, but they need to be deprived. Now git on out there. I hear Paul's old truck limping into the yard. He'll be bringing the players."

As it turned out, Paul was the best banjo player in the county, if not the state, and his presence guaranteed the attendance of several other musicians, as well as a fair-sized crowd. Larkin had thought to organize the dancing, maybe teach them all a few shag steps, but after an awkward demonstration from her, Ben stepped in and suggested a local fellow call a few squares. The next thing Larkin knew, she'd lost all semblance of control.

At first she was annoyed. This was supposed to be her gift to the community, but as she joined in the dancing—which even included a few old country dances—she realized she was having a wonderful time. As she and Ben partnered to dance a reel the length of the building, she found she didn't care what she was wearing or that her hair was coming out of its pins. There was no pretense about these people, and she wanted to live like this always.

As the evening wore on, Ben finally had to pretty much force the musicians to stop and everyone to pack up and go home. Sleepy children were slung over shoulders, courting couples slipped away hand in hand, and the old women stopped talking long enough to wake their drowsing husbands so they could walk out arm in arm.

When Maude finally exited with a drooping Kyle, Larkin looked around to determine if the mess could be left until morning. But there was no mess. The little bit of remaining food had been packed up and put away. The furniture had been relocated to its usual places, and the fire had even been banked.

"It's all done," she said, eyes wide.

"Respect for the church building," Ben said. "And maybe for the newcomers—that'd be you and me. With a few notable exceptions, folks around here take pride in never being what you might call a burden."

"That's why no one will let me help them." It wasn't a question. Larkin thought maybe she finally understood. Tears rose. "Will I ever be any good to these people? I thought I was going to make a difference in their lives. I thought I was going to help the poor and take care of hungry children. Why am I even here?"

Ben snugged an arm around her shoulders. "I think you do help, just not in the way you imagined. You've been good for

Granny, and I think you gave Kyle incentive to keep doing his exercises so he'd get stronger. And this dance was a blessing to lots of folks. Paul lost his job just before Christmas. The mandolin player's wife died last summer—he's raising four children with only his mother to help." He squeezed her arm. "There are a dozen sad stories I know of and probably twice that many I don't. Just having you around for a distraction helps more than you realize."

Larkin looked down at her simple dress and put a hand to her falling-down hair. "I guess I am something of an oddity, although being a circus sideshow wasn't what I had in mind when I braved Daddy's wrath to join you here."

"Life almost never has the same thing in mind that you do. Try to roll with the punches, little sister."

Granny Jane summoned Larkin to her cabin the following day to share every detail of the evening before. Larkin wore her new dress, which seemed to delight the old woman.

"That cloth come to me when my aunt Maybell passed. She left some household sundries to me, and I never could decide what to do with yeller cloth. I don't look good wearing that color and it seemed too fine for curtains." Granny waved a hand at her bare windows. "When I got the idea to have Lucille make it up into a dress for you, I was so excited I could hardly hold it in." She cocked her head one way and then the other. "Might need to nip it in a bit at the waist there, but I guess Lucille did alright not having you to measure firsthand. And that gold goes good with your hair."

Larkin raised a hand to smooth her hair back where it was fastened in its usual ponytail. "It's the most comfortable thing I've worn in years. I danced in it last night and I think I could have kept going until the rooster crowed. I just wish . . . well, it doesn't matter."

Granny nodded, leaned forward, and laid a hand on Larkin's knee. "Child, there's a shadow on your heart, and I'm thinking you'd feel better if you told me about it."

Larkin felt tears prick her eyelids. Granny knew her better than she knew herself. "Yes, ma'am, there is something worrying me."

Granny tapped a stool with her walking stick, and Larkin perched on it. "Considering what I know of you, I'd guess you're missing a certain tall, dark feller with dimples in his cheeks."

Larkin grinned at that. So Granny wasn't immune to Judd's charms, either. "He's determined to stay in South Carolina, and I'm determined to stay right here—except I'm not sure I'm really meant for this place anymore. I keep trying to be a help, but no one will let me. Except you." She laughed. "And I think you're just taking pity on me."

Granny rocked and hummed what Larkin thought she recognized as "Rock of Ages." Finally, the older woman slowed to a stop and pointed at Larkin. "Do you love him?"

Larkin's eyes went wide, and she felt a flutter of panic. "I . . . I don't know."

"Hunh. Nobody knows *but* you and the good Lord. You go on back to the church hall, get on your knees beside your bed, and ask your Father in Heaven to clarify the matter. And if you do love him, you'd best git to South Carolina and let him know. Good men are few and far between, and from what I seen of that boy, he's a good 'un. God has a plan for you, and might be Judd Markley is a big part of it." She laid her head back against her chair and started rocking again. "God will take care of you no matter what. If He wants you here keeping me company, He'll tell you so. And if not, you'll just have to visit now and again."

That evening, Larkin did as Granny suggested. Kyle was mostly living with Maude now—the older woman said he was a big help around the house, and it was obvious the pair adored

230

each other—so it was just Larkin and Ben rattling around the
church hall. He'd given her the curtained-off bed with its little
side table and wardrobe. Most of Larkin's luggage sat un-
touched in a corner. She'd only pulled out the clothing she
needed and her sturdiest pair of shoes, which weren't nearly
sturdy enough.

She knelt next to the narrow bed, grit digging into her knees
through her skirt and the woolen stockings Ben had rounded up
for her. She folded her hands and tried to think how to begin.
Ben had gone out to tend to a few chores, and she wanted to
do this while she was alone.

Squeezing her eyes shut, she tried a few words. "Dear God,
Granny Jane said I should talk to you about Judd—about where
you want me. You probably know I think I'm in love with him,
but I'm afraid it's not a good idea. We seem to have switched
places, him going south and me coming north, and I don't want
to miss my calling because of"—she smiled to herself—"a tall,
dark feller with dimples."

She sighed. Laying it all out made the idea of running back
home just because she *might* have a future with a man she barely
knew seem foolish. She guessed Granny was right about talking
things over with God. It was already helping her see more clearly.

"So anyway, God, I was thinking maybe you'd make it all
work out if that's the best thing, but I can certainly see why it's
not. Maybe you could make me care for him less, if we're not
supposed to be a couple." She pressed her palms more tightly
together. "I do thank you for this place and these people and
letting me come here. It's what I wanted most and I appreciate
the chance." She paused. "Amen."

Larkin pulled herself to her feet, staring at her bed without
seeing it. God may have given her what she most wanted a few
months ago, but now she found herself wanting something
more. She waited for God to take the longing away—a longing
that pierced even more deeply than the desire to be useful ever

had. She thought of the day the two of them spent together working around Granny Jane's place. That might very well have been the best day of her life, even if she had ruined lunch. And then the day Judd kissed her on the beach—he'd needed her that day. She'd been useful and helpful in a way she hadn't even known was possible.

A single tear slid down Larkin's cheek and she brushed it away, straightening her shoulders, and tossing her ponytail. She'd made her own choices and now she'd live with them. She'd just have to keep asking God to take away this longing in her heart.

Ben banged through the door and set the coal bucket down near the stove. He held his hands out to the heat while Larkin came over to take his coat and hang it up. She was certainly a help around here and that was blessing enough. Or so she told herself.

"Hey, check that inside pocket. I stopped by the post office today, and they had a letter addressed to the both of us. Just about forgot it."

Larkin fished the envelope out, recognizing her mother's monogrammed stationery. Perhaps a note from home would cheer her up. She sat at the table, slid her finger under the flap, extracted the crisp linen paper, and frowned. This wasn't her mother's handwriting.

Ben and Larkin,

I thought you should know your mother has cancer. Her doctor found a lump in her bosom and will cut it out some time next week. She didn't want to tell you, but since you are her children I thought someone should write and let you know.

What you do with the information is up to you.

George Heyward

Larkin looked at Ben, stricken. "I have to go to her."

Ben slid into the chair opposite and took the letter from her hand. His eyes scanned it, then met Larkin's. He wet his lips. "I agree, although I'm suspicious of our father's intentions." He grimaced. "Which isn't very generous of me. Yes, you should go. Having you here has been wonderful and I hope you'll be able to come back once Mom is well, but I think she needs you."

That night, Larkin slid into bed with a plan in place. Ben would drive her to the nearest town with a bus stop, and within two days she'd be back in Myrtle Beach where she could help take care of her mother. Peace flowed through her in spite of her worries about cancer and surgery. She smiled, realizing it was the very peace she'd longed for earlier. Maybe God was answering her prayer. And maybe, just maybe, His answer had something to do with sending her to where Judd Markley was.

She slid out of bed into the chill air and knelt in her too-thin cotton nightgown. She whispered a prayer of thanks, asked God to watch over her mother, and finally said, "And God, if Judd's the one for me, please let me know. On the other hand, if he's not, please make that clear, as well." She climbed back under the heavy quilts, snuggled in, and fell into a deep sleep.

CHAPTER
28

Judd knocked on Pete's front door Friday evening. He could smell whatever Sally had cooked for dinner and thought about his own bowl of canned chili back in his room. He really needed to see about renting a place with a kitchen if he was going to stay here. Probably should have done it before now.

Sally opened the door, and a smile bloomed across her face. "Come on in, Judd. I was just about to dish up some cake and coffee—you'd be most welcome to join us."

"Don't mind if I do," Judd said, scuffing his boots on the doormat.

"Pete, it's Judd. Why don't you boys settle in the front room here and I'll bring you dessert and coffee?"

Pete wandered out from the kitchen and shook Judd's hand. "About time you came around. You ready to throw old man Heyward over and come work for a real outfit?"

"Oh, well, I don't know about that," Judd said, settling in an armchair.

Pete flopped onto the sofa across from him. "You wanna play some cards?"

"If you want to, but mainly I came to talk to you about this lawsuit I hear you're bringing against George Heyward."

Pete gave a short bark of laughter. "That's Judd for ya. Straight to the point." He sat forward and pointed at Judd. "That's what I like about you. Don't have to wonder where I stand." He settled back again. "Yeah, this attorney thinks we can squeeze some cash out of the old man. 'Course, what I really want is my daddy's land—and anything that's on it—back, but if I can pry a few dollars loose, well, that wouldn't hurt my feelings none."

"But didn't Mr. Heyward buy the land fair and square?"

Pete leaned forward again. "What he did was take advantage of a drunk's moment of weakness."

Judd nodded. "But that isn't really illegal, is it? It might've been wrong, but it's not something you can take a man to court over."

"Attorney says I can."

"What's in it for the attorney?"

"Whatcha mean by that?"

Sally came in and handed Judd a plate with a thick slice of chocolate cake. "You take your coffee black, right?"

"I do," Judd said. He forked a bite of cake into his mouth and looked at Pete, who waved Sally off. He swallowed. "I mean, I have yet to meet a lawyer who wasn't trying to make money or get ahead in some way."

Pete made a scornful sound and took the cup of coffee Sally handed him. She set Judd's cup and saucer on an end table near his elbow.

"Don't be so suspicious. Some people just want to set a wrong right. And this wrong goes back further than you know."

Judd wondered what Pete meant by that but knew asking him outright would only turn his friend coy.

Pete slurped his coffee. "The old man send you over to see what you can find out?"

"No. I just don't want to see you get into trouble."

Pete puffed his chest out. "I can take care of myself. I don't need Waccamaw Timber Company, and if the old man ain't careful, he's going to lose more than his kids."

"What do you know about his kids?" Judd bristled.

"I know Ben's supposed to run the company and he's not interested. And I know the old man has a backup plan that involves that girl of his."

"Larkin?"

"Yeah. Guess you know her some." He leered at Judd over the rim of his cup. "Good-looking, ain't she? Wonder if her daddy might not mind her finding a real timberman to settle her down."

Judd felt something in him harden against Pete. "She's joined her brother doing church work back in Kentucky."

"That how it is? Maybe the old man'll have to do something about that if he wants to keep the business in the family."

"What do you mean?"

Pete's eyes shuttered and he swallowed some more coffee. "Nothing. Just wouldn't trust that man any farther than I can throw him with one arm tied behind my back."

Judd ate his last bite of cake and washed it down with bitter coffee, wishing he hadn't come.

💧💧💧

Larkin stepped down from the bus, grateful for the driver who invited her to sit behind him where he could keep an eye on her. Over the long ride there'd been a fellow or two who looked at her in a way that made her uncomfortable. The driver on the last bus looked old enough to be her grandfather, and he'd treated her like family. She puffed out a breath and claimed her suitcase. She'd left quite a few of her belongings back in the church hall. Somehow all those things hadn't seemed as important as she traveled south to see to her mother.

She'd used a pay phone at the last stop to call Hank, asking him to keep her arrival a secret so she could surprise her mother. He'd been reluctant, but finally agreed. Now he waved at her from the parking area and hurried over to carry her bag.

"Sure is good to see you back in South Carolina," he said.

Larkin hugged him and kissed his cheek. "It's good to be back and it's such a relief not to be shivering."

Hank laughed. "Haven't adjusted to the frozen north?"

"No, but I'm working on it." She climbed into the cab of Hank's truck. "Have you seen Mother or Daddy lately?"

Hank fussed with her luggage, settled into the driver's seat, and seemed intent on adjusting the mirrors.

"Hank, I asked you a question."

He sighed. "Mr. Heyward's been a terror, and I haven't seen your mother." He started the truck. "I'm sorry she's sick."

"I'm hoping it's not serious. Daddy didn't exactly give a bunch of details."

"Straight home?" he asked.

Larkin pressed her back into the cool of the seat. "Yes, please." She straightened her skirt and waited for Hank to pull into traffic. "I'm assuming Daddy's at the office?"

"Last time I saw him."

"I'm thinking it'll be nicer to surprise Mother while he's not there."

Hank nodded. "Sounds right."

They drove in silence until Hank pulled up to the two-story house with its camellias in full bloom. Larkin noticed how the spent blossoms were scattered across the lawn. Mother normally gathered them up every other day or so. Maybe she could help with that.

Larkin let Hank hand her suitcase out of the back of the truck and then sent him on his way. He seemed reluctant to go, but she assured him she'd be all right. Leaving her bag sitting in the driveway, she headed for the back door. Her car was parked in the garage, looking dusty and forlorn. She pictured Judd behind the wheel and wished he were here to greet her. But that was silly. Why would Judd be at her parents' house—especially after their parting at Christmas?

Pushing open the door, Larkin tiptoed inside. She listened intently, trying to determine where her mother was. A rustling from the den sent her creeping down the hall. She peeked around the corner and saw her mother flipping through a magazine. She was wearing beige slacks and a winter-white sweater with pearls. Larkin smiled. Of course her mother would be dressed perfectly to read a magazine, alone in her own home, on a Tuesday afternoon.

Larkin felt a smile spread across her face. It was a relief to see her mother looking so very normal.

"Any good recipes in there?"

Mother jumped and crumpled a thin page. "Larkin—where in the world did you come from?"

Larkin laughed. "Kentucky."

Mother stood, more slowly than Larkin would have expected, and hurried over to her daughter. She cupped her face in her hands. "Oh, my darling, it's so good to see you. Is Ben here?"

"No, it's just me." She leaned into her mother's palm. "Daddy wrote and told us that you . . . need surgery."

"Oh. He did? He wrote to you?"

Larkin took her mother's hands in her own and led her over to the sofa. "Yes. He said it might be cancer."

Mother laughed, but it sounded thin. "Maybe not. Dr. Endicott found a lump." Her hand lifted to her right side as though of its own volition. "He wants to cut it out so he can know for sure if it's cancer." She leaned into Larkin. "But I don't think it is. And somehow, now that you're here, I'm not worried about it at all."

"Mr. Heyward wants you back at the office at eleven-thirty." Chuck found Judd changing the oil in one of the trucks on Thursday morning.

He slid out from under the vehicle and looked at the foreman. "What for?"

Chuck shrugged. "Beats me. He sent word, not an engraved invitation." He laughed. "Ain't that always the way?"

Judd smiled, nodded, and pulled himself back under the truck. George Heyward had a reason, sure enough. He'd just have to wait to find out what it was . . . and tread carefully along the way.

Judd wished he'd had time to change his oil-spotted shirt before going to see Mr. Heyward, but he didn't suppose his employer would care one way or the other. He stepped into the warmth of the office from the cool February afternoon. It wasn't cold exactly, but the moisture in the air seemed to carry what cold there was straight to his core. He shivered and hung his jacket on a hall tree.

"That you, Judd?" Mr. Heyward stepped to his door and stuck his head out. "Come on in here."

Judd rubbed his palms on his shirt and followed his boss inside. Mr. Heyward retreated behind his oversized desk and sat, waving for Judd to do the same in one of the leather chairs facing him.

"How long have you worked for me now?"

Judd thought about that, tapping his fingers one by one against his leg. "Six months or so."

Mr. Heyward nodded as though he already knew. "And in that time you've moved from laborer to mechanic to forestry commission liaison. Seems you've done alright here at Waccamaw Timber Company."

Judd didn't suppose that needed an answer, so he just nodded.

"Hank and Chuck agree you're a hard worker and honest as they come. I've seen some of that myself." He looked uncomfortable, then cleared his throat and shifted in his chair. "I'd like to promote you to chief mechanic in a supervisory position. You'll be training and overseeing several other men. This means a significant increase in pay, and I'll expect you to hold all those workers to the same high standard you've been meeting."

Judd pondered this turn of events. While he'd determined to do his best to get ahead in his new line of work, he hadn't been expecting a promotion. And while he was grateful for the opportunity, it felt a little too easy. He rubbed a hand along his jaw, feeling the stubble there and wondering if his boss had something up his sleeve.

Mr. Heyward clearly expected a different sort of reaction. "Well? This is good news, man. An honor."

Judd cleared his throat. "I understand that, sir. I'm just a mite taken aback by it all."

Mr. Heyward waved a dismissive hand in the air. "No need for a show of humility with me, son. You just live up to my expectations and we'll both be satisfied." He stood, and Judd took the hint, rising from his chair.

Mr. Heyward walked him toward the door, glancing at his watch as they went. "Of course, as a senior representative of the company, you might need to spend less time with, say, anyone involved in litigation against us." He emphasized that last word.

Judd began to feel the light dawning. He was still confused, though, since he was pretty sure Pete didn't actually have a case. Could there be more to the situation than he knew?

They were almost to the front door when it flew open and Larkin burst in. "Daddy, am I late? Mother and I got to talking and I—" She froze when she saw Judd, and he thought her cheeks, already rosy from the fresh air outside, turned a shade pinker.

"Larkin." He didn't trust himself to say more than her name.

240

And even that might have been too bold. He should have called her "Miss Heyward."

"Mother's ill. I came back to help take care of her." The words rushed out of her.

"I'm sorry to hear that." He glanced at Mr. Heyward, who looked from one to the other of them, then snapped his fingers.

"Say, Judd, I was planning to take my daughter to lunch, but something's come up. Why don't you see to her?"

Judd tried to keep his jaw from scraping the floor. "I'd best be getting back to work," he said, glancing at Larkin. Did she look disappointed?

"Nonsense. I'll let Chuck know not to expect you back until later this afternoon." He elbowed Judd. "If at all."

Judd half expected him to wink, but thankfully he didn't. He just leaned over, gave Larkin a peck on the cheek, and said, "I'll see you at home this evening." Then he left them standing there staring at each other.

Larkin was the first to recover. "I'm sorry Daddy stuck you with me like that." She spoke softly, presumably so her father wouldn't hear. "There's no need for you to take me to lunch if you don't want to."

"I . . ." Judd meant to say something, but he lost it as soon as he opened his mouth. The smell of motor oil wafted up to him. He waved at his stained shirt. "I've been working on an old truck. I'm really not fit to be seen in public." He thought to add *especially with a girl like you*, but his tongue froze up again.

"Is that all? By the look on your face, I was afraid Daddy had assigned you something awful in taking me out."

"No, no, I'd be honored to take you to lunch," he said, looking down again, "if I was fit."

Larkin's laughter sounded like a church bell pealing. "I know just the thing." She looped her hand through his arm and tugged him out to the parking lot where her car was parked next to his truck.

She headed for the truck, and Judd wished he'd cleaned it out that weekend. He was a reasonably tidy man, but his work gloves were lying on the bench seat, a thermos and lunch sack sat on the floorboards, and some tools rattled around loose. Somehow he had the presence of mind to reach out and open the door before she could. She scooted in and shoved his junk aside like she was used to it. Judd pictured Ben's rattletrap of a truck and supposed she was. He went around and climbed behind the wheel, finally looking her full in the face.

"Where to?"

She smiled and gave him directions.

CHAPTER
29

Larkin thought her father would probably have a heart attack if he knew she knew about the diner where working men gathered for "meat and three" each lunch hour. She'd discovered it when a patient at the hospital practically begged her to go and bring him back fried pork chops. She'd gone for him several times while he was recovering from awful burns down his left leg, and the owner, who was also the cook, had gotten to know her.

She walked in with Judd, craning her neck to see if Mason was working the grill. He was and spotted her immediately.

"Well, bless my soul if it ain't Larkin Heyward. Don't tell me Jackson's back in the hospital?"

"No sir, haven't seen him in months. This time I've brought you a mountain man to feed." She tugged Judd forward. "This is Judd Markley, down from West Virginia. He's working for Daddy and he's powerful hungry."

Judd looked like he was going to protest but held his peace.

Mason came out from behind the counter and shook Judd's hand. "Missing your mama's cookin', are ya?" He didn't wait for an answer, but waved them into a corner booth. "Food, and plenty of it, comin' right up."

Judd slid onto the cracked Naugahyde, his stomach rumbling as his nose tried to sort out all the wonderful smells, including seared meat, baked bread, and all things fried. A waitress appeared and set tall glasses of iced tea in front of them, then hurried away.

"Don't we need to order?" Judd asked.

"I have a feeling Mason's already decided what we're having. Don't worry, I have yet to eat anything that wasn't good." She made a face, keeping a close eye on Judd. "Except the chicken livers." She tried not to laugh out loud when Judd struggled to hide a look of horror. "Of course, they might be your favorite."

"Nooo." Judd drew the word out. "Can't say I much care for innards."

Larkin giggled and was rewarded by a deepening smile from Judd. When his dimples showed, she felt like she'd won a prize. She could hardly believe she was sitting here across from the man she hadn't been able to stop thinking about the last few weeks. It was almost as though Daddy had engineered it. But of course he hadn't. Why would he?

The waitress returned with several plates and some small bowls she somehow managed to carry all at once. She arranged everything in front of them, gave Larkin a pat, and then went to refill coffee cups.

Larkin watched Judd take in the array of food, thinking she could live on his look of wonder for a week. There was fried chicken, pork chops smothered in gravy, a slice of meatloaf, popcorn shrimp, turnip greens, macaroni and cheese, stewed squash, potato salad, pinto beans, corn bread, and a dish of spiced apples.

Larkin leaned her head toward the counter where several cakes and pies waited under glass domes. "Don't forget to save room for dessert."

"The smell's almost enough to satisfy a man," Judd said,

a note of reverence in his voice. He lifted a fork and speared an apple.

"Wait." Larkin held up a finger. "Would you say grace?"

Judd looked at her a moment, set his fork down, and reached for her hand. Larkin felt a thrill as their fingers touched. She bowed her head lest Judd see the emotion in her face.

"Lord, thank you for this day, this food, and this woman who shares the joy of living wherever she goes. Bless her and guide us both in all that we do. Amen."

Larkin felt a lump rise in her throat and took a drink of tea to try to wash it down. "Thank you," she whispered. Then louder, "Now dig in. We'll have to eat most of this if we don't want to hurt Mason's feelings."

◆ ◆ ◆

Judd wasn't sure he could do the food justice when all he wanted to do was take in Larkin sitting across from him, practically glowing with . . . what? Contentment maybe? She was the prettiest thing he'd ever seen, and although he couldn't quite make sense of how he'd come to be sitting opposite her eating more food than some folks back home saw in a week, he was glad to be here.

"Is your mother's illness serious?" he asked.

A shadow passed over Larkin's face, but she didn't let it stay. "Mother's having surgery. I think she'll be fine, but I wanted to come home and help take care of her." She laughed lightly. "All that candy-striper training is finally coming in handy."

"I'm real sorry to hear she's sick." Judd reached for the potato salad. "If there's any way I can help, I'd be more than glad to."

"I don't know that we need anything at the moment, but I'll let you know if we do."

Somehow, Judd got the feeling she might actually call on him if something came up. It made his heart light. "So you'll be in town for a while?"

"Yes. I don't know how long Mother's recovery will take, but I'm not going to leave her until she's well." Larkin bit into a chicken leg and looked thoughtful. "I wish I could've brought Granny Jane with me. I'm thinking she knows how to take care of people."

Judd pictured the old woman sitting in her rocking chair, dispensing wisdom to anyone who crossed her path. "She's a treasure," he said and meant it. He felt a pang at the thought that there was now one more person in his life to care about. After Joe died he'd been determined to distance himself from those he loved and not to let anyone else in. Somehow he'd failed in that and he had the strangest feeling Larkin had something to do with it.

Larkin leaned back and laid a hand across her belly. "Oh my. I'm not sure I can eat much more of this, but I hate to disappoint Mason."

"Well, I'm not done yet." Judd swirled some shrimp in tartar sauce and popped them in his mouth.

Larkin watched him eat with a bemused expression on her face. "I missed you while I was gone."

Judd thought the food he'd just swallowed might get stuck and kill him. Or at least embarrass him. He gulped some tea. "You did?"

"Yes. I was pretty determined not to, but . . ."

Judd held his breath, afraid if he spoke he might interrupt her train of thought.

"But that place reminds me of you in so many ways. Those mountains and the people . . . they're straightforward. What you see is what you get. Goodness knows they've made it clear they can get along just fine without me." She leaned forward. "Except with you . . ."

Judd cleared his throat, hoping his voice wouldn't break. "Except what?"

"Mostly I know where you stand on things—you don't pretend

246

or try to fool people. But I'm not sure where you stand on . . . well, me."

"I'm not sure what you're asking."

"I'm going to go out on a limb here, Judd Markley, and tell you that I like you. A lot. I'm just wondering if maybe you feel the same about me."

Judd felt the way he had when the first glimmer of light reached his eyes that day in the mine. Hope bloomed in him, spreading into dry places that he didn't even know needed watering. He could almost hear Joe laughing at him, struck dumb by a pretty girl saying what she felt. For him.

"I . . ." He wanted to stand, to kneel at her feet, but he settled for taking her hand where it rested on the tabletop. "I think you're the most wonderful person I've ever met. You're like sunshine on water. When you went on back to Kentucky, I thought I didn't have a chance. I thought I'd lost you." He gulped air. "Do you really . . . could you really care for me?"

Larkin's laughter was like the sound of rain on a tin roof at the end of a long, hot day. Judd felt soothed, comforted . . . alive.

◆ ▲ ◆

Courting a girl was difficult when that girl was determined to spend every possible moment with her mother as she prepared for and underwent surgery. Judd managed to take Larkin to a movie once—a waste, he thought, since they spent the whole time looking at a screen instead of each other. Then he'd brought flowers and candy the day before Mrs. Heyward's operation. Five days later, he was itching to see "his girl," but didn't want to take her away from her self-designated role as private nurse.

As he headed for his truck on Friday afternoon, pondering the wisdom of stopping by the Heyward home, Hank caught up to him.

"Larkin sent word that if you're free this evening, she is, too." He tilted his head to one side. "You seeing the boss's daughter?"

"Trying to," Judd said, his heart lighter than it had been all week.

Hank nodded and pulled out a pocketknife. He started trimming a ragged fingernail. "You think that's wise?" Before Judd could speak, he hurried to add, "Not that I don't see why you'd want to. Just wonder how it might affect your employment."

"You were there when Mr. Heyward gave me permission to call on her."

Hank nodded, folded his knife, and tucked it deep in a pocket. "I've seen George Heyward make a hundred offers to all kinds of men. I've never seen him come up short in the end. I don't know what he's after—I hope it's nothing more than a good man for his daughter—just thought I'd throw out a word of caution." He slapped Judd on the shoulder. "Not that you'd heed any man's warning when someone as special as Larkin is waiting for you to come take her out." He winked. "If I were you, I'd get cleaned up in record time and get on over there to pick that girl up." He paused. "Say, you know what she'd like? They have dancing at the Kozy Korner, plus you can get a great steak."

Judd nodded. "I'll think on that."

Hank's eyes flicked to Judd's leg. "'Course, dancing isn't for everyone."

"Right," Judd agreed. "I'd best be getting on."

Hank shoved his hands in his pockets. "Sure thing. Hope everything works out for you."

Judd climbed in the truck thinking about how his leg bothered him less these days. Maybe he would take that girl dancing.

💧💧💧

Larkin wondered if Hank had passed her message on to Judd. Surely he would. He'd never let her down before. She changed into a pale-green sweater set with a tweed skirt and brown pumps. She thought it struck the right chord between

248

dressy and casual. Fastening her ponytail, she wondered if it was too soon to leave Mother alone. She'd come home from the hospital the day before in excellent spirits. The doctor was optimistic that the lump he'd removed was benign, and Mother was healing quickly. Larkin dabbed on some lipstick. It might even be time to go back to Kentucky soon. She felt a stab of sorrow at that. As much as she wanted to get back to work helping Ben, leaving Judd behind didn't feel right.

She closed her eyes and whispered a prayer that God would send Judd back to the mountains with her. She opened her eyes when she heard the doorbell. Yes, Judd coming back with her wasn't so very farfetched. After all, that was his world back there in the hills and hollers.

Larkin bounced down the stairs to find Judd standing in the entry dressed in slacks and a shirt open at the collar. He was holding a bouquet of carnations and had a hopeful look on his face.

"These are for your mother," he said, holding out the flowers.

Larkin gave him a quick hug and led him into the kitchen where she put the blooms in a vase. "Mother's napping, but she's doing ever so much better. These will please her when she wakes up." She put the arrangement in the middle of the dining room table and then turned to Judd. "I hope it's not presumptuous of me to invite you to take me out."

"I'm glad you did. I wasn't sure if it was too soon with your mother just getting home."

Larkin smiled. "It was her idea. Now, where are we going?"

Judd's dimples showed. "Come get in the truck and I'll show you."

Larkin squealed and clapped her hands when Judd escorted her into the Kozy Korner. Steaks sizzled, and couples were already on the dance floor as the jukebox pumped out "Mr. Sandman" by the Chordettes.

"Oh, dancing! You remembered."

"Seems like you dance just walking across the floor. Thought you might like to have some music to go with it."

Larkin could barely contain herself as they found a booth and ordered steaks with baked potatoes and salads. As soon as the waitress left, Larkin looked at Judd. "Can we . . . maybe we could squeeze in a dance while we wait for our food?"

Judd laughed and it sounded like it came from somewhere deep inside where it had been trapped for too long. "Don't see why not."

Larkin charged onto the dance floor, then caught herself. "Do you—do you know how?"

"Joe loved to dance and showed me a few steps I think I can remember. I'm no Gene Kelly, but I can manage."

Beaming, Larkin caught his hand and they danced. Judd was right, he wasn't going to win any contests, but he was willing and Larkin had a feeling that was significant for him.

Larkin could have kept going, but after three dances, Judd tugged her back toward the table. "Food's going to get cold if we don't go eat it."

"Oh, have they brought it already?" Larkin felt breathless, not so much from the dancing as from how perfect the evening felt. She followed Judd back to the table, and this time he took her hand and bowed his head without her asking.

"Father, thank you for your many gifts. For Mrs. Heyward being on the mend, for this food, and for the chance to share it with Larkin. Amen."

Larkin wasn't sure she could get any food past the lump in her throat. Judd didn't say a great deal, but what he did say tended to be exactly right. She blinked moisture from her eyes and dug into her steak, realizing she was hungry enough to eat every bite.

◆ ◆ ◆

Judd drove Larkin home, palms sweaty against the steering wheel. He thought the evening had been just about perfect and he wanted to close it out by kissing the angel seated beside him. But the very thought made his heart skip a beat and his vision feel blurry. He swiped a palm on his slacks, hoping she wouldn't notice.

He pulled into the driveway and leapt from the truck, practically running around to open her door before she could even think of opening it herself. She smiled and her ponytail swung as she dropped to the ground, her hand securely in his. He tucked those fingers through the crook of his elbow and walked her to the door. Stars twinkled overhead and the moon hung low, as though as eager to see what would happen as he was.

Larkin set her feet on the bottom step, which still didn't quite raise her up even with Judd. She turned to him. "I had the loveliest evening. Thank you for taking me dancing."

Her eyes danced as prettily as her feet. Judd stopped wondering if it was the right moment and simply leaned in to kiss her perfect, pink lips. She kissed him right back, and Judd thanked the God of second chances for returning her to him.

She sighed and pulled away as if she were sorry about it. "I'd better go in and check on Mother." She giggled. "She said she wanted to hear all about our date, but maybe I won't tell her quite everything."

She gave him one more quick kiss before disappearing inside. Judd just stood there for a moment, basking in moonlight and listening to his heart sing.

CHAPTER

30

"Mother, we'd better get going if you don't want to be late for your appointment." Larkin saw her mother wince as she raised her right arm to style her hair. "I can do that for you."

"I know, but I feel so much better, I want to show off."

She finally picked up a hand mirror and examined her coiffure from all sides. "Oh, I suppose it'll do."

"I doubt Dr. Endicott will even notice your hairstyle."

Mother smiled. "No, but his nurses might."

Larkin laughed. "I had no idea you were quite so vain."

"Didn't you? I thought everyone knew." Mother giggled like a girl and took Larkin's hand in her own. "Let's take your convertible. I know it's too cool to put the top down, but it sounds like fun."

Larkin agreed and tucked her mother in the passenger seat. She was grateful for such a quick recovery and tried to be glad that she could go back to Kentucky soon. But thinking of leaving left her blue. She thought she'd have a clearer picture of what she was meant to do by now. What would it mean for her blossoming relationship with Judd? She hoped he would consider going back home or maybe even coming to Logan. Ben could certainly use

252

his help. She supposed she'd have to talk to Judd about the future soon. Maybe that would clarify the situation for her.

They didn't have to wait long at the doctor's office. Dr. Endicott examined Larkin's mother and then invited both of them into his office.

"I don't often say this sort of thing, but I'm astonished at how well you've done. When we first discovered the lump, I felt certain it was cancer and you would be facing an uphill battle." Larkin darted a look at her mother, who refused to meet her eyes. "I expected . . . well, it doesn't matter now. I'll want to see you again in six weeks, but I genuinely believe you're going to be just fine."

Mother stood, thanked the doctor, and led Larkin out of the office. Once they were in the car, Larkin turned to her mother.

"You said it was nothing."

"And so it was." Mother fished a compact out of her purse and reapplied lipstick.

"But the doctor didn't think so. Why did you tell us it was nothing serious?"

Mother looked at Larkin. "Your father knew it might be serious. I suppose that's why he wrote to you. And I'll confess I was worried myself. I even wondered what would happen to your father if I . . ." She trailed off and took Larkin's hand. "But once you arrived, I had the most amazing peace about everything. And now here we are, and I was right to stop worrying." She touched the tip of Larkin's nose. "And not to worry you and your brother."

Larkin shook her head. "I suppose we could say all's well that ends well, but I hope you won't keep things from me in the future."

Mother laughed and gave her a pointed look. "Only if you promise not to keep anything from me."

Larkin blushed and started the car.

♦♦♦

Judd had been invited to dinner at the Heywards' house again, only this time it wasn't business. This time he was court-ing the boss's daughter and he thought he might throw up. He tried to think what Joe would tell him, but Joe rarely took anything very seriously and nothing helpful came to mind. He walked over to the hall mirror to check his tie again. Floyd ambled toward him.

"Must be something important."

Judd grunted and smoothed down a curl of hair that wouldn't cooperate.

"Job or a girl?"

Judd glanced at the older man. "Girl."

Floyd nodded. "Gonna marry her?"

Judd froze, then lowered his hands. "Might if she'll have me."

"Kind of thought you looked like a man planning to ask somebody's daddy a hard question."

Judd blew out a breath. "You're smarter than you look."

Floyd chuckled. "Life'll teach you some things if you let it. Can I give you a word of advice?"

"Sure, I can use all the help I can get."

"Don't take no for an answer." Floyd slapped Judd on the back. "From either one of them."

◊ ◊ ◊

Dinner was less painful than Judd had expected. George—he asked Judd to call him by his first name—was friendlier than he'd ever been. Mrs. Heyward—Augusta—was welcoming, and Larkin was . . . well, Larkin, which was more than enough for Judd. After they ate, Larkin helped her mother clear the dishes while George invited Judd into the den.

"Care for a drink?" he asked, pouring something amber-colored from a sparkling decanter into a stubby glass.

"Don't believe I do," Judd said. He wasn't sure if he should sit since George was still standing, so he ambled over to the

254

fireplace and admired a photo of Larkin and her parents. He wondered if this was the right time to have that talk with Larkin's father.

George stepped up beside Judd. "She's a fine girl. Maybe a little too wrapped up in dancing and that Pavilion, but a fine girl all the same."

Judd stiffened. "I guess anybody who volunteers at a hospital and goes off to Kentucky to help folks can get away with a little dancing now and then."

George grunted and swallowed some of what was in his glass. "To be honest, I might prefer it if she stayed around here doing her volunteer work." He paused. "What about you?"

"I sure do enjoy having her here," Judd said, not sure where this conversation was headed.

"I was hoping you might be thinking to try and keep her around."

Judd swallowed hard. He wasn't going to get a better opening than that. "Well, sir. We haven't been courting all that long, but I have been thinking about the future. And how I'd like Larkin to be part of that." His mind raced for the right words. Usually, he had no problem saying exactly what he meant without wasting too much breath, but this evening he was having a rough go of it.

"Yes." George nodded helpfully.

Judd figured he'd better spit it out before he choked on it. "When the time's right, I'd like to ask Larkin to be my wife."

His boss chortled and slapped him on the shoulder. "I was hoping you were headed there."

"You were?"

"Sure thing. Good man like you, moving up in the company, taking on more responsibility. There's a real future for you at Waccamaw Timber, and the more we can keep things in the family, the better."

Judd felt confused. He was talking about Larkin, while

255

Mr. Heyward—George—was talking about the company. He rubbed the back of his neck. He could see that the two were tied together, but he hadn't fully considered what that meant until now.

And just like that, a lightbulb went off. If he married Larkin and kept her in South Carolina, she—or perhaps he—could continue being part of Waccamaw Timber. And maybe they would produce an heir to take it on one day. His first thought was to chafe under the weight of such a responsibility, but the more the idea percolated, the more he thought he might enjoy helping to develop the timber company. He'd learned quite a bit already and he thought maybe he could see some ways to improve things—especially for the workers. Yes, if keeping the business in the family through his daughter was what George had in mind, he just might be open to the idea. Could be he didn't need Joe's dream anymore. Could be he had a dream of his own.

George finished his drink and went to pour another. "Sure you won't join me?"

Judd let one corner of his mouth lift. "Maybe I will."

"That's right, celebrate a little." The older man winked and handed Judd a glass that felt cool and weighty in his hand. He liked it. He might even get used to it.

Judd and Larkin walked down to the beach. She'd grabbed a sweater against the cool of the late March evening but hardly needed it. The glow she felt from her mother's recovery, the time with Judd, and her father's apparent approval of their budding relationship was more than enough to keep her warm.

They passed the shuttered Pavilion and stepped out onto the boardwalk. Judd seemed nervous, which Larkin chalked up to dinner with her parents. She was still getting used to the fact that her father was not only tolerating Judd's suit but might even be encouraging it. She hugged herself, and Judd wrapped an arm around her shoulders.

"Cold?"

"Nope, I'm just right."

They gazed out at the moonlit foam curling at the tips of the waves. Larkin breathed in the sharp salt air. It was cooler here, with enough of a breeze to make her glad for the sweater after all. She'd missed the ocean while in Kentucky, though she was surprised to find it didn't tug at her heart the way it once had.

"Larkin, I don't want you to go back to Kentucky." The words poured out of Judd like he hadn't meant to turn them loose.

"You don't?"

He shook his head. "I know working with your brother means a lot to you, but I . . . I was hoping you might want to stick around here." She saw his Adam's apple bob. "With me."

She laughed lightly. "Why, Judd Markley, what are you suggesting?"

He grasped her hand and looked into her eyes. "I'm hoping you might consider . . . being my wife."

Larkin found she couldn't quite process the words. She looked blankly at Judd.

"You don't have to answer me right now. You can think about it. Think about it all you want. I'm just hoping one of these days, maybe when I have a little more money saved up, you might—" he gulped—"marry me."

Larkin laughed, and this time the sound took flight. "Of course I will," she said. "I just didn't think you'd ask."

She thought she saw moisture—could it be tears?—in Judd's eyes. He wrapped both arms around her, pulling her snug against him. "And you'll stay here, in South Carolina, with me?"

Images of Granny Jane and Kyle sitting in the pews while Ben stood behind the pulpit of the little church flicked through her mind. Now it was her turn to swallow hard. "If that's what you want," she whispered. "Where my husband goes, I go."

Judd let out a whoop that startled and delighted Larkin. She giggled, but the sound was stifled by Judd's kiss. She leaned into him with a sigh and tried not to think about Kentucky and everything she was giving up.

CHAPTER

31

"We should tell your parents," Judd said, leaning back but not releasing Larkin.

She raised her eyebrows. "I suppose we should, but I'm surprised you're so eager. What if they don't approve?"

Judd tucked her head against his shoulder. "I asked your father for permission."

"You did?" Larkin was more shocked now than when Judd proposed. "And he agreed?"

Judd shrugged. "He might have even encouraged me."

Larkin tried to enjoy the feeling of being held in Judd's strong arms, yet something niggled in the back of her mind. "Daddy's usually not so . . . cooperative."

A deep chuckle rumbled under her cheek. "Don't I know it? Might be he's hoping I'll keep you around here."

Larkin stiffened. Of course. Daddy knew she was drawn to his hired mountain man and saw his chance to pull her back home for good—after luring her back with news of her mother. She was partly annoyed that her father was manipulating her and partly confused that he'd want to. Did he dislike his own son so much that he didn't want Larkin to have anything to do with him? She glanced up at Judd, who was gazing out to sea with a contented look on his face as he tangled his fingers in her ponytail.

Sighing, Larkin whispered that they'd better head on home. She didn't understand what her father was after, but she supposed she should be glad that their desires seemed to be coinciding for once.

◆▲◆

After the news of Judd's engagement to Larkin got around, the men at work treated him differently. He tried not to mind but felt as though everyone were tiptoeing every time he set foot on a job. Even Hank and Chuck acted different.

On the first Monday in April, Hank swung by the work site around lunchtime. Judd eased down beside him where he sat on a log eating a sandwich. Judd unwrapped two pieces of cold fried chicken and bit into a leg. Larkin had started fixing his lunch several times a week, and he had to admit it was nice to have something other than Vienna sausages and saltines.

They ate in silence a moment.

"You and Larkin set a date yet?" Hank asked.

Judd tried not to grin but couldn't help himself. "October. I'm ready to marry her tomorrow, but it seems her mother needs at least six months to plan a wedding." He laughed. "Might be in over my head."

Hank ate his last bite of sandwich and dusted his hands together. "You mind if I ask you something straight out?"

"Nope."

"You taking over Waccamaw Timber Company?"

Judd tossed a chicken bone back in the weeds. Of course Hank would know details like that. "Don't rightly know."

"If you were anybody else, I'd suspect you of marrying that girl to get in with the company." Hank sighed. "Guess I trust you more than Mr. Heyward, though. Don't get me wrong. I think Larkin's lucky to have you, and I'm betting you'd do a fine job of managing the company." He braced his elbows on his knees and stared at the ground between his feet. "At the same time, I've worked with George Heyward a long time and seems like he's usually working an angle." He looked at Judd sideways. "Keep an eye out."

Judd nodded. "Been through a mine collapse and a hurricane in the past year. I can handle myself."

Hank laughed, but it sounded hollow. "Natural disasters got nothing on George Heyward when he sets his sights on a target. You just make sure you don't find a bull's-eye painted across your chest one day."

∴

Larkin tried to take an interest in choosing colors for her wedding. A few years ago, this sort of thing would have been a dream come true. Colors and clothes and cake and flowers and music, and oh, why did it feel like a gauntlet she had to pass through rather than the joy she'd once imagined?

"We'll have roses, of course," her mother was saying. "Ivory for the base color, but we can spice it up a little. What do you think of burgundy? Or would you rather go lighter and have more of a peachy-orange color? If you can keep a tan, it would look lovely with your skin."

"Lighter would be nice," Larkin said, trying to put some thought into it.

"I was hoping you'd lean that direction. Now, I called Nell and Patty to see if they could go dress shopping with us tomorrow. We'll have lunch at the Dunes Club and then shop all afternoon if need be." Her mother was practically brimming over with excitement. "Won't this be fun?"

Larkin smiled, unable to resist her mother's enthusiasm, especially since she'd given them such a scare. "Yes, it'll be fun to go shopping with Nell and Patty."

Her mother wasn't really paying attention. "Take these magazines and see if you can find a hairstyle you like. I think you should wear it up, maybe with a small tiara or comb, but that's up to you."

Larkin almost laughed out loud. She was marrying a West Virginia mountain boy, and her mother thought a tiara would be appropriate. She'd much rather put on a nice dress, scoop her hair into its usual ponytail, and stand up in front of the justice of the peace. Judd wasn't going to know what to make of all this fuss.

Taking the magazines, Larkin went out and sat on the back steps, where she could soak up the April sun. She glanced at the Debutante Camellia Mother planted the year she had her coming out. She thought how it would be covered in delicate pink blooms in October. She wished she could persuade her mother to let her pick a bouquet of her own to carry down the aisle.

Then she looked at the shrub more closely. Quite a few of the leaves were yellow, and too many had fallen to the ground. It even looked a bit wilted. Furrowing her brow, Larkin went to the gardening shed for clippers and maybe some fertilizer. She'd have to pay more attention—she didn't want her camellia suffering because she was too busy to tend it.

$$\bullet \spadesuit \spadesuit$$

"Our dresses are so pretty. I can't believe you just let us pick what we wanted." Patty gushed as she sat with Nell and Larkin on the Heywards' screened porch, sipping lemonade and discussing the day's finds.

Nell let her head fall back against the cushions. "I feel like a package all wrapped up for Christmas with that luscious coral sash."

Patty giggled. "Would that be a present for my big brother by any chance?"

Nell flushed. "Don't talk like that unless you think he might, you know, ask me."

"Leon has never been quick to catch on, but I'm thinking all this wedding talk might give him an idea." Patty leaned forward. "Say, Larkin, you and Judd should double with Nell and Leon, maybe give my poor brother some hint about what he should do next."

Larkin forced a smile. "Sure, we could do that. Maybe get a hamburger and see a movie." Not that she wanted to. All this wedding nonsense was giving her a headache. Nearly every day. It all seemed so frivolous, while Granny Jane was sitting in her cabin with a wardrobe that would just about fit in Larkin's overnight bag. And Kyle had never eaten in a restaurant or seen a movie.

"Do you think your mother will give in and let you get that tea-length dress?" Patty was eager to continue talking about the wedding.

Larkin sighed and tried to care. "I don't see why not, so long as the wedding's in the afternoon." She wanted to roll her eyes. Wedding etiquette was beyond frivolous.

"I thought you were going to have an evening ceremony with a sit-down dinner. That's what I'd like to do." Nell looked wistful.

"That was Mother's idea, but I'd prefer something simple in the afternoon with just cake and a few light refreshments afterwards. I don't think Judd would know what to do at a formal dinner." She felt a genuine smile spread across her face. "And I'm kind of glad about that."

"Aren't you the rebel," Patty said. Then she wrinkled her nose, looking at the table next to her. "What happened to your green thumb? I thought you could get anything to grow, but this spider plant is positively awful looking. You need to pitch it and start over."

Larkin frowned as she pinched a wilted stem between her fingers. She'd been fussing with this poor plant all week and it was getting worse. She couldn't think what she was doing wrong. Not to mention the poor camellia outside.

She shrugged. "Oh well. Mother said that thing was taking over out here anyway. Maybe it's time to let it go."

Patty's attention had already turned back to bridesmaids' gowns and bouquets. Larkin did her best to take an interest.

CHAPTER

32

J udd combed his hair, trying a dab of pomade one of the men at work recommended. It wasn't something he'd ever thought to put in his hair before, but he wanted to fit into Larkin's world, and those fellows he'd seen down at the Pavilion last summer had fancy hair.

He climbed in his truck and considered whether or not he ought to trade it in for a sedan. The truck was more practical, but maybe Larkin would be more comfortable in a four-door something or other.

He pushed the thought aside and drove through the streets that were getting busier as the weather grew warmer. Most of the evidence of the hurricane had been removed or repaired, yet there were still signs of it here and there. A gap where a business once stood. A house still being worked on. A view to the ocean that was inexplicably different. Healing took time, even for a town.

It would be summer again soon, but first Judd had to get through the anniversary of Joe's death. He gripped the steering wheel tighter. Thank goodness he had Larkin's love to see him through. He hadn't mentioned to her that the date was coming up, but he would tonight and he felt certain she'd understand the confusing mix of emotions percolating through him.

Larkin was quiet as he handed her up into the truck. He suggested they go see a drive-in movie, and she nodded like she wasn't quite paying attention. He parked, settled the speaker on his open window, and offered to go get some popcorn. Larkin nodded and smoothed her skirt over her knees, staring out the windshield, but somehow Judd got the feeling she didn't really see the screen up ahead.

Returning, Judd handed the popcorn to Larkin and settled a soda with two straws on the seat between them. He sat and rubbed his leg where he could still feel scars beneath the fabric of his slacks.

"Almost the anniversary of the day I busted this leg," he said.

Larkin turned, looking interested for the first time all evening. "You mean when the mine caved in?"

"That'd be the day," Judd said. He ate a piece of popcorn, quiet settling in the cab like dust on a still afternoon.

Larkin gasped. "Which means it's been almost a year since Joe died."

Judd felt his eyes prickle. "Yup. It's been weighing on me lately. I feel kind of, I don't know, guilty that my life's turned out so good and his is . . . gone. It's almost like I've taken on what should have been his."

Larkin touched his hand where he held the soda bottle. "From what you've told me, he'd be awfully glad to know you're doing well." She smiled and swiped at her eye with her other hand. "Got a good job, got a girl." Her voice softened. "Getting married."

Judd wanted to wash the lump in his throat down with soda, but no way was he going to pull away from Larkin's touch. "Joe always did like a party—even the kind where folks ended up married at the end." He tilted his head back and blinked his eyes. "He would have been my best man."

Larkin slid across the seat, scooping up the soda and setting it on the passenger-side floorboard. She snuggled under Judd's arm. "I'm glad you told me. I'm glad we'll get through this anniversary together." She tilted her face toward his. "And I'm even more glad you're still alive."

Judd felt something break loose in his chest. He'd tolerated being alive for the past year. Tolerated breathing and eating and working because he didn't know what else to do. Went to sleep each night and woke each morning because it was what his body demanded. But gazing down into Larkin's blue eyes swimming with unshed tears, he felt, for the first time in a long time, glad just to be alive.

"Me too," he whispered and then kissed those soft, pink lips.

Larkin told herself she could do this. She could get married and stay in South Carolina and do volunteer work and learn to play bridge at the country club and live the life she'd once thought she wanted more than anything. She could do it for Judd.

Who would have thought a lanky fellow from the mountains of West Virginia would be the reason she held on to her life as a socialite rather than giving it all up to do mission work in Appalachia? The irony was not lost on her.

Never mind that, except in those moments when she was alone with Judd, she thought her old life might suffocate her. She promised herself it would be different once they were married. Surely they would have children and then she'd be too busy for anything else. That brought a smile, but Larkin barely trusted herself anymore.

She resumed fitting items into a pasteboard box to send off to Logan, Kentucky, where Ben would share it with Granny Jane and Maude and Kyle and anyone else who needed socks, coffee, tea, a new Bible, or chocolate. Larkin smiled. Actually, the chocolate was for Granny and Kyle to share. She'd explain that in the letter to Ben.

Her brother had already promised he'd come home for her wedding, but Larkin wished he could bring everyone else from Logan with him, too. It astonished her how quickly she'd become attached in the short time she was there. Granny would love sleeping in the guest bedroom, not to mention experiencing indoor plumbing. But she supposed that wasn't to be. Sighing, she went to the desk to begin writing her letter.

∘◆◆

Judd was worried about Larkin. She just didn't sparkle the way he'd gotten used to. He remembered the first time he'd seen her, glowing like she not only absorbed the sunshine but internalized it and sent it back out into the world. Lately she seemed cloudy. Judd was on his way to church and Sunday dinner with the Heywards and he meant to get a few minutes alone with Larkin to ask her if she was sure she wanted to marry him. He hoped it wasn't cold feet, but he thought he'd better ask.

During church, Judd only half listened to the songs and found it difficult to focus on the sermon. Then Pastor Brearley said something that hit Judd right between the eyes. Or rather, he read it. "'The people that walked in darkness have seen a great light: they that dwell in the land of the shadow of death, upon them hath the light shined.'"

The shadow of death. Judd had felt that shadow there in the mine and maybe it had been the shadow of Joe's death hanging over him ever since. But now that he'd asked Larkin to marry him, his world was getting ever brighter. He glanced at Larkin, gazing at the pastor with an expression that told him her mind was elsewhere. It was as if she'd taken on the shadow he'd been carrying around.

As soon as they stepped out into the April sunshine after the service, Judd grasped Larkin's arm. "Let's walk back to your house. Pretty day for a stroll."

She nodded and smiled, but it didn't light her eyes. "Just let me tell Mother."

In a moment, she was back by his side, linking her arm through his and strolling along the sidewalk in her pale-green dress with the dark green ribbon accentuating her waist. A waist Judd thought might be even smaller than it was a month before.

"Been thinking about home lately."

Her eyes lit briefly, then dimmed again. "Because of Joe."

"No. Well, some. But mostly I've been thinking about home because of you."

Larkin looked a question at him.

"I've never seen you as happy as you were helping those folks back in Kentucky." Laughing softly, he added, "Maybe not even when I asked you to marry me."

"Oh, Judd. Marrying you is what I want more than anything, but I can't deny I have the strangest longing to go back to Logan. I don't understand it and I trust it will pass, but that place felt like . . . home to me."

Judd laid a hand over hers where it rested in the crook of his arm. "Might be I know something about wanting what you can't have. And maybe I haven't wanted to go back to the mountains because that's where Joe's supposed to be." He squinted up, watching a sea gull swoop and circle before heading on out to sea. "But maybe there's room to build something new back there. Maybe even in a town where Joe never set foot but with people he'd like almost as good as his own family." He glanced down at Larkin, who had the most hopeful expression on her face. "People like Ben and Kyle and Granny Jane."

Larkin squealed and threw her arms around Judd's neck. "Are you saying we can live in Logan?"

"I'm saying it might be worth a shot. Might be good for both of us."

She laughed so loud that people driving by turned their heads. "When can we go?"

"Now, hold on there." Judd wrapped his arms around her and eased her back down on solid ground. "First, we'd better get married and I'd better save every penny your father's paying me so we'll have a little something to live on. There's timbering in that part of the country, but I doubt it pays what it does here." He chuckled and eased Larkin away so they could resume walking and not create more of a spectacle than they already had. "Plus, your family may not be too happy with this turn of events."

Larkin flipped her ponytail and practically skipped along beside him. "They'll be fine, I just know it." She gasped and turned to look Judd in the face. "I could go back there now, spend a month or two finding us a place to live, and Ben could ask around about jobs."

Judd wished he could put the brakes on this train, but since he was the one who started it down the tracks, he guessed he'd have to ride along. "We can talk about that, sure." He glanced down at his soon-to-be bride, wondering if giving up the running of a timber company was a smart thing to do. But then he saw that Larkin's light was back on and sunshine shot from her fingertips. He smiled and supposed whatever trouble they were about to walk into would be worth it.

◊◊◊

Larkin bought a bus ticket for the following week before she told her parents, or even Judd, exactly when she planned to leave. She thought she'd need the assurance of an escape route to steel herself.

On Sunday, she sat down to breakfast with her parents. Mother stared out the window as Daddy read the paper. Larkin scooped some eggs and sausage on her plate and cleared her throat.

"So Judd and I agreed that I'd make a trip back to Kentucky this week to check on Ben and some of the folks back there." She focused on buttering a slice of toast as her father's paper slowly lowered.

"I don't see as that's necessary," he said. "I'll have a word with Judd."

Larkin felt panic stir in her belly. "We've already decided, and I have my ticket." She tried to think how to reassure her parents but couldn't come up with anything short of lying, which she was maybe doing a little bit already.

Now the paper was completely down, Daddy crumpling it. "You'll stay here and help your mother prepare for this wedding."

Larkin sipped her coffee. "The wedding is well in hand. Mother doesn't need me. I need to see that Kyle's doing his exercises and help Granny Jane get her garden ready."

Her father's face turned red and he stood. "Of all the ridiculous . . . I will have that word with Judd and you won't be going anywhere." He pointed a finger at her but spoke to her mother. "Augusta, if she leaves the state, I will hold you personally responsible." Then he stalked from the room.

Larkin exhaled and slumped back in her chair. She looked into her mother's sad eyes. "I need to go."

Mother leaned forward and took her hand. "Your father has already seen one child defy him, and now you're headed down the same path. I'm not saying he's right, but he's surely struggling. Give him a little time. Try to understand what he's feeling."

Larkin squeezed her mother's hand. "If he's feeling frustrated, then I know exactly what he's feeling."

◆ ◆ ◆

Judd whistled as he sharpened a chainsaw. The sun was shining, Larkin was happy again, and he'd soon be married. Things might not be working out exactly the way he'd planned, but they were mighty fine nonetheless.

"Markley."

Judd jerked his head up at the brusque voice calling his name. Mr. Heyward—George, he reminded himself—was striding toward him. This was odd. He'd seen the boss on a jobsite only once before.

"Yes, sir." He opted not to use his boss's first name based on the thunderclouds in his face.

"What's this nonsense about Larkin going back to Kentucky?"

Judd tensed. "She's been so unhappy—I'm sure you've noticed—and going back is what she wants more than anything."

Mr. Heyward looked as though he might be about to have another fit like he did in the country store. He breathed in deeply and held the air a moment. Then he exhaled and spoke softly. "The only reason I agreed to let you court my daughter was to keep her here. If you can't manage that, you're of no use to me."

Judd felt like he'd been struck. "I don't understand."

"Keep her in South Carolina or I'll find someone else she can marry. You understand that?" Mr. Heyward turned and walked away.

Judd hitched his pant leg and sat on the tailgate of the truck where he was working. He watched his employer climb in his car and drive away. This clinched it. George Heyward only wanted him as a son-in-law so he could hold on to the company by way of Larkin. And if he and Larkin went to Kentucky, Mr. Heyward would be right back where he started with the future leadership of his business in limbo.

The problem was, Judd had come to care what happened to Waccamaw Timber Company. Larkin might be anxious to go back to the mountains—and Judd had no doubt she'd go regardless of what her father wanted—but Judd was only considering it to please her. He looked around the jobsite at the men muscling timber into place. He breathed in the scent of cut pine and listened to the hum of machinery. He'd come to enjoy his work and was pretty good at it. Mr. Heyward had given him more opportunities than he ever had when he worked the mines. He'd managed to take his brother's dream and turn it into a solid future. But back in the mountains . . . it was sure to be rough going. He'd have to scratch out a living above ground or reconcile himself to mining. He hopped down off the tailgate and went back to work. He found himself hoping this trip back to Kentucky would help Larkin get her need to do good up there out of her system once and for all. Folks hadn't exactly welcomed Larkin's meddling with open arms, so maybe if things didn't go so good . . . well, it surely would simplify things.

CHAPTER
33

Judd and Floyd sat in dining room chairs in front of the boardinghouse. Judd seemed to have way too much time to think and not near enough clarity about what to do. When he tried to talk to Larkin about her father's stance, she said it didn't matter a bit. Then she got on a bus and left for Kentucky. That was a week ago, and Judd still felt torn between his love for Larkin and his loyalty to Mr. Heyward. Judd whittled a stick, aimlessly sending shavings into the dry grass while Floyd smoked and told stories about working tobacco. Judd thought it sounded just about as bad as mining coal.

A pickup truck rounded the corner, and Hank pulled to a stop in the street. He climbed out and walked toward Judd, head down, feet dragging. Something deep inside Judd seized up.

"Judd, Mr. Heyward sent me over here." Judd swallowed hard. Might be he was fired. He wondered if George Heyward had enough pull to ban Judd from the state of South Carolina.

Hank continued. "They just got a phone call from Ben up there in Kentucky." He shoved his hands in his pockets and took a deep breath. "Larkin's gone missing."

Judd found himself on his feet, almost nose to nose with

Hank without remembering standing up. "What do you mean, 'missing'?"

Hank rubbed the back of his neck. "Apparently, she and some boy went off on a picnic or some such, and they have yet to come home."

Kyle. Judd would bet his last dollar it was Kyle she'd taken on a picnic. And here he was back in South Carolina hoping things would go badly for her. He set his mouth in a grim line. Guess he'd gotten his wish.

"Sounds like most of Logan is out looking for them. Mr. Heyward thought you'd want to know."

Judd squinted at the sky. It was after lunch on a lazy Sunday afternoon. If he started now, he could be in Logan before midnight. He debated leaving with just his wallet and the clothes on his back, but decided to take five minutes to throw a duffel together.

"If you want, you can tell the Heywards I'm on my way up there." He took a step toward the door. "I won't be in to work tomorrow. If Mr. Heyward doesn't like that, he can find another man to fix his equipment. Might be he's going to anyway."

Hank nodded, then reached out and grasped Judd's forearm in a firm but gentle grip. "I have a feeling if anyone can find those two, it's you. George Heyward's a fool at times, but I expect he had a fair idea what you'd do when you heard the news."

◦ ◦ ◦

Judd pulled up at Ben's living quarters behind the church just after midnight. Late as it was, the whole place was lit up and people milled around. He could see Maude through the window, carrying plates of food to men who looked dirty and tired. Judd watched, hope welling, as though he might spy Larkin helping and discover it had all been a mistake. But her figure didn't appear and he went on inside.

Ben spotted him immediately. "I had a feeling you'd show up."

"Any word?" Judd felt his brow furrow and mouth tighten, but he couldn't smile for all of Solomon's gold.

Ben shook his head. "Afraid not. Saturday was so nice, Larkin decided to take Kyle for a picnic lunch. They were supposed to follow Kettle Run till they found a pretty spot, then come on back in plenty of time for Larkin to help with supper. We started looking for them around five when there'd been no sign of them." He blew out a breath and shook his head. "We've been looking ever since."

"Have you found anything? Any sign of where they might have gone?" Judd felt desperate, as though if he asked the right question, it might free Ben to give him an answer he liked.

"Found where they had their picnic, we think. There were some eggshells and the grass looked mashed down. At one point, we thought we had their trail, but . . ." Ben's voice faded to nothing.

"But what?"

Ben scrubbed a hand through his hair. "There was some torn fabric. I'm pretty sure it was from Larkin's skirt." He hung his head. "Had blood on it."

Judd strode toward the door. "Show me where."

Ben darted after him and laid a restraining hand on his arm. "Judd. It's pitch-black out there. I'm not sure I could even find the place in the dark. We need to wait until first light."

Judd stared out into the inky darkness. He could feel the people in the room staring at him. They wanted to find Larkin and Kyle almost as bad as he did and they knew this country. He let his shoulders sag. "First light."

"Good. Eat a bite and see if you can get some sleep." Ben started to turn away, then stopped. "And pray. God knows where they are."

Judd didn't doubt it. He just hoped it wasn't because they were with God.

💧💧💧

The stars mocked Judd. He tried to sleep after choking down a bowl of stew he knew he'd need to keep his strength up. Finally, he slipped outside while Ben and Paul—Maude's son—snored on their cots. The rest of the crowd had gone home, promising to return with the sun.

Judd tilted his head back and considered that it was Monday now, April eighteenth. One year ago tomorrow he'd walked into a mine he'd been carried out of before nightfall. As had Joe. Only his brother wasn't breathing, wasn't marveling at how bright a lantern could shine after utter blackness. Judd wished he could gather up light and carry it with him now. Not just a flashlight or a lantern, but the kind of light that shone into all the dark corners. The kind of light he'd seen as the sun rose over the ocean, falling against everything in its path, defining whatever it touched. Larkin carried light like that, and he realized he'd go anywhere and do anything just so her light could shine on him. He bowed his head, closed his eyes and prayed that wherever she was, her light was still shining.

◊◊◊

"Ready?" Ben offered Judd a cold biscuit with a slice of ham.

"Been ready," Judd said, shaking his head at the food.

Ben wrapped the biscuit in a handkerchief and pushed it at Judd. "You'll want something to eat eventually."

Judd took it and dropped it into the pocket of his hunting jacket. He'd hardly needed a coat in South Carolina all winter, but it felt good on this cool, spring morning.

"What's your plan?" Ben asked.

"Show me where they ate and we'll go from there."

Ben nodded, motioned for Paul to join them, and headed for the bottoms where he picked up a trail along Kettle Run. They hiked briskly, warming quickly as the pale light gave way to day. Judd considered eating his biscuit after all, but didn't want to be slowed down even a second. He'd slurped a mug of coffee before they lit out and he could feel it sloshing against his ribs, giving him a sour feeling.

"Here." Ben pulled up and pointed to a grassy spot where the trees opened and water splashed into a small pool.

Paul crouched down and poked at the grass and leaves. He didn't have much to say, which suited Judd just fine. He looked around. He could almost see Larkin sitting on that rock, a handkerchief over her knee while she peeled an egg for Kyle. He closed his eyes, and when he opened them again, it was almost as if the sun glowed brighter there, where he imagined her sitting and smiling back at him. He blinked his eyes and noticed a gap in the brush opposite the clearing.

"That a trail?"

"Animal trail most likely," Paul volunteered. "Some of them other fellers followed it a ways, but couldn't find nothing promising."

"Let's try it again," Judd said.

They headed out along what was little more than a narrow groove worn through last year's leaves. Branches slapped at Judd's face, but someone smaller, more petite could pass through here without too much trouble.

The trail grew steeper and the hillside rockier. Judd stopped to get his bearings. He looked around, listened so hard his head hurt, and tried to think where a curious boy and a woman who'd grown up on flatland might have gone.

A bird hopped on a branch and flashed red-spotted wings at Judd. It was a red-winged blackbird that had found a patch of sunlight where he could trill his *oh-ka-lee* over and over. Judd felt a smile quirk his lips and fought it. Larkin would love to see that. He was a little surprised to see the bird in the woods like this—they usually preferred the edges of pasture-land. The blackbird flew down the hill, and it occurred to Judd that a boy and a woman unaccustomed to climbing probably wouldn't climb. He scanned the terrain, saw a mass of rhododendron up ahead, and figured that would have turned them.

Judd looked back at Ben and Paul, who stood waiting as though they had all the time in the world. Larkin and Kyle had been missing most of two days now. Judd fought the panic that welled up inside him. He tilted his head down the hillside, and Ben nodded. Choosing a likely path, Judd curved back down toward the creek.

As they went, he noticed the trees opening up and the woods getting brighter. He stepped out and saw the red-winged black-bird perched on a dead tree, its head back and throat wide open. A brown, speckled female flitted nearby and answered. There was an old, overgrown road coming in from the far side.

Paul brightened. "Hey, I know this place. They's an old mine around here somewheres. Local folks used to come scrounge coal. Been a few years since I been here, though."

Judd's gut twisted. Kyle had mentioned abandoned mines, and he'd warned him in no uncertain terms to stay away. If he remembered being a boy rightly, that would make showing them to Larkin more tempting than ever. He turned slowly, examining the terrain all around. The hill sloping up from the creek was steeper here, and Judd thought he saw something dark up among the branches.

"That the mine opening up there?" he asked.

Paul squinted. "Seems about right."

Judd felt something cold squeezing him from the inside out. He'd planned never to step foot in another mine. Much less a run-down old mine that probably hadn't ever been stable to begin with.

"Guess I'll go have a look-see," he said, climbing up the hill. Ben and Paul clambered after him.

Judd pushed some overgrown brush away from the opening and examined it closely. He thought he could see scuffs in the dirt—like someone had knelt and crawled inside. He shuddered.

Might have been an animal. What kind of fool would crawl into an abandoned mine? He pictured Kyle with his bright, curious eyes and his penchant for getting involved in whatever they were doing. He guessed he knew what kind of fool, and Larkin was just the sort of fool to go in after him. The very best kind of fool. He took a deep breath. And that was the kind of fool he wanted to be.

CHAPTER
34

A in't safe to go in there." Paul stood well back from the opening.

"Don't I know it," Judd said.

"If they went in there and haven't come out on their own . . ." Paul trailed off. "Don't bode well for 'em."

"I know that, too." Judd took in Ben's pinched expression. "Might just be some animal sign, but we won't rest easy until we check."

Ben nodded and moved toward the opening. Judd reached out and laid a hand on his chest. "I have more experience crawling into a hole in the ground than you do." He looked around. "Don't suppose you have a rope or a flashlight tucked up in your pocket?"

Ben chuckled like he'd been waiting for something to take the pressure off. "I surely don't. If you want to wait a minute, I can go back to the church and see what I can find."

"Naw. Let me see if it looks likely, then you might send Paul back for tools, along with water and some blankets just in case."

Ben smiled, but it didn't quite reach his eyes. "Thinking positive. I like that." He stepped aside to talk to Paul.

Judd crouched down and peered into the opening. It got dark quick in there. He felt something cold creep along his spine and burrow deep in his belly. Entering that black hole was just about the last thing he wanted to do.

Then he pictured Larkin, all coppery hair and glowing skin. Maybe there was at least one thing worth crawling into hell after. He gritted his teeth and eased through the opening.

Inside, it was clear the mine had never been big enough for a man to stand in. He felt the walls all around. It hadn't been shored up properly, either. He called Larkin's name, but his voice sounded hoarse, low. Clearing his throat, he tried again, louder this time. He stopped to listen, straining his ears, and shuddered at how much it reminded him of those first conscious moments after the cave-in. He'd listened with every fiber of his being then, too. And heard the same thing. Silence.

Judd moved deeper, wishing for any kind of light. The darkness was far worse than the tight space. Maybe he should have waited until Ben could go round up a flashlight. He felt his pockets, hoping there might be a book of matches he'd forgotten about. All he found was the biscuit that he couldn't choke down if he wanted to, dry as his mouth was. He kept going, trailing a hand along the wall to his right to make sure there weren't any side tunnels.

"Larkin." He tried again. "Larkin and Kyle, if you're in here, I'm coming to get you."

Judd felt certain the shaft wouldn't go very far or deep, and he tried to keep mental track of the distance. He was calculating in his mind as he crawled when his hand came down on some loose stone. He stopped and felt all around. Could be a dead end or a cave-in. The rubble at his knees made him think the latter.

"Larkin, Kyle, you in here?" His voice sounded thin, like it wasn't going anywhere. He called louder. Nothing.

Judd began to shift loose rock, taking care so as not to set off a worse fall. He doubted he could move enough to tell anything—even if it was a cave-in, he had no way of know-ing if it had happened recently or five years ago. He held his breath as he dug a little deeper with his bare hands.

After a few minutes, Judd realized this wasn't getting him anywhere. He needed to go get a light, a rope, and some tools. Then he could come back and decide if this was a likely spot to find Larkin and Kyle.

Judd turned and placed his left hand on the wall. He blinked. He could have sworn he saw a light. He knew how staring into the darkness could sometimes make your brain send false light to your eyes and told himself that's all it was. But just to be sure, he looked back at the wall of rubble. Yes. There. The softest glow. He blinked some more, but the faint luminescence near the top of the tunnel to the right didn't fade. Judd scuttled back to the mine entrance, told Ben and Paul to get lights, picks, shovels, and men to help.

"I saw . . ." He started to say *light* when he realized how crazy that sounded. "I saw what looked like a recent cave-in. Could be them."

Ben nodded, Paul shrugged, and Judd turned to reenter the dark opening.

"Best wait on us," Paul said.

"Not on your life," Judd answered and crawled as fast as he could back to that dim, almost indiscernible light.

💧💧💧

"Glowworms."

Paul, headlamp bobbing, was the first to reach Judd, whose digging had slowed. He could feel where he'd torn a nail and knew his flesh was raw. Paul pressed a pick handle into his hand and waved toward the hint of light lingering beyond the circle of the lamp.

"You sometimes see them worms back in caves and such. Strange critters."

Judd felt like he couldn't get a full breath. He stopped, hung his head a moment, and rested on his haunches. "Anyone else out there?"

"Ben and two other fellers. I come in to spell ya. Ben said he'd come in once you come out."

"I wasn't planning on leaving here until we find them."

Paul shrugged and handed over his headlamp. "I'll let Ben come in and take a stab at it, then. Can't say as I like it in here." He disappeared back up the shaft, following the rope he'd brought down with him.

Judd shined the light over what he'd done so far and was disappointed at how pitiful his progress was. He almost wished Ben would stay outside. There wasn't much room for shifting dirt and rocks with just him there. He blew out air and swung the pick as best he could, dislodging a satisfying mass of debris. As it fell away, he thought he felt a puff of air, cool and soft, brush past his cheek. He closed his eyes, leaning into it. Then he switched off the headlamp and opened his eyes again.

Light. He could see light. Must be a whole herd of glow-worms. He swung the pick again and again, hurrying now, feeling an urgency to gain on the fall before Ben reached him.

"Help."

Judd froze. Had he heard something? A voice whispering in the dark?

"Larkin? Kyle? You in there?"

"I want my mama."

Judd heard the catch and the sob. That was Kyle, sure as anything. He worked like a man on fire, talking as he dug.

"Kyle, you hang on." Swing, jerk. "We're almost there." The pick sunk in, barely moving any dirt this time. "We'll have you out in no time." Swing, jerk, and the sound of rocks falling. "Larkin with you?"

Judd stopped, chest heaving. He listened with every ounce of his being.

"Yes."

"Is she okay?"

There were snuffly sounds, and Kyle was quiet too long. Finally, he said, "I don't know. She's awful still."

Judd felt as if a hand had closed over his throat, and he wanted to reach up and pry it away, finger by finger. He steadied himself with the pick and told himself Kyle was just a child. He didn't know what he was talking about. The important thing was that they'd been found.

A hand—a real one—closed over Judd's shoulder.

"I hear you talking to someone. Hallelujah. Our prayers have been answered."

Judd switched on his headlamp so he could see Ben as well as the fall of dirt before them. There was an opening at the top— just enough to talk through. Judd examined the shaft all around.

"Need to be careful about opening this up. There's instability here. Could make it worse if we're not careful."

Ben blew out a slow breath. "Let's pray."

Judd felt a moment of confusion, then bowed his head. Couldn't hurt.

"Father, we're in a tricky spot here, but you sent a coal miner in to do the job. Please guide us in the work you have set before us. In your Son's holy name, amen."

Judd raised his head and looked at Ben. It wasn't the prayer he'd expected. His own prayer might have been more along the lines of God seeing to it that Larkin left this dark hole in the ground unscathed. But he guessed maybe God had brought him here and given him a job to do.

"Let's get to it," he said. They began to work the opening larger, little by cautious little.

◆ ◆

Kyle crawled out first. Ben showed him the rope leading back to the opening and told him to start up the shaft slow and easy.

"Maude should be out there by now. I'll be surprised if she doesn't have some good food and a warm blanket just for you."

The boy looked at them, his face serious. "I'll be staying here to help you get Larkin out."

Judd nodded and crawled through the gap to where he could see Larkin's feet in shoes never made for walking in the woods, much less going into a mine. She was so perfectly still. He heard Ben urging Kyle to go on, they'd be out in a minute, but the conversation was soon lost in the roaring coming from somewhere inside him. He laid a hand on Larkin's ankle. Cold—so very cold. He shined the light along the length of her, noting her torn skirt, spotted with blood. He forced himself to keep looking until he came to her face.

Her eyes were closed, expression serene. Her hair glinted through the grime, and she was somehow brighter than the lamp he wore. He reached out a shaking hand to touch her cheek and was surprised to leave a smudge of blood and dirt there. He glanced at his torn, dirty hand, noting the damage and not caring.

"Larkin."

She didn't move. Not even a flutter of an eyelid.

Judd crawled closer and held his hand beneath her nose, trying to feel for breath. He wasn't sure. Couldn't be sure. He lowered his face until his cheek was almost touching her lips. He closed his eyes, tears washing his face.

And then . . . a puff of air. He could feel her breath whispering in and out. It was like suddenly coming awake from a nightmare—reality was disorienting and hard to grasp. He brushed a wisp of hair from her cheek. This time her eyelids fluttered.

"Judd. I knew you'd find us." Her voice was rough, hoarse, and utterly beautiful.

"Never any doubt," he said.

Tears welled in her eyes. "Is this the anniversary?"

Judd furrowed his brow. What was she talking about? Was

286

her mind addled? Then he remembered. "Joe. That's right. No, tomorrow will be a year since he . . ."

"Died in a mine." Larkin pushed herself up to lean on one arm. "In a cave-in. And I had to go and drag you back down into the dirt and the dark." Tears tracked her grimy cheeks. "I'm so sorry. Kyle was playing a trick on me—hiding in the mine. I could hear him giggling, but he wouldn't come out so I followed him in. It was a ridiculous game."

Judd gathered her to him, wrapping her tight in the confined space, cradling her against his chest where she cried out fear and grief as though for the both of them. He rocked her gently, soothing himself as much as her, relishing the feel of her alive in his arms.

When her tears subsided, they sat silent for a moment. Then Judd took what felt like his first breath since noon on Sunday. "I don't think I've ever felt so clean and bright as I do right now, sitting in a dark, dirty mine with you. I thought I'd die when I lost Joe. And I thought I'd die if I lost you." He reached down and tipped her face up into the circle of light from his headlamp. "But when I saw you there, so still, I . . ." He choked, cleared his throat, and continued, "I knew I'd always carry your light with me, no matter what. The same way I carry Joe's. I've kept any light in me buried for a long time, but somehow you've brought it to the surface, helped it break through the crust of my tough old heart."

Larkin gazed at him, cheeks now rosy in the glow of his lamp. "Why, Judd, that's pure poetry. Are you courting me still?"

"Always. I will court you always."

CHAPTER
35

I t's just a scratch," Larkin insisted once Judd had her out in
the open where he could count her fingers, see her stand—
briefly—and assess the damage to her person. Dr. Baldwin arrived while they were still in the mine, but Judd figured he could
wait his turn. Finally, he stepped aside so the doctor could clean
the cut on Larkin's leg where she'd tripped and torn her skirt.
Now he was probing her scalp, which featured a gash and a
goose egg.

"I'd be surprised if this didn't cause a concussion, but you
seem pretty well over it if it did," he said. "Get some food, water,
and a hot bath and I think you'll do just fine. This bump will
stay tender for a few days, but both of you are in surprisingly
good condition considering how long you were down there."
He snapped his leather bag shut and winked at Judd. "I'm
guessing you'll have more than adequate nursing from here on
out." He started to walk away, then turned back. "I told Ben
he's welcome to stop by the house and use the phone to call
your parents and let them know you're alright."

Judd managed a smile, although he hated to see the dried
blood matting Larkin's burnished hair. He reassured himself

that the cut wasn't bleeding and the bump was likely a good bit smaller than it had been two days earlier. Maude wrapped a blanket around Larkin's shoulders and took the tin cup she had already emptied.

Kyle sat on a log near the creek, eating Judd's ham biscuit and watching them intently. Judd scooped Larkin up and carried her over to sit beside the boy.

"Are you alright?" Kyle asked Larkin. "I didn't mean to get us in trouble like that." Tears welled in his eyes.

She cupped his cheek. "What we did was foolish, but I'm grateful for how brave you were." She turned to Judd. "He told me stories and sang songs to pass the time." She smiled at Kyle again. "All I wanted to do was sleep, but Kyle kept me going."

Kyle puffed his chest out. "You'd best eat something, Miss Larkin. I know I was powerful hungry."

Maude walked over with bowls of soup for them all. She waited until they'd each tasted the thick ham-studded beans before nodding and going back to pack up her supplies.

"I take it what Dr. Baldwin said means Daddy didn't come?" Larkin raised her chin high, yet Judd could see tears glistening.

"Guess not." Judd considered offering a possible excuse, then decided that wasn't his place.

"I've disappointed him. Ben and I both have."

Judd grunted. "Might be he's disappointed some folks, too."

Larkin turned her attention to her bowl and swallowed some more soup. She was eating slowly, and Judd wanted to pour the nourishment into her, to heal her by force if necessary. He felt anger well up in him against George Heyward. How could he have let the man turn his head with the notion of one day running the timber company? Here was what mattered. A woman he loved, people who came together in a time of need, and a little boy falling asleep sitting up on a log.

A memory of Joe drifted into Judd's mind. They'd been to

a barn dance where they'd each taken a turn with every pretty girl in the county and maybe a few who were on the plain side.

"That Miranda Watson's got a crush on you bigger than the sky," Joe had said as they walked home under a canopy of stars. "When you gonna settle down?"

"When are you gonna settle down?" Judd asked.

"Me? Never. I'm not built for it. But you—you'd make a good husband and father, too. Miranda's a fine girl and she'd do you proud."

Judd remembered looking at the moon where it hung down near the horizon. "Guess there's time for all that. No need to hurry."

Joe stooped to pick up some flat stones and skim them across a pond. "Judd, there's a whole pile of things I don't know, but one thing I do know is this—there's never as much time as you think."

Judd sat on the log and settled the sleeping boy against his side. He wrapped his other arm around Larkin. He held them there, not speaking, and whispered a prayer of thanks for this moment in time that would soon disappear, like a startled deer, into the woods. But he'd remember it and would try never to take a moment like it for granted again.

◆ ◆ ◆

Larkin woke and stretched under the weight of the quilt Granny Jane sent over. She'd go see Granny today and tell her goodbye. She'd made up her mind sitting on that log yesterday, marveling at the sky and the trees and the ferns pushing through last year's dead leaves. She'd breathed the fresh air and for a moment thought she caught a whiff of salt. But that was impossible. Even so, it awakened something in her and she knew it was time to go home and face her father. Sometimes the people who needed the most help didn't look like they needed any help at all.

She slipped out of bed into the cool morning. Although it was nearly May, mornings could still be frosty. Back home in South Carolina it would be as good as summer. She pulled on a nubby sweater Maude had given her over her nightclothes and pushed aside the curtain that separated her bed from the larger room.

Ben sat at the table, Bible open before him, sipping a cup of coffee. She didn't see Judd.

"Hey, little sister. How you feeling this morning?"

Larkin stretched, testing her arms and legs. "I'm a little stiff and sore, and this bump on my head is still tender, but otherwise I think I'm right as rain."

Ben smiled, probably recognizing one of Maude's favorite sayings. "There are biscuits and sausage in the warmer. Maude sent Kyle over with them early. Coffee's in the pot."

Larkin made a sandwich with a biscuit and the ground pork, loaded with sage. She'd been part of the hog killing that made this food possible and she realized how grateful she was for that pig as her mouth watered in anticipation. She'd felt so hungry and sick at the same time when they'd been stuck in the mine. Eating whenever she wanted was a luxury she'd long taken for granted.

"Is Kyle still here?" She spoke through crumbs and didn't care.

"He and Judd went out to do something or other. I think Judd was worried the boy would wake you."

Larkin felt her cheeks pink at the mention of her intended. Somehow marrying him was more real now. She wished they could skip the big to-do back home and just let Ben wed them right here.

The door opened as Judd and Kyle clattered in with an armload of wood to keep the cookstove going. Kyle rushed to Larkin and flung his arms around her.

"I feel better this morning. I ate three biscuits, and me and Judd have been chopping wood." He leaned back. "Do you feel better, too?"

"I do," Larkin said with a laugh. "Although I'm not sure I've recovered my energy the way you have."

Kyle grinned and slid into a chair. Ben offered him a mug of mostly milk with a splash of coffee, and Kyle accepted it with what Larkin had come to think of as his "manly look." Judd stepped over to the table and dropped a kiss on top of her head before sitting.

He took her hand and looked into her eyes. "I need to go back to South Carolina and set things straight with your father, but as soon as I'm done I thought . . . well, I thought I'd come here and we could stay until the wedding."

Larkin marveled that this man would give up being a key part of a lucrative business just to make her happy. "Actually, I've got a few things I need to set straight with Daddy, too. I'd like to go on back home with you. We can sort out where we'll live later. I'm beginning to see that I can be happy wherever I am just as long as I'm doing what God made me to do."

"And what did God make you to do?" Judd asked, trying to keep his dimples from showing.

"To help people and to . . ." She glanced at Ben, who just sat there grinning like a cat with cream. She made a face and looked back to Judd. "To love you."

"Sounds right to me." Judd kissed her quick.

"In the meantime, I've had the most marvelous idea." She could feel the joy flaming up inside her. "Let's get married right here, right now. Ben can perform the ceremony, and we won't have to bother with a big church wedding back in South Carolina."

Judd kept hold of her hand, his face turning serious. "Larkin, that sounds awful good, but . . ." He looked at the floor, then back to her. "I don't think it would be right to leave your parents out. Or to spoil all the plans your mother's already made. I'm ready to make you mine right this minute, but I guess I ought to respect the way you've been theirs up until now."

Larkin was astonished. "I . . . well, I suppose you're right. It's just I suddenly felt like I couldn't wait another minute."

Judd tugged her hand and pulled her over to sit on his knee— scandalous in front of Ben and Kyle. "Then you know exactly how I feel. I'm not saying I'll kick up a fuss if you get your mother to move the date up from October, but either way, you're worth the wait."

She swatted at him and leaned into his shoulder with a sigh. "You know, I suppose I am at that."

Ben laughed and clapped his hands together. "You tell me the day and I'll be there."

Kyle piped up, "Can I come?"

"Oh, I don't know about that—" Larkin began, but Ben cut her off.

"You just wait and see if I can't make that happen. Now, when are the two of you leaving?"

"No time like the present," Judd said. "The sooner we go, the sooner we can come back."

"I'll drink to that," Ben said and downed the last of his coffee.

CHAPTER

36

Augusta Heyward waited in the open door as Judd pulled into the driveway with Larkin riding beside him in his truck.

"My darling, I was so frightened." She wrapped her daughter in a hug. "I'd be willing to have cancer five times over just to know you're safe."

Larkin surprised them all by bursting into tears in her mother's arms.

Augusta spoke over her daughter's shaking shoulder. "Thank you, Judd. George meant to be here to thank you as well, but"—her eyes darted away—"business was pressing." Then her eyes darted back briefly. "I think it had something to do with a former employee. Pete something or other."

Judd's ears perked. What was Pete up to now?

"Won't you come in and stay for dinner?" she asked.

Judd considered it, but decided it might be best to leave the initial meeting of father and daughter to family only. "Not today, but I'll be back around tomorrow."

"Good. We'll count on you staying, then."

Judd tipped his hat and drove to the boardinghouse, torn

between leaving Larkin to fend for herself and wondering which hornet's nest Pete had poked this time.

◊ ◊ ◊

Judd didn't have to wonder about Pete for long. Hank was waiting for him on the front porch of the boardinghouse, and he didn't waste any time with small talk.

"Sure am glad you got Larkin home safe and sound." He rubbed the back of his neck. "I hate to ask you this, but you been spending much time with Pete lately?"

Judd sat on the top step and leaned back against a post. "I try to keep up with him, but I guess it's been a while since we last visited."

Hank nodded. "Pete's in some trouble over this land he says Mr. Heyward stole from his father."

"You talking about the lawsuit?"

"That's probably part of it. The main thing is, Pete got arrested for trespassing. He was out there in the woods late at night with a shovel and some other tools. Refuses to say what he was doing, but the consensus is it wasn't anything good."

"He was pretty upset last time I talked to him."

"You think he might try to tamper with the machinery—maybe shut the job down?"

"I don't think so. He wasn't exactly everyone's best friend, but I don't think he'd do anything to put the other men at risk."

Hank sighed. "I didn't think so, either. And the funny thing is, he wasn't even around the machinery. He was out in the middle of those woods, stumbling around with a flashlight. Somebody who lives on an adjacent plot saw the light bobbing around, got worried and called the police. You got any guesses as to what he might've been up to?"

Judd thought back to his last conversation with Pete when they'd discussed the lawsuit. "Seems like Pete said something about wanting the land and anything on it. I assumed he meant the trees, but maybe there's something else out there. He has mentioned treasure a time or two, but I figured that was just talk."

Hank looked thoughtful. "You know, there was a story I remember hearing as a kid about a wealthy family living out that way during the War Between the States. Supposedly they hid some gold or jewelry or something like that when the Union soldiers came through. Hid the best stuff and left the everyday silver plate and some cheap jewelry lying around for the soldiers to find." He tapped his lip "Now what was the name? Oh, right—Bennington."

"How would Pete's father have ended up with some wealthy family's land?"

Hank shrugged. "Don't know. Plus I'm pretty skeptical about there actually being any valuables hidden. Treasure hunters look for that stuff all the time. If there ever was anything, it's probably gone by now."

Judd stretched out his leg. "Pete strikes me as the kind of feller who'd look just the same."

"Maybe," Hank agreed. "Either whichaway, it's got him locked up. Thought you'd want to know."

"Appreciate it," Judd said and went inside to his lonesome room.

◆ ◆ ◆

"Daddy usually isn't this late," Larkin said, looking at the table set for three.

"Especially not when his baby girl's come home after a harrowing experience in the wilds of Kentucky," Mother said with a smile. "I'm sure there's a good reason."

"Oh, it wasn't all that harrowing. Not looking back on it now. Although it did help me get some things straight in my mind, and I really do wish Daddy would come home so I could talk to him."

Her mother wrapped an arm around her shoulders and pressed her cheek to Larkin's. "This is hard for him. He's not used to being defied. Are you . . . planning to come home to stay?"

"At least until Judd and I can get married." She felt hope rise in her mother. "Which I'd like to see happen sooner rather than later. I know you had a big wedding in mind, but honestly we'd prefer something small and . . . soon."

Her mother sighed. "I remember being in a hurry to marry. It is so very hard to wait when you know it's what you want."

"You couldn't wait to marry Daddy?"

"I thought I'd die if we didn't get married, I loved him so much."

"Do you still . . . love him like that?"

Mother moved back into the kitchen and began putting food in serving bowls. "Oh, not exactly like that, but I still love him very much. I just wish—"

Her wish went unspoken as Larkin's father came through the back door, a gruff expression on his face.

"Larkin," he said.

She went to him and he wrapped her in a hug, tears springing to his eyes. "I'm so glad you're here," he said in a hoarse voice.

They settled in the dining room and passed the dishes of pork chops, butter beans, rice, and salad. When all their plates were full, Larkin cleared her throat.

"Daddy, would you say grace?"

He paused, loaded fork halfway to his mouth. "Very well." He folded his hands and closed his eyes. "Lord, we thank you for the food before us and for returning Larkin safely home. Amen."

It wasn't quite the eloquent, heartfelt prayer Larkin hoped for, but she was grateful all the same. If she was going to have a difficult conversation with her father, it was best to begin with prayer. She whispered one of her own as they began eating.

"Daddy, we're thinking of moving up the wedding date."

He laid down his fork. "Now that is good news. Judd's a good man." He cleared his throat. "Will you, uh, be returning to Kentucky afterwards?"

Larkin did her best to hide her surprise. "We haven't quite decided."

He nodded. "Larkin, I'll tell you the truth. When I told Ben he was no longer a son of mine, I felt certain he would see the error of his ways and come home. Obviously, he did not. When you ran off and found him, I hoped . . ." He pinched his nose where his glasses sat. "I hoped he might realize what he was giving up and ask for my forgiveness. But instead he began to woo you away, as well."

"Daddy, I—"

He held up his hand. "While I wished Judd had a little more ambition when he first arrived, I couldn't deny that he was smart, hardworking, honest, and just the sort of man I'd want to groom to take over Waccamaw Timber one day." He laughed. "In a way, his lack of ambition made him perfect. Once I saw how smitten he was with you, it was easy to steer him toward greater responsibility and I think, as he sampled what might be his, he came to want what I wanted."

"What's that, Daddy?"

He leaned back in his chair and fiddled with a fork. "A successful business that other men respect. A legacy that continues for generations after we're gone. Just one page in the annals of history noting that I was here and changed the world at least a little." He dropped his chin. "Not to be passed over and forgotten."

Larkin swallowed hard. She thought about what Mother said about Daddy's own father giving everything to the church, even at his son's expense. She guessed maybe Daddy just wanted to be seen, for his efforts to be acknowledged.

"As long as I have anything to do with it, you will not be

forgotten," she said. "You have quite a legacy in Myrtle Beach and in this family." She reached over and took his hand. "And I think maybe part of that legacy is having children who care about people and who also want to change the world. Just maybe in a different way."

Daddy took a hitching breath. "I can see there might be truth in that," he said. "Just don't expect me to come around all at once."

Larkin grinned. "There now. I feel like I've changed the world already."

◊ ◊ ◊

Judd tried not to feel uneasy as the jail door clanged shut behind him. He was here to see Pete and could leave anytime he wanted. The deputy showed him to a sort of communal room where benches were attached to metal tables. It was gray and plain and smelled of disinfectant. Judd considered sitting but opted to stand for the time being. A few moments later, Pete shuffled in behind another guard. He gave Judd a dark look and slouched at one of the tables.

"Come to see the monkey in the zoo?"

"I was worried about you, Pete. Thought I'd come see if there's anything I can do." Judd slid onto the bench opposite his friend.

"You got a metal file in your hip pocket?" Pete's laugh sounded rusty. "Aw, just kidding. I'd be out of here already if I could've paid the fine." He straightened a notch. "Say, there is something you could do. Go on by and check on Sally. This is harder on her than me."

"I'll do it as soon as I leave here," Judd said. He tapped his fingers on the cool tabletop. "What exactly were you up to out there in the woods?"

Pete got a cagey look. "Nothing. Just trying to figure out how to get back what's mine."

Judd nodded. "Hank said there was some story about trea-sure out that way. You weren't hunting it, were you?"

Pete stuck his chin out and crossed his arms over his chest. "Seems like if there were anything worth finding, it'd been found by now."

"That's what I thought," Judd said.

"You'd best get on over and check on Sally." Pete's expression softened. "Tell her I'm real sorry I embarrassed her like this."

Judd nodded and shook his friend's hand. "Hope you get out of here real soon."

Pete stood and walked slowly back to the door he'd entered through. He banged on it until a guard opened the door and let him back into the depths of the jail. Judd remembered feeling trapped in the mine and supposed Pete had an inkling of what that felt like, too.

CHAPTER
37

I thank you for coming," Sally said as she ushered Judd into the front room where he'd played cards with Pete so many times before. "I can't hardly understand what Pete was thinking." She perched on the edge of a sofa cushion and waved Judd to a nearby chair. "What did he hope to gain?"

Judd shrugged. "He wouldn't say when I spoke to him. Just asked me to check on you and to tell you he's real sorry."

Sally gave a dismissive wave. "I'd rather he just tell me what he's up to, but Pete always has been stubborn as a mule."

"Do you have any idea how his father came to own that property?"

"It was a gift from his mother—Pete's grandmother. I think that's part of why losing it was so hard on Pete. He doted on his grandmother."

"So she's gone?"

Sally nodded. "The story is, she didn't much like anyone but Pete. Her name was Eugenia, and Pete said her family was well-to-do back in the day. She married a man who was killed young." Sally lowered her voice. "Shot for cheating at cards, they say. Anyway, she must've used up most of what she had just to

301

get by. We've got her wedding picture—she was real elegant."
Sally opened a drawer in an end table and pulled out a small
photo album made of paper. Flipping it open, she handed it to
Judd. "There you go. Folks always looked so grim in those old
photos, but you can still tell she was something."

Judd took the album and admired the photo of a regal woman
sitting poker-straight and looking into the camera with a steely
gaze. He started to hand the book back, but the photo fluttered
free and fell to the floor. Judd stooped to pick it up and noticed
writing on the back. There, in a flowing hand, it read, *Eugenia
Bennington Dixon*.

"She was a Bennington. Hank said there was a family named
Bennington that hid their valuables from soldiers during the
Civil War."

Sally looked surprised. "Pete said his grandmother came from
a wealthy family, but I don't know anything about valuables.
Seems like they'd have gone back and got whatever it was as
soon as the war was over."

"That does seem likely," Judd agreed. He visited a little while
longer, promised to take Sally to see Pete later that week, and
then headed back to the boardinghouse. He needed to get
cleaned up and go see how Larkin had fared talking with her
father.

♦ ♦ ♦

"I don't think any of this has turned out quite the way he'd
hoped," Larkin said as she and Judd strolled along the beach.
Tears glimmered in her eyes. "I hate to have been part of spoiling his plans."

Judd took her hand. "I guess maybe God has a plan bigger
than any of us. Maybe your father needs to figure out how to
be more in line with what God wants from him instead of the
other way around."

"What do you think God wants from us? You and me, I mean?"

Judd stopped and wrapped an arm around Larkin's shoulders, turning her so that they were looking out over the ocean. The May sun was already hot. Soon the summer crowds would return in force.

"You know, ever since that day we crawled out of the mine, I've been thinking about the story in Genesis where Jacob wrestled an angel. He was running away from his father-in-law while his brother—who was likely still angry about his stolen birthright—was waiting up ahead. Jacob had tricked his father-in-law into letting him leave with his family and herds of animals. But then he was scared of his brother, so he sent gifts up ahead to try to smooth that out." Judd breathed in the salt air and watched a gull swoop down after something in the surf. "He'd gotten out of one pickle—barely—and he was about to face another. He sent everyone else on ahead and was left all alone. That's when an angel showed up and wrestled with him."

Larkin laid her head against his chest, and he could feel the warmth of it even more than the sun. She waited for him to go on.

"Me and Joe and Abram used to have wrestling matches. I was pretty good, too. Could beat 'em most of the time. But Jacob, he wrestled an angel—or maybe it was God himself—until the angel cheated in my book. He touched Jacob's hip and knocked it out of joint. But even then ole Jacob wouldn't quit until he got a blessing. So the angel changed Jacob's name to Israel and blessed him."

"I remember that story," Larkin said. "I never really understood what it was about."

"I wondered myself. But the thing is, Jacob—Israel—had a limp from then on." He thumped his leg. "Kind of like me. I've been wrestling with God for a while now, and maybe your father is, as well. I had Joe's death dogging me from behind and the fact that everyone else I love is gonna die, too—including me—waiting up ahead." Judd put both arms around Larkin and pulled her snug against him. "But you marrying me—well, I think that's the blessing. That's the thing I've been struggling for without even knowing it. Not because it fixes Joe dying, but because it proves we're still alive and love goes on . . . well, forever."

"I like the sound of that."

Judd kissed the top of her head. "Maybe your father's hip is just about out of joint by now. Maybe he's not too far off from figuring out what blessing he's after."

"I hope so," Larkin said. She tilted up her head so that Judd saw he had no choice but to kiss her soft lips.

The next day, Judd started back to work for the timber company. He wasn't sure how everything was going to shake out, but he figured he had an obligation for the time being. Chuck took him out to work with the crew on the Bennington tract. Judd tried not to feel like he was somehow betraying Pete, but it nagged at him just the same.

"Skidder's down," Chuck said. "I don't suppose you could just flip a lever like you did that first time and have her back up and running?"

"A feller doesn't usually get that lucky twice, but I'll give her a look."

Judd had been looking all morning and still hadn't figured out exactly what was wrong. He'd never been so glad to see lunchtime approaching when there was a shout from some of the cutters out in the woods. Everyone ran in that direction, the first thought being that someone had been hurt. But instead of seeing a man down, Judd saw three men standing near the jagged stump of a freshly cut tree. They were all staring, hands in pockets or hanging slack.

Chuck got there first and whistled. Judd stepped up behind him and saw that the tree was about half hollow, which meant that as soon as they'd cut through the solid part, the weight broke the tree off, exposing the cavity.

"Man alive, it's a miracle no one got hurt when that came down," Judd said, but no one responded.

He pushed closer to see what they were looking at, and there, inside the hollow of the tree, sat what looked like a small barrel.

"Nail keg, I betcha," Chuck said. "Old too. You don't suppose . . . ?"

"I saw it first." One of the men spoke up.

The other two immediately began offering arguments for why they should get a share of whatever was inside.

Chuck whistled, loud and sharp. "Hold on there, boys. That keg belongs to the owner of the property."

The men looked disgusted, though none of them seemed willing to risk their job for what might, or might not, be inside the keg. Finally, the one on the far right kicked the stump. "Well, can we at least open it and see?"

Chuck darted a look at Judd and licked his lips. "Probably ought to let Mr. Heyward do the honors. Judd, reach in there and see can you lift it out?"

The keg was about eighteen inches high and maybe ten wide, and Judd found it to be plenty heavy. He grunted and staggered back toward the landing with his hands under the bottom of the keg. He could feel the wood shifting, ready to give way, but thought he could make it. He thumped his cargo on the tailgate of his truck, since it was the first one he came to.

They all stood there staring at it. Judd could almost hear them wondering if this was the Bennington treasure.

"Judd, why don't you take it on to Mr. Heyward? These boys aren't going to get a lick of work done so long as it's around here."

Judd pushed the keg up against the side of the truck and braced it there with some wood blocks. He hoped it would hold together until he got back to the office. He drove slowly, wondering what Mr. Heyward would think. He also wondered what Pete would think if this did turn out to be Bennington family treasure. Would he have a rightful claim? Judd hoped, with all his might, that the keg held nothing but rocks and dirt.

◆ ♦ ◆

"I don't think it'll hold together to get it inside," Judd explained to Mr. Heyward. "Best come on out to my truck and see what you think."

His soon-to-be father-in-law grumbled as he followed Judd out to the truck where the keg did look like it might fall to pieces. Dirt had sifted out around the edges, and Judd guessed whatever was inside was doing more to hold it together than the wire twisted around the outside.

"Probably some old moonshiner's stash. You could have opened it yourself."

Judd scratched his head. "Well, with all the rumors about the Benningtons' Civil War treasure, Chuck and I thought we'd best bring it on over here."

Mr. Heyward rolled his eyes. "Pry it open."

Judd found a small pry bar behind the truck seat and gently tapped at the wooden top of the keg. Mr. Heyward grabbed the bar, jamming it inside along the edge and pushing up. Punky wood and dirt sprayed Judd, and he swiped his face with his hand.

Mr. Heyward continued wrecking the keg, which was indeed full of dirt and something else. He reached out and sifted through the mess to pull out what looked like a well-worn pocketknife.

"Doesn't look like much." He handed the knife to Judd, who applied his bandanna to it.

"Something else in here. Looks like a box." Mr. Heyward clawed at the debris, extracting something rectangular wrapped in several layers of oilskin. He folded back the leathery material.

"No. It's a book." He eased it open. "Diary maybe." He glanced at the mess in the back of the truck, then at Judd. He held his hand out for the knife, which Judd thought looked like it had a staghorn handle. "It's surely no treasure, but I'll hang on to these and get someone to look at them. Never know when you're going to find a museum piece."

Judd watched the older man walk back inside without a backward glance. He was awful glad to be marrying Larkin, but he thought his in-laws might prove to be a challenge. He sighed and backed the truck up into some bushes so he could sweep out the mess Mr. Heyward left behind. He debated saving the wood—might be able to do something with it—but decided it was too far gone. He tumbled it all out into the shrubs, and as he did, he saw something glinting back at him.

Bending over, Judd poked around and found a jaw harp. He held it up, swiped it against his shirt, and started to put it to his mouth, then thought better of it. He'd clean it proper before trying it out. He looked toward the door Mr. Heyward had passed through and debated taking the item inside, but decided against it. Surely an old-time musical instrument wasn't important, and he didn't feel like dealing with his employer any more today. He shrugged. He could always give it to him later.

CHAPTER

38

June eighteenth," Larkin said. "Mother has agreed to a wedding on June eighteenth. And the best part is that we don't have to invite everyone I've ever met. It can be just family and close friends. I called the store in Logan and they're getting word to Ben, so he and Pastor Brearley can do the ceremony together." She squeezed her hands together. "What if he can't come?"

"I have a feeling he'll manage," Judd said. "And I'll get word to Abram, although they might not come. It's a long ways with two little ones."

They were walking to church on the last Sunday in May and Judd was trying to will himself not to sweat. Although he wasn't sure which was making him hotter under the collar, the sun or the thought that he'd be wed in less than three weeks. He still didn't know where they were going to live. Would it be here or in Kentucky? Or maybe even back home in West Virginia, for that matter.

"Are you sure we're ready for this? Seems like quite a few things still need figuring out."

Larkin stopped and faced him. "You mean like what we're going to do with the rest of our lives?"

"There's a start."

She threw her arms around his neck and kissed him, short and sweet. "I think we should start by loving each other more every day."

Judd wanted to be put out with her, but how could he? Gently unwinding her arms, he started them back toward the church. "My room at the boardinghouse isn't much of a honeymoon suite, and until we decide once and for all where to live—"

Larkin cut in. "We can live in the apartment over the garage until we find something of our own."

Judd frowned. "Over your parents' garage?"

"Yes. Granny Ben used to live there when I was little. It's been empty for a while, but I went up there yesterday and I think it'll do fine. Just needs some sprucing up. There's even a tiny kitchen where I can make you dinner every evening now that Granny's taught me how to cook." She glanced at him and squeezed his arm where she'd tucked her hand through his elbow. "I know it's not ideal, but I think it could work for now."

"But . . . your family. I don't want to be beholden."

Larkin smiled. "Oh, I think when we tell Daddy we're staying right here in South Carolina, he'll be more than happy for us to live in the apartment until we find our own house."

Judd blinked. "We're staying?"

"Unless you don't want to. I still think Daddy's been manipulating everyone, but that doesn't mean you shouldn't take advantage of a chance to be a partner in his company." She looked up at him through long lashes. "I think you can handle him just fine now that everything's out in the open. He won't be trying to trick us into staying or getting married or anything else." She shrugged one shoulder. "It just so happens that what we want and what he wants coincide." She shook her head. "Isn't it funny how all that worked out?"

Judd didn't comment. He was still trying to get a handle on whether getting what he wanted by staying in South Carolina and becoming a businessman was really and truly what he wanted. Everything was moving fast, and suddenly he felt a deep homesickness for mountains and valleys, for tumbling streams and rhododendron thickets.

"Are you sure you want to stay?" he asked.

Larkin stopped, the church just a block away. "I'm sure I want to be where you are. If that's here, then yes, this is what I want. If you'd rather be in Kentucky or West Virginia or Timbuktu, all I know is I'm going with you. I can be of use wherever we go. All I have to do is look around and see who needs an extra measure of love, then pitch in."

She smiled up at him, and Judd thought his heart might stop. But no, it was only pausing before taking on a new rhythm— one he thought most likely matched hers. As they entered the church together, Judd realized that three weeks was an awful long time to wait.

⸵

Sunday afternoon, Judd picked Sally up and drove her to see Pete. It looked like he'd get off with time served, but he had a few more days to go. Judd personally thought it would be better if Sally just waited until Pete got home. Yet if she was determined to see her husband, Judd would take her.

Inside, she stayed so close, she kept bumping up against him. Her eyes were wide and her face pale as the last door clanged shut behind them. Pete shuffled into the day room, head down, and slid onto the bench opposite them. No one spoke for several beats.

"Guess you'll be heading home soon," Judd said.

"Looks that way." Pete rested his forearms on the table.

"Judd's been looking out for me while you've been . . . away," Sally said.

"I thank you for that." Pete finally lifted his eyes to meet Judd's. The sorrow there was deep.

"I showed him a picture of your grandma Dixon." Sally blurted the words as though she'd been casting for something to say and they were the first to rise to the surface.

Pete's eyes narrowed. "Why'd you do that?"

Sally looked nervous, as if realizing this might not be the safest topic of conversation. "He was asking about your family and . . . that land."

Pete squinted at Judd. "Did Heyward put you up to that?"

"Of course not." Judd glanced at Sally and sighed. He'd rather not have this conversation in front of her but guessed there was no time like the present. He reached into his breast pocket and pulled out the jaw harp, pushing it across the table to Pete. It had nearly been confiscated on the way in, but the guard deemed it a harmless item to share with a short-term prisoner.

"Heard a story about the Bennington family hiding valuables when the Union soldiers came through back during the war. You mentioned something about treasure a time or two. Wondered if maybe hunting it was what made you decide to trespass."

Pete acted like he was only half listening. He picked up the jaw harp and turned it over and over in his hand. "There's more than one kind of treasure," he said, almost to himself. He looked to Judd. "Where'd you get this?"

"Men found an old nail keg in a half-hollow tree they cut. That was in it along with some kind of diary and a knife."

Pete lunged across the table, grabbing Judd's shirt. "Where are they?"

A guard materialized and shoved Pete back down onto the bench. "Enough of that. Visit's over."

"But I need—"

"Don't care, don't matter," the guard said, jerking Pete to his feet. "Get a move on."

311

"We'll pick you up on Thursday," Judd called as Pete disappeared through a door.

Sally fought tears all the way to the truck, finally letting them fall once Judd had her settled inside.

"You're the best friend he's got," she sniffled. "Why'd he get worked up like that?"

"Aw, it's my fault. I should've waited until Thursday to talk to him. Something about that property has Pete in a state, and I'm thinking there's more to it than just the loss of the land and the money it might have meant."

Daddy was making an effort to take an interest in the wedding without harping on the future of Waccamaw Timber. Larkin appreciated that he was at least trying. She kissed his cheek as she sat down at the breakfast table.

"Your mother tells me I'm to walk you down the aisle on the eighteenth."

"I was hoping you would." Larkin buttered a slice of toast and reached for the peach preserves.

He grimaced. "Of course I will. I might even go so far as to say I'm looking forward to it." He reached for his coffee cup but only twisted it in the saucer. "And whatever you and Judd decide to do after you're wed is fine by me." He finally sipped his coffee. "I'm afraid the company may mean more to me than it should. I've been . . . thinking about some things I may need to set to rights before long."

Larkin let a smile slide across her face and decided it was time to let him off the hook. "I thought we'd move into Granny Ben's apartment while we look for a place of our own." She laughed at her father's stunned expression. She stepped around the breakfast table to wrap her arms around his neck, then sat on his knee and leaned her head against his shoulder. "Judd and I plan to stay for now. I think we'd like to be part of Waccamaw

Timber Company. But I don't think you can count on Judd being a silent partner. He has ideas of his own."

Daddy squeezed her tight. "Wouldn't have it any other way." He smiled. "Although it may take some time for us to get used to each other."

"He's pretty easy to get used to," she said.

◆◆◆

Something was niggling at the back of Judd's mind. Pete sure seemed to know that jaw harp, and the way he got worked up when Judd mentioned the diary and knife didn't make sense. It certainly wasn't any Civil War treasure, but if he didn't know better he'd guess those items were exactly what Pete had been hunting.

"Penny for your thoughts," Larkin said.

They'd eaten supper with her parents and were taking inventory of what they'd need in the little apartment over the garage. It was nice enough, but Judd saw he'd be ducking rooflines and doorways once they moved in.

"Aw, Pete's got me worried, but I'd rather not stew about that right now." He scooped her into his arms. "It's gonna be a haul to carry you up those stairs and over the threshold."

She giggled. "I think you can manage." She gazed around the main room. "Granny Ben sure would like knowing we're using this place. She loved it here."

"That sure is a funny name for a woman," Judd said, releasing Larkin and opening kitchen cabinets to see what more they'd need.

"It was short for her last name."

Judd straightened, brow furrowed. "Last name?"

"Bennington. My grandmother's maiden name was Lavonia Bennington." She grinned. "Ben is named for her—his full name is George Bennington Heyward. Maybe if we have a girl one day—"

313

"Your grandmother was a Bennington? As in the Benningtons who owned the land your father's timbering?"

Now it was Larkin's turn to furrow her brow. "Could be. I'm not sure."

"Pete's grandmother was Eugenia Bennington Dixon. Could they have been kin?"

Larkin tapped her lower lip. "Granny once mentioned a sister of Grandpa Victor—that makes her my great-aunt—who married a no-good gambler and was never heard from again. I tried to get her to tell me more, but she refused. Seemed to be a sore spot for her." She smiled. "I do remember a story about how, during the Civil War, they hid the good silver and jewelry out in the woods, leaving just enough silver plate and costume stuff to fool the Union soldiers."

"That sounds like the Bennington family that owned the land we're working now." Judd stopped to piece it all together in his mind. "So maybe your great-grandparents left the land to the daughter whose husband didn't take care of her. Your grandparents were doing alright in timber and turpentine." He thought some more. "And then Pete's father, Wade, who might have been a good bit like his own father, ended up selling the land to . . . George Heyward, his cousin by marriage. Which means Pete . . ." He did some calculating. "Pete might be your second cousin."

Larkin seemed delighted. "Really? Can I meet him?"

Judd thumped down on an overstuffed, floral sofa. "Don't you see? If Pete's your cousin, that would explain why he's so worked up about this timber tract and why he thinks your father pretty much stole it from him—even though they were family. It also raises a few questions about that nail keg we found and the diary that was in it. He's been going on and on about needing to find something that would set the record straight."

Larkin's eyes sparkled. "A mystery—how intriguing. But

you don't really think Daddy did anything wrong in getting that land, do you?"

Judd tugged at his ear. "There's wrong and then there's not right. And your father seems to have been walking on both sides of many a fine line over the years."

CHAPTER

39

Sally was busy preparing a feast for Pete's return, so Judd drove to the jail by himself. Pete met him at the curb, hands shoved deep in his pockets, squinting into the hot, early June sunshine.

He climbed into the truck. "Thought to wait inside so's nobody would see me, but where I been lately ain't exactly a secret."

"Sally's cooking a mighty fine meal to welcome you home."

Pete slouched low. "I don't deserve that woman. That's why I need to get ahold of that diary you mentioned." He glanced at Judd. "You know anything more about that?"

"I might."

Pete sat up straighter. "Can you take me to it? I need it real bad if I'm going to do right by Sally."

Judd signaled for a right turn and glanced at Pete. "What's written in there?"

Pete shrugged. "Don't know for sure. But I hope it's my grandma's diary. Pappy kept it close and I always figured it was mainly sentimental to him. But one time, when he'd been drinking worse than usual, he told me there was something in there that would make me rich one day. I figured he was talking out of his head, but not long after that, I didn't see the book anymore." Pete stared out the window. "I asked him about it and he said he hid it on the land that belonged to his mother. She was still living then. Not long after that, she died and Pappy said he inherited the land." Pete thumped his fist against his leg. "Then the fool sold it to George Heyward. Acted like he thought we'd get it back one day. 'Course, then he died." He thumped his leg again. "Sorry cuss."

"You don't have any idea what might be in the diary?"

"My grandmother was disowned by her family when she married my grandfather. All she got from the Benningtons was that tract of land. Her father didn't know it would grow up into some good timber one day. Or maybe he did." He rubbed a hand over his eyes as though bone-weary. "I think that diary somehow shows I have every right to the Bennington land—that Pappy sold it out from underneath me."

Pete fished the jaw harp out of his pocket, tucked it between his teeth, and played a few mournful notes. "This belonged to Pappy. Can't think why he'd hide it in a tree. Probably too drunk to know he'd done it. Probably didn't even remember." He plucked the instrument again, and Judd's own jaw tightened.

He felt torn. On the one hand, Pete deserved to know who his family was—that he was George Heyward's cousin. On the other hand, he didn't want Pete to cause trouble for the timber company—the one he was about to have a pretty serious stake in. The whole business was a convoluted mess. Still, Judd always did prefer the truth, no matter how inconvenient.

Judd was still wrestling with what to do when they pulled up to Pete's house. The magnolia tree was blooming, and the clean, fresh scent greeted him as he opened the truck door. He was also met by a car that looked a lot like the one George Heyward drove.

Pete walked over to the car, eyes narrowed. "You know this car?"

"Might be it looks familiar."

"What I thought," Pete said and headed for the door.

George Heyward met him on the top step. Pete froze, lip curled like a worried dog. "What in blazes are you doing here?"

"We need to talk," Mr. Heyward said. Then he went back inside, leaving Pete and Judd to follow if they chose.

◦ ♦ ◦

Judd looked at Pete and debated blurting his information but then decided to wait and see how this thing played out. Pete inhaled deeply, turned and went into the house. Judd followed close on his heels.

Inside, Sally stood in the doorway to the kitchen, wringing her hands. She looked to Pete, and he stretched an arm out toward her. She scooted to his side and tucked in close to him. Pete turned toward George, who stood with his hands braced on the back of an armchair.

Pete gave George a dark look. "I'd invite you to sit, but I'm not sure you'd do it even if I asked. Why don't you just say whatever you have to say so we can get on with my homecoming." He spat the last word like tobacco juice.

George glanced down at his hands. "Maybe we should all sit." He looked back up. "Seeing as how we're family."

Pete staggered and tugged Sally down onto the couch beside him. "What's that you say?"

George looked to Judd and then moved around to the front of the armchair and sat, as though he'd been carrying a mighty weight. Judd slid into a ladder-back chair near the door and kept his peace.

George pulled the diary from his coat pocket. "This belongs to you as much as anyone," he said to Pete. "I've read it—every word, and it made me think pretty hard about the way I've handled my family."

Pete bristled, but George held his hand up. "Now, don't get your dander up. Eugenia was your grandmother, but she was also Augusta's aunt. I've known it for a long time. It's why I hired you on. I wanted to do right by you since you're my wife's cousin. But maybe my idea of what's right got a little twisted along the way."

Although Judd had guessed the truth, hearing George say it out loud just about made the hair stand up on the back of his neck. Pete was about to become his cousin by marriage.

"Grandma Eugenia was . . ." Pete couldn't seem to piece it all together.

"Augusta's aunt—her father Victor's sister. I knew there was a younger sister who married the wrong man, but the Benningtons never talked about her and somehow I thought she was dead. 'Course, I eventually met Wade Dixon and figured out the truth. I never did say anything. I thought it would be best if everyone really did think that line had petered out." He looked Pete in the eye and thumped the book. "But that's not what happened."

"Pappy and Grandma Eugenia. That means Pappy was your wife's first cousin."

"He was, and while I don't care to speak ill of the dead, he never was the sort of man to hold a . . . steady job. And while I knew who he was, Augusta didn't, and I hoped it would never matter."

"Why's it matter now?" Pete had a suspicious gleam in his eye.

George held the diary up and looked toward the ceiling, as if what he wanted to say might be written there. "I have come much too close to losing my family over my desire to preserve the business I helped build. It just might be that I've misplaced my priorities." He took a breath and looked Pete in the eye. "You, sir, are my family and I intend to do right by you. Let me read you something."

He gently pressed the crinkling pages of the diary open, smoothing a particular page over and over—to buy time, Judd suspected. Then he cleared his throat and began to read.

"'Peter is gone and I cannot bring him back. Perhaps Victor was right when he said I was a fool to marry him, but he was so full of life and I was so full of love. Now Wade and I must carry on, bearing the shame of his manner of dying, as well as the horrors of surviving with no regular income—not that it was regular when Peter was with us.

Father has given us the land where an old slave cabin sits, most likely to appease his guilt. It will have to do. He also gave Wade his pocketknife. I don't suppose he can blame the boy for the sins of his father. Or his mother, for that matter. I could probably sell that knife for enough to feed us a good while, but I swear I never will. It and this sorry, swampy land are all we have to remind us of who we are. Who we were. Who we might be again. We have lost a great deal. I will see that my son does not lose any more.'"

George looked up, eyes moist. "It's dated November 6, 1902." Pete had taken Sally's hand at some point. He sniffed loudly. "I was named for my grandfather even though he was shot down the summer of 1902 for cheating at cards. I think Pappy hoped it would please Grandma Eugenia—the name. I guess Pappy wasn't much better than his own father, but he did love Grandma." He pulled out a handkerchief and blew his nose loudly. "And I surely loved her, too. It would've made her madder than a hornet to know Pappy sold that land."

George reached in another pocket and pulled out the knife from the nail keg. "I'm guessing this is the knife she mentioned. There are initials carved in the handle—H.B. Augusta's grandfather, your great-grandfather, was Howard Bennington." He

320

rubbed his thumb over the initials. "Your grandmother cared more about the family legacy this knife represented than she did about cold, hard cash. Made me take a long, hard look at what matters most to me."

He flicked the knife open, then shut it again and passed it over to Pete. "Seems like this ought to be yours now."

Pete took the knife like it was a sacred relic. He flipped it open and ran his fingers over the staghorn handle. "I remember Pappy carrying this. Always wondered what happened to it."

George cleared his throat. "There's more in that diary. It continues right on up until she died—after you were born. Your grandmother meant for the land to pass to you. I'd say she was aware of Wade's propensity to drink and fritter away anything he had." He fished a piece of paper out of his pocket and held it out. "I was able to buy the land because no will was ever found after Eugenia passed, leaving any property to fall to your father. I'm not sure if that diary would stand up in court, but it surely says straight out that she planned to leave everything to you." He laughed, dry and hard. "Guess maybe ole Wade thought he had an ace up his sleeve. Sell the land to me, then let you get it back through the courts." He handed Pete the piece of paper.

Pete unfolded it and scanned the contents. He looked at George, a furrow forming between his brows. "I don't understand."

"That's a deed showing I've signed the land over to you. It's yours—the way your grandmother meant it to be—and we'll split the profits on the timber just like I would have if you'd sold it to me." He darted a look at Judd. "Things got a little tight with the company after that blasted hurricane and I needed the harvest, but since then a contract has come through from the state, thanks to Judd buttering up the forest service."

Pete squinted at him. "How much are we talking?"

"I wrote the figure down there at the bottom of that paper."

Pete whistled low and showed Sally, whose eyes got big and round.

"What's the catch?" Pete asked.

"No catch. Maybe just take good care of that pretty wife of yours and come have dinner with us after all this wedding business is over. I know Augusta would enjoy hearing about Eugenia."

Pete relaxed back against the sofa cushions and looked at Sally, then Judd. "What do y'all think?"

"Oh, Pete, I think it's wonderful. Like getting your family back and then some," Sally said, tears glistening in her eyes.

Judd nodded. "My mother used to say, 'The Lord gives, and the Lord taketh away.' Seems to me, this time, He took away and now He's giving back. I know I'll be glad to call you cousin."

Laughter suddenly burst out of Pete. He stood and spread his arms wide. "Me and Sally always have wanted a big family. This one just might work out."

CHAPTER
40

Two days before the wedding, Ben rolled into town with Granny Jane, Maude, and Kyle. Larkin was beside herself with excitement. She put Maude and Kyle in the apartment that would soon be her home while Granny Jane stayed in the guest bedroom.

"Law, child, I don't know what to do with all these frills. Afraid I might muss 'em if I ain't careful." Granny circled the room, touching things with just the tip of her index finger.

"Oh, Granny, I've imagined how wonderful it would be to show you all these luxuries. I wish I could give you eyelet curtains and indoor plumbing every day."

"No, thank you. I might never leave the house if I had all this, and I like getting out too much. No, I'll keep my cabin and necessary out back." She gave Larkin a toothy grin. "But I surely will enjoy all this while I'm here."

The day before the wedding, Abram and Lydia arrived at Judd's boardinghouse. "We left the young'uns with Charlene Cutright. She always has doted on 'em, and although they wanted to come see the ocean awful bad, we said it'd have to wait until next time," Abram said. He slapped Judd on the shoulder. "Couldn't let my baby brother get hitched without a Markley or two in attendance."

Judd grinned. He'd always thought of Joe as his baby brother, forgetting that's what he was to Abram. He let himself wish, for just a moment, that Joe could be there, too. And somehow it felt like maybe he was.

◊ ◊ ◊

The wedding wasn't as fussy as Judd feared. It was in the afternoon—Larkin explained that it could be less formal that way. She could even wear a tea-length dress, an explanation that mystified Judd. There was only a handful of people, and Judd knew more of them than he thought he would. He glanced around the sanctuary as he took his place up front. Pete and Sally sat near Hank. Chuck was here with his wife, who couldn't cook but by golly she was awful pretty. Granny Jane kept gawking at the windows and the rafters and the candles. Lydia blushed every time Abram looked at her, and even George and Augusta held hands like they must have when they were young and first in love.

Joe was the only one missing, but Judd felt as though he were present in a new way. Joe lived on in everyone who remembered him, and Judd seemed to recall something new about his brother every day. He could just picture Joe sitting there in the second pew, laughing at Judd stuffed into a brand-new suit and tie.

Which made him think about his tie and how maybe it was a little too tight. He ran a finger inside his collar, finding he had difficulty swallowing. Plus it was all-fired hot in the church, and those gardenias, which he'd thought smelled sweet when Larkin showed him some, were about to knock him over with their perfume. He fished out a handkerchief and dabbed at the sweat beading on his forehead, all thoughts of Joe fleeing as he glanced toward the door at the back of the sanctuary. What if Larkin changed her mind?

Abram, wearing a tie he'd borrowed from Hank, grinned like a monkey and poked Judd in the side. Judd darted a look at the rear doors, praying that they would open and this show would get on the road. Ben stood, Bible in hand, next to Pastor Brearley. He winked and gave Judd a nod that he supposed was meant to reassure him.

Then the music swelled, and the doors at the back opened to admit first one girl in a frilly dress, and then a second. Judd kept his focus on the doorway, looking for Larkin. Finally, she stepped forward on her father's arm in the prettiest white dress he'd ever seen, with a bunch of roses and a wide smile. She even had her hair down, curling over her shoulders, and Judd wanted to reach out and touch it.

He started to lift his hand, but something was wrong. It was like the church was suddenly filled with thick fog, and stars sparked beyond the corners of his eyes. He tried to move, but felt like he was stuck in mud up to his armpits. Then blackness—mine-deep blackness—began to close in on him until all he could see was a pinprick of light. He tried to stare down that light, make it grow, but he feared it was a losing battle.

"Dearly beloved, we are gathered here today, in the sight of God . . ." The voice traveled down a long tunnel, and Judd felt panic rise, a tide of fear that he thought might wash him out to sea.

Then he heard Joe laughing. And not just a little. It was a deep, full belly laugh. It had been the last time they went deer hunting before Joe died. They'd shot a doe out of season and loaded it in the back of Joe's beat-up old Jeep—not exactly hidden, but not advertising what they'd done, either. Joe was driving when they came up on a checkpoint. A game warden sat in his car, keeping warm. Judd thought they were done for when the warden waved them down.

"You boys seen anybody hunting out of season?" he asked through his open window.

Joe, calm as could be, leaned out his own window and began having a conversation with the warden. They talked hunting and fishing, and Judd thought they might start in on farming when finally another car came along and the warden waved them off.

Judd collapsed against the back of his seat. "Are you out of your mind? All that feller had to do was stand up and he'd have seen the deer in the back."

That was when Joe started laughing like he'd just heard the best joke ever. "He couldn't. I pulled up too close for him to open his door."

Judd felt something like joy bubble through him where he stood there in the church, and the pinprick of light started to get a little bigger. Then a hand touched his. A warm, gentle twining of fingers tugged him forward. The warmth traveled up his arm to his heart and on to his head. His vision began to clear, and when it did he saw not his baby brother, not the gleam of daylight, but something even better. It was the love of life brimming in Larkin's blue eyes. And just like that, Judd felt himself come out into the open. It was like stepping into the stillness in the center of the hurricane. Chaos lurked on every side, but here, protected by a love bigger than any of them, all was well. He took a deep breath, let it out again, and pledged his life to the woman who filled his every day with pure light.

Author's Note

The Ocean View Memorial Hospital didn't open until 1958, four years after Hurricane Hazel swept through. One of the pleasures and prerogatives of writing fiction *based* in history is tinkering with that history. I don't do it often, but I wanted Larkin to volunteer at a hospital, and the one in Loris was too far away. So I moved up the date. Of course, the hospital was also just a few blocks off the ocean and would likely have been severely damaged if it had been around for Hazel, but it sure was handy to have a refuge available for those displaced by the storm. The hospital closed after just twenty years, unable to keep up with the rapid growth of Myrtle Beach.

Acknowledgments

My first job out of college was as a public relations assistant for the Myrtle Beach Area Chamber of Commerce. This was when I learned that without Hurricane Hazel, Myrtle Beach, SC, would probably not be the tourist destination that it is today. In 1954, Hazel took a sleepy little seaside town and literally wiped the slate clean. Where private homes and cottages once stood, little remained but sand and rubble. Estimates are that eighty percent of oceanfront buildings were either damaged or destroyed.

Except for the Pavilion.

When I was in high school in Buckhannon, WV, the coolest place you could go on vacation was Myrtle Beach, and the coolest place in Myrtle Beach was the Pavilion. My family did finally take several memorable trips to the beach, much to my delight. One year I got the worst sunburn of my life. Another year I took a girlfriend, and she let me try my first—and last—cigarette while sitting outside the hotel's pool overlooking the ocean.

But I never did go to the Pavilion. Too wild, too many boys, and really, Dad was probably right. The Pavilion of the nineties was far different from the Pavilion of the fifties. And what I really wanted was to go to the Magic Attic—the upstairs nightclub where other people were clearly having more fun than I could even imagine.

Well. Probably not.

I finally made it to the Pavilion, thanks to the chamber and my job helping to promote the annual Sun Fun Festival. That's where I met Vanna White (a native of North Myrtle Beach) and Roy Clark (*Hee Haw* was required viewing back home). They paled in comparison to the edifice that opened its doors in 1948 and then fell to the wrecking ball in 2006.

That's right. Hurricane Hazel left her standing, but time and the economy did her in. The Pavilion is no more.

Except . . . I can clearly see Larkin there on a quiet September night after the tourists have gone for the season. She's doing the shag to music only she can hear, and time is standing still.

My thanks go to Doug Bell, who gave me that first job and believed I was a writer—maybe before I did. Also to Angel Frantz McAllister and Julie Bostian, who made Sun Fun 1994 an absolute blast and spoiled me for real jobs.

Of course, this book is also about a West Virginia coal miner. My love and appreciation go to all the miners in my family— especially Uncle Harry, Uncle Judd, and Grandpa Rex.

I couldn't have written the timber industry bits without my baby brother, Daniel, who broke his leg TWICE during his timbering career. Thanks for going into a *slightly* safer line of work. If anything in the story sounds off, it's because I didn't listen to you carefully enough.

To my husband, Jim, thank you for actually gasping the first time I read the introductory pages aloud. I can't think of any better encouragement. Although the many mugs of tea are a close second.

If it weren't for the amazing teams at Bethany House and Books & Such Literary, I'd be writing for my own amusement alone. Dave and Wendy, I hope you know how much I appreciate your partnership.

Most importantly, I thank God for orchestrating the story of my life that continues to unfold day by day. While the unexpected plot twists often take me by surprise, I know there's a happy ending, and I can't wait to see what the next chapter holds.

Sarah Loudin Thomas is a fund-raiser for a children's ministry who has also published freelance writing for *Now & Then* magazine, as well as the *Asheville Citizen-Times* and *The Journey Christian Newspaper*. She holds a bachelor's degree in English from Coastal Carolina University and is the author of the acclaimed novels *A Tapestry of Secrets* and *Until the Harvest*. She and her husband reside in Asheville, North Carolina. Learn more at www.sarahloudinthomas.com.

You May Also Like . . .

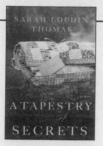

Perla Phillips has carried a secret for over sixty years. When she sees her granddaughter Ella struggling, Perla decides to share her story—then suffers a stroke. As Ella and her aunt look into Perla's past, they'll learn more than they expected about Perla, faith, and each other.

A Tapestry of Secrets by Sarah Loudin Thomas
sarahloudinthomas.com

Fleeing a stalker, Kaine Prescott purchases an old house with a dark history: a century earlier, an unidentified woman was found dead on the grounds. As Kaine tries to settle in, she learns the story of her ancestor Ivy Thorpe, who, with the help of a man from her past, tried to uncover the truth about the death.

The House on Foster Hill by Jaime Jo Wright
jaimewrightbooks.com

Telegraph operator Lucy Drake is a master of Morse code, but the presence of Sir Colin Beckwith at a rival news agency puts her livelihood at risk. When Colin's reputation is jeopardized, Lucy agrees to help in exchange for his assistance in recovering her family's stolen fortune. However, the web of treachery they're diving into is more dangerous than they know.

A Dangerous Legacy by Elizabeth Camden
elizabethcamden.com

When paid companion Gertrude Cadwalader is caught trying to return items pilfered by her employer, her friend Harrison's mother jumps to the wrong conclusion. But Harrison quickly comes to Gertrude's defense—and initiates an outlandish plan to turn their friendship into a romance.

Out of the Ordinary by Jen Turano, APART FROM THE CROWD
jenturano.com